Note on the Author

Emma Hannigan lives in Bray, Co Wicklow with her husband Cian and their two children Sacha and Kim. Her ongoing battle with ill health has left Emma in no doubt that each day is there to be appreciated and lived to the full. That doesn't rule out the fact that she gains huge solace from her faith in the power of chocolate. Her first novel *Designer Genes* was a bestseller.

D0996225

Also by Emma Hannigan

Designer Genes

Published by Poolbeg

Acknowledgements

For me writing the acknowledgements for a book is almost more difficult than writing the rest of the novel. Suddenly the blank page facing me becomes a minefield. There are so many people I want to thank. So many people who make each day of my life better.

Firstly thank you to Sarah, Gaye and everyone in Poolbeg, especially Paula Campbell, whose name should really be Dorothy. Everyone should own a pair of red shoes like hers. Thank you to my agent and cheerleader Sheila Crowley for taking me aboard the Curtis Brown bus. I hope we will have a long and lively journey together.

Without my husband Cian I would be a dribbling mess. I can never express my gratitude to him for his unbending support. I promise to do my best not to get cancer again. Although I think we're getting used to it at this stage, the joke is getting a bit old. Please know I never take your love for granted.

To Sacha and Kim, my children, my friends, my joy, my angels on earth. Nobody else has the ability to fill me with love, rage, frustration and laughter all in the space of thirty seconds.

My parents Denise and Philip are my backbone. Without their unconditional love and support, I would be lost. I love you both and thank you for carrying me through the tough times. You are always on hand to help with the practicalities like groceries, babysitting and general grandparent duties. Not to mention the convenience of your living next door, so the children don't have to cross a dangerous road to run away from home when they need to. No dictionary possesses a word to express how much you both mean to me.

Thank you to all my in-laws the McGraths, especially my-father-in-law Seán who drove to the airport to buy airside editions of *Designer Genes* the day it was released.

Thank you to Robyn and Steffy for being the best sisters a girl could wish for. Thanks to Timmy for being my favourite brother, and to Hillary for putting up with him.

A special mention and big thank-you to all the teachers at St Gerard's Junior school in Bray for teaching and nurturing my children. Especially Deirdre Farrell principal of the Junior School who is now Dr Farrell woo-who! You're amazing! Also my sincere thanks to Tom Geraghty headmaster of the Senior School for all your support and kind wishes.

Big love to all my cousins, especially Andrew, Patrick and Tom Rhatigan, Jessica Freeney, Max O'Donoghue, Reiltin and Iseult O'Hagan and Evie Seavers. To my nieces Camille Allen and Molly O'Bric and my goddaughters Ari O'Donoghue and Trudie Barker.

Thank you to my oncologist Dr David Fennelly and his team at Blackrock clinic. To Dr Cal Condon, Dr Frances Stafford, Dr Declan Magee, Dr Micheal Moriarty and his team, and all the other jaw-droppingly clever and dedicated medical experts who have kept me alive so far.

Thank you to all my wonderful and supportive friends, may the coffee and wine continue to flow. Thank you to Chris Upton and Sarah McSharry for stepping in as baby-sitters so I could do *The Late Late Show*.

Love and gratitude to Sinéad Desmond and Mark Cagney of TV3 for minding me the first time I ever went on television. Thank you to Ryan Tubridy who allowed me to tell my story both on radio and television. Even though I thought I might die of fright, you made it all seem normal. Thank you for the most memorable birthday surprise ever, affording me the chance to appear on *The Late Late Show*. I promise to tell my grandchildren about it ad nauseam when the time comes!

Thank you to Mel Doyle for taking my photographs and making it fun, I haven't forgotten about the marmalade kitten.

Thank you to the people of Hughes and Hughes for your support and belief in *Designer Genes*. The day your doors closed for the last time brought me great sadness. Many thanks to Eason, Dubray, Waterstones, Borders, Tesco and all the book stores who supported me. With a special mention to Hilary in Bridge Street Books in Wicklow town, a little piece of book-lovers' heaven run lovingly by a true lady.

Thank you to my friend, mentor and fellow shopping addict, Cathy Kelly. You guide me and encourage me all the time. Not so good when we're in a shop, great when I'm writing and in all other aspects of my life! You were sent to me by a very wise angel.

Finally, I cannot believe the amount of warmth and support I received from people I've never met. None of this writing lark could continue to work without you, my dear readers. Thank you from the bottom of my heart for spending your hard-earned cash on my book. I hope you enjoy *Miss Conceived*. I would heartily recommend strong coffee and an obnoxiously large bar of chocolate to accompany it!

Lots of love
Emma

For my children Sacha and Kim

With all my love

Mum x x

1

tweeting@angiebaby.com
*I do not need a man to make my life complete . . . I am a modern
woman . . . I will learn to be happy with what I've got . . . I am in
charge of my own destiny . . .*

Even bloody Seamus was married. Come on! He wore brown
nylon trousers and had two pockets of white spit on either side
of his mouth. Granted, his wife looked scarily like Shrek, but all the
same they'd found love. *Well,* Seamus did what he was told and his
wife was only short of poking him with a cattle prod by way of
communication. But, at the end of the day, they had each other.
They had *someone.*

As she looked around the dimly lit room, Angie sighed.
Eyeballing the Bacardi and Coke she'd just paid far too much for,
she was tempted to pour it into the plastic pot plant beside her and
leave.

"All right there, Angie baby?" Ken from Accounts staggered
towards her, with one eye shut, spilling his pint up his own sleeve.

"Not really, Ken – in fact, I'm about as far from all right as I've
ever been." She downed the drink, figuring she might as well get the
value out of it at this stage.

"Ah, what's wrong with you? Tell me all about it!" Ken tried to
sit on a bar stool, but the combination of his jockey-sized physique

and ten pints meant he shunted sideways and drenched his own shirt and the front of her skirt. "Oh no, I'm such a gobshite! Angie, I'm really sorry. I'll wash your frock for you – bring it in tomorrow and I'll get it back to you as good as new." He bit his lip.

Angie took a deep breath. "It's okay, Ken, could happen to a bishop. It's just another disaster to add to the multitude of others that I call my sad life." She slumped forwards to lean on the bar, resting her chin in her hands.

"Hello!" Seamus was standing like he'd a pole up his arse and waving like a clockwork dolly from the end of the bar. His wife, who was actually more manly-looking than he was, elbowed him and he swiftly turned his attention back to her.

"At least you're not with someone like that yolk Seamus has to endure." Ken shuddered.

"Shrek, you mean?" said Angie. "That's true."

But, deep down, Angie would settle for a mongrel on a piece of string and living in a shoe box if it meant she could find a decent man. She was starting to wonder whether she had an invisible, negative, magnetic force surrounding her. For years she had attracted all the wrong men. Cheapskates, don't-give-a-tossers, I'll-call-tomorrowers. Liars, every one of them. Maybe she should go to the doctor and ask if there was a scan available to tell her whether or not she's been chipped by aliens with a "nice guy" repellent.

Ken began to tell her about his new flat-screen TV. "Ah, you'd love it, Angie," he slurred.

"Um-hum." Angie sighed inwardly, thinking about the line-up of men in her life. From time to time, she'd manage to convince herself that she could get a man. How hard could it be? She wasn't too picky. As long as he possessed dangly toilet parts and could mutter "I love you" occasionally, he'd do. But over the years, she'd never found The One.

Her first boyfriend was in school in Senior Infants, when she was six. His name was James and he'd stolen his mother's engagement ring and brought it into school to give to her. They'd been in the toilets "getting engaged" when the teacher had found them. In fright, James had swallowed the ring so he wouldn't get caught having nicked it. His mammy had given him two tablespoons of castor oil and he'd had to shit into a sieve for two days. Hardly the makings of a wonderful relationship. But at least he'd given her a ring.

Lately, as her thirties were slipping into her forties, the pickings were getting slimmer. She'd go out on the pull, full of intentions of scoring, just to prove a point. But, *wham* (or dead silence to be exact) – nothing. Not an available mutant in sight. Instead, to avoid feeling like a reject, she'd decided it was better to take the assertive, defensive approach. She maintained to all and sundry her firm assurance that all men should be evenly covered in dog poo and then rolled in leaves.

"You've the right idea, Angie," one of the girls in work used to say to her. "Steer clear of men. You've got your super-cool apartment, a gang of friends and you're your own woman. A lot to be said for being your own woman, I can tell you."

That was all very well for her to say – she had a husband and three kids at home. But who was Angie trying to kid? Here she was, at the after-conference drinks with the people she worked with day in day out, and even now she couldn't manage to relax and enjoy herself.

"What the hell is wrong with me?" she asked Ken. "Okay, quick CV, correct me if I'm wrong at any stage, right?" Choosing to ignore his pained look, she decided, fuelled by the Bacardi Bus, that right here and now was the right time to get some answers.

"Well, in fairness, Ange, I bat for the other team so I'm probably not the best choice to be asking."

Ken was one of the few people in the world who Angie didn't feel the need to be Superwoman with. He was her emotional crutch when times were fractious – usually after several units too many of mixing the grape and the grain, which was of course a total no-no.

"No, Ken, you're spot on. You're a man but you're gay, so you won't be foggy in your judgement. Just hear me out and let's work from there, yes?"

That day the team-building conference had been about trust and communication, which Ken had been all fired up about, but he hadn't thought in his wildest dreams it would mean having to listen to Angie's man troubles. Feeling more than a little boxed-in, he tried to resist the urge to lie on the floor and fall into a loud snoring drunken slumber. Keeping his focus away from the floor tiles, which looked alarmingly enticing, he turned his attention back to Angie, who was going hell for leather on the ranting front, God bless her.

"I'm an honest, decent and fairly intelligent woman. I have a sense of humour, I can laugh at myself." She lurched a little and snorted to demonstrate this fact.

Ken nodded with a fixed smile.

"Okay," she held her hands up, "I know I mightn't be Elle MacPherson, but am I offensive-looking? Especially in the right light, with enough make-up on and assuming the fella has a few drinks on board?" She tried to stand up straight, keeping her tummy in and her boobs out.

She could see herself in the mirror over the bar. She had shoulder-length brunette hair. (Well, that's how the magazines might describe it. In reality it was the same colour as a muddy puddle and, no matter what hairstylist she went to, it stubbornly remained unkempt and not-bothered-with-looking.) She had piercing blue eyes, which Ken felt were her best feature.

"You're a real firecracker, Angie, you have stop-'em-dead eyes and all you need is to give it a bit of time." Ken rubbed her arm, hoping to God she'd melt and thank him, and shut the hell up. No such luck.

"So," she slurred, "why is it that the only men who are attracted to me are either comparable to pond life, mentally deranged or, recently, non-existent? I'm nearly forty, Ken. My body clock is ticking so loudly sometimes I feel myself looking around to see if anyone else can hear it."

She was gripping his arm so tightly by this point that Ken was becoming increasingly alarmed.

"Another drink?" He smiled and tried to release his arm, which was in danger of bruising.

Ken ordered some of those tiny mouse's-pints-of-Guinness cocktails, which Angie hated at this stage of attempting to get ossified.

"They take half an hour to mix, two seconds to drink, they cost an arm and a leg and they have the potency of a Mr Whippy. I'm ordering us some real drinks. Tequila time! Barman, if you please, two shots of your finest tequila!"

"You, my dear, are going to end up in a pool of your own vomit. I am merely trying to slow you down a bit and provide a sophisticated little tipple that we can actually enjoy the flavour of."

The mouse's pints arrived and Ken made her giggle as he raised his pinkie and downed his in one.

"I'll see your posh fairy drink and we'll hammer this night home," said Angie, swaying a little as she grabbed a tequila shot from the barman. "Are you a man or a mouse?"

"I'd settle for the fairy description," Ken winked.

Angie had started working with Ken and Seamus at Stacks and Co IT eight years previously. It was a small company which had grown steadily over the years. Situated in a Georgian house just behind Shandon church in Cork city, the main office was open plan, with big blue screens dividing her and Ken's desks. Her area was usually messy and laced with chocolate wrappers, while Ken's was pristine and orderly.

Angie had grown up in a small remote village, with a higher ratio of cattle to people. So when she'd first got her job at Stacks, she'd shared with a college friend, Ed. His parents owned the flat and he subsidised his dope and lack of work by renting the spare room to Angie. Within two years she had moved from her shared accommodation into her own one-bed place. The sale of the last ten acres of land meant her parents were able to give her enough for a decent deposit on her apartment.

She thought back to those first few months in her lovely apartment. She was like a child in a sweetshop. The sheer joy of not having to label her milk and cheese in the fridge was beyond exciting. There was nothing worse than coming home from work to find her hairy, smelly, stoned flatmate sitting in *her* sweatshirt, eating the only food she had left. Ed was a lovely guy, but he had long dark hair which congregated in the plugholes and he was usually too stoned to go outside, and so he'd help himself to her stuff. Her flat was decorated in a minimalist way, which translated as having only the absolute necessities in place. A battered old sofa her father had found in a barn, an old iron bed and very little else. As she balanced her beans on toast on her lap, while watching the tiny portable TV with the coat-hanger stuck in the top (not a satellite dish in sight) she couldn't have been happier. There were no carpets on the floors and, as yet, no curtains on the windows, nor was there a resident stoned hippy. Best of all, the sinks weren't full of Ed's tangled dark hair. No more brushing her teeth and then retching when she discovered the plughole looking like a spider colony. She'd got on the right side of the builder and managed to get him to throw in her white goods in exchange for a cheaper bathroom suite. When she put food in the pristine new built-in fridge, it was still there when she came home from work. She could walk around in her underwear. In fact she could walk naked from the bathroom to her bedroom and decide what to wear without being confronted by a confused druggie with the munchies. She could leave her toiletries in the bathroom. (Ed used to use her toothbrush if she left it in his.)

"I was so happy when I moved to my flat, Ken. I don't know why but I thought that if I had my own place the man and babies would follow." She slumped and drained her drink. "My round. Thanks for listening and I'm sure you're dying to go the toilet and you're sick to the back teeth of listening to me moaning. No doubt you're ready to head home and wrap your arms around Barry and thank your lucky stars you're gay," she sniffed.

Ken made some limp attempt at telling her he was glad she'd talked to him, before excusing himself, tapping his watch. "Sorry, hon, you know I'd love to stay and chat for longer, but Barry will be worried and it's a work night and all that jazz." He kissed her cheek and tried not to trip on the carpet as he ran out.

She sat in the bar watching the work crowd. Not just Seamus but one of the new girls who was sweet and all that but certainly no supermodel – and she was engaged.

For the first years after she'd taken possession of the apartment, every spare cent was put back into making her place more homely.

But now that she had full furniture, matching towels, pretty bed linen and even optional extras like a coffee table and a tiny patio table with chairs for her miniscule balcony, she knew she wanted the most important accessory – a man.

She'd arranged to meet a group of friends in the city's newest and trendiest tapas bar. She wasn't a fan of all those tiny bits of stuff that could be a marinated rat's arse covered in spicy tomato sauce and presented on a big cocktail stick, but it seemed to be all the rage, so there might be some choice men floating around. Her friend Rachel was also single, and she and Angie were a great twosome. There were fewer and fewer "going out" buddies still unattached.

Slinking out of the work drinks, which had emptied out considerably at that stage, leaving only Seamus, Shrek and some other randomers, she tried to fix her lipstick as she walked. There was no sign of a taxi, so she strode steadily towards the city-centre bar. It was late July but, as it was Ireland and nobody had told the weather it was supposed to be summer, without warning the skies opened and the rain bucketed down.

"Bugger it," she muttered, trying without any success to shield her hair, face and body with the light jacket she'd brought. She was, of course, not organised enough to own a little handbag-sized umbrella, so instead she got soaked. Unlike in the movies, when the women get wet and look all sexy with stunning corkscrew curls framing their delicate features, making them look vulnerable and in need of love from a heroic, toned man, Angie just looked a state. By the time she reached the bar she was more haystack than Audrey Hepburn. Her hair was matted and wiry, her eye make-up was careering down her face, and the front of her trousers was soaked.

Angie hugged her friend hello. "Have you managed to have a scope around? Any nice-looking men?"

"Jesus, girl, what have you been drinking? Your two eyes are facing different directions already," said Rachel. "And you look like something from Fossetts' Circus – what's all over your face?"

"I touched up my lipstick on the way." Angie fished in her bag for a mirror. Sure enough she looked like she'd been attacked by a visually impaired toddler with a crayon. "Here, grab us some drinks, I'm going to fix myself." Angie shoved a note into Rachel's hand.

Spreading her make-up all over the sink in the toilets, she tried to make herself look half-decent. She was always aware that tonight might just be the night she met Mr Right. (Or even Mr Sort of Okay).

She began to panic then. She wasn't one of those people who could mix and match clothes and come up with a stunning outfit. She never knew what clothes suited the occasion. She was happier in her work suits, with a clean shirt and her black shoes. Her "going out" gear was safe to say the least. In fact, all she was missing was the wooden cross and the rosary beads and she would have passed for a nun. Even when she'd just had a shower and dried her hair and put on make-up, she never looked polished or svelte. She unintentionally sported the just-got-dressed-in-the-dark look. When she saw an outfit in the window of a shop, she had to buy the whole thing. Picking up "key pieces" and making them her own just never happened for her. If she tried to move away from black and went for a gorgeous pink skirt or top, she just ended up looking like a nun going to a special occasion, or a policewoman who didn't have the right shirt clean to put with her uniform. Much as she hated to admit it, she knew she lacked natural style.

She'd always had friends, both male and female, but the boys always seemed to treat her as either a confidante or one of the lads. They never seemed to fancy her. None of them wanted to date her, vie for her attention or make a move on her. They were all more likely to challenge her to a pint race, followed by a congratulatory dig in the arm, than try and put their hand up her skirt.

Feeling a bit hungover already, she tried to dry herself with the hand dryer and gave up, spritzed herself with perfume and said a silent prayer. *Please God, let me meet my soul mate tonight.*

Everyone said it happened when you least expected it, that love came along when you weren't looking. Well, she would make sure she looked as carefree and unsuspecting as possible.

"I don't have a drink problem as such . . ." It was midnight and she was hugging a pillar in the bar with one arm and slurring to

Rachel, who was equally trollied, "I just find it can work as a kind of anaesthetic for my broken heart, ya know?"

"Don't you need to have actually had some sort of catastrophic relationship-tragedy to be broken-hearted?"

"That's just it, Rachel, I'm such a disaster that I can break my own heart."

"Ah, come off it, you're not a total disaster. If you asked me to rate you, I'd say above Mother Teresa and below Joan Collins." Rachel giggled so much her sangria came out her nose.

"I'm actually two steps above Mother Teresa, I'll have you know. One relationship lasted two months, and the other almost three!" She did exaggerated counting on her fingers for effect.

"Ah yeah, but you were always the one to make all the effort, and still ended up being dumped in the end," teased Rachel. "It's been two years since a man stayed in that neat, minimalistic, tasteful, built-in-a-good-area apartment, with outdoor space overlooking Shandon."

"Now that was harsh, Rachel. It's hardly for a lack of effort. You and I," Angie poked herself and Rachel repeatedly, "would go to the opening of an envelope, at four in the morning on a Tuesday night, up the back of a field, if we thought we might meet a nice guy. Isn't that true?"

"It's true for you, girl," Rachel agreed.

"I think I'm good fun too. It's not like I walk around with a sandwich board on my back, with 'desperate for a husband,' in big black letters written on it. But, if the truth be known, all this being an independent woman looking out for myself is bloody boring and fecking exhausting. I'd love to come home even one night a week and have someone else make the dinner. To come home and be met with something other than silence would actually do it." She felt too drunk, quite sick and utterly miserable.

* * *

At two o'clock that morning, she swayed and shut one eye as she wrestled with her key, trying to make it fit in the lock of her apartment,

"I don't understand why this fucking key won't work," she slurred loudly to herself.

At that moment the door opened and a rather bleary-eyed man stood there in a pair of striped boxer shorts, staring at her with his arms folded.

"What the hell are you doing in my apartment?" she shouted.

"I live here," he answered rather snottily.

"I think you'll find you've made a mistake. This is my apartment and I've been living here since it was built. Now if you'll kindly move aside!" She shoved him out of the way and pushed her way in rudely. "What have you done with all my furniture?" she asked, feeling really confused.

Then it dawned on her.

"Oh Jesus, Mary and Joseph, I'm on the wrong floor, aren't I?" She turned around and met his gaze. "I am so embarrassed. I think I'm a bit drunk and I decided to take the stairs instead of the lift and I don't think I went up enough flights . . ." She trailed off feeling like a complete idiot.

"I'm sorry I'm such a spanner – if it helps you at all, I do intend on going to the vet tomorrow morning and having myself put down."

"Don't worry about it, could happen to a bishop," he replied yawning. "Will you be able to find where you live?" He scratched the back of his head.

"Yep, that'll be no problem. So, sorry again, you go back to sleep – I'm off to slip into something a little more comfortable, like a coma." She staggered away. She was glad she was so pissed, otherwise she'd have died with embarrassment. He was bloody cute too, more was the shame. But, odds were, he was probably either gay or married, so there was no point in even thinking about him.

* * *

When the alarm clock went off at six forty-five the next morning, Angie did hear it but it was very far away and quite muffled. By the time her brain managed to register it was intended for her, it was seven fifteen.

"Oh God," she groaned. Hauling herself out of bed, she berated herself for getting so drunk last night. She hardly ever drank mid-week any more, it just wasn't worth the hassle. She knew she would spend the day shovelling in junk food, washed down by dissolvable painkillers, counting the hours before she could go to bed again.

She'd staggered halfway to work by the time she recalled all the events of the night before. Her heart stopped as she halted.

"Oh God no!" she said out loud, to no one in particular. She felt her cheeks flush with embarrassment. She would have to move house. She would definitely have to sell her apartment now. There was no way she could risk seeing that man ever again. The shame of it, how was she going to cope? She couldn't even go home alone in a dignified manner.

By the time she reached work, her boss was standing at her desk looking agitated.

"Oh Angie, there you are. Nice of you to join us. You look rough. Come into my office when you've had a cup of coffee and made yourself look halfway decent. The team-building days are meant to be a positive thing, not an excuse to get yourself inebriated and insult fellow colleagues. Seamus mentioned to me this morning that you were comparing his wife to an ogre last night. I'm not impressed, just chalk it down." He looked her up and down and walked off muttering.

Brian O'Leary was an utter prick. There was no two ways about it. He had balls of steel and that was why he'd made so much money. His company was going strong and he paid well, but he had the personality of a pre-menstrual she-devil and Angie had always felt he had it in for her. How typical that Seamus and Shrek had overheard her talking to Ken. She'd a good mind to stomp over to Seamus and tell him to keep his whingey little trap shut. What was he like? Telling on her like that?

Angie had worked hard to get to the position she had now, but being head of marketing was no easy feat. Especially when she was dealing with Brian O'Leary. She'd never forgiven him for his snide comment when she'd sent in her CV for the job application. He'd phoned her to organise a meeting, way back when he was only getting going and didn't have a shower of minions to do his dirty work.

"Your credentials look promising on paper but, looking at your passport photo, if you actually look like that in reality all I can say is that what you need is a holiday!" He'd proceeded to snort and laugh at his own wit.

Only her foresight that the company might be a good place to climb the success ladder made her hold her tongue. She could easily have hung up saying, "Give my regards to your arsehole if and when you remove your head from it." Instead, she'd made an extra-special effort just to prove him wrong and had done a great interview and secured the job.

The jury was still out on Brian O'Leary all the same. Angie wasn't convinced that he was definitely human. She often wondered what might happen if the fire-extinguishing sprinklers were ever activated. Would sparks fly out the back of his head?

Snapping back to the present time, putting her contempt for her boss aside and doing her best to look neutral as opposed to seething, Angie staggered into the bathroom and frightened herself. In fairness to O'Leary, she did in fact look like she'd just survived a holocaust. Riffling in her handbag, she found the makings of a face. Concealer, blusher, mascara, eyeshadow and lip gloss. Her skin had that ruddy, post-boozy complexion which no amount of product bar building materials could rectify. Knowing she was simply wasting her make-up, she knew she had to be seen to make the effort nonetheless. In the hope of feeling fresh, she spritzed herself with perfume, which she knew would just clash horribly with the smell of stale alcohol emanating from every pore. Lastly, she finished off by pulling a brush through her hair. Surveying her work, she grudgingly admitted that she felt and looked a damn sight better.

Taking a deep breath she strode purposefully towards Creepy O'Leary's office. He'd been in his pacing-panther mode, which always meant either a big deal on the cards or trouble in the camp.

She knocked on his door and he answered in his usual abrupt tone.

"Come in!" he barked. "You look slightly more human. Sit down, Angie."

The bloody nerve of him! With his old-fashioned trousers, greasy grey comb-over, and his patchy reddish beard. He was hardly Brad Pitt himself. More like an ageing fox with a dose of the mange. Cheeky bastard.

"I'm going to cut right to the chase here. There's a big deal coming through the pipelines. I need a strong team on board. How would you feel about relocating to Dublin for a year?" He was eyeing her like a vulture.

"Well, I don't know. I'm not sure. Why?" Angie looked astonished. Why the hell did he have to dump this on her today? Why in the name of God did she choose last night to go out and get rat-arsed? She hardly ever went on the batter on a work night and this was exactly why. She couldn't cope with the aftermath. She was a mess. On cue, her stomach did one of those dreadful angry-sounding gurgles as she felt cold sweat engulf her.

O'Leary was on the move again. Striding up and down his murky oatmeal carpet, in his squeaky cheap shoes, hands clasped behind his scrawny back.

"Okay, the deal is this. I need you to head the marketing strategy. You are the best person for the job. You've headed all the big campaigns over the last eight years – with ease and talent, I might add. You are well able to do the job. There's a good package in it for you to boot. I'm collaborating with an American company on this one. I've swung your rent in Dublin, as well as your mortgage to be paid here in Cork while you're away. A good expense account – in fact, you could eat in a Michelin-starred restaurant every night if you like. Your current wage and a ten-thousand-euro bonus at the end for your trouble. Will you think about it?" He was smiling, which was actually rather unnerving.

He was so unaccustomed to being cheerful, it really didn't suit him. In fact he looked a bit like a deranged squirrel, with his strawberry-blonde beard, as he revealed little sharp teeth. He stroked his bristly beard and then leaned on his desk to focus on her.

"I'll need to think it over. When is all this supposed to go ahead?" Angie asked, her hungover head reeling with this information overload. Not to mention her discomfort at having O'Leary in such close proximity, being all thrilled with himself.

"The deal is done. I need you to sign and agree to move to Dublin in two weeks' time. I know it sounds rushed, but believe me it will be worth it. These guys are big time. If we do well with this deal, it could become a regular trade-off. Why don't you go home, get some rest and mull it over? See me back here at three o'clock, and for Christ's sake, Angie, take the boiled sweet out of your hair, girl. If you're going to be a real high flyer, you'll have to get the finger out."

Angie reached up and felt around her head in confusion. There, nestled in her stringy locks, was a half-wrapped, sticky cough sweet, which must have been suctioned to her hairbrush at the bottom of her bag.

O'Leary never told anyone to go home, so she didn't wait to be told twice. She grabbed her coat and told her secretary she would be out for the morning.

The muggy city air hit her nostrils but it still felt fresh in comparison to the stuffy building. She headed straight for a coffee shop, knowing she needed some soakage before she could even begin to think about this opportunity. Intending to buy a low-fat bagel and black coffee, she waited in line at the nearest café. Of course by the time she reached the counter all ideas of being sensible and health-conscious went out the window. She figured her liver was already in distress after the night before and her growling stomach needed some proper sustenance.

"A breakfast roll, a piece of double-chocolate fudge cake and a large cappuccino with an extra shot to go, please." She dumped her bag on the sliver of counter space available in front of the cash register.

As she fumbled for her wallet, her oversized faux-leather supposed-to-be-a-handbag-but-really-should-have-wheels bag decided to empty itself all over the hard tiles of the crowded shop. Close to tears, she bent onto her hunkers, her head throbbing at being tilted at such an angle, and tried to steady herself while shoving her personal items back into the privacy of her bag.

"That's twelve euro and eight cent," the bored Eastern European girl, with jet-black hair and enough make-up to secure tiles to a bathroom wall, stood with her hand rudely shoved out.

"Can you just give me a sec? I'm trying to put what's left of my belongings into my bag."

"Next!" the girl yelled, as Angie put her smashed eyeshadow compact away.

"*Shiiiiit!*" she cursed under her breath as her leg got showered in greyish glittery powder which she stupidly tried to wipe, causing a greasy stain on her good work skirt.

She paid and tottered home, trying to sip her boiling coffee, which she reckoned would melt metal it was so hot, and flopped on the sofa feeling violated. The salt of the bacon and sausages, followed by the dense sugary cake, at least helped with her shaking hands and eased the hollow churning in her stomach.

This time in Dublin could be just what she needed. She knew it sounded sad, but it would also mean a fresh start. New men to meet, a new scene to crack into. Maybe this was Cupid's way of lining up his bow for her. Rachel could come up to Dublin on the train and the capital city would be their new playground. Sighing, firstly with relief that her hangover was shifting slightly and secondly at the thought of what could lie ahead, Angie felt hope springing forth.

2

tweeting@serenasvelte.com
A day without wine is a day without sunshine — let's sunbathe!

Serena O'Keefe marched up and down the arrivals area in the airport. She wasn't in the mood to wait for her fiancé Paul and his clients. She swished past a couple of backpackers emptying out a scabby rucksack. The state of them! Serena whirled her Prada coat past them. In a cloud of Chanel No 5, garnished with glittering rocks bigger than Jelly Tots, she pulled her Hermes scarf downwards, flicking invisible particles of dust away from herself.

It would all be utterly unbearable if it weren't for Paul. As she pictured him in her mind's eye she softened. A couple of times a month she found herself in this very position, waiting for him to land with various business clients. The last lot had been all men, New Yorkers with very little sense of humour and even less time for women. Of course she'd managed to charm them and Paul had told her afterwards that they'd expressed their envy.

"You landed yourself a real little trooper of a lady there, Paul!" The MD had banged Paul on the back. Women were afraid of Serena, men adored her. It had always been that way. She seemed poised and older than her twenty-eight years.

Growing up, she'd always acted like she was the eldest, even

16

though her sister Adele was thirteen years her senior. Their parents had sent them both to a private school for girls and ensured they'd graduated fluent in French and Spanish, with the ability to conduct themselves impeccably in any type of company. And she was beautiful, she knew that.

She was also very impatient. She couldn't bear this feeling of expectancy as she watched the arrivals area like a hawk. This evening Paul was on his way back from London. He was bringing in one of his biggest clients along with his wife. They'd met before, so at least Serena knew what to expect. Not that this kind of thing daunted her in any shape or form. In fact, this was what she did best – looking after Paul.

Paul owned an engineering company. He had set up his business in the mid-nineties. He'd been full of ambition and enthusiasm. Like any young guy starting out on his own, he'd hoped to be successful, but he'd never dreamed just how well he was going to do. It had been a real case of right place, right time, with the right ideas. Jumping on the bandwagon right on the back of the Celtic Tiger, he had firmly grabbed the proverbial beast by the tail. Now, fifteen years later, he and his company were worth millions. Millions the downturn hadn't managed to touch.

Serena and Paul had met at a charity ball, which Paul had sponsored along with Serena's father. Working as her father's personal assistant, Serena had organised everything from the colour of the tablecloths to the endless list of wealthy attendees. The proceeds on the night were to go to a local women's refuge centre, which her family had supported for many years.

It was a gala evening incorporating an auction, boasting fabulous prizes.

She introduced herself with ease, offering her slender hand for him to shake. "Hello there. Serena O'Keefe. We've spoken on the phone. My father is so pleased that you've kindly agreed to lend your support to this worthy cause."

"The pleasure is all mine, Serena," he said, smiling.

As he took her hand she jerked slightly in a manner she knew he wouldn't have noticed. But she was affected by him. He was the right balance between rugged and pretty, just the way she liked her men. Suave and sophisticated, yet definitely not effeminate. He was taller than her, well built without being overweight.

Paul coughed softly and then stood with his hands behind his back, taking her in. She was so self-assured, and from his couple of brief telephone conversations with her on the run-up to this evening, he'd been more than impressed with her organisational skills.

Serena knew he was admiring her. She wasn't being arrogant in knowing she was stunningly beautiful. She was the image of her mother, who had done some part-time modelling in her day. Like her mother, she had olive skin and silky brown hair like a polished conker. Her eyes were pale green and startling against her sallow complexion. She was tall and slim and carried herself with confidence and pride. She was always immaculately presented, smelled like an expensive fragrance hall, and smiled with such warmth she stopped Paul in his tracks. He had never expected someone so beautiful to have such a warm smile.

"It's great to be able to give a little back," Paul went on. "Jim mentioned the charity to me when my company was rewriting his computer system and I was more than happy to help out, especially when the lady pitching the idea was so charming."

"Daddy feels passionately about helping the less privileged and I'm always glad to organise these worthwhile events," Serena said, smiling at the compliment. "I was just going to the bar – would you like to join me for a drink, or are you waiting for someone special?" She regarded him with her head to the side. She'd been dying to meet this guy. Her father had told her he was dynamic and clever, and urged her to call on him for charity support, but he'd neglected to mention how deliciously gorgeous he was.

"No, I'm not waiting for anyone." He looked her in the eye. She was almost as tall as him. "Please, let me buy you a drink." He placed his hand on the small of her back and led her to the bar.

They chatted amicably and Paul was pleasantly surprised at how witty she was. They both liked spicy food, good wine and Quentin Tarantino movies.

He was disappointed when the bell was rung for dinner and he had to leave her to find his seat. He found it even more difficult than usual to talk to the person beside him at his table and, after dinner, he was longing to finish the speech he had to give and find her again. As he stood up to talk, his eyes scanned the room for hers. She gave him a slight nod as she sat with her hands clasped under her chin, taking in every syllable he spoke.

Just after the compère thanked him for co-sponsoring the night and making such an informative speech, a net of balloons and tiny twinkling streamers were released onto the dance floor amidst a huge round of applause. Just on time the band struck up with an opening rendition of "Brown Eyed Girl". As the sounds of glasses clinking mixed with laughter and music, Serena surveyed the room with satisfaction. The auction had exceeded her expectations and after a few bars of the song only a couple of the tables were still occupied. The dance floor was heaving with happy punters.

Paul excused himself and went to the bar to buy a nightcap. Usually he would slip away at this point. His duty was done – he didn't have to hang around. Most people were langers drunk anyway, so any relevant conversations he needed to have were well over by this stage of the proceedings. Jim and Kate O'Keefe, Serena's parents, hadn't attended the function. They were in their house in Cap Ferret in France, so Paul decided he'd done his duty for the evening.

As the barman placed his whiskey on the counter, he heard her throaty voice behind him.

"Is that for me?"

"If you'd like it to be." He picked up the glass and handed it to her. He ordered another drink then led her out of the noisy function room to the hotel foyer.

"So was that fun, or did you feel it was as much fun as having a toe removed without an anaesthetic?" She raised an eyebrow, using his moment of laughter to drink him in fully, as he stood pulling his fingers through his dark mane of hair. He was sharply dressed in a kind of corporate shop-dummy sort of way but, my God, he could do with a woman's touch! There was no matching handkerchief in his suit pocket and his shoes could do with polishing. If he were with her, for instance, she'd see to all of that.

"Well," he exhaled dramatically, "I'm not overly comfortable with social gatherings – in fact I hate them. I find it so much of an effort to talk to people I don't know. I'm happier with the business end of things. To be honest, these evenings frighten the living shit out of me. All those people who want to know all about 'the real Paul'. I don't want to tell them my business. I like to keep myself to myself if you know what I mean?" He took a large swig of his drink and regarded her.

She stared back at him with amusement. "I'm the opposite. Ever since I was a little girl, I used to watch my mother getting ready to go to functions. Putting on her make-up, dressing in beautiful clothes. Wearing high heels and matching handbags, fastening sparkling jewels around her throat, and finally spraying herself with exotic perfume. I envied her and wanted to go with her. I always thought she was like Cinderella going to the ball. I longed to be old enough to go too."

An image of her mother flashed through her head. She was the one person that Serena had never felt at ease with. Her sister Adele had been their mother's favourite. Serena used to long to have a mother like some of her school friends. A confidante, someone she could go for coffee and lunch with. But Kate O'Keefe had never been affectionate or even terribly interested in her younger daughter. For all her beauty, her mother had been cold. So Serena had been closer to her father growing up.

"And now that you are old enough, do you still like it, or is it all a let-down?" he asked.

"No, it's not a let-down at all. I adore socialising. I love meeting people and finding out new things." She sighed happily. "Everybody has a story of their own. All you have to do is unlock their minds. Delve into their heads and usually they have a funny or sad or moving tale to tell." She flicked a speck of lint off her dress and raised her eyes to meet his. "For instance, I now know that Paul Davenport is an antisocial git, who would rather talk to his computer bits than people!"

"I don't mind talking to you." He moved towards her and kissed her. She didn't pull away.

* * *

20

Serena's thoughts were pulled out of the past and into the present as she caught sight of Paul and his clients at last. Grinning, her previous impatience was all forgotten. She rushed forward to greet him.

"Hello, darling. How was your trip?"

As they kissed, she inhaled his familiar musky scent and leaned against him. Every time he returned, even if he'd only been gone a couple of days, she was reminded of how much she loved him.

"Claire, how lovely to see you again. I hope you're not too exhausted, although it's only a short hop from London to here. I must admit to serious coat envy." Serena air-kissed the glamorous lady.

"Don't draw too much attention to it – Walter will wonder how much I spent on it!"

"And well you look too, Walter," Serena went on. "I'm glad you're keeping your good wife in the style she's become accustomed to."

Paul grinned, as he silently thanked his lucky stars for his fiancée. The flight had been short but Paul had still found it a trial. He was so bad at small talk and the general social niceties that Serena oozed naturally.

"I wasn't sure how hungry you'd all be," said Serena, "so I've booked a table in the bistro at your hotel, Claire. I figured that the big luncheon we have on for tomorrow might be enough formality for twenty-four hours."

Paul put his arm around her shoulder as they made their way from arrivals to her car. It was always appreciated when he asked Serena to do the meet and greet thing. People felt it was more of a personal approach. Besides, Paul loved to show her off.

3

tweeting@angiebaby.com
*The city lights are shining brightly . . . I am now a Dublin gal . . .
anyone know any good pubs for meeting people? . . . all work and
no play is making Angie a very dull girl . . .*

Angie felt like she was dreaming. One minute she was feeling disgruntled with her stale life in Cork and the next she was living in Dublin. Wiping the sweat from her brow, she dragged the last box out of the lift and into her new home. Picking up the phone, she dialled Rachel's number.

"Hello, you are now speaking to a Dublin resident, do I sound any different?" she giggled.

"How's it going? What's the flat like?" asked Rachel.

"Well, put it this way, the estate agent called it compact and that actually translates as being poky and the correct size for a gerbil to live in rather than a fine Corkwoman like myself, but I didn't spot any drug addicts or hobos sitting in the foyer and there's a taxi rank right outside." Angie leaned out the Velux window for a better view.

"Is the décor all modern and cool?" Rachel wanted to know everything.

"It's kind of plain, needs a bit of jazzing up, I would have thought, but sure you'll see it soon enough when you come for a visit." The girls chatted for a while longer and Angie agreed to call her friend soon to arrange their maiden voyage in the capital city.

* * *

Any kind of social life had to be better than the one she'd left behind. The final straw had been her fortieth birthday party. Three days before she'd left for Dublin, she'd reached that milestone age that she'd been dreading. She'd decided against having a big bash, as she didn't have a husband or significant other to organise it lovingly for her. She didn't want to advertise the fact that she was still left on the shelf.

Instead, she'd invited seven close friends to join her for dinner in an upmarket restaurant. There was no cake and no banners with *"Oh no, the big 40!"* decorating the walls. She'd wanted the whole event to slip past as quietly as possible. In her dreams as a little girl, she'd assumed she'd be a yummy mummy, in a beautiful house in the suburbs with a work-obsessed husband by the time she'd hit forty.

She'd had visions of herself putting her hand to her mouth and being all coy and shocked as she opened the dark velvet box her thoughtful husband had handed her, or even better having the waiter remove the silver dome from her starter to find a stunning necklace instead of the scallops she'd ordered. She'd envisaged envious sighs as her friends looked on as she dabbed at her eyes, overcome with emotion and love, at the gorgeous gesture by her man. She'd make a speech along the lines of, "Hubby and I don't always see eye to eye but it's times like these that have kept us going this long . . . we may not be perfect but we sure as hell know how to make each other laugh . . ."

Her adoring friends would all dab their eyes and the men would cough awkwardly, suppressing their huge emotion. Her hubby would then invite all concerned to raise their glasses in a toast to his "beautiful and dynamic wife".

Alas, instead, she'd gone to Marks and Spencer's and used her own wages to buy herself a "classic cut" black dress, which was sculpted to her curves with the help of a pair of hold-it-all-in-knickers and some slightly edgy-without-being-trashy high heels. She had her hair and make-up done (because she was worth it) while sitting on a high stool in the make-up department in a shopping centre.

Deflated inside, she'd sat for the evening in the upmarket restaurant with glued-on false eyelashes to match her false smile.

Before she'd even managed to swallow a mouthful of food, Deirdre, an old school friend and particularly smug married person had dropped the first clanger.

"I really admire you, Angie, do you know that?"

"Ah thanks, D. That's nice of you to say so," Angie had said, smiling.

"Yeah, like, I know if I were you, I'd rather sit at home and hide under the bed than have to organise my own party and come by myself. I'm *so* relieved I married Ronnie because I'd be a basket case if I were in your position. Fair play to you, you're a real little belter, isn't she, Rachel?"

How Angie didn't stand up and whack the bitch with her chair was nothing short of a miracle. Perhaps it was the intervention of a piece of asparagus being coughed out Rachel's nose in astonishment but her moment of violent tendencies passed.

Knowing she didn't want to get into making speeches or drawing attention to herself, any more than necessary, Angie had warned Rachel not to allow any surprise birthday cake which might have the potential to stop the other people in the restaurant and make them all lean in their chairs to look at her. As the dessert was served, without a candle in sight, she was about to exhale with relief, when the lights went out.

"Happy, Happy, Birthday,
To a girl with lots of pluck,
Tarzan's here to say to you,
How about a f***!"

"Stop! Please!" Angie flung her chair back and put her hand over the mouth of the puny and rather bald-looking attempt at Tarzan. "I'm sorry, I know I'm being a bit prudish and it's probably all a great laugh, but there are other people in this establishment trying to eat. So thank you all, or who ever organised this, but I think I'd like him to go now!"

Luckily the other guests at the table had drunk far too much champagne and wine to notice her pain. Instead, they all banged the table and shouted about how mean she'd been to poor Tarzan.

"At least give him an auld snog before he goes!" one of the men shouted from the other end of the table. Rachel had come to her rescue and ushered Tarzan (who happened to have a very strong Knocknaheeny accent and had probably never owned so much as a spider plant, never mind coming from the jungle) out, slipped him a tenner and sent him on his travels.

Angie felt like flinging her napkin onto the table and running out onto the road and diving in front of the first speeding truck.

She wanted to stamp her feet and yell, "No, this is all wrong! This isn't what I wanted. Where's the loving husband and the cute dog-eared pictures of little Jimmy and his baby sister Fiona?"

Then, in her dream world, she would drift into the lovely banter of reminiscing over the births of the children and how after "their wedding" they'd been the most wonderful days of her life. Instead she'd gritted her teeth until it was time to go home, Rachel had jumped into the taxi with her and they'd gone back to her flat and polished off a bottle of vodka.

"Oh God, that was awful wasn't it, Rachel?" Angie asked her friend mournfully. "Argh, and when that bitch Deirdre started going on about how she envied me I could've shoved my napkin in her mouth."

"Don't mind her, Angie," Rachel said loyally, "we've loads of time to find men. She's only jealous because she's married to that gimp of a creature."

When Rachel had gone home, Angie had thought about what she'd said. But Rachel was only thirty-five, it was different for her.

* * *

Relieved that was all behind her, Angie was more than ready to embrace her new venture in Dublin. It was the first time she'd worked with this new American team, and my God, were they cutting edge! They paid well, sure, but Jesus they expected 110% in return. In Cork, she'd been head of a team of six. At times that had been difficult to juggle. But it had all been chicken feed compared with these guys. When they said they wanted a list of figures ASAP, they didn't mean over the next couple of days they meant right now. In fact, five minutes ago. They didn't "do" the usual Irish attitude of putting things on the long finger. She was well able to keep up with them and was more than capable in her job, but she was still unaccustomed to their zero-tolerance, impersonal approach.

"Thank you, Angie, we'll see you here tomorrow morning at seven. Please have all the proposals ready for us to go through." Mr Crispin, one of the American team shook her hand and left the room.

She fully realised that the money she would make from the whole experience was going to be seriously worthwhile, but she wasn't sure if she'd have the energy to enjoy it.

None of the American team were drinkers. She figured that out early on. She had enough cop-on to realise that they wouldn't look kindly on her if she ended up trollied any time they took her for dinner. She was determined to avoid being the typical *Irish* stereotype in their eyes, she wasn't going to let herself down by looking like a beer-guzzling buffoon in their company.

Work was one thing, but her life outside the office was bordering on depressing. Needless to say, nothing had changed. No men were throwing themselves at her, even though she'd splashed out on new work suits. She still went to work, came home via the shop to buy a dinner for one, which she ate, while still wearing her coat, directly from the heat-and-serve packaging.

She'd tried to chat to the gum-chewing girl at the cash desk in the supermarket on the way home this evening. "I suppose I'm not the only one buying these meals for one, or you wouldn't bother selling them?"

"Right." The girl wasn't up for a chat.

Feeling like a leper, Angie had stuck her dinner in the microwave, opened a bottle of wine and stood watching her chilli con carne turning round and round. Grabbing the remote control, she flicked from one channel to the next. She'd been excited when she'd spotted the sky dish in the living room, but somehow she couldn't ever seem to find anything of interest to watch.

By nine o'clock, she'd eaten, finished a glass of wine, ironed her blouse for the next morning, had a shower, and found herself at a total loss. As she sat on the tiny balcony, she tried to listen for any signs of life in the apartments above or below her. Either everyone else was out having fun, or the block was mostly unoccupied. The city sky was awash with orange and white lights, blighting the sky and stopping the stars from being able to twinkle.

Wrapping her arms around her legs, she crouched in the plastic garden chair and wished she was at home on the farm. Even though there would be no noise of traffic and no streetlights for miles, she wouldn't feel this alone. At least the stars would shine and make pretty glittery patterns, of animals, faces and all sorts of evolving images. Here she was surrounded by the sound of an impersonal fabricated world, where no one would even miss her if she expired at that moment.

4

Serena stood with her hands on her hips and surveyed Paul's apartment with satisfaction. She really had worked wonders on it. A pity they would have to move out after the wedding. They would need something more appropriate to the lifestyle of a successful couple than an apartment, however lavish.

When she moved in at first, the apartment was slightly drab.

"Darling, it's lovely, but it needs a woman's touch," she'd said. "Would you let me do it up a bit?"

"Be my guest. I have neither the time nor the inclination. I'd be delighted if you want to do a bit of redecorating." He was thrilled she wanted to look after him.

She took off, phoning and driving to interior shops. Within a month, she had turned the place into a home. She picked luscious deep shades for the bedroom. Calm comfortable tones for the living room. She changed the hard leather sofas for plush deep couches. She had the ready-made curtains removed and added sweeping velvet drapes which pooled luxuriously on the floor, making the room look opulent and impressive.

She was a dab hand at organising caterers and florists to come to the apartment and create flawless evenings for Paul and his clients.

The first time this happened was something of an emergency.

"Hi, Serena, I know it's very short notice, but I've a client coming from the UK today. I can't get into Guilbaud's restaurant tonight – is there any way you could organise a meal"? Paul held his breath waiting for her response.

"Of course, honey. What time will I expect them here?" she said soothingly.

"Well, around eight, I suppose," he replied and felt himself relax.

"No problem, I'll be ready and I'll have everything organised. See you later." She hung up and hummed to herself. Picking up the phone again, she set about organising the evening.

The ease with which Serena did all this impressed Paul beyond belief. He had been lacking hugely in this department and she was an enormous help to him. She was always stunningly turned out, her hair and skin immaculate, her clothes always the best of everything. She was the missing link that he had needed in his life. She had taken the sting out of his world. He was now in a position to concentrate on his ever-growing business and leave the part that unnerved him to her flawless capabilities.

It seemed like the most natural thing in the world when Paul proposed. He'd booked their favourite table in the Four Seasons and, as she'd clinked his glass and toasted him, he'd looked around. The maître d'hôtel was approaching with a large platter covered by a silver dome.

"I believe this is for you, Madam." He bowed formally.

Serena was taken completely by surprise. "But we haven't even ordered yet."

The maître d' raised the silver dome to reveal a stunning diamond ring.

Before Serena could utter another word Paul got down on one knee, to the applause of the onlookers. "You are the light of my life, Serena. Will you do me the honour of being my wife?"

The one-and-a-half carat diamond looked perfect on her slender, brown finger.

* * *

Serena immediately flew into action, organising their wedding.

"Paul, hi, love, I know you're up to your eyes, but hear me out. I'm in the Four Seasons with Victor, that old pal of Mummy and Daddy's who just happens to be the current manager of this wonderful establishment! Guess what? They can offer us a date in October. Too rushed or will we just go for it?" Serena tapped the table in the reception room with a perfectly manicured nail.

"Erm, yeah, you know me, I'm never going to jump for joy at the thought of a large function, but I do want to marry you so your call, my sweet," he grinned. Serena really didn't "do" waiting around, he mused. She gave out about her sister Adele and how impatient she was, but the girls had more in common than they realised.

Every detail had to be precisely managed, and it would be. Serena's determination and attention to detail would shine through. She travelled to London to purchase her wedding gown. It was a buttery cream satin sheath, which would accentuate her figure and skin tone. She ordered cream roses for her bouquet, the church and hotel flowers. It would all be tasteful and simple, yet impossibly elegant.

There was only going to be one bridesmaid and one flower girl in the bridal party. Serena had plenty of friends she could ask but there simply wasn't time to organise too many people, if she wanted it all to be perfect the following month. Besides, she wanted to be the centre of attention. This was her moment to shine.

Serena wanted to feel confident and relaxed on the day. Although they were both stunning, she wanted her only sister and her darling niece Ruby to be by her side. Feeling excitement bubbling inside her, she dialled Adele's number.

"Oh gosh, I'm a little surprised I must admit. Would you not prefer to have one of your girlfriends?" Adele replied. "You're sweet to ask but would I not look utterly foolish at my age, swanning down the aisle looking all mutton dressed as lamb?"

"Well, I wasn't thinking of putting you in a one shouldered thing held together at the sides with large safety pins. I just happened to see the most divine creamy coloured Chanel suit that has the most subtle hint of gold threaded through it. The minute I saw it, I just thought it had your name all over it. Coupled with a tightly bound posy of roses, I think it would make you look elegant and far less tacky than a row of young ones in garish matching dresses! I'd love to have Ruby as a flower girl too." Serena waited for her sister to mull it all over.

"That sounds like a wonderful idea. I'm honoured, thank you." For a split second, there was a warm moment between the sisters. "I would be delighted to accept."

"And what do you think about Ruby? She'll be so thrilled, I hope!" Serena was getting little butterflies of excitement now.

"Yes I suppose that'll be fine, just so long as she's not wearing something inappropriate. She's still only fifteen, don't forget. I understand that girl thinks she knows it all, but she's too headstrong for her own good. Keep it tasteful, won't you?"

"Adele, why do you have to assume that I'm going to dress her in a bandeau of lycra and six-inch heels? Do I dress like a tart? Would I even consider putting Ruby in something that doesn't suit her? Give me a shred of credit, please. Why would I go to the trouble of having a gorgeous gown for myself, putting you in Chanel and making Ruby look like a hooker? I have acquired the palest gold heavy silk satin and was hoping to have a designer make her a bodice and down-to-the-floor skirt. I would never want Ruby to feel any thing but happy and pretty. One last thing, this is *my* wedding, so don't you forget that." Serena slammed the phone down feeling stung to the core. She'd really hoped that by asking Adele to be part of the wedding that it might make things a little more friendly between them.

Adele was just jealous, she decided, so she called Noelle, one of her oldest friends, to chat about all the wedding build-up.

Herself and Noelle had been "best friends" in school. Her parents were also very wealthy, and there had always been some underlying rivalry between the two girls. When Serena was given a convertible Golf GTI for her seventeenth birthday, four months later Noelle arrived in school driving a Volvo. It was a silent game of anything you can do, I can do better, bigger and costing more.

Knowing they were in the same league, they pushed the limits with each other all the time. When Serena had her eighteenth birthday party, she had a big marquee in her parents' garden. She invited two hundred guests and the night was a roaring success. Four months later, Noelle did the same, except she also had stilt-walkers, fire-eaters and a lady doing tango dance lessons.

Now Noelle was already married and had a baby, so Serena was beyond relieved that she was now finally following suit. Paul was a lot more of a catch than Noelle's husband, in Serena's mind, so she felt she should be entitled to a small gloat, in the circumstances.

"Meet me for lunch tomorrow at twelve in that little Italian off Grafton Street and I'll fill you in," Serena gushed.

* * *

Serena had some swatches of fabric in her Louis Vuitton handbag, ready to show her friend. She was just finishing her glass of sparkling wine when Noelle arrived.

"I'm sorry – I'm not late, am I?" Noelle pulled up her sleeve to check her watch.

"Not at all, darling, I was early, had some details to go through and thought it would be easier to do it here," said Serena smiling. "You'll join me in a glass of bubbly, won't you?"

"Of course, sweetie. God, I've had a terrible morning, I went just after nine to get my hair done, and my usual guy wasn't in, so they made a total hames of my head and I've only just escaped."

"Poor you but it's nothing a couple of glasses of vino won't fix." Serena patted her arm while motioning to a passing waitress.

They finished their bubbly and ordered chicken Caesar salads. Serena and Noelle were never outwardly nasty to each other, but there was always the underlying feeling that the competition was there all the same.

"Bring us a bottle of Chablis and a bottle of Evian water, please," said Serena. "Make sure the Chablis is very cold, I hate warm white wine." She flicked a smile at the waiter and turned back to Noelle. "As it's going to be October when I get married, Adele will be fine in her Chanel suit. I think Ruby should have sleeves on her dress or at least a bolero jacket for the church. Nothing annoys me more than people flapping about with slipping and sliding pashminas so that will rule out all that fumbling."

"I think you're rather brave, to be honest." Noelle gazed out her long-lasting false eyelashes at Serena.

"Why? What do you mean?"

"Well, Adele is impossibly elegant at the best of times. Dressing her in Chanel, is that wise? And Ruby hardly has a face like a smacked bottom! She's so young and stunning. Are you not worried she'll steal your limelight?" Noelle raised an eyebrow, with a smirk playing on her lips.

"Don't be so ridiculous, Noelle. Adele has her own look which is going to look impossibly attractive I won't deny, but believe me my gown is showstopper enough to compete. Ruby is only a child and, besides, I don't want some total pug ruining my wedding album. I wouldn't have anyone else as my flower girl. Ruby is my niece and the light of my life. Life isn't a competition when it comes to the ones we love." Serena smiled falsely. "Anyway, you're one to talk, you had myself and Julie as your bridesmaids."

"Hum, yes, I did, didn't I?"

The wine arrived and was promptly poured, diverting any further catty comments.

5

tweeting@themercedesking.com
Pints all half price at 'The Orb' club Mon to Thurs all this week —
come on down the price is right.

Damo loved his Merc. He never tired of sinking into the plush leather seat and gliding towards one of his many establishments. Tonight was going to a biggie. His most prestigious club was renowned for its mega laser-light display, and even more so the VIP backroom area.

Anyone who was anyone in the music and film industry ended up in the rear-positioned, elevated VIP section of The Orb. Damo made sure the area was strictly monitored so the celebs could relax and feel like they were in a private arena.

The front of the special room boasted a large smoked-glass circle, so although it was slightly raised above the rest of the club, punters could still get the odd glimpse of their favourite celebrity, should they choose to pose near the window.

Today Damo was buzzing. Beyoncé was in town playing a sell-out gig that very evening. The venue was less than twenty minutes from The Orb and her publicity people had been on to him that afternoon to confirm her interest in an after-show party.

"Now, you understand that we'll have to pull out and take her somewhere else if there are too many paps around," said her PR woman. "We'll have our own security, but you'll have to make sure you have enough people on site to keep the crowd from getting too close."

"Rest assured," said Damo, "that we will treat Beyoncé with the utmost respect and she won't be put in any danger from the public on my premises. The place will be crawling with security. We have a rear entrance if she wants to come in that way, or if she would prefer the red carpet I can have that roped off and security lining either side of it at the front. All that depends on how many pictures you are aiming for in the papers."

"I'll have to check that and let you know. I emailed you her list of guests earlier – did you receive it?"

"Yeah, I have that here. I've me iPhone on all the time, so just mail me again if you want to add anyone. You know yourself, the old rule is still golden," and Damo put on a very bad cockney accent, "'If you're not on the list, you're not comin' in'."

"Yes, I see. I'll let you know if there are any changes."

"Did you get my backstage list? It's just my two daughters and three other girls in total. Along with my good self of course," said Damo jovially.

"Yes, we have all the names. See you later on unless I think of anything else in the meantime." The click let him know she'd hung up.

Letting himself into the club via the rear entrance, he inspected the area, making sure it was all spotless. The staff were putting the finishing touches to the exotic flower displays on either side of the bar.

"Jaysus, that yolk looks like it'd jump down and bite me. Are ya sure Beyoncé likes that kind of thing?" Damo stared at the orange birds of paradise arrangements being slid into place.

"Ah yeah, they're all the rage now, Damo. People like the fresh-flowers touch. Adds a bit more class." Nina looked after the VIP bar and she'd never let him down before.

Whistling, Damo continued to pace through the club, casting his expert eye over every nook and cranny.

But it was far from flash cars or unusual floral arrangements that he'd been raised. He'd done well for himself. No one could argue with that.

He'd been with Noreen since they were nineteen. With a baby on the way, getting married had seemed like the right thing to do.

"I'll make sure the baby has everything it needs. I'll look after yous," Damo had vowed.

They had a brilliant wedding. Real flash. It was in The Regal Hotel in the city centre. They had three hundred guests. Damo organised a horse and carriage to bring Noreen and her sisters to the church.

"Ya look legend, love," he told her as she stood beside him at the top of the aisle. Sniffing the air, he had to ask, "What's the smell?"

"Me bleedin' veil got dipped in horse wee just as we got out of the carriage!"

They started giggling and they couldn't stop. All through the ceremony they got wafts of horse, which set them off again. Luckily the priest was elderly and one of those eyes-mostly-shut ones, so he'd mistaken their mirth for loved-up emotion.

The reception had blown everyone away. He'd gone all out with decorations.

"Would you like flowers or balloons on the tables, sir?" the banqueting manager had asked.

"Both. And make sure there's loads of little presents on the table so people have a ton of gear to take home." He'd paced up and down the function room, imagining how impressed everyone would be.

"We can get a new thing done, where they personalise boxes of matches, actually print your name on them. Would you like that?" the girl had asked tentatively.

"Yeah, mega. Do it all. Then put all that sparkly stuff all over the tables too. I'm getting some of those new yolks for each table as well. Instamatic cameras – have you seen them? You press the button and they spit out the photo, there and then. Deadly they are, I'm putting one on each table and getting people to take pictures so we have a taste of the action, as well as the formal ones."

The banqueting manager had looked wildly impressed with the ideas and Damo had felt a hundred feet high.

"Jaysus, Damo, ya really know how to throw a bash!" his mates had told him the night of the wedding. They were all dead impressed with the spread – roast beef with all the trimmings – not to mention the free bar all night. It was the best piss-up they had ever been to.

The wedding cake had eight tiers on it, with a little water feature running out of the top layer, with a little bride and groom standing gazing into each other's eyes.

As they cut the cake, he'd winked at her. "I couldn't find a figurine that looked up the pole, so you'll have to use your imagination."

"Cheeky bastard!" Noreen had cackled.

Noreen's belly wasn't that big and it didn't stop her having a few drinks to celebrate the day.

"I'm managing the crème de menthe with me crushed ice, but this child has put me right off me fags. I miss them, especially on a day like today, but I'll be back on them as soon as it's born," she'd confided to Damo.

"Please God, pet." Damo had patted her leg. "You love them fags and it's hard to see you wanting one and not being able to enjoy one on your special day."

As the DJ turned on the flashing lights and Elton John and Kiki Dee sang, "Don't Go Breaking My Heart," the fourteen bridesmaids, all dressed in mint green, dragged the eager groomsmen onto the dance floor.

Noreen had decided to let the wedding party lead the first dance, on account of her bump. "I can't jump around just after me dinner. I'd end up yakking all over me wedding dress. Let the girls and the fellas get things going," she'd advised.

"They look like a colony of penguins at a toothpaste factory, don't they?" Damo nudged Noreen as he watched them, and as the two of them laughed he stood behind her and hugged her close.

That was all nearly thirty years ago now. Damo had kept his wits about him since then. As he made money, he invested it in another business, and so on. He rarely touched a drink so he was able to stay on top of his game. Fair enough, he used the odd line of coke to help him keep his eye on the ball. But that was normal in his books.

Himself and Noreen had three kids. Alexis (the wedding bump) now twenty-nine, Elvis twenty-five, and the baby, Mariah, almost sixteen. He'd given his kids everything. They lived in a five-bedroom house in Blackrock, a posh suburb of Dublin.

The kids all went to private schools. Santa came every year and left most of the toy shop on their large patterned sitting-room carpet. It was all worlds apart from the life he'd grown up with. Santa had stopped coming when he was five and if there'd been a roast chicken on the paper tablecloth at Christmas they'd have been doing well. In Damo's house they had a turkey the size of an ostrich, half a pig, enough potatoes to reverse a famine and more desserts and sweets than they'd eat in a lifetime.

He was happy with Noreen. She was a grand girl in fairness to her. She never moaned and kept to herself. He never had any long-term affair, although he'd plenty of girls throwing themselves at him over the years. But none of them ever lasted too long. He was more concerned with looking after his own at the end of the day. Himself and Noreen never talked about the young ones, but they had their own understanding.

Being a good provider for his family gave him more of a buzz than anything else. Noreen could have whatever she wanted, he minded them all like a caveman, and they never wanted for anything. His kids had the best parties for miles around – he knew they were the envy of their buddies. He loved that. He knew what it felt like to be the son of a redundant biscuit packer and a ma who looked like she carried the worries of the world on her scrawny nylon-clad shoulders.

For Elvis's twenty-first, he'd pulled out all the stops. They'd had a marquee in the garden, with a thick red carpet at the entrance. Fire-eaters and stilt-walkers greeted the guests. Inside there were two champagne fountains. Each table was set out with goodies. Gold chains for the girls and watches for the lads. Caterers made and served the food. The dinner was followed by a top class DJ.

Then he'd made his speech.

"I'll never forget the day my son was born. I was the proudest father alive. When I was growing up, I didn't have much, so I wanted Elvis to have it all. He was named after The King, and that's exactly what he is to me and his ma. Thanks for coming tonight and for making the party a success so far. For your entertainment tonight, I'd like you all to give a warm Dublin welcome to P Diddy."

The crowd went wild. The inside of the marquee was in total darkness apart from the tiny twinkling lights in the roof, which made it look like a starry sky. As Puff Daddy took to the stage, a huge laser light show took off. The kids screamed and clapped and jumped around like wild animals. Damo was delighted for Elvis. It was the party of the century and he'd be a hero among his mates. That gave Damo a warm feeling inside. He never wanted his son to feel like a low-life scumbag, the way he'd felt as a kid.

Not a bad show for a little fecker from the north side, Damo congratulated himself.

When the American rap star finished his set, he paused briefly for photos before being whisked away.

Next came the feathered bikini-clad burlesque dancers.

"Thanks for all the enthusiasm – are yous having a good time?" Damo held the microphone out.

"*Yeeeeeees!*" The guests nearly lifted the roof off.

"If yous'll all follow me outside, I'd like to give our Elvis a little birthday pressie." The crowd shuffled outside, where Noreen came around the corner beeping in a large black BMW jeep, complete with a huge red ribbon and balloons.

"Omigod!" Elvis was stunned. His friends cheered and clapped and all said how they wished they had parents like his.

"Well done, love, that went really well." Damo hugged Noreen.

"Sure you're the best da in the world, Damo. You've them kids spoilt rotten, but they love you for it. MTV, eat your heart out!" Noreen had laughed.

The disco went on until the early hours of the next morning. The champagne flowed all night, as did the full bar. Dublin had met Hollywood as Damo pulled out all the stops.

"This is for you, my love." He handed Noreen a velvet box.

Inside was the thickest gold chain she'd ever seen. It would have looked more at home as a choke-chain for a wild dog, but Noreen squealed with delight.

"It's massive, Damo, thanks, love!" Her eyes shone with glee.

He'd bought himself a matching one, which he'd put on that night over his white T-shirt, with a smart pinstripe Hugo Boss jacket. His jet-black hair (helped along by his trusty bottle of Grecian 2000) which he styled with wax, set off the whole look.

He looked around proudly at the whole set-up. He'd come a long way since the days he'd lugged beer kegs around a smelly cellar.

"You're one in a million, Damo. You look after us all like a real pro." Noreen had looked up at him in awe. "The chain sets off me rings and all. Brings out the lovely leopard-skin nail-art on me fingers too. Thanks, love." She kissed him passionately.

* * *

Now, speeding in his Merc through Dublin on his way to his night-club, Damo thanked his lucky stars that he was as far away from the world he'd grown up in as possible.

As a kid, he used to see the men driving around town in big fancy Mercs like the one he now owned. Real businessmen, in expensive suits, ones custom-made by Louis Copeland. Guys who'd made it in life. Who had big fancy houses in the suburbs, not like the damp two-bed council house he'd grown up in.

Fair enough, his ma and da had done their best for him and his two brothers. But the biscuit factory where his da worked was never going to make him a rich man.

When he was fourteen, his da was made redundant.

"You'll have to leave school and find your own way now, son – we can't manage unless you bring a few bob into the house," his ma had told him.

Most of the time he didn't bother going to school anyway, so he figured he might as well try and earn a few quid. He got himself a job packing in a warehouse down the docks. The pay was shit, but it was better than nothing. It also beat sniffing glue or drinking cans with the other lads from his neighbourhood.

He kept his head down and stayed out of trouble. When he was seventeen, he got a job in a nightclub. He moved from stacking the bar with bottles to being allowed to pull pints. He soon realised that smiling at the ladies and being quick off the mark with the men gained him tips.

"Yes, darlin', what can I get you? You're lookin' lovely if you don't mind me sayin'." He winked at the pissed girl who was swaying and waving a twenty in his face.

"Tanks, love, and sure have one yourself," she smiled back at him.

Damo leaned over and kissed her hand. Swerving around, he threw the price of the drink he'd been offered into a small plastic lunch box he kept under the counter. On a good week, he managed to clock up over two hundred pounds in tips.

Some of the people who came to the club were loaded. Throwing fifties around like they were used toilet paper. Drinking more in one night than he'd earn in a week. He never let it get to him all the same. Instead of getting ratty with the rich bastards, he played them. He charmed them and they paid out. He didn't *get* the way they behaved, pissin' their money against the wind, pouring their wages down their necks or snorting it all up their nostrils, but that was their lookout. He always hoped he'd manage to earn enough to open his own club one day. Then he'd really be in a position to drag himself out of this drudgery of a life. Unlike most of his peers, he was going to use drink and people who poured it down their necks as a stepping-stone out of the gutter and onto the bright side of the road.

The night of the fight, Damo was behind the bar as usual. He was straining to hear the man in front of him as he was ordering a round of drinks. The music was pumping, the strobe lights were flicking like mad and the smoke was thick and grey in the air.

"You'll have to speak up, bud, I can't hear ya!" Damo put his hand behind his ear to try and cup in the sound of the man's voice.

As he leaned over to try and take the order he felt a hot searing pain rip through the side of his face. The heat was followed by a dull thud and then silence.

When he woke up, he was in a hospital bed with two nurses looking down at him. The smell of disinfectant hit his nostrils, the bright strip-lighting hurt his eyes. The noise of metal trolleys being shoved around rang through his head.

"Hi, Damian, you're in the hospital. You got caught in the crossfire of major bust-up," said the nurse.

"There was a major fight in the club where you work. The police think it was two drug dealers fighting over their patch. You've been glassed in the face and hit over the back of the head with a baseball bat," said the other nurse.

Damo put his hand up to his face. He was like a mummy, bandaged and bound. His head felt like he'd been hit with a sledgehammer. Well, it had really.

"Is me face fucked?" he asked the nurse.

"The surgeon did what he could. You're going to need a lot more surgery, but they managed to save your eye," said the nurse.

"What do mean, save me eye?" he asked horrified.

"They got you right down the side of your temple, hooking the side of your eye on the way. Your cheekbone was also exposed by the jagged glass."

"Jaysus, the pricks! What will me boss say? When will I be able to go back to work? I don't want to lose me job," he fretted.

"The compo you're going to get from this will mean you won't be working for a very long time unless I'm very much mistaken," one of the nurses said, smiling at him. "That's probably the only positive thing that can be taken out of this whole situation. You try and get some rest. The police want to talk to you, but we'll try and hold them off for another while so you can get your head together." She patted his arm and walked out of the cubicle.

His progress had been slow and, by the time the court case came up, he was still in a bad way, unable to work and about to go utterly doolally cooped up in his ma's damp council house, being subjected to cups of tea with Mrs Wilkins from over the road and an endless ream of TV soaps. If he didn't get out of there and back on his feet rapidly, he'd most definitely be up in court for murder – starting with Donal, his ma's budgie. The little green fecker spent its time clawing its way around the tiny cage in the corner of the dark sitting room.

"Hew-r-ya, Donal?" his ma would twitter and poke the poor little bastard through the bars. Once a day, she'd let him out for a quick fly. Every day, Donal did dive-bombing poos all around the place, hitting everything from the little scary ornaments to various parts of Damo's body.

"He's a useless yolk," Damo had fumed. "He either pecks repeatedly or makes constant noise and then finishes off his exercise in futility by shittin' all over me and the entire bleedin' room. What's the point of him, Ma?"

"Leave Donal alone, ya great big bully! Don't mind him, Donal, he's only a gobshite." She'd stick her finger in the side of the cage and make kissy noises at the bird.

As it happened, the air of hopelessness and Donal-infused depression that emanated from Damo swung things in his favour in court.

"Look at him, he's a shadow of his former self, Your Honour," his wig had expounded. "He used to be a real get-up-and-go sort of a fella. The trauma of this attack has sapped the life out of him and left him frustrated and nervous." When all the wigs and lads in suits had looked at Damo for proof, he felt like he wanted to crawl into a hole and die. He was morto – he hated being stared at, especially by all these posh, up-their-own-arses legal guys.

Taking pity on the poor cowering lad in the ill-fitting nylon suit and plastic slip-on shoes, the judge had decided to make an example of the cocky, drug baron who'd glassed and beaten him. Damo had ended up being awarded sixty thousand pounds in damages, which in 1980 was a fortune.

Damo didn't let the money go to waste. He seized the opportunity to set himself up. He wasn't going to piss it against the wind and leave himself open to ending up like his da. If it was the last thing he did, he was going to get the hell out of the depressing budgie toilet he called home. He bought a pub of his own, in a central location, along the docklands in Dublin. The area was fairly rundown but Damo saw the potential and got a huge premises for a song.

It took him nearly a year to renovate the three-storey building into a bar, nightclub and members-only club on the top floor. He spent a good wedge of cash on the publicity. The night of the opening, he invited loads of the well-known businessmen. The press were there to take their pictures. The champagne flowed and the seeds were sown. Before long, it was the "in place" to be seen. His private, members-only bar was a hit. All the pop stars dropped in when they were in town. And Damo was always there to look after the ladies, in more ways than one.

* * *

As he paced around the main part of The Orb, Damo's echoing footsteps rang across the large dance floor. In just a few hours' time, this entire place would be a heaving mass of scantily clad clubbers.

A ripple of excitement fluttered through him. It wasn't just about money. The buzz of being Damo McCabe, the successful businessman, never wore thin for him. Slipping into the gents' toilet, he quickly fixed himself a line of coke. With a bit of luck tonight's concert would attract a good after-show crowd. The recession had hit him like a sledgehammer. But Beyoncé was a sell-out and, once people were dressed up and on a night out, it generally meant they didn't want to go home too early.

Alighting from the cubicle in the men's room, he washed his hands and checked his face in the mirror. Satisfied there were no tell-tale signs of white powder around his nostrils, he clapped his hands, rubbed them together and strode towards the back door and his beloved Merc.

He'd enough time to fly home, have a shower, put on one of his new designer suits and make sure the girls were ready to go to the show.

Grinning to himself, he could nearly hear the giggles and squeals of excitement already. Noreen was probably having a cuppa and a fag in the kitchen, while all hell was breaking loose upstairs with make-up and hairspray a-plenty.

"You are the main man." He pointed at his own reflection in the tiny mirror in the visor of his car. As he turned the key in the ignition, the stereo pumped out an upbeat tune.

6

tweeting@rubytuesday.com
Beyoncé beckons! Bring it on! if I weren't me, I would be pea green with envy!!!

Ruby twirled around to check herself out fully in the mirror. Her mother had taken her to the most exclusive boutique in South Dublin. She was in third year in St Brigid's secondary school for young ladies, the most salubrious all-girls school in Dublin. At the age of fifteen she thought she knew it all, and that her mother was put on this earth to get on her wick.

"I love, love, love it! It shows off my figure and all those years of pony camp have made sure I have the legs to wear it too." She slipped into the customary pair of heels that were left in most changing rooms – hard, high and the size of boats.

"I don't know, Ruby, I think it's too old for you. It's like something Tina Turner would wear. I think your father would have heart failure if he saw you in that." Adele bit her lip. Her daughter most definitely had the figure for the dress but she was still only a child. If she'd had her way, she wouldn't be going to this concert with her friend tomorrow night. But Harry had overruled, saying that she would probably get out the window and go on her own if they didn't give her a bit of leeway. Besides, her friend's father would be there to keep an eye on them.

45

"Mariah is going to die when she sees me in this! Can I get a pair of kitten heels too?" Ruby used her puppy-dog-eyed look to win her mother over.

Mariah's dad owned The Orb, which made him just about the coolest father on the planet. Mariah had met Robbie Williams, Take That, The Script, U2 and a whole host of other A-listed stars. Her dad had managed to sneak her in the back door to the club any time he'd got the nod from one of the big PR companies. Until today, Ruby's mother had held firm on the matter of her going too.

"You're too young, Ruby. When you hit seventeen, and have at least done your Junior Cert, we'll consider it. Besides, it's illegal for you and Mariah to be on those premises." Adele had been adamant. "You don't have that much time for hanging around – you have pony camp coming up. Daddy spent a fortune on that horse you have up at the stables, so don't even consider leaving it standing in a field like a recluse."

"I was up there this morning, I have all my dressage course learned off, so don't annoy me," Ruby sighed. Her mother was getting more and more nagging, and she hadn't a clue about horses in the first place. All she did was drop Ruby to the stables, without so much as placing her Jimmy Choos on the ground. Her Range Rover had never been allowed to have so much as a speck of mud on it. So her mother was not in a position to lecture *her* about horses.

Tonight, Mariah had invited Ruby to come backstage to a Beyoncé concert, followed by the invitation-only after-show bash, at The Orb.

"Mum, Dad, I'll die if you don't let me go!" Ruby had pleaded. "I'll be sixteen in three months' time. You need to face facts that I am not going to stay a child forever. You still see me as a tiny kid but I've moved on. I don't want to end up as a total dork with no friends. Everyone in school is queuing up to go to this gig. I've got free tickets and will even be in the same room as Beyoncé. You have to let me go!"

Harry, Ruby's dad had been suitably impressed and even expressed serious interest in going himself. "If your mother continues to say no, can I go with Mariah?"

"Harry, you're not helping matters here!" said Adele. "Will you phone Ruby's house and ask to speak to one of the parents and find out the exact schedule? I can't let her go if they're going to be left on their own hanging around clubs and concerts. I know you all think I'm the most fuddy-duddy person in the world, but I happen to think I know what's best for my daughter. If you feel the supervision will be fairly sound, I'll consider it." She held her hands up in defeat.

Harry had made the call.

"I bring all the stars into the club, Harry. It'll be a blast for the girls to see Beyoncé. It'll be cool."

Damo McCabe made Harry feel like an ancient old git. This guy was happening and seemed to know everyone there was to know in the business.

"Eh, right so," Harry mumbled.

"It'll be a first-class gig – the entourage and PR crew she's using are second to none. The guy who's staging the show is a good buddy of mine and I've told him the girls are coming down. They'll be treated like royalty. My older daughter is going with a couple of mates too. They'll have a blast. You're only young once, what?"

"Yes, I suppose. We're just concerned because Ruby is still only fifteen and she hasn't grown up rubbing shoulders with the stars. Her mother and I only want what's best for her, you know?"

"Yeah, sure thing. I'm with you all the way. But, believe me, they'll be a notch higher in the cool stakes when they go back to school on Monday. The kids would all give anything to be going to this thing tonight. A bit of street cred is where it's at with the young ones, wha?"

Harry didn't like Damo McCabe. He seemed to have a very high opinion of himself, acting like he knew everything. Harry knew he'd made his money on clubs and bars, but no amount of money could buy class, and Harry felt that was the one thing the other man was lacking.

Finally he agreed he'd drop Ruby over to the McCabes' at six o'clock the night of the concert. Ruby was to stay over with Mariah, on condition she'd be back home before ten the next morning.

Now Ruby flew up to her room to gather half the house to take over to Mariah's house. She'd got false eyelashes, brush-on body-shimmer stuff and the new colour of Juicy Tubes lip gloss. To keep her mother happy, she cycled over to the stables and took Biscuit her pony out for a quick hack.

She'd been riding since she was four and up until now her pony had been her life. She still loved her beautiful bay mare, but as she hacked towards the big back field where she would go for a gallop, her head was filled with the thoughts of seeing the pop star and all the cool people that night.

"When you see me next, I'll be one of the 'in set'," she told the pony. "It's all thanks to you that I'm not like a huge big dumpling in my dress either. Let's go for it, girl!" She squeezed her legs to urge the pony to quicken her pace. She felt as free as a bird as the wind whooshed past them and they cantered across the field.

After she'd finished walking Biscuit to cool her off, she gave her a quick brush-down, put on her rug and put her into her stable.

"You have a few nuts, Biscuit. You're the best girl." Ruby kissed her velvety nose and gave her a firm pat on the neck.

Hopping on her bike, Ruby cycled home to have her shower, wash her hair and get ready to go to Mariah's house.

Her dad was giving her a lift, so her mother had one last fuss at her in the hallway.

"Please be careful, Ruby. I know you think you know it all, but you're at a very vulnerable age, and there are a lot of weirdos out there. Keep your head and no drinking alcohol, and if you get a coke or orange or something, don't leave it unattended. There are too many stories of people having drinks spiked and waking up days later in dingy flats with God knows who!"

"Mum, I'm going to have fun, not to get stabbed, drugged or attacked. Chill. Okay. I might be only fifteen, but I do actually possess a brain!" Ruby rolled her eyes to heaven.

"I know, darling. Sorry, I just worry, that's all."

Outside the McCabes' house, Ruby leaned across to give her daddy a kiss, before jumping out and emptying the boot of all her bags. Harry smiled to himself. Ruby could've been moving out for a year, with all the stuff she'd brought with her.

Herself and Mariah hugged and air-kissed and squealed, before tearing in and thundering up the stairs to Mariah's room.

"Ohmigod, that dress is u-mazing. You're going to look so cool!" Mariah stroked the gold sequin mini-dress enviously. "Those gold hoops are perfect with it too."

"Yours is stunning!" Ruby looked at Mariah's full-length black backless number. "We are going to have the most amazing night ever!"

Damo walked into the house and smiled. As he'd predicted there was a thick fog of perfume, hairspray and nail polish, mixed with deafening music.

"Hiya?"

There was no answer. Taking the stairs two at a time, he called through Mariah's door as he made his way to his and Noreen's en suite.

"Hi, girls, we're out of here in twenty minutes!"

"Hi, Daddy, we can't wait! This is going to be the best night of our lives. We're nearly ready." Mariah appeared in a towelling dressing gown with a cordless GHD straightener wrapped around the front of her fringe.

"Hi, Ruby, how's it going, love?" Damo got a glimpse of the girl in Mariah's room. Not looking too shabby, he mused.

"I'm in here." He heard Noreen calling from the separate bathroom she loved so much. He'd had the bath put in especially for her. It was pure class. Gold taps, a lovely shade of pink and deep as a hot tub.

"Hiya, love. I'm flying! Don't know where the afternoon went." He stuck his head into the steamy room for a split second.

"Do you want a sandwich or something before you go? I'm only after sitting in here."

"No, I'm not hungry. You enjoy your bath and I'll get me shower. Did you iron that Hugo Boss white shirt for me? Don't want me making a show of you in front of Beyoncé, do ya?"

"It's in your dressing room, and I wouldn't flatter yourself. I'd say Beyoncé will have more on her mind than you."

As he kicked the bathroom door shut, he grinned at Noreen's

giggles. She was mad about him, bless her. If he's asked her, she would've jumped out of that bath and gone to make him a full dinner. She was a grand cook but the anticipation coupled with the line of coke had removed his appetite altogether.

It suited him that his wife wasn't into the club scene. It meant she wasn't breathing down his neck all the time. It was great for Mariah, he mused, that she was getting into the club scene. You only live once and life was for living, according to himself.

7

tweeting@angiebaby.com

A night on the town awaits . . . bring it on!

Angie had been thrilled when Rachel rang to ask if she could come and stay the weekend.

"It'll be a bit squashed, as the flat is tiny, but I'd so love to see you," she squealed.

The hours were mental. Angie never finished on a Friday before nine, and they expected her to be on call pretty much all weekend, so it had proved impossible to go back to Cork at the weekends as she's originally planned.

Rachel knew Dublin well from her college days, and agreed to make her own way to the city and call her when she arrived.

"There are a couple of friends I'd love to hook up with," said Rachel. "Would it be okay with you if we all met for a bowl of pasta and a bottle of wine?"

"I'd love that, and maybe I could make a new contact outside of work," Angie enthused.

* * *

On Friday, Angie felt like the day would never end. All afternoon she willed her American boss, Tom, to leave. At least if he made an exit, she could finish up at a reasonable time.

At six, Angie was shocked when Tom leaned back in his chair and stretched, saying, "Let's call it a day, you've been here long enough, go and experience some of the famous Dublin nightlife," he smiled.

Grabbing her bag and saying a quick good bye to the other guys, she speed-walked back to her apartment. She was thrilled about seeing Rachel and the prospect of being able to relax with non-work people for a change.

Angie's phone beeped to tell her a text message had come through.

In Flanagan's pub, meet me here ASAP x x Rachel

Angie was so excited as she hurried out of her apartment. They were meeting in one the most famous and trendy bars in the city. Angie had been dying to go there but hadn't dared go by herself. It took her a couple of minutes to find Rachel in the thronged pub. They hugged and squealed and Angie ordered a drink.

Rachel looked her up and down. "You look fantastic, Angie! You've lost a ton of weight – are you not allowed eat on top of all the crazy work hours?"

"It's probably all those sad single-girl dinners I've been heating in the microwave every night. I'm so knackered by the time I leave the office, I fall into the supermarket, grab the first thing I see, shove it in to heat, and that's it. I'm not snacking during the day, because they just don't do that. There's no such thing as going for a latte and a Danish, so all that's cut out. And I barely drink any more. There's no point in opening a bottle of wine on my own and I haven't hit the bars at all." Angie paused and bit her lip. "Sorry, I know I probably sound like such a saddo. I'm just so thrilled to see you." She hugged her friend.

"Would you stop? It's me you're talking to! I know you've been a bit out on a limb – I remember when I moved to Dublin for college. It's a fairly daunting place when you're a fish out of water. Give it time, you'll be grand, girl. You'll take it all in your stride. Besides, I'm here now."

"I'll drink to that." Angie grinned as she sipped the glass of wine the barman handed her.

"Angie, this is Lauren and Kelly. Girls, this is Angie, my oldest pal in the world."

"Less of the old!" Angie quipped as she shook hands with the others.

"So you've just made the move to the big smoke – how are you getting on?" Kelly shoved up in her seat to make room for Angie.

"So far I can't really comment. I've been pretty much a hamster on a wheel, if you know what I mean. I go from bed to work and back again. The high-light of my day is stopping off in the express supermarket near my apartment to grab the essentials. I'm under contract to an American firm who believe I should give 100% and then somehow magic another entire reservoir of expertise from my arse pocket." Angie suddenly heard herself moaning. "Sorry, girls, I'm sounding like a right grumpy old biddy. Cheers!"

"Oh God, now you're putting the wind up me." Lauren looked scared.

"How's that, Lauren?" Rachel swirled the end of her drink in her glass.

"Well, I've just accepted a job in New York – I figured it's now or never. I'll be forty next month and things aren't happening the way I'd always envisaged, so I decided to go for it. I'm having mixed moments of excitement, trepidation and after hearing how much poor Angie here is being pushed by her American bosses, I think I'll add fear to the equation."

The two girls were chatty and easy to get along with, but Angie was a little disappointed. Lauren was off to her new life in New York and Kelly was heading back to her hometown Aberdeen in Scotland.

"I only ever intended staying here for college. I've spent ten years here now and I want to get home. My parents aren't as young as they used to be and my sister has three small children who need an auntie. I feel the time is right."

Still, it was great to be out and about and after a round of vodka and Red Bull, the girls decided to skip food and head straight for a club.

Angie had expected the Dublin clubs to be totally different to her native Cork ones. But it was a serious case of same shit different day. They had a really fun time and Angie had managed to attract the attention of a rather touchy-feely older gentleman.

"At least you were getting a feel, which is more than any of the rest of us managed!"

The girls were linked arms and swaying as they searched for chips.

"He was old enough to be my father though!" Angie shuddered.

"Jesus, I hope to God we're not in our sixties and still having to haul our asses into clubs in search of lurve!" Rachel pulled a horrified face.

"We'll be well settled, with rich husbands." Kelly grinned.

"Or what about our own award-winning multi-million-dollar companies?" Lauren suggested.

In her own head, Angie had different priorities right at that moment in time. They involved a duvet, plump pillow and no alarm clock going off before midday.

8

tweeting@rubytuesday.com
When I grow up, I want to BE Beyoncé . . . she is totally amazing!

As Damo McCabe pulled up outside the concert venue, one of the security guards approached.

"I've organised with Kiko to leave the car here. Damo McCabe!" he yelled out the window.

"Sure, Mr McCabe, here are your backstage passes. The security is massive so keep them on at all times," the man instructed.

"Fair enough, that's for yourself," Damo shoved a fifty-euro note into the guy's hand and they drove in.

The girls leapt out of the car almost before he had parked.

"Right, girls, this is it. Show time!" Damo rubbed his hands together.

As they ran up the stairs into the green room at the back of the stage, Ruby felt like she was going to vomit she was so nervous and excited. There was no sign of Beyoncé as she was apparently having her hair and make-up done in her dressing room, but there were small groups of really cool people in leather jeans and scanty sparkly dresses. Ruby and Mariah clung to each other, more than a bit overcome.

"Relax, girls. You're not in the zoo! Chill, have a few glasses of bubbly and you'll get into it." Damo brought over a bottle of champagne and opened it expertly, pouring it into the two glasses he had threaded through the fingers of his left hand.

"Thanks, Daddy," Mariah kissed his cheek.

"Thanks, Mr McCabe," Ruby blushed. She'd never had champagne before, let alone in the back room of a world stage.

"Cheers, girls, and less of the Mr McCabe stuff, Ruby! It makes me feel old and God knows we all hate that." He rubbed her arm. "Damo will do just fine, wha?"

He told the girls to stay around the area and said he was just shooting off to say hello to a few people.

"God, your dad is so cool. I wish my dad was like him," Ruby whispered to Mariah.

"Yeah, he's all right I suppose. Come on – down the hatch and we'll feel less like tools in the corner!"

They clinked glasses and gulped the drinks. The fizz was dangerously close to coming out Ruby's nose, and she struggled not to cough and splutter. Mariah filled their glasses again, managing to avoid letting it bubble all over the place.

Shortly afterwards, there was a lot of commotion as Beyoncé was ushered through the room towards the stage. Although she didn't make eye contact with either of the girls, they felt a shiver at being in such close proximity to her.

The gig was electric and the girls peered at her from the side of the stage. The crowd were loving her and being able to observe them made it even more special.

The whole night flashed past so quickly that Ruby couldn't believe it when the lights went on in the auditorium.

"Right, girls, Beyoncé is changing so we need to get out of here and back to the club to get things ready for her. Grab your coats, let's fly!" Damo clapped and jigged from side to side.

Ruby had lost count of how many glasses of champagne she'd had. As she sat in the car and Damo drove at top speed, she felt very queasy. She opened the window slightly, drinking in the cool night air, hoping to God she didn't vomit down the back of the driver's seat. By the time they made their way up the back stairs to the club, she was beginning to feel slightly less ill.

"James, this is our Mariah and her mate Ruby. Keep an eye, yeah? Give them whatever they want, but only for themselves." He turned and winked at the girls. "Yous can have anything for free, but don't take the piss and get stuff for other people, and don't accept drinks from anyone else. Any sniff of hassle and you tell James here – he's a black belt – or you come and get me. I'm on the radio at all times." Damo connected the radio-controller to his ear, tweaked Mariah under the chin and strode away.

Beyoncé arrived about half an hour later. She only drank water and didn't speak to many people. Damo was joking with her and the bodyguard, not to mention half a dozen others who were shadowing her. Ruby and Mariah sat on high stools, looking on in awe.

"Your dad is a real people person, isn't he?" Ruby gazed at him enviously.

"Hum? Yeah, I suppose so. I'm going to chat to those guys over there. The one on the left works here from time to time, his old man owns that new Italian restaurant off Grafton Street. He's nineteen but I think he'd be just perfect boyfriend material. Coming?"

"I'll follow you in a minute," Ruby nodded. "I want to go and check my make-up, you go ahead."

As she exited and walked towards the ladies', Ruby spotted Damo. He was leaning against the wall with a tall smooth chocolate-coloured girl, who looked like a sleek supermodel. As Ruby was about to say hi, she witnessed Damo whispering something to the stunning beauty before they kissed passionately.

Ruby was rooted to the spot. Knowing he would spot her any second, she scurried by and found safety in the cubicle. Trying to calm her breathing, she tried to convince herself she wasn't shocked. The sound of laugher approached, the door to the ladies' opened and she could hear the click-clack of high heels on the tiled floor.

Emerging, Ruby spread some make-up out beside the large marble sink.

"Hi there! Ooh, I love that Mac eyeliner, would you mind

terribly if I borrowed a bit?" It was the beautiful dark girl Damo had been kissing.

"Eh yeah, sure. Be my guest." Ruby couldn't help staring at her.

"Do you get your Botox done here in Ireland?" The girl was looking at Ruby's eyes.

"No, I've never had any, to be honest," said Ruby, startled.

"Lucky cow! I'm getting to that stage already and I'm only thirty. Pisser, isn't it? Thanks for that. Want a line? It's really pure." She seemed to be staring right into Ruby's soul.

"Sure, thanks." Ruby smiled easily, even though she had no idea what the lady was talking about. The look of relief and warm smile she got in return made her think she'd said the right thing.

"This club is such a blast, isn't it? Not to mention the owner. God, that guy is just the business. Do you know much about him?"

As the girl took a pouch of powder out of her purse and began to chop it up with her credit card, Ruby's blood went cold. What the hell had she talked herself into?

"Damo is a family friend. Listen, I'm actually going to pass – you go ahead, I'll catch you later."

Ruby turned to walk away when the girl grabbed her wrist. "Are you hidden security or something? If you shop me to the management, I'll deny it," she seethed. "I thought you were cool – you better not fuck me about!"

"Hey, it's cool! I just feel a bit too pissed, that's all. Too much bubbly in too short a time, you know yourself?" Ruby tried to smile.

"Well, in that case, this will sort your head quick smart. I'd recommend it. Clears your head like nothing else. You'll be able to drink your body weight in bubbly and you won't feel a thing. I'm Jude, by the way. What's your name?" She held her hand out, with one perfectly plucked eyebrow raised.

"Ruby." She could barely breathe.

"So want some?"

"Okay."

9

tweeting@angiebaby.com
A girls night in! Just what the doctor ordered!

Angie lit the four scented candles she'd picked up in the accessory store on the way home from work. It was another Friday night but she'd spent most of the day at work – again.

"This won't be forever and you're being paid double for any overtime. Please try and play ball with these guys." Brian O'Leary was trying to calm her down over the phone.

"I have no problem working hard, Brian. That's not the issue. My gripe is that these men seem to think that I shouldn't have a life outside of the office. I've been working sixty and sixty-two-hour weeks since this began. But asking me to come to the office for an hour and only being able to leave seven hours later – not on."

"Ah yes, I hear you. Hang in there. Good woman yourself, you're playing a blinder."

Angie exhaled loudly. There really was no point in talking to O'Leary. All he wanted was to see the money rolling in. If she ended up with her eyes hanging out of her head as a result, or worse, in the funny farm due to lack of head-space, that was quite clearly her own lookout.

That morning, she'd texted Kelly and Lauren, the two girls she'd met with Rachel, to see if they'd like to go out for a meal.

Lauren was heading off to New York early the following week and Kelly was also working, so they'd arranged to convene at Angie's place for a Chinese delivery and a couple of glasses of wine.

Bar Rachel, Angie hadn't even shared a cup of tea with anyone yet in her Dublin apartment. So she was humming happily as she made the place homely.

Dialling her parents' number, she smiled at the sound of her mother's voice.

"Hi, Mammy, it's only me." Even though she was forty, she still felt a little tugging on her heartstrings when she chatted to her mother.

"If it isn't yourself! How are you, lovie? How is Dublin city treating you? I suppose you're off out on the tiles with a gang this evening, are you?"

"I wish! But no, Mammy. I've been working most of the day so I'm having a couple of girls Rachel introduced me to over for a bit of dinner."

She could hear her mother's voice relax as she felt reassured her daughter was settling into her new life in Dublin. Angie knew Mags, her mother worried about her, especially about what the future might hold.

All Angie's talk of not needing a man and how the times had changed quite frankly scared the life out of her mother. Who would she turn to when they were long gone? Surely Angie must harbour maternal urges? She might have the best job on the planet, the most modern apartment known to woman and the most loyal pals imaginable, but Mags knew that nothing in the world could come close to the feeling of holding your own child.

The unfamiliar sound of the buzzer made Angie jump.

"Oh sweet Jesus, that's the door, Mammy. I'll ring you again soon. God bless!" Angie hung up and quickly rushed to answer the intercom.

The two girls arrived together and hugged Angie warmly. It was a real shame they weren't going to be staying in Dublin.

By the time the local Chinese restaurant managed to deliver their food, the three were more than a little squiffy.

"Do you ever think about having a baby?" Lauren threw it out to the other two.

"I do," Angie answered a little too quickly for her own liking.

"I do too," Lauren was just as quick to respond. "That's one of the reasons I'm taking this job in the States. I'm giving myself two more years, and if I don't find Mr Right, I'm going to seriously look into artificial insemination. It's much more commonplace over there and I don't want to miss the opportunity of being a mother, even if it means doing it alone."

"Well, if I don't manage to meet my Mr Right in a shining sporran, I think my options are going to involve taking up the offer made to me by my brother's drunken gay pal." Kelly made a gruesome face.

"What on earth?" Angie looked astonished.

Kelly sighed. "He's always wanted children and we made a drunken pact, sealed by a pinkie promise, that we'd avail of a turkey-baster and 'create' a baby if I was still single by the age of forty-three and looking to become a mother. At the time, I hugged the guy and laughed myself silly. But the conversation is getting to be less of a joke as time marches on."

The three women had a very open discussion about the fact that so many women were having babies well into their forties.

"I know some people are actually choosing to do so, to allow time to develop a career first, and some like us haven't met the right partner," said Kelly. "I know my slightly quirky offer is what could be described as slightly unsavoury, excuse the pun, seeing as we're discussing a turkey-baster." She giggled along with the other two women. "At least it makes me feel I have an outside chance of being a mother some day."

Angie crunched on a prawn cracker looking suddenly pensive. "How old are you now, if you don't mind me asking?"

"Forty-one in eight weeks' time. Not that I'm counting." She shrugged, looking a little miserable at the thought of it.

"Well, take heart, girls!" said Lauren. "My sister has just given birth to her second child, at the age of forty-three. A perfectly healthy baby girl. She had major fertility issues and little Catherine was the result of their third IVF attempt." Lauren smiled as she passed her phone to Angie to look at the photo of the baby.

"That is heartening, I have to admit. I'd hate to feel that my chance of having a family is shot already." Angie admitted.

"To the modern woman!" Kelly toasted. "Fingers crossed we will all achieve our hearts' desire in the next five years!" Holding up her hand she added, "With or without a turkey-baster!"

While Angie wasn't convinced about the alternative use of the kitchen implement, she took comfort in the notion that she wasn't running out of time just yet. All joking aside, she wasn't a bit enthusiastic about the thought of climbing onto that "shelf" that Rachel often pontificated about during particularly negative drunken moments.

10

tweeting@themercedesking.com
Under 18s party night at 'The Orb' . . . the only place to be in Dublin tonight.

It was a week after the Beyoncé night and Damo was issuing his usual warnings to Mariah. She and all her friends were coming to The Orb, for one of those underage, no-booze events. Damo wasn't mad about them. They didn't make him much money and there were always fights. The kids all brought in bottles of booze in their bags and they were all on "E's". But it was only from seven till half ten, so it would be over in time for the real money-spinner at eleven.

"Make sure ya don't take any drugs, mind you!" Damo warned his daughter, standing in front of her with his arms folded. "All ya need is one dodgy "E" and you'll be fucked. I've seen the state of some o' the young wans in me clubs. A few pints'll do, d'ya hear me?"

"I don't do drugs, Daddy, and I wouldn't be seen dead drinking pints. What do you think I am – a skanger? I'll be celebrating with all the Transition Year people, so I'll be drinking champagne." She turned on her heel and marched into her bedroom to start straightening her hair.

Damo chuckled to himself. He loved her posh accent and the sassy attitude she had. He was dead proud of her. She was a real little looker too. He'd be watching all the spotty little gits who thought they could get their paws on her later on. If any of them even laid a finger on her, he'd toss them out.

He'd stay for the whole time, just to make sure there was no messing. Once his clubs opened, he usually went from one to the other, to keep the staff on their toes. If they thought the boss was coming, they were less likely to act the maggot or rob from the tills. He trusted nobody, and it had worked for him so far. He'd a couple of new kids from an up-and-coming girlband coming into the VIP bar later on. The press would be around, which was always good. He'd hopefully get a few photos in the back of a social mag and a couple of the colour supplements on Sunday. That always brought in a good bit of business. Besides, one of the girls from this band was a right racy little goer. She'd given him the eye last time he'd let her in so if he plied her with a few glasses of champers, maybe she'd show him a good time.

Music began to emanate from Mariah's room upstairs. Damo decided to go and have a quick workout in the gym. He'd bought their house over ten years ago now. It was one of those big five-bed places, detached with a big garden. He'd done a lot of work on it too. He'd put in his own bar and a gym in the extension at the back of the house. The bar was a really classy place, with leather stools and plenty of rugs.

It was nice and clean-looking with loads of white and gold accessories. "Contemporary" as the designer had called it. He had those tiny speakers set into the ceiling too, so the sound was amazing when he pumped out the tunes. All his mates thought he was a real showman, with his own pumps, serving creamy pints of Guinness any time of the day or night. The coloured lights were deadly at night-time too. It was just like his own mini nightclub. He only drank orange juice himself, but he still liked the feeling of pulling a good pint for one of the lads. He got his buzz from feeling like he'd made it, rather than from pouring booze down his neck.

Changing into his gym gear, he strode into the white tiled area and flicked on some music. After doing a few stretches, he began to do some bench presses. Adjusting the weights, he pumped until the muscles in his arms and torso burned.

As he moved onto the treadmill, he admired himself in the mirror. He was in good shape, even if he thought so himself. He was taut and a decent weight for his height. Some of Mariah's friends had fathers who looked ancient. All flabby and grey, wearing old-fart outfits: brown trousers and boring shirts, with auld-fella shoes with rubber souls. Not him! He was a trendy git. He wore Ralph Lauren and Hugo Boss. All the top gear. He used that shampoo stuff which kept his hair nice and dark and shiny too. The sunbed in the corner of the gym kept his skin nice and tanned. He looked great and he felt even better. He was at the top of his game. Life was good, the money was still rolling in and he was a happy man. He'd two nice girls on the go at the moment, both foreign. They were easier to deal with. He favoured the Eastern European ones – they'd rarely any family nearby and they were happy with a bit of attention. They all idolised him too. It kept him young and made him feel like he still had what it took to be The Man.

By the time Mariah was finished doing herself up and spraying perfume and putting make-up on, Damo had done his workout and had his shower. Putting some wax in his hair, he called in to his daughter.

"I'm leavin' in ten! If ya want a lift, hurry up!" he yelled.

"I'm coming! Can we collect Ruby on the way? Her mum said she can't come unless we pick her up and drop her home!"

"No worries! Text her and tell her to be ready. I'm not pissin' about waiting for her and I'm not going into her house either. Her mother's a stuck-up cow and I'm not standing around being made to feel like a tosser." Damo splashed his face with aftershave and hocked up some phlegm. He hated yer woman's ma. One of those bitches who always looked at him like she'd a bad smell under her nose. He was fucked if he was going to give her the chance to dis him. She was one of those uptight no-sense-of-humour types, who spent her time giving out. Naggin' her poor bastard of a husband and always at the young one, Ruby. Telling her to behave and stand up straight, and be polite and blah, blah, blah! Fuck's sake, she was only a kid! The dried-up old bag was probably just jealous of her daughter.

He smiled when he pictured Ruby the other night after the Beyoncé gig. She certainly didn't take after her mother. Jaysus, she'd been dynamite in the club. She could certainly move. She'd been flooring the cocktails too – well able to hold her booze. The men had been mad for her. She was a funny kid too, with a great sense of humour and not afraid to chat in the car on the way home.

"I'll tell her to come out to the gate," Mariah assured him.

"Right. Noreen, we're outta here!" he shouted in to his wife. "See ya later. I won't be back till around four. I'll send Mariah back in a cab when the kids' disco finishes!"

Noreen appeared in the hallway. "Right, love. Take care now and I'll talk to you in the morning." She was dressed in her usual: a tracksuit and slippers. She'd plenty of jewellery on though. She loved her gold chains. She had three she wore all the time around her neck, including the heavy one Damo had given her at Elvis's twenty-first, and two bracelets, one with her name engraved on it. Damo gave that to her years ago, when the kids were small. The other was a charm bracelet. He bought her another gold charm any time they had an occasion. Christmases, birthdays, that type of thing. They used to joke that Noreen didn't need to lift weights with all the gold she heaved around on her neck and wrists.

She wasn't a bad-looking woman for her age. She was small, only five feet, with clear skin and big brown eyes. She'd been like a little elf when he'd met her years ago. Gorgeous she was. All the fellas fancied her but he'd got her. Granted they'd got caught on the hop and she'd ended up pregnant with their Alexis. But all their friends were having kiddies, so it was fine really. It had given him the incentive he'd needed to do well for his family.

Noreen suited him grand. He could have his bit of fluff at the club, and she didn't get involved in his dealings outside the house. She was as innocent as the day they'd met, and didn't know about the workings of the club. He looked after her, made sure she had all the stuff she needed, and in turn she was a good wife and mother.

He gave her a quick kiss. Her hair was a bit brassy from all the dye, but she wasn't fat and she always wore make-up. She was a quiet kind of girl. Never liked the drink, apart from the odd shandy or whiskey and red lemonade, and wasn't that into going out. She rarely came to his clubs. In fact, she preferred to go to the bingo with Sharon her best friend rather than go to the pub. Especially since that smoking ban. Noreen loved her fags and she couldn't see the point in going out, now that she had to spend most of her night outside with her puffa coat on, being blown to be-jaysus on the side of the road in the cold. No, she'd sooner go to the bingo and bring the girls back to their bar.

"No feckin' smoking ban in my bar, wha?" she'd giggled with the girls.

"Yeah, and we can play Barry Manilow and the Bee Gees with no-one annoyin' us," Sharon had agreed.

Noreen stood in the hall, lighting another ciggy as she said goodbye to her husband and youngest child. Mariah was growing up so fast it brought a little tear to her eye.

"Bye, Mum, see you later on." Mariah hugged her mother.

"See ya, love. Have a good time and behave yourself."

Damo revved up his Merc and spun out of the drive.

Ten minutes later, as Ruby got into the car, the waft of perfume filled his nostrils.

"Hi, Mr McCabe, I mean Damo," Ruby greeted him.

"How're ya, Ruby love, in ya hop!" Damo called over his shoulder as she slid into the back beside his daughter.

The girls chatted animatedly the whole way to the club.

"Mariah, you will not believe the outfit I'm wearing to my Aunt Serena's wedding!" Ruby buzzed. "It's a pale gold two-piece with a bodice and then the skirt goes straight down, and the whole thing kind of falls in onto the floor, making what looks like a pool of fabric. And it's being designed by this really cool, like, famous designer that my aunt knows. Do you want to come to the fitting with me next time?"

Pulling in the side lane to the left of the club, Damo jumped out and led the two girls in the side door.

"Come over to the bar and I'll get yous a drink!" he called to the girls. As Mariah and Ruby stood at the bar, he glanced at Ruby. Jesus, she was a little ride. She was going to break some hearts when she was older, and judging by the way she commanded the floor the other night, that time wouldn't be too far away. He told the barman to open a bottle of champagne.

"Yous'll have to drink it outta tumblers, just to be on the safe side," he winked at the girls, "in case we get raided by the cops. It's supposed to be an alcohol-free event."

"Thanks, Daddy," said Mariah, kissing him on the cheek.

"Yeah, thanks, Damo," Ruby smiled at him.

"Stay away from tossers and drugs and I'll see yous later on. I'll be over at the door if ya need me!" he called as he left.

"Ruby," Mariah hissed, "wait until you see Yaakov! He's this new bouncer my dad hired. He's from Outer Mongolia or Eastern Europe or one of those places. But he is to *die* for!"

Ruby drank her champagne and shrugged. She'd never really ventured down the boyfriend route. Up until now all she'd really cared about was pony camp, clothes and her school friends. She bit her lip as she remembered the other night upstairs in this very club. She'd taken the lead from the dark girl, put the rolled-up banknote to her nose and inhaled the gritty powder.

She'd felt her nose throb and it was like the times she'd got water up her nose in the swimming pool. Within a few minutes, however, she'd felt like she could take on the universe. She'd been the life and soul of the party and had put all the years of stage school and dance classes to use.

"You can really move, young lady!" Damo had said as she joined him at the bar. "If you're looking for a summer job, I'd hire you as a dancer in a shot. Fair play to you!"

Ruby, in turn had felt like she was on top of the world. So many cool guys had bought her drinks and she'd known she could have had her pick of men.

"This is what life's all about, Ruby. Life can't be bad when you're hanging out with rock stars. You stick with me, kid. I know where the fun lives."

But that was last week. This was the here and now. An entirely different experience. All the people in the club tonight were her own age. Ruby guessed that most of the boys here hadn't spent a night upstairs in the VIP bar, snorting coke with a girl who looked like she'd stepped out of a page of *Vogue* magazine. Instead of feeling like a fumbling and wide-eyed kid, Ruby felt empowered by her previous night in this very club.

Ruby tucked her little clutch bag under her arm, the way she'd seen the older girls do it last week, and sauntered towards the side of the dance floor. Swaying to the beat, she was just working her way up to showing off her hottest dance moves, to wow the boys, when she felt Mariah's elbow jabbing her ribs.

"Enough of wasting your energy on that lot – come with me. This guy is simply to die for."

The two girls sauntered towards the cloakroom at the main entrance of the club.

"Hey, Yaakov, do you remember me? I'm Damo's daughter, Mariah!"

"Hallo, and who is this lovely lady?" Yaakov was staring at Ruby.

She desperately wanted to appear cool and sexy, but she felt her cheeks flushing and sweat beading her forehead.

"Hi!" She waved her hand lamely, immediately wishing she could rewind the clock and start again, with a funny or cute retort, like "the lovely lady is charmed to make your acquaintance".

They hung around chatting to Yaakov for a few minutes but, as the club began to fill up, he had to plug in his headset and do some work.

But, even though she could see he was busy, Ruby found herself gravitating back towards Yaakov. He looked Italian, with hazel slightly cat-like eyes, a quiff of dark hair like Elvis at his finest, and although he wasn't the tallest man in the world, he was muscled and toned-looking. Even in the black trousers, white shirt and black puffa coat uniform, he stood out.

All the girls her age were talking about him too. In the loos Ruby applied some more Juicy Tubes lip gloss and listened to a group of other girls ranting about him.

"Oh-mi-god, did you *see* that delicious guy on the door?" One tall leggy blonde was waving a mascara wand around as she spoke.

"I have *never* seen such an amazing-looking guy! Even if he was a girl, he'd still be beautiful!"

Ruby finished checking her make-up in the mirror and slipped out the bathroom door. As luck would have it, there was Yaakov. He winked at her as he spoke into the tiny microphone on his headset. Ruby crossed her arms and fixed her gaze on him. Fuelled by a couple of tumblers of Damo's secret champagne, she came into her own.

She stood boldly in front of him. "Where are you from?"

"Russia." He gazed slowly down her body and back up, drinking her in. "Unlike you, pretty lady – you came straight down from heaven."

Ruby knew it was corny as hell but anything uttered by this man could be deemed cool and sexy.

"You'll have to do better than that. I also didn't come down in the last shower!" She put her hand on her hip and stared out from under her false lashes at him.

"What is 'the last shower'?" He looked confused and slightly perplexed that Ruby wasn't just beguiled by his charms.

"It means, I wasn't born yesterday or, for a direct translation, I'm not stupid, so you'll have to step up your game to impress me." She tossed her head to the side and with one hand on her hip, strode away, doing her best supermodel walk. As the disco music enveloped her, she could hear Yaakov bellowing with laughter.

Ruby wished she felt as confident as she sounded. The other night, after she'd taken even that tiny amount of coke, all her inhibitions had melted away. She didn't feel all sluggish and sick like with alcohol. Instead she'd felt a new clarity and sense of knowing. All in all, Ruby wasn't enjoying this teenage disco half as much as she's enjoyed the VIP back bar last weekend. Being on the main dance floor with boys her own age just didn't have the cool-factor of the previous week. The designer-clad older girls and the gorgeous twenty-something men she'd rubbed shoulders with before just had the edge.

Some of the kids here tonight were acting like such an embarrassment. They were making up dances and doing that stupid thing where they ran and bashed off each other's chests. The girls were clapping and screaming when a song they liked came on.

None of the ice-cool crew from last weekend would have raised an eyebrow even if Beyoncé had decided to give a spur-of-the-moment concert on the spot. It just wasn't the done thing.

Two hours later The Orb was heaving. Tons of kids had turned up. Unlike Ruby, Damo was thrilled with how the night was going. He might make this a more regular thing. So far they were all behaving themselves. Two fellas had started a scrap so he'd fecked them out on their ear. Apart from that it was all going okay. He could charge a fortune for minerals and bottles of water, so it would be a nice little earner by the time half ten rolled in. Fair enough, he'd had to tell the bouncers to calm some of the kids down a bit. All that young blood and rampant hormones meant they were prone to tearing around the place more than the usual punters.

"If yous want to run around playing chasing, go to the park. Tone it down a bit and stop jumping on the couches. Yous wouldn't behave like that at home, so don't do it in here." Damo had put on a real grumpy face. The kids had looked terrified he was going to feck them out and had immediately apologised and gone back to dancing.

Looking at his watch, he realised he only had twenty minutes to go before the DJ stopped and the main lights went on. Assuming he could get them all out, he'd be home and dry.

If they wanted to fight or stab each other once they were off his premises, that was their prerogative. He just needed to keep them all nicey-nicey while they were on his insurance.

"Hi, Damo!" There stood Ruby, with a big smile and a very small tight dress on.

"Ah, how're ya, Ruby. All right? Enjoyin' yourself, love?"

"It's okay. Not really the same buzz as the other night, but I suppose we can't hang out with Beyoncé all the time," she shrugged.

"True. Listen, that new girl band are coming in later on. Do ya want to check if Mariah wants to hang around for a while? I can easily get the taxi to drop yous home later. I'll text Noreen and your ma will never know the difference. Would that put a smile on your face again?"

"Sounds great." Ruby felt her heartbeat quicken. This evening was looking up. She staggered a little to the right.

"Are you feeling all right?" said Damo. "Do you want to sit down for a bit? Lay off the booze for a while, there's a good girl. We don't need you falling and suing me." He grinned and tweaked her cheek.

Ruby stood and held her hand on her cheek where he'd touched her. "I'd prefer to stay here with you. All the guys are idiots. They haven't a clue. I'm just not interested in all those spotty little gits my age!" She staggered again.

"Hang on a minute till I get our Mariah. I think you're a bit langers, pet." He nodded and smiled. He could really get to like this kid, but even he knew it was a bit close to home. He appreciated the little glances and the bit of flirting all the same.

"I'm not in the least bit langers! I just want to stay here with you. Do you mind?" She tilted her head to the side and raised one eyebrow.

"Eh, no, no, that's grand if that's what you want." Never one to look a gift horse in the mouth, Damo put his hand on her elbow to steady her. "I'm just going into the office!" he called to the doorman, who was a large tank of an ape wearing a tux and dickey bow.

The office was small and quiet in comparison to the hallway. He could hear the thudding of the music and see the lights flashing under the door.

"Stay here for a minute and I'll get you some water. Don't drink any more booze, love, ya hear?"

Ruby sat on the wooden desk and kicked off her shoes.

Another fight had broken out and it was escalating into a big brawl at the side of the dance floor. All the bouncers raced towards the young men, to move the action outside and disperse it.

"Yaakov, Mariah's little pal Ruby is a bit jarred – she's in my office. Get her some water and look after her, will ya?" Damo called over his shoulder as he lunged towards the action on the dance floor. "Don't let her drink any more, or I'll be shot. Her ma's a real boot and I'll never hear the end of it!"

Ruby was passed out on Damo's desk, looking like a broken dolly, when Yaakov found her.

"Hey, Ruby, you need to wake up now! You drink water, you try to stop feel so very drunk, yes?" Yaakov was pulling as much English as he could muster out of his limited reserve of vocabulary.

She groaned and tried to focus on him. God, he was gorgeous! Why had she got herself so pissed? Now she probably had make-up streaming down her cheeks and was making a total ass of herself.

"Here, you want little bit of Charlie to make your head more clear? You don't tell boss man now, yes?"

Yaakov lined up some coke and she lunged forward to sniff it. Even though she felt queasy and ready to puke, the butterflies in her tummy were overtaking the nausea. The night was looking up. All she needed was to convince Mariah to stay on for a while and she'd be back on form.

"Yaakov, would you do me a favour? Can you find Mariah for me?"

"You no can tell her I have the gear, in case she tell the boss man. I get kaput from job then." He held his hands up in resignation.

"No, no. Nothing like that. I need to make sure she stays a bit later, that's all." She winked. "This is our little secret, yes?"

11

tweeting@rubytuesday.com
I'm late, I'm late, for a very important date! To Russia with love . . .

Ruby could hardly believe her luck when the text had come through on her phone the day after the junior disco.

Hi Ruby, it is me Yaakov, u wud like date with me? U can c me on Wednesday? I have work so we can go coffee shop after ur skool?

Ruby smiled at his spelling and her heart flipped. Running to find Mariah, she could barely contain herself.

"Look, look! What do you say to that then?"

"How did he get your number, you jammy cow?" Mariah looked suitably jealous.

"When I ended up hammered the other night, your dad asked him to drive us home and he asked for my mobile number as I was falling out of the car," Ruby fibbed.

"That's so unfair," Mariah pouted. "I've put so much effort into flirting and chatting to that man – he meets you once when you're off your trolley and he's asking you out. Bitch!"

"Ah don't be like that! You and he were just not meant to be! Cover for me?" Ruby clasped her two hands in mock prayer. "Pleeeeeese!"

"Go on then, where and when?" Mariah sighed. Ruby was petite and pretty and the boys just loved her sassy, whatever attitude. She sighed inwardly. Yaakov was beyond divine and Ruby was going to just soar in street-cred if she could bag him.

"One thing to watch out for, Rubes. He's older – he's going to expect you to do the wild thing, you know? So keep it brief, this little fling, or you'll end up in the sack, my girl, you mark my words!" Mariah wagged her finger.

"And what if I want to end up in the sack?" Ruby raised one eyebrow. "Besides, I'll be sixteen soon. What harm? Some girls are on to their third or fourth partner at our age!" She tossed her hair back.

* * *

The following day after school, Ruby rolled up to the coffee shop in town and tried to make herself look cool and collected while being just about to have a mild heart attack, as there was no sign of Yaakov outside.

"Hallo, lovely lady, it's so nice to see you once again!"

She jumped as he came up behind her. He kissed her on both cheeks and she inhaled his lemony scent. He was even better-looking than she'd remembered. "Are you feeling a little less, how we say, crazy, today?"

He smiled and Ruby thought she might expire. All her cocky confidence had disappeared with her hangover the other morning.

"I'm fine, thanks, sorry about the other night. I think it was all the champers, I'm not usually that bad," she stuttered. "Thanks for dropping me back," she added, raising herself up and pushing her chest out, to show confidence she didn't actually feel inside.

"You need to mind yourself, pretty Ruby. Some men are not as, how you say, control as I am. You will meet bad boy who will not treat you like a lady, you understand?" He brushed a strand of hair from her eye, stroking her cheek. "You should let Yaakov look out for you. By the way, would you like to have little bit of your own, you know, stuff?" He winked.

"Eh, sure. How much is it?"

"I can give you good price, because you are friend, no?"

"All right then."

They went inside for a coffee and time flew by.

Ruby's phone beeped in her pocket. Two new messages.

Ruby where are you? Call me asap x Mum

Shoot, it was ten to six and she was going to face the wrath of her mother if she didn't get home, and quickly. The second message was from Mariah.

Hey R, call me l8r, ur mum is havin a skitso, get ur ass home x x M

"I have to go, Yaakov," Ruby told him.

Outside, she agreed to meet him in the club the following weekend.

When he put his hand on the small of her back and pulled her into a deep kiss, right there on the side of the road, Ruby struggled to keep her stance.

"Hey, take it easy, cowboy!" She wasn't sure if she wanted him kissing her. She wasn't sure about a lot of things she was doing at the moment, come to think of it.

* * *

Luckily, Adele was so hassled by Ruby coming home late, she didn't notice the change in her daughter.

"Where on earth have you been? I've been texting you!" She paced up and down the hallway. "The stable yard called – you never went up to take Biscuit out today. That's simply not fair to the poor pony, Ruby. If you're not interested, Daddy and I will take her away from you." Adele expected Ruby to burst out crying and promise to go first thing after school the next day.

"I told you already, I had extra drama after school, to try out for that play, remember?" Ruby stared her mother down, hand on hip.

"No, but if you say so." Miraculously Adele backed down. "Go and get on with your homework, dinner is nearly ready. Daddy and I are going out so Serena is popping over to watch a DVD with you."

"Mum, I'm nearly sixteen. I don't need a baby-sitter for crying out loud!" Ruby pouted.

"Serena loves to spend time with you – don't deny her, Ruby. Besides, you are fifteen and very young and vulnerable, in spite of what you may think."

Ruby scowled at her mother and ran upstairs. She didn't really mind Aunt Serena coming over. Serena was really cool and chilled out, unlike her fuddy-duddy mother. She could tell her all about meeting Yaakov and Beyoncé and all the cool people at the club. Serena would understand – well, most of it at least.

Without even considering doing even a tap of homework, Ruby lay on her bed daydreaming. Instead of Yaakov or any of the boys in her class, though, she pictured Damo. She knew there was an age gap, and the fact that he was Mariah's dad was a bit iffy, if she allowed herself to think of that. But when she saw him work the floor in the club, rubbing shoulders with the biggest stars in the world and having them all high-five him and treat him like a God, it gave her the shivers. He wasn't like anyone else's dad, he was so good-looking and sophisticated. Ruby had no interest in starting off with boys, not when there were *men* like Damo on the horizon.

Her mobile phone snapped her back to reality.

"Tell me every second of it all," Mariah breathed.

"What do you mean?" Ruby's voice was like ice.

"Jesus, don't bite my head off! Your coffee with Yaakov, how did it go? Did he not show up or something?"

"Oh that! It was cool. He's a nice guy. He wants to have a drink with both of us on Friday. He's not on at the club, but said he'll come in and say hello. Do you think your dad would get us in again?"

"I suppose. God, I'm *sooooo* jealous. It's just not fair! Will your mother let you go again?"

"I'll ask. Maybe we can say we're working on a project together and not mention going out again, just for this time. I don't want to push it. I'll tell you what. I'm not really that into Yaakov, to be honest. Why don't we meet him, then I'll act all snotty and you can move in for the kill. He's more your type and he did ask about you twice today." Ruby felt mean lying but she wanted to see Damo again, not to mention use the promised little bit of powder.

"I don't know, Ruby. If he'd liked me in the first place, he wouldn't have asked you out today. I don't want to come across as some desperate geek who needs her friend to toss her unwanted leftovers her way."

"He's hardly my leftovers, Mariah. Nothing has happened between us. We had coffee, end of story. I know I'm not into him, you are, so where's your big issue?"

"I dunno. My dad mightn't let us into the club again anyway. Leave it with me and I'll text you in a while when I've talked to him. He's in the gym at the moment. When he's finished his shower, I'll try and catch him off guard. I would adore to see Yaakov again . . ."

Ruby clapped inwardly that she was going along with the plan. With a bit of luck, Yaakov would go for Mariah too, and then she'd have a perfect alibi from here on in.

Just after ten that night the chiming of Ruby's phone with a new text made her jump.

All sorted, Dad in gr8 form. Yaakov, here I come. Dad will cover for u 2! Result. C u in school x x M

Sweet. Ruby was beside herself with excitement. She could barely do her homework, as she envisaged herself strutting her stuff on the dance floor on Friday night. Plugging in her iPod, she slid her mirrored wardrobe shut, and danced. Some of her moves looked stupid, so she made a mental note not to do those on Friday night.

* * *

The following day in school, Mariah came rushing over with her phone.

"Look, I have two pictures of Yaakov from the other week. I was just showing the girls in my German class. They all think he's one of the best-looking guys they've ever seen. Look at him and tell me he's not perfection."

Ruby looked at the sullen dark-eyed guy but he just didn't do it for her. She had her sights set much higher than him.

"Okay, he's seriously cute. But, we are best friends, you saw him first so you get first shot at him. Deal?" Ruby held her hand out.

Mariah shook it and then hugged her friend.

"What will I wear?" she asked. "If I'm supposed to be trying to entice him, should I go for a short dress or something more sophisticated?"

"I'm not sure. I'll tell you what, I'll bring over a load of my stuff and we can swap if we need to," Ruby squealed.

Friday night felt like it would never come.

By the time Adele dropped Ruby at Mariah's house just before six, both girls were ready to explode.

"Don't stay up half the night chatting, Ruby. You've a jumping competition at three tomorrow, and you promised Serena you would meet her to go over some details for the wedding," Adele reminded her.

"Okay, Mum. Don't fuss, I'll be there." Ruby kissed her goodbye.

Damo was already gone to the club to set up, so Ruby could concentrate on getting ready and chatting to Mariah. They pulled out nearly every stitch of clothing from Mariah's wardrobe and tried it all on. Eventually, three whole hours later, they emerged from the bedroom.

"Where are you going dressed like that?" Elvis was coming out of his room to go out too.

"We're going to the VIP bar at The Orb, if you must know!" Mariah spat.

"Off to look at the Italian Stallion, along with half of Dublin, I presume," he teased.

"Firstly, he's not Italian, and secondly, we're meeting him there. As in, a date. Aren't we, Ruby?" She looked to her friend for back up.

"Whatever," said Elvis, bobbing down the stairs bellowing with laughter.

Ruby had convinced her mother to give her money for a pizza, which she had tucked into her purse along with a twenty-euro note her Aunt Serena had given her the other night and some other coins. Damo always gave them free drink and they wouldn't need to pay the extortionate entrance fee to The Orb. By hook and by crook, Ruby had managed to scrape the forty euro together that Yaakov had told her she'd need in exchange for her magic powder.

"I'm starved," said Mariah. "Will we go to the Chinese on the way? We don't want to be sitting there like dweebs waiting for the lights to come on and the first punters to arrive. We need to make a bit of an entrance."

"Okay, whatever you think. I'm broke though. I've no money 'cos my parents don't know I'm going out tonight, remember?" Ruby didn't really care if the whole world turned in a different direction, just as long as she got the same feeling as before and managed to impress Damo a little.

"Don't worry about that, I've got cash."

The Chinese was packed but the owners knew Damo, so the girls were ushered past the huddle of waiting diners and seated quickly. Raising their glasses of orange, they clinked them and toasted each other.

"To finding the love of our lives tonight!" Ruby hunched her shoulders in anticipation.

They ate noodles and, one by one, went through everyone they knew deciding if they'd done it yet or not. They came to the conclusion that about half the class were virgins and the other half weren't.

"So would you do it then?" Ruby asked Mariah, chin leaning on her hands.

"I don't know. It depends on who it's with, I suppose." She sipped her orange.

"Okay, say if Yaakov took you to his apartment and asked you to, would you go all the way with him?"

"Oh Jesus, I can't answer that. Besides, I don't want to sound like a slut or anything." Mariah blushed. "What about you then?"

Ruby thought of going all the way. It scared the living daylights out of her if she was honest. But with the help of a little of her magic dust, she'd probably be well able to handle it. "It would really depend on the circumstances," she answered honestly.

Mariah misunderstood her friend. "Yeah, me too. It'd have to be a long-term boyfriend and someone who I knew loved me. Not just a fling. It would have to mean something."

"But, if you just *knew* you were in love, then it would all make sense." Ruby knew it was wrong but she was so infatuated by Damo that she'd even thought about what it might be like if he was to leave Mariah's mother and live with her. She knew Mariah would be really annoyed with her at first, but they were best friends. So it would all work out in the end. Mariah would come around to the idea. It *could* work out. Even if they didn't tell anyone until Ruby was, say, nineteen. By that stage, they'd be together a few years and people would see that it wasn't just a sordid affair, but true love.

* * *

Damo was in bad form. One of the girls he'd been seeing had gone back to Poland. He'd really liked her – she wasn't like the others, just looking for money and all that. She had been really sweet-natured and clever too. He'd given her money to help with her studies, not to mention one of the flats above his pub in Rathmines.

She'd finished her course and buggered off. Just like that. The knowledge that he'd been used didn't sit well with him. If he was honest, he was hurt. He'd thought he'd meant something to Jana but she'd taken him for a fool. At least nobody much knew about her, so he wouldn't be jeered or laughed at. He did a quick line of coke and smoothed his hair back. Checking himself in the mirror, he stepped out of his office just as the girls strode in with Yaakov and a friend of his.

"Hiya, girls, how was your dinner?" Damo hugged Mariah.

"Great, Daddy! We're going up to the VIP bar. Yaakov and his mate are with us, okay?" Mariah did the big wide eyes at her father.

"Grand, girls, all right. Yaakov, mind those two now or you'll have me to answer to!" Damo gave the Russian guy a playful dig in the arm. "All right, Ruby, love. Lookin' hot!" He winked at her and strode off. That kid was going to break some hearts, he thought to himself.

Even though the club was only open half an hour, the VIP bar was almost full. The girls found a seat and the hostess brought them a bottle of champagne and glasses.

"Your father said you're to take these too, just in case the place is raided," she whispered to Mariah. She unloaded two glasses of coke from her tray and set them in front of them, then spun around and waddled off in her pencil heels.

Yaakov was lapping up the attention from Mariah. Ruby sat nervously eyeing him, waiting for a chance to give him the money she'd folded into a neat rectangle in her purse.

"I'm going to the loo. Coming, Rubes?" Mariah motioned to her to follow.

"Yeah, I'll be there in one tick, you go ahead." Ruby smiled sweetly and pretended to search for her purse under the table. The second Mariah's back was turned she shoved the money at Yaakov. He grinned and winked at her. Following Mariah to the bathroom, she felt excitement prick her skin.

"What do you think? Does he like me?" Mariah was fit to burst with delight. "He's laughing at all my jokes and he's put his arm around my shoulder twice. Oh my God, Ruby! What will I do if he tries to kiss me?" She bounced up and down, before rushing to the sink to check her make-up.

As Mariah locked herself into a cubicle to pee, a dark girl came into the loos and stood brushing her hair slowly. "Ruby?" she whispered.

"What? Yes." Ruby was shocked. She didn't know this girl at all.

"From Yaakov." She shoved a piece of white paper into Ruby's palm and walked out.

Ruby just managed to lock herself into an adjoining cubicle beside Mariah before her friend emerged.

"Rubes?"

"Yeah, I'm in here! You go on – get back to your flirting, you minx!" Ruby called out.

"Well, if you're sure. I can wait for you if you like?"

"No, honey, I'm fine – go for it!"

Ruby's hands shook as she unwrapped the magic dust. Not sure what to do next, she stood dumbfounded and stared at it. It was like a pile of icing sugar. Remembering the trick with the note, she balanced the paper on the sanitary disposal unit and luckily found a last five-euro note in her purse. Rolling it into a tight tube, she put the lid down on the toilet, sat down and snorted as much of the cocaine as she could manage.

Her nose fizzed and hurt, she coughed and the taste of bitterness made her gag. Her eyes watered and she heaved. This wasn't as much fun as the last time. Maybe it was because she was on her own and a bit panicked. Once she finished it and got back inside to the music and other people she'd be fine again. The fun would start. The dancing would kick in. She'd be beautiful and confident again.

It took her another few minutes of fumbling to get the rest of the powder up her nose.

"Ruby?"

Oh shit, it was Mariah looking for her.

"Yes, I'm coming! I just got my monthly, so I had to get stuff from the machine. Sorry for keeping you. I'll be right with you!"

"Okay. I'm going back outside."

Luckily, Mariah was so busy being charmed by Yaakov when Ruby managed to stumble back out, she didn't notice how flustered her friend was. She perched on the side of an armchair and took deep breaths, hoping to feel the whoosh of fun and confidence flood her.

"Come on and dance, Ruby, I love this tune!" Mariah grabbed her wrist and dragged her along with her. Yaakov smiled slowly and watched the girls like a Cheshire cat from the plush sofa.

Ruby didn't feel the love. She didn't feel like she was in a great place, a better one than anywhere else. Suddenly, she didn't want to feel like this. Her heart was racing, she was beginning to really panic.

Yaakov sidled over to her. "What's the matter with you?"

"I feel awful. I feel like my blood is going to rush out my ears and my brain is going to blow up. I don't like this, Yaakov!" she hissed.

He stared at the young girl with eyes like saucers and half smiled. "How much did you take?"

"All of it. Why? How much was I supposed to take?" She shivered with a sudden fear.

"Oh shit, Ruby! You should have spaced it over the night. Here, drink some of this water– it will calm you. Just try and go with it. You'll be good, eh?"

She drank everything she could get her hands on, from

champagne to beer to other putrid and sour drinks, not caring whether they belonged to people.

"Hey, back off, that cost me an arm and a leg!" screamed one woman when she caught her downing her drink. "Get your own!"

Ruby staggered away, feeling like she was in a big plastic bubble.

"What's the suss, Ruby?" Damo's face appeared in front of her.

God, he was so gorgeous!

"I've no drink and I just tried to take a sip of one and that lady got all snotty!" Ruby chewed the inside of her mouth. God, she was thirsty!

"Okay, calm it down a small bit there, girly. You can't go around stealing drinks – someone will get really pissed off with you. What do you want?" Damo put his hand in the small of her back and led her towards the bar. "How about a Smirnoff Ice? Not too strong, all the young ones love them?"

At the bar he called one of the girls over.

"Get this girl a Smirnoff Ice, darling. Put it on my tab." The girl sauntered to get the drink while holding eye contact with him for as long as possible. "Cheers, Sandra! You're looking fab and doing a great job tonight!"

"It's Sheila."

"It doesn't matter what your name is when you have a face like you do." He cupped her face with his hand momentarily as she passed the drink over the bar.

Ruby watched every move, envy spiking her to the core.

"See ya later, girly." With a grin and a wink, he strode off.

Mariah spotted her and came over. She cupped her hands over Ruby's ear to shout.

"I'm heading back to Yaakov's place – are you coming?"

"No, I'll hang on here. Do you think it's wise going off with him? You hardly know the guy."

Ruby tried to focus on Mariah but her head was too whizzy.

"He's lovely, and besides he works for my dad so he's not going to do anything I don't want," Mariah giggled. "But right at this moment, there's not a lot I don't want him to do!"

"Okay, but you'll have to meet me back here or your dad will have an eppo," Ruby warned.

Perhaps it was the alcohol kicking in or else the cocaine just calmed down a bit, but Ruby suddenly felt a lot better. She made her way on to the dance floor to strut her stuff, as she'd rehearsed in her bedroom. But suddenly it wasn't quite as much fun, with Mariah gone. The other women were giving her dirty looks and some were even smirking at her.

Like a shining beacon, on the side of the floor, she spotted Damo chatting to a man in a dark suit. He caught her gaze and held it. As if under a spell, she found herself gravitating towards him.

"How's the head?" he asked.

"So, so!" She rocked her outstretched hand to indicate.

He took her hand and led her out the back of the bar into a private office. "Take a seat." He poured himself a glass of water.

Ruby couldn't sit still, she felt like she'd lava running through her veins instead of blood. She was so drawn to Damo and found him so unbelievably attractive, she simply *had* to make a move.

"What a day from hell," he began.

"I could try to cheer you up, if you'd let me," Ruby purred.

A slow smile spread across Damo's face. Maybe this was God's way of closing one door and opening another.

12

tweeting@angiebaby.com
Work, bed, work, bed. Please God, let there be a break in the savage routine that I now call life.

Angie blew her fringe out of her eyes as she surveyed the chaotic desk in front of her. The pages were four and five deep, and no matter how many hours she put in, she never felt on top of the work. The office was bright and spacious, with large windows overlooking the city. At first she'd been blown away by the sophisticated look of the place, mixed with the American accents of her colleagues, but she was starting to realise that living in Dublin wasn't as much fun as she had thought it was going to be. The job was a level above anything she'd ever done before and left her knackered every evening and fit for bed and very little else.

Just as she'd decided that she would be better off bringing a sleeping bag to the office and giving up on any idea of a life outside work, Rachel had come to visit again. It was Saturday afternoon and Ireland was due to play England in rugby. The pubs were packed to the gills and the atmosphere was electric.

"This gang are great craic and they're always up for a bit of fun, so I'll introduce you to them today and at least you might have one or two people you can call if you want to go out for a drink or bite to eat. They're all very laid back and not in the least bit cliquey."

"Are any of them planning on staying in Dublin or are you going to introduce me to another group of really fun people who are also moving further away from me than you are?" Angie quipped.

"No, this lot are all natives as such. So unless they've all been made redundant in the last month, you should be safe enough. Let's find them first and then we can grab a drink!" Rachel took Angie's hand and guided her through the throngs of revellers.

The small group looked up as the girls made their way to the corner. They all either shook hands or waved across the high round table and carried on chatting among themselves.

One of the guys Rachel introduced her to was a real cutie.

"Hi, Angie, I'm Troy." He ignored her offered hand and leaned forward and kissed each cheek gently.

He seemed sweet and his messy tumbling curly brown hair and small round glasses framed his boyish-looking face. He was casually dressed in a grandfather shirt and sleeveless jumper. His brown cords were finished off by a pair of brown suede shoes. He looked a little bit like a cross between Paddington Bear and a little boy making his First Communion. He had that "dressed by his mummy" look. He certainly wasn't what would be described as sex on a stick.

"Oh, hi there," she managed, feeling like an utter tool.

As Troy leaned away to grab his pint, Angie felt herself blush, much to her own dismay. It was so long since she's been kissed, the harmless greeting brought colour to her cheeks. It was lucky he wasn't exposing himself or trying to play tonsil-tennis with her – she'd probably have had a heart attack. She felt a bit like a nun who'd just been released from a silent convent on a rugged remote island.

She smoothed her blouse and fiddled awkwardly with the gold chain around her neck. Jesus, she was behaving like a twelve-year-old at a church-hall disco. She really needed to get out more. Sitting at home with nothing but reruns of *Friends* on satellite TV was having a dire effect on her self-confidence.

Outside of herself, Rachel and Troy, there were four people in the group. They were friendly enough, although they were a bit intent on talking solely about the wild parties they'd had in college. While that was understandable, Angie found herself a bit left out of the loop.

Once the rugby match started, all eyes were on the big screens. Being an avid fan, Angie became so sucked into the game her inhibitions disappeared.

"You've a fine set of lungs on you, I'll give you that." Troy smiled at Angie as she finally sat down and relaxed at the end of the match.

"I wasn't sure what you were going to say there!" she said.

Troy went the colour of beetroot and looked like he'd like the ground to swallow him whole.

She was going to point out that she was only trying to tease him, but he was so awkward and shy she felt she'd only make matters worse.

"I'm starving actually, is any one else hungry?" Rachel asked the celebrating lads. Ireland had beaten England and the mood was euphoric.

Much to Angie's relief the gang decided to go to an Italian restaurant nearby. As they were making their way up the street, Rachel jumped onto one of the guy's back and the remaining three proceeded to play horse-racing.

Amidst all the whooping and shouting, Troy fell into step beside Angie.

"I hope you don't want me to jump on your back and pretend to whip you all the way to the Italian restaurant?" Angie smiled at him. "Don't get me wrong, I'm as thrilled as the next person that Ireland won today, but I think hitting forty has put a stop to my gallop – well, that type any how, excuse the pun."

"Eh, no, you're okay. I'm happy enough to walk, boring as that might seem. I'm with you!" He shoved his glasses back up his nose.

"They all seem like a nice group. Did you know them before college or what?"

"Yeah, I was in school with Mick but the group only meets up every now and then. Every time we do, they spend the whole night reminiscing about their young, free and single days. To be honest, I didn't enjoy college that much and I'd prefer to talk about something else. The other thing is that it was all twenty years ago – I wish they'd just let it drop already."

"What would you like to discuss then? World peace? Interior design? The dropping price of houses? The failing economy?" Angie supplied helpfully. She felt a bit drunk, although it was nice…

"Uh, well, I don't think I can do much about the state of the world personally. Interior design wouldn't be my forte and I share a house with three run-of-the-mill lads, not a celebrity, entrepreneur or genius between the lot of us. We're all nice enough guys, but nothing mega to write home about, so I'm probably not the best conversationalist." He smiled awkwardly, stuffing his hands into his pockets and pulling his shoulders up to his ears.

"I've just had a few weeks of being on my best behaviour and watching my 'p's' and 'q's,' and I could really do with not having to talk too much, and concentrate on getting langers instead. Like to join me?" Angie smiled at him. He was a sweet, gentle kind of fellow. Not the type to ever exactly rock her world but he was endearing in a shy unassuming way. He seemed equally grateful to have someone to chat to and was gracious enough to laugh quite enthusiastically at all her jokes. Even if he had a tendency to snort a bit and bob his head slightly frantically, while shoving his glasses back up onto his nose, he was "grand" as they'd say in Cork. In any case, he was preferable to her own company or the high-flying Americans. At least he didn't click his fingers and smile at her in that come-up-with-the-goods-or-we'll-fire-you-as-quick-as-look-at-you stare.

Eventually they managed to get a table. The meal was average. It was the usual buckets of pasta with sauce that was probably from a jar, with garlic bread that was so crispy it resembled Styrofoam. But it was cheap, filling and washed down with plenty of wine. Most of all, Angie enjoyed the fact that she didn't have to eat it on her own.

During the meal, Angie and Troy sat beside each other. The conversation, although not exactly a hoot, did flow.

"So, if you were handed a ticket for anywhere in the world, where would you go?" Troy leaned on his elbow and waited for her reply.

"Oh, let me see, probably China. I know it's meant to be hot and intensely overcrowded and all that, but I'd love to see it. What about you?" she added, figuring she ought to be polite.

"Probably Australia. It's always had some sort of draw for me – besides, I'd really like to see the water running the other way when you flush the toilet," he mused.

"That's not a reason to want to go to a place, unless you have some mad fetish with toilets that nobody knows about." In spite of herself Angie giggled.

Afterwards they walked, or more to the point, staggered back towards his house, which was close by. She found him a bit dull, but totally inoffensive and a bit like a grateful puppy dog because she was bidding him the time of day. In a strange way, it was nice for Angie to feel like the stronger person for a change. She was usually so nervous around guys and always ended up feeling a bit inadequate. She felt kind of confident with Troy. She knew she was probably being rather obnoxious, elbowing him and thumping him on the arm a lot, while she took over the conversation. She also knew she was talking utter twaddle, but he wasn't objecting so she gladly kept it up.

"If you were an animal, what would you be?" Troy asked, trying to focus on her.

"Ah for fuck's sake, can you not think of any thing more original than that? It's not twenty questions, is it?" she snorted.

"No, I suppose not." Instead of looking put out or even upset, Troy just grinned at her.

"Let's go to that club we danced the night away in last time with the girls!" said Rachel, still enjoying swinging out of Mick, the guy she'd been playing horsey with earlier.

When Angie didn't whoop with outward joy, Troy shyly asked her if she'd prefer to accompany him back to his place.

"I'd say the lads are all out still, so we might have the flat to ourselves. If you'd rather go dancing, that's cool."

He was a sweet guy and nothing like his friends. Angie knew that by that time (a quarter past one) the nightclub would just be crowded, boiling hot and messy.

"Rachel, I'm going to head back to Troy's gaff for a drink. What are you thinking of doing?" Angie tried to say it all quietly.

"Ooh, do we have a little match made in heaven?" Rachel swayed. "No, you go on, I was never one for being green and hairy. I've got your spare key so don't rush home on my account." Rachel bear-hugged Angie and skipped off singing a really raucous rendition of "The Fields of Anthenry" with the others.

Several hours and six glasses of cheap red wine later, Angie found herself in bed with Troy. She knew it wasn't love – in fact she had no desire to even see him again. But she wasn't going to turn down the chance of a quick shag. Besides, it was be so nice to feel the touch of a man again.

What they did together could not have been classed as making love, by anyone's standards. It was all very fumbly, with him making more than his fair share of grunting noises and blowing out his nostrils like a warthog. He was fairly well endowed, but she had to guide him rather a lot as he seemed to be missing the beat most of the time. She put it down to both of them being scuttered, rather than either of them being bad in bed. Feeling at a bit of a loss, and only realising the whole thing was over when he slumped asleep heavily while still on top of her, she managed to shrug him over to the side, squeezing her eyes shut as she hoped he wouldn't fall onto the floor with a thump. Sitting up for a second to check that he was still actually breathing, she lay back down beside him, feeling kind of skuzzy, wearing only her bra, with all her make-up on.

Feeling too pissed to move, she fell into a buzzy slightly sweaty sleep. The nylon bedclothes on the single bed were stale-smelling and the bed was springy and uncomfortable. Through her drunken mist, she allowed herself to feel slightly smug too. It had been too long since she'd had sex, even if it had been a total anti-climax in every sense of the word.

* * *

As light filtered through the nylon curtains the next morning, she peeled her dry eyes open and felt like an idiot. She tried to cheer herself up by thinking she'd now had a one-night stand, a good thing really, because how could she be a proper modern woman without one? As she edged her way out of the bed, she tried not to even breathe, terrified he'd wake up and she'd have to speak to him. It had all been okay last night, when sense, soberness and any form of her usual normality had been well and truly pickled with booze. But this was a whole different kettle of fish.

Mercifully, his flat was small, so she managed to find her knickers and the rest of her clothes easily. As she creaked the bathroom door shut, she lowered herself on to the toilet and tried to pee quietly, which proved to be nigh impossible. Dropping some sheets of toilet paper into the loo, she hoped that might help to buffer the noise. Then she was faced with the dilemma of whether she should flush or leave it as it was.

Her head was splitting and she felt like she wanted to vomit, but most of all she wanted to get the hell out of there and make her way back to her own apartment. A thought suddenly struck her. She was on her own here with Troy. What if he'd been an axe murderer? He could have severed her limbs and chopped her into little bits and stowed her in a suitcase and flung her in the canal.

Vowing to take serious mental notes to never, ever allow herself to do something this stupid again, she took a deep breath and said a little silent prayer of thanks that she was still alive. With her shoes in her hand, so as not to make any noise, she grabbed her handbag and let herself out the front door into the dewy morning air.

13

tweeting@serenasvelte.com

Here comes the bride! Who is the luckiest girl in the world? You guessed it . . .

Serena looked at herself in the mirror on the morning of her wedding. Her heart skipped a beat as she thought of Paul. By the end of today, she would be Mrs Davenport. The build-up to this day had been wonderful. She had enjoyed every second of it. All the attention was on her as she floated down the aisle on her daddy's arm. Her dress was a stunning buttery-coloured satin sheath, which showed off her perfect figure to a tee. The heavy antique lace veil with tiny seed pearls contrasted beautifully and showed off her dark hair.

Paul took her hand from her father and kissed her cheek at the top of the aisle.

"You look simply beautiful," he whispered to her.

She knew she did, but it was nice to hear him say it. "Thank you, darling, and you look most dashing!" She gazed at him adoringly.

The wedding was flawless. Adele was poised and oozed style and effortless elegance. But, as Serena mused to herself, that was Chanel all over. Ruby was like something from fairyland, her elfin features delicately framed by the beautiful pale-golden slick chignon. For a brief moment that morning Serena was about to ask the beautician to put a little more blusher on her cheeks. She wasn't sure if it was her imagination but she thought Ruby looked a little bit peaky. Serena figured the poor little thing was just nervous at the thought of walking up the aisle first. Not to mention the fact that Adele had been snapping at the poor girl non-stop.

"Stand up straight, Ruby. You don't want to ruin your lovely outfit by looking like you've got scoliosis." Adele pulled at the back of Ruby's bolero jacket.

"We're all a bit emotional here Adele, let's try and keep it calm, please." Serena gave Adele one of her get-back-in-your-box stares. Not wanting to start an argument with her sister just before she walked up the aisle, Serena stroked Ruby's arm gently.

"You're all right, aren't you, darling?" she asked her niece.

Ruby didn't meet her gaze. "Sure, why?"

"You look a tiny tinge pale." Serena held her fingers half an inch apart to demonstrate.

"I'm just so excited, Aunt Serena. It's all so overwhelming, isn't it?" Ruby smiled angelically.

"Yes, pet, it is." Serena clapped her hands with the pleasure of it all. "Do you know, I will be the luckiest person alive if I can have a daughter like you some day." She stroked her niece's cheek. Bar Paul, Ruby was Serena's favourite person on the planet. She wasn't a huge fan of kids or babies but Ruby had always melted her heart, from the first second they'd met.

Serena had it all worked out. First and foremost, when they came back from the honeymoon in Hawaii, she was going to find a proper home for herself and Paul.

"Mummy wants us to live near their and Adele's houses in Blackrock," she had told Paul. "They've both commented that married people need a house to live in. I do agree. It's okay for a courting couple to live in an apartment but once we're married, I think a house would be more fitting."

"Fair enough. I'll tell you what, you can sort that out for us. No better girl!" Paul patted her bottom, delighted in the knowledge she would organise a perfect home for them.

Then, Serena planned, as soon as she had a house organised, she'd get pregnant. She was already off the pill. She'd hire a nanny and get a personal trainer to make sure she didn't end up looking a mess after the birth. Hopefully it would be a girl, one that looked and acted like Ruby. That way she would adore it instantly.

She wasn't going around in hideous maternity clothes either. She was going to go with her mother or Adele to Paris and buy chic clothes, which skimmed over her growing tummy. She certainly wasn't going to go around in awful tight T-shirts, shoving her large swollen tummy in people's faces. She couldn't understand why anyone would want to do that. It was quite revolting really. She shuddered as she thought about all the fatness she'd have to endure.

It would be worth it in the end though. Just imagine how proud of her Paul would be, if she produced a little son or daughter for him. It would all be just perfect. She shrugged her shoulders in excitement at the thought of it all.

Pulling herself back to the here and now, this was her day to shine. She waltzed into the Four Seasons, working the red carpet, and accepted a glass of champagne with glee.

This was the best day of her life. All her friends and their parents' friends were oohing and ahhing at her. Telling her she was stunning and complimenting her diamond-encrusted wedding band.

"I just love it," she oozed, linking Paul's arm. She felt him stiffen slightly as they followed the bagpipe music into the huge function room.

"Please be upstanding for the bride and groom, Mr and Mrs Paul Davenport!"

Serena relished the applause and attention. Paul shrank and looked like he wanted to crawl under a rock.

"Just smile and wave, darling. You can do it – they're all here for us." She looked into his eyes and he knew she would carry him through.

As they took their pew at the top table, Serena flew into action.

"Paul likes red wine only, don't pour him that white," she said to the foreign waiter. "Be a darling and bring him a bottle of Gigondas. I don't want him having to ask for it. Thanks so much, sweetie!" She smiled at him and he ran off to do what she'd requested.

With smooth ease, she downed a glass of white wine and then chatted easily to Paul's father, who was sitting on her right. Normally quite a shy man, he found himself relaxed with his son's gorgeous wife. At the end of the meal, when the speeches began, Paul came into his own. Taking the microphone, he commanded the room, speaking with confidence and aplomb about his life and career.

He ended by addressing Serena.

"None of this would have been possible without my wife."

The crowd applauded his use of the word wife.

"She's the light of my life and I know we are going to be very happy together. We make a great team and, being a businessman, I know I've made the best deal of my life today." He raised his glass. "To my wife!"

Jim O'Keefe was a well-known businessman and was both respected and liked. When he took to the microphone he glowed with pride.

"Today is a bittersweet day for me as a father. Serena and I have a wonderful bond. Apart from her mother, who is of course a pro at manipulating me, my youngest daughter takes the prize. She was the first to drive a Golf GTI in her class, the first to own a diamond ring and the first to receive a standing ovation at a function she organised aged twenty. She has determination by the bucketload, she is beautiful inside and out, and I wish her all the love and happiness that Kate and I have experienced during our marriage. Paul, all I can say is, welcome to the family, and the best of luck. You're going to need it!"

The room laughed and clapped as Serena pretended to be offended.

"Please raise your glasses for the final toast today. To Serena and Paul!"

The room joined in and the sound of clinking glasses rang out. Serena basked in the positive attention.

After they finished cutting the top tier of the five-tiered cake, she caught the waiter's arm as he passed. "Be a darling and bring me over a large brandy." She winked at him and sauntered back to her seat.

14

tweeting@themercedesking.com
It's probably the forbidden fruit that tastes the sweetest . . .

Damo took a deep salty breath of sea air. He felt on top of the world as he marched along the prom, avoiding the piles of dog poo and gazing enviously at the boats. He allowed himself to think about the other night. He really hadn't meant to make a move on Ruby. It had all happened before he could blink. The club had been filled to capacity, which hadn't happened for ages. The recession was taking its toll on everyone but people had been shying away from the club for months. At last the place seemed to be heaving and he'd needed to clear his head in the back room. Ruby had been looking a bit out of it, so he'd only been minding her.

One of the barmen had come to him and told him Mariah had left with that Yaakov fella. He was a useless worker and could barely string a sentence together, but the ladies all thought he was a looker, so he'd been good for business. Having said that, he was not the type he wanted his child hanging around with.

"Your daughter's just left with the Russian lover," Matt had reported.

"You're not serious, ah Jaysus, why didn't you stop her, you dozy git? Find out where they're gone and find them, will ya?" Damo was agitated.

Ruby had been there, all smelling nice, with a showstopper of a rig-out on, and she wanted him. He could see that. He'd fleetingly thought he should probably stay away. He'd end up getting his fingers burnt if she told Mariah or Noreen. But the couple of lines of coke he'd taken earlier on were talking louder than his common sense.

She'd kept telling him how cool he was, how much she wanted to be with a man like him, not a kid. That she'd been watching him for ages. That she wanted it. So, needless to say, he'd obliged.

Afterwards, she'd gone off like a thing possessed onto the dance floor. He could get to like her. She wasn't demanding and seemed to be the same as him – out for a good time and a bit of pleasure along the way. Fair play to her.

* * *

Ruby found herself thinking obsessively of that night too as the days went by.

She had been high as a kite by the time Mariah had arrived back with the Russian, looking rightly pissed off.

Mariah was fuming. "Ruby, did you tell my dad I'd gone off with Yaakov?"

"Hell no, what do you take me for?" Ruby retorted.

"Well, one of his asshole doormen just burst into Yaakov's flat and dragged me out. He said Yaakov is fired and then he punched him in the eye. Now I'll never see him again!" Mariah burst into tears.

Ruby flung her arms around her, making her stagger backwards into the wall. "It's fine, Mariah, don't you worry about him. He's just a flash in the pan! You'll find true love soon. Come on, dance with me!"

Ruby yanked Mariah onto the dance floor and left her with no choice but to join in. Mariah was mildly surprised by the madness emanating from her friend, but put it down to the Smirnoff Ice she was swigging.

By the time Damo tapped Mariah on the shoulder and told her the taxi was waiting outside, she'd had enough anyway.

"Come on, Ruby, Dad's organised us a taxi, let's go!" Mariah shouted.

"What? Already? No way. I'm staying here!" Ruby clapped her hands and tried to dance away. Damo scooped her up in his arms and carried the giggling girl down the back stairs, as Mariah went to grab their coats and bags.

"When can we see each other again?" Ruby relished being in his strong arms.

"Soon," Damo grinned. This one was a little ball of dynamite, there was no denying it.

15

tweeting@angiebaby.com
Burning the candle at both ends? It used to be my forte, now it's my failing. I just can't do it any more!

Angie had been delighted to hear that Rachel was coming back to Dublin for another weekend. Dublin was a cold place when you didn't know anyone. It wasn't as if she could go into a bar or a restaurant on her own and hope to meet people. It just didn't work like that here.

But unfortunately, as it turned out, this weekend Angie hadn't felt up to anything much.

"I know I sound like such a Granny-bag but I'm still playing catch-up after our escapade three weeks ago. I can't do heavy drinking sessions with very little sleep, sandwiched between incessant work any more," she moaned.

She'd felt fine until they'd gone out the night before. They'd had a nice meal, with a couple of glasses of wine. She'd enjoyed that bit.

"Let's go to a club!" Rachel had said when they emerged from the restaurant. She was dying to scout around and look at the Dublin talent again.

"Do we have to?" Angie had groaned, feeling wrecked. "My bed is calling to me. I've had all fourteen-hour days this week. I'd really

100

prefer to just curl up with a bottle of wine and have a chat," she pleaded.

"We can chat on the phone any time. You're the one who's always saying you want a husband. I hate to be the one to break it to you, but Mr Angie isn't going to jump out of the kitchen press and sweep you off your feet. Staying in is a one-way ticket to the shelf." Rachel was tottering towards the nearest nightclub.

"What shelf?" Angie asked, trying to keep up with Rachel.

"The one we're going to be left on if we don't get out and shake our asses!" Rachel called over her shoulder.

Knowing it was futile arguing, Angie followed her.

Rachel bounded up to the bar in the nightclub and leaned over to shout to the barman. "Shots!"

Angie groaned. She really didn't feel up to this.

Rachel was twirling around with one arm above her head and squealing, "This is it, girl! Let's go for it and see what the night brings!" She snatched up the tiny shot glass from the bar and tossed it backwards, draining its contents in seconds. "Two more!" she yelled to the barman.

Angie downed the shot and had to cover her mouth. Retching horribly, she closed her eyes and tried to breathe through her nose to stop herself from puking.

"Come on, girl, all work and no play makes Angie a very dull girl!" Rachel teased.

Knowing her friend wouldn't notice, Angie poured the next shot into an empty can which was sitting on the bar. As she followed Rachel onto the dance floor, she felt rotten. Her tummy was like a balloon, tender and crampy. Maybe she was getting her period. She was so irregular, she never knew when it would come, but now that she thought about it, she hadn't had one for a while. Even for her, it seemed a very long time. Her boobs were very tender too. No wonder she was so knackered.

It was after four when she'd finally managed to drag Rachel home to her apartment. They'd had to stop for chips on the way. Rachel was on top form and had hung around chatting to the customers.

"I'd invite you back, but I'm staying with my friend, the cranky one over there," Rachel was giggling. Staggering over to Angie, she whispered, very loudly, "Do you mind if I bring that fella back for a nightcap?"

"Yes, I do. He's a bloody tramp for crying out loud! You're not bringing him within an ass's roar of my place. He'd probably clear the place out while we're asleep, not to mention stabbing us for a teabag. You're pissed and obviously visually impaired. Now get your chips and shift yourself. I've had enough, we're going home. On our own!" The poor git stank to high heaven, had holes in his trousers and was almost totally gummy. Talk about beer goggles! Rachel was wearing telescopes if she thought Bill Sykes in the corner was a runner.

Angie had fallen into bed, too tired to even wash her make-up off. Rachel was still babbling away in the bed beside her as she'd drifted into an exhausted slumber.

"Here, Ange, let's sing something! What'll we sing? Angie, come on, wake up!" Rachel was jabbing her in the ribs.

"Piss off," she mumbled. "You're like having a small child pumped with sugar to stay. I'm wrecked. Now shut up and go to sleep."

"Ok-ay, how about a Spice Girls song?" Rachel began to croon.

"You sound like a gremlin on speed. Please, shut the fuck up!" Angie croaked. "If you want to stay awake and be annoying, go in and watch the telly!"

Rachel was now clapping and poking her simultaneously, while singing, "Wannabe". "Come on, sing with me, la, la, la, la!" She was then erupting into giggles, finishing with snorts, which she also found hilarious.

Angie felt like hitting her. She must've fallen asleep, because the noise stopped soon after that. Thank Christ, Angie thought as she burrowed into her soft pillow and tried to ignore the snoring. No wonder Rachel was still single. She'd have to end up with a deaf giraffe if the relationship were to last. At least then his head would be far enough away from her and his hearing would be bad enough that he couldn't hear her. Christ, the noise could make it onto the Richter scale.

* * *

As it turned out, Ruby and Damo didn't cross paths again until a few weeks later. He'd thought about her, sure why wouldn't he, but he was busy with the clubs, and Mariah hadn't asked to go out since. She was in a bit of a strop over that Russian. Damo had fired his ass, and sent a message to say that he wasn't to show his face again unless he wanted it rearranged.

He was at home, running on the treadmill, sweating like a bastard, in his gym, when Ruby had appeared behind him.

"Hi, Damo." She looked less cocky than before. She was looking at her shoes. She looked like shite. All pale and iffy. She looked like a kid again. None of the sassy attitude or the sexy dress or make-up like the night in the club.

"Ah, there ya are, Ruby! All right, love?" He slowed the treadmill down until it came to a halt. Grabbing his towel, he mopped his brow and wiped his nose on the back of his hand as he jumped down off the machine to talk to the girl.

"I'm not really all right. I'm not okay at all, to be perfectly honest with you!" She burst into heaving sobs.

"Ah Jaysus, Ruby! Come and sit here and tell me what's happened to ya. You'll be grand, love." He walked over to the bench press and motioned for her to sit there.

"I'm pregnant," she sobbed.

"Yer wha? Wha? Ah fuck, no! Since when?" Damo felt the room spin. Now this was messy. But judging by the way she'd been with him, she probably didn't have a clue who the daddy was.

"Since the night in the club."

"You've got to be kidding me." Damo looked at her like she was speaking a foreign language.

"I wish I was," she sobbed. "But, maybe we can work it out. You see, I'm in love with you. I don't want any of the kids my age. You have it all, Damo. I could leave school – we could get a place together. We could be perfect, you and me. I know our families will be a bit upset at first but they'll come around. To be honest, Mariah isn't talking to me at the moment anyway, 'cos she thinks I told you she went off with Yaakov, so she's really annoyed."

"Whoa, wait one minute there. What the hell do you think you're saying?"

"This is all insane, Ruby! We were only having a bit of a laugh, you and me. It doesn't mean anything. I'm married to Noreen. That's the way it is. The rules are that it's okay to have a bit of fun, but at the end of the day I'm a family man. Nothing is going to get in the way of that. Never has, and never will."

To Ruby, Damo didn't look as nice as he had before. He was angry and sneering, looking down his nose at her.

"But I thought you loved me too!" Ruby was shaking and sobbing like a baby.

Damo was walking up and down the room like a caged animal. "Are you keeping it?"

"Yes, I'm keeping it. I've told my parents. They've booked me an appointment with a gynaecologist in a private clinic. I'm not having an abortion." She shuddered at the thought.

"You've told your parents! About me!" Damo exploded.

"No! Just about the baby!" Ruby cast her mind back to the dreadful conversation and subsequent events of the previous day.

* * *

"Please, tell me you are making this up?" Adele's eyes had widened and her voice had risen to a very loud shrill tone.

"I wish I was but I'm not." Ruby had stood and stared at the floor. "I found out yesterday. I bought one of those testing kits in the chemist …"

"Which chemist? Not the local one, I hope? Did anyone see you buy it?" Adele was now shouting. Her face was all red and she was pacing up and down, muttering.

"No, I got it at the shopping centre. Please, Mum, try to stay calm. It's not the end of the world and – ."

"Stay calm! Ha, that's a bloody joke for a start, and believe me, Ruby, it's the end of *your* world! You can bet it is. How could you be so stupid?" Adele spun around and faced her daughter. Her face was hardened. "You've ruined everything, you silly little slut!"

The simultaneous noise and sting shocked Ruby to the core as her mother slapped her face. She raised her hand to her face slowly as tears began to seep down her cheeks.

"Your father is going to be devastated. Well done, Ruby," Adele whispered through gritted teeth, eyes like flints.

Ruby had run from the room and up the stairs. She'd stayed in her room for over two hours. She kept expecting her mother to come up and apologise for hitting her and calling her stupid and a slut. But there were no sounds of footsteps on the stairs, her door didn't open gently. Her mother didn't come. Instead, she heard the car door shut on her father's car outside. She heard his key opening the front door, swiftly followed by a loud slamming sound.

"Ruby, get down here!" he bellowed.

Feeling terrified, ashamed and embarrassed, Ruby emerged from her bedroom and dragged herself down to the kitchen. Her mother was sitting at the kitchen table. She had a purplish, puffy complexion from crying. Her hands were shaking and she had a big ball of scrunched-up tissue in her fist.

"I think you have some explaining to do, young lady. What the hell has been going on? Start at the beginning and make sure you tell the truth."

Her father was like steel. His blue eyes were like ice. Her normally loving and doting father had gone away. In his place was this pacing, angry, hassled man.

"Daddy, it was all a mistake, I never meant this to happen." Ruby's voice was barely audible as she spoke.

"Look at me when you speak and stop muttering!" Harry banged the table with his fist.

Standing at the opposite side of the table to her dad, Ruby could hardly talk she was so scared.

"It happened at the disco. The boy is from Russia, he was there working at Mr McCabe's place. He's gone now. He got fired, you see." Ruby was trying to bide her time until she spoke to Damo and worked out their future.

"Bloody marvellous!" Harry was taking deep breaths and staring at her. "Give me Damo McCabe's home number – that man has a lot of questions to answer. We told you that you could go to that cesspit of a club on the condition that he took responsibility for you. Where the hell was he? Drunk in a corner?"

"No, he was working! I went out with Yaakov. I snuck away and came back to the club before the taxi was due to bring us home. Mr McCabe knew nothing about it!" Ruby was shaking so violently she could barely speak. "You both hate me, don't you?" She started to sob.

Her mother answered, speaking for the first time since her father had come home. "No, we don't hate you, Ruby. It would be a lot easier if we did, believe me. We are beyond disappointed and, right now, we don't particularly like you. But don't tell us we don't love you. At least spare us the wounded animal routine."

Harry took over from his wife. "Your mother rang me at the office and told me, and I stupidly thought, no, not our Ruby, she wouldn't be so irresponsible and selfish! I drove home thinking I'd get here and the whole thing would be a big mistake. Ruby, what the hell have you got us into? Have you any idea what you've done? You're fifteen years old. You have your whole life ahead of you. You've just wiped it all out."

The way her father looked at her at that moment made Ruby want to curl up and die. The look of adoration and love was gone. She'd killed it all.

She had tried to leave the room.

"Don't you dare walk out of here, my girl!" said her father. "You've made your bed and you will lie in it now. Running away is not going to help this situation. We will all have to sit and decide what's going to happen here." He pulled a chair out and pointed at it. "Sit."

Ruby had done as she was told and they'd talked to each other as if she wasn't there. They'd discussed abortions. Ruby had tried to interject and say she didn't want that. But they weren't listening to her.

Her mother had said she couldn't live with herself if they did that. "We'd have to take her to England to a clinic. I don't think I could bear it," she had sniffed.

"Adele, it would be difficult, but it would be a couple of days of grief and this mess would be over and done with. She could have counselling. She'd get over it."

"No, Harry. It's wrong. It's murder. I can't be a part of that." Her mother began to cry again.

"I don't want to kill my baby, Daddy, please!" Ruby burst out.

"Do you have any clue how wrong that sounds, Ruby? You're only a bloody baby yourself. Why did you do this? What's wrong with you that you had to do this to us and to yourself?" Harry was trying to nail down a black-and-white reason for the whole thing.

But there wasn't any premeditated reason why she'd done it. She had never in a million years thought she'd end up pregnant. She knew the facts of life and all that. But it had been her first time and she really hadn't thought she'd get pregnant the first time. Besides, Damo was the love of her life. They would be together forever, so there were no downfalls to sleeping with him. It had felt like the most natural thing in the world at the time.

"Okay, Ruby, so, say you keep this poor child. What then? Who raises it? Who pays for its food, clothes, education? Who pays the rent? Shall I tell you? Me, that's who!" Harry jabbed at himself repeatedly to emphasise the point.

"Okay, Harry. That's enough. This child is going to be our grandchild. We can't say things we'll regret later. We all need to calm down and try to let this sink in a bit." Adele ground at her eyes with a tissue and tried to steady herself, by taking big deep breaths.

"Can I go back to my room now?" Ruby asked in a small voice.

"We'll call you in a while." Adele didn't look at her. "Daddy will want to talk to Mr McCabe. He was meant to be watching out for you and minding you – we'd like to hear his side of the story on this."

Ruby ran up to her room and buried her head in her duvet. All her fears and worries came spilling out. She sobbed like a baby. She was stupid and thoughtless, her dad was right. Her life was over. None of her friends were going to want to hang around with her when they heard she was pregnant. They wouldn't want someone with a huge tummy going for hot chocolate with them.

None of her Juicy Couture mini-dresses were going to fit her anymore. Oh Jesus, she'd have to wear old ladies' maternity clothes! Those manky big smock things that made women look like walking sofas. The pain was going to be horrendous too. How was she going to manage the birth? She rolled over onto her back and ran her hands down past her hips. She was too small to push a baby out. Fresh tears sprang from the endless fountain she seemed to have acquired in her head.

I've no credit - can u ring me? My life is over - so much to tell u. R x

Ruby thanked God for the "free texts to your friends" service on her phone, as she sat praying Mariah had some credit to call her back. She needed to fill her in and warn her that her parents were on the warpath.

Then there was Aunt Serena. She'd have to be told. Ruby had always been her pet, she'd stuck up for her in the past, or bought her cool stuff her parents had refused her. But this was different. She was going to be so let down by her behaviour. She'd look at Ruby in a different light now. Ruby wanted to die. She wanted to turn the clock back and make the whole situation go away.

"Hey Rubes, what's the big panic?" Mariah was lying on her tummy painting her nails, with Snow Patrol booming in the background.

"I'm pregnant." The words hung in the air like a bad smell.

"Wh-aaaaa-t? Oh sweet Jesus! Hang on a minute, will you? I'm going to turn down the music." Ruby heard the music stop abruptly.

"Oh holy shit, Ruby, what are you going to do?"

Ruby didn't know what to say. She was going to talk to Damo but she couldn't let Mariah know that.

"Ruby? Can you hear me?"

"Yup, oh Mariah, what have I done? This is a total shambles. Things like this don't happen to girls like me. This happens to other people, not me. I can't believe it, and now my parents are angry with your dad," she sobbed.

"Why what's it got to do with him?" Mariah was horrified.

"It happened at the club. When you went off with Yaakov, I went out the back with a guy. I took some cocaine and then one thing led to another and I suppose they just want someone to blame, so my dad wants to talk to your dad, yadda, yadda! What am I going to do? Nobody will want to talk to me ever again, none of the guys will want to go out with me, like ever. I have to learn how to be a mum, Mariah. This is totally insane!" Ruby's chest hurt from crying.

"Oh God, I don't know what to say. I knew you were acting really weird when I came back that night. You were like a woman possessed. Ruby, how could you be so bloody stupid? Do you have this guy's number? What's his name? My dad can probably track him down."

"No. I'll sort it. I got myself into this mess, I'll sort it out. It'll be fine. I'm sure of it. This all seems like a big black hole right now, but I know the guy loves me. It's Yaakov. I'm sorry, Mariah. He came back to the club after the bust-up with your dad's bouncer and I met him in the corridor. If it helps at all, I wasn't trying to make a fool of you. I knew you really liked him but when I saw him again, I realised I had feelings for him too. Coupled with the drugs, I couldn't help myself. I'm not proud of myself and I know I've overstepped the mark by going off with him when I knew you liked him. But we've been friends forever. We'll get through this, won't we?"

"Whatever you say, Ruby. I wouldn't hold out much hope if I were you." Mariah's voice was as cold as ice.

"What would you know, Mariah? You're still a bloody virgin!" Ruby yelled.

"Yeah, and who's better off? Me or you? Eh, I think we both know the answer to that one. I don't need 'friends' like you, Ruby. Don't come near me again. We're through."

Ruby couldn't take anymore. She slammed the phone down and threw herself on the bed and cried.

Ruby's bedroom had grown dark by the time her mother came up to speak to her. The huge shadows from the outside branches cast deep dark fingers across her ceiling. The sound of children screaming with glee outside filtered through the windows.

Her mum came over and sat on the end of her bed.

"Ruby, I've spoken to Dr Sullivan – he's the doctor who delivered you. He's agreed to see you. We're very lucky he's taking you on. Usually –" Adele's voice cracked and she took a minute to regain her composure. "Usually, he doesn't see anyone under eighteen but he agreed because I am already a patient. Daddy and I would prefer if you didn't discuss any of this with anyone until we see Dr Sullivan in two weeks. You can go to school tomorrow as usual. We have to try and keep everything as normal as possible, for as long as possible." Adele stood up and left the room.

* * *

Now, sitting in front of Damo in his customised gym, she sat rocking back and forth, wailing like an injured animal. Damo didn't know what to do with her.

"But tons of young wans go and have abortions. I'll organise a private clinic, a real posh one in the UK. I hear they're real nice to you and it's all over in a jiffy. Before you know it. Then you can get on with your life. I've a good few mates in London – maybe you could have a nice night out for yourself if you made a weekend of it? I'll sort it all for you, a few quid to spend and cheer yourself up. This baby'll be a noose around your neck. Your life is over if you go through with this, Ruby." He didn't need this kind of hassle. He had enough to sort out with his own kids and the business. "Are you sure your parents don't know I'm the father?" He spun around, suddenly envisaging a huge row.

"No, I told them it was Yaakov and that he's gone now." She ground her eyes with a screwed-up ball of tissue.

"Right, nice one, love. Good girl. Your parents wouldn't understand and it'd only cause hassle. So I'll sort you with a clinic and nobody needs to be any the wiser." He walked over and patted the sobbing girl's back.

"I didn't come here so you could tell me what a mess I've made of my life! I've easily worked that out for myself. The only reason I'm here is to tell you I'm pregnant and that you are to expect a call from my father, who seems to have decided that you are solely responsible for all this mess, as you're Yaakov's employer!" She began to wail again.

Fuck's sake, Damo thought. He'd thought Ruby was a great little one but this was all a different territory. He'd have to up the incentive for her to go to England. He'd think about it more carefully and get back to her. Meanwhile, he'd be ready for the call from Lord Snot, the father. He'd sort him too, by agreeing what a toe rag your man Yaakov was and offering to help out. That way, he'd come out of it all smelling of roses. Problem solved.

"You go on home, Ruby. I'll have a think, you just stick to your story and I'll look after ya. You can trust me, love. Look at me." He gently lifted her chin in his hands. "You're beautiful, you're going to break some serious hearts, you mark my words. You're special, do you know that?" He grinned at her and winked.

Ruby stopped crying and her heart soared. He *did* care. He thought she was beautiful. He thought she was special. She'd just give him time to see that he wasn't able to live without her, then it'd all work out. For now, she'd do as he suggested and keep her parents believing it was Yaakov.

16

tweeting@serenasvelte.com
What are you supposed to do when there is something you want and it doesn't seem to be happening? Not only am I not used to this – I hate it.

The honeymoon had been wonderful and relaxing and romantic. Two full weeks of having Paul to herself, with no work, no distractions and all the time in the world to bask in the sunshine and roam around the beautiful island of Hawaii.

Serena had returned and concentrated on looking for the perfect home. With her unlimited budget and her father's connections in the building trade, she found a magnificent six-bedroom home in Blackrock.

The interior had to be totally redone, as it just didn't meet with Serena's standards. The colours were too dark, and there was far too much red everywhere. Serena hated red.

"Just use your imagination, darling," she enthused to Paul when they went to view it together. "I know it's a little shabby at the moment but it will be gorgeous when I put my touches to it. Especially when I get rid of all that red – God, it's just so garish!" She flew from room to room gesturing and explaining what she was going to do.

Paul just followed her in amazement and slight amusement. The house was already a showpiece. Every finish was to the highest standard, and to even employ the word "shabby" when referring to the place was a joke. But if Serena thought she could do better, who was he to argue?

"Just imagine how much our children will love to grow up here!" She slid her arms around his waist and pulled him to her.

"That'll be wonderful all right," he smiled at her. Although it would probably be great when it happened, he wasn't hell bent on the whole kids issue. But if it made Serena happy, then he was happy.

The icing on the cake for Serena had been Adele's face earlier that day. Herself and her sister had met the estate agent and walked around the house for the final time before Serena brought Paul to view.

"It's a stunning property," Adele admitted enviously. "It's very big though. We wouldn't bother with such a large place, with only one child. I hope you and that husband of yours are planning a large brood to fill this place. Otherwise I don't think I could justify it, personally."

That did it. If she had to sell her body, Serena wanted this house.

As she felt the familiar cramps, telling her she was getting her period, Serena did feel disappointed. Although they'd only been officially "trying" for two months, she was really planning on being pregnant by now. Deciding not to leave it to the gods, she phoned a private clinic and made an appointment to have herself checked out. Serena didn't "do" waiting, and this issue was no exception.

* * *

Dr Sullivan was one of the top gynaecological consultants in Dublin. He was a tall thin man with neat hair and was immaculately turned out. Serena felt immediately relaxed in his presence. He had his rooms in a renowned private clinic in Blackrock. His rooms were tastefully decorated in soothing pink tones and the place always smelled of expensive perfume. All the well-to-do ladies of the area attended him. He was known to be one of the best in his profession, but there was no doubt that the prestigious surroundings attracted the ladies who lunch.

He'd taken a couple of blood tests on the spot.

"I need you to go for a pelvic X-ray and an ultrasound examination." He scribbled the necessary information on a card and handed it to her.

"Well, I see no point in waiting around with anything in life, let alone something as important as conceiving," Serena smiled.

"Come back in two weeks' time – make an appointment with my secretary on your way out. Hopefully, if there's any problem it will show up in the tests. Between now and then, try not to worry." Dr Sullivan patted her arm gently as he accompanied her out of his office.

"Thank you, Dr Sullivan, I'll see you then." Serena shook his hand in a very business-like manner.

After making her appointment with the secretary, she bustled through the waiting room with her eyes averted, desperate to avoid the row of women with pregnant swollen bellies, smiling smugly at her. How she hoped she would be able to join them soon!

Now that she had begun to worry about the baby issue, everywhere she went she saw pregnant women. From young girls to women who looked like they should be grandmothers rather than mothers. Pregnancy seemed to be rife everywhere except in her house.

The problem could always lie with Paul of course. The idea flashed fleetingly through her mind. She wouldn't like to bother Paul with all this however. Unless he had to, he wouldn't have time to trot in and out of clinics. She didn't think he'd like to have to sit and talk about his bits to a stranger either.

Knowing it would help to calm her nerves a bit, she took a little hip flask from her bag and took a small mouthful. She didn't drink that much during the day, especially when she needed to drive. The police were so annoying about all this drink driving issue now. Why they were all so hung up on it all she'd never know. A little drink didn't hurt anybody.

Taking another quick swig of vodka, she felt the liquid burning as it travelled down her throat and hit her stomach. Although the taste was kind of putrid, it was amazingly comforting. Closing her eyes for a few seconds to steady herself, she called Paul.

"Hi, darling, how are you?" She tried to sound as cheerful as possible.

"I'm fine. What are you up to today?" he asked.

"Oh, I've a bit of shopping to do and I need to have my hair done for the ball tonight. Do you need anything picked up? I have your tuxedo and shirt ready." She hoped he wasn't going to notice the tension she knew was in her voice. Luckily he was up to ninety, with the four-hundred-person function he was speaking at that night.

"Okay, darling, I'll be home at six for a quick shower, so be ready to leave at around half past." He hung up without noticing her anxiety.

She supposed it was her own fault, he wasn't a mind reader. She really needed to sit down and talk to him, and explain what she was going through. There was no way he would ever pick up on her inner worries. He was too busy for all that. It wasn't that he didn't care or didn't notice her. He was a wonderfully caring and loving husband, but he was also exceptionally busy and important.

She hated the thought of having to tell him that she might have problems conceiving. It just wasn't her style to have something *wrong* with her. She made things happen. She was the utmost in style, chic and organisation. If she couldn't have children, it just wouldn't fit the picture. Pointing out to her husband that she might have a slight flaw wouldn't be on the agenda unless totally necessary. Besides, this Dr O'Sullivan was the best in the business – she'd let him sort it all out. He had reiterated over and over during her consultation that some people needed to try for at least a year before they got pregnant.

"Please try not to worry, Serena. You've only been trying for such a short time, and the only reason I'm even doing this test is to help you rule out any problems in your own head. The more you relax, the higher the likelihood of you managing to conceive."

Taking a deep cleansing breath, she tried to convince herself that this little, unfortunate blip would be over soon. With a bit of luck, she'd never need to mention this unpleasantness to anyone. Besides, highlighting one's shortfalls was dreadfully common and garish.

Serena looked at her watch as she pulled into the shopping centre where she was having her hair done for that night. Before she could stop herself, she realised she was standing in a beautiful children's boutique. On one side there were stunning, teeny-weeny little pale ice-cream pink and powder-blue outfits. As she stroked a soft velour Babygro, she felt her heart contract in her chest.

"Can I help you with anything?"

"No, I very much doubt it!" Serena spat at the shocked shop assistant.

Running from the shop, she had to walk up and down the shopping mall to calm down.

Trying to regain her composure, she strode into the hairdresser's.

"Hi, Serena." The receptionist smiled at her. "Tom will see you in just a few minutes. Come on over and we'll get you ready."

A smiling girl took over from the receptionist and draped a protective gown around Serena. Then the girl turned sideways to tuck a towel into her collar. And there, mocking Serena, was a baby bump.

Serena stared at the girl coldly. "Are you expecting a baby?"

"Em, yes, actually. I'm nearly five months gone." She rubbed her lower back as she spoke. "It's really killing me this time. At least on my first, I didn't have another child at home to contend with as well."

"Oh, stop showing off! I get the picture. You're just a walking pile of fertility, aren't you?" Serena put her hand up to her mouth as soon as she spoke.

"I'm sorry, I wasn't trying to annoy you . . ." The poor girl looked shocked at the attack.

"No, it's me who should be sorry. I'm having a stressful day and I shouldn't have taken my bad mood out on you. Forgive me!" Serena took the girl's hand and felt relief flood through her when she was rewarded with a smile.

"Don't you worry. I feel like stabbing someone half the time at the moment. My hormones are running wild, even though I'd never admit that to my husband!" She finished tucking towels and fastened a nylon black gown around Serena's neck before waddling away.

Serena berated herself. She'd have to be more careful. She

couldn't go around yelling at people like that. She had to control herself. She couldn't let anyone know what was going on. She'd prefer to walk naked down Grafton Street on a Saturday morning than let anyone know she was having trouble conceiving. What was she going to do if she couldn't reproduce? Would Paul leave her? Trade her in for a more fertile, younger model?

There was no point in panicking until she had the facts. She hoped in two weeks' time she'd at least have something to work on. Between now and then, she'd just have to keep it all together and look after Paul.

She accepted a cup of coffee and tried to relax and look at the pile of glossy magazines she'd been handed. Much to her dismay, the first article she opened was all about how to achieve the latest season's looks while pregnant. The whole world seemed to be able to get pregnant except her.

Maybe she would talk to her mother about it. They were away at their villa in France, and Mummy didn't really like to be bothered when she was relaxing, but she needed to talk to someone. She supposed Adele would be sympathetic if she called her, but she was in such dreadful form at the moment even Paul had commented on it.

"Is there something going on with your sister?" he'd asked, looking a little stunned as Adele had rung to cancel Sunday lunch at the last minute.

"What, more than usual?" Serena sighed. "There's always something wrong with that woman. Why? What did she say?"

"Just that she's sorry to leave it so late to call us, but something has come up and she'll call you later in the week. I told her to hang on, that you were in the other room, and she said she didn't have time to chat right now." Paul shrugged.

That had been two days ago, and Adele hadn't bothered to call, so Serena wasn't going to make the first move.

Knowing the noise of the hairdryers would shield her conversation, she dialled her mother's mobile phone number.

"Hello, darling," her mother answered, sounding like she was half-asleep.

"Hi, Mummy, how are things in Cap Ferret?"

"Delicious. The sun's shining and I'm beside the pool with Marjorie. Daddy and Seán are golfing while we take it easy. Where on earth are you? You sound like you're in the middle of a building site. Don't tell me Paul has you roped into a job working for him? You're a married woman now, Serena. Your job is taking care of your husband!"

"Of course I'm not on a building site! I'm at the hairdresser's waiting to have my colour done. Listen, Mummy, I went to see Dr Sullivan in Blackrock today –"

"Oh wonderful, don't tell me, am I about to be a grandmother again? Although I'm not sure I'm ready to be called Granny yet. Ruby still calls me Katie, I think I like that better. We seem more like friends that way. Especially in light of the fact I've just had that chemical peel. That's rather exciting all the same – can I tell Marjorie?"

"Mummy, I'm not pregnant. That's the whole point. That's why I went to see Dr Sullivan. Things aren't happening for me, so he did some tests and I've to go back in two weeks' time." She felt her eyes fill with tears. She was overcome with emotion at finally being able to voice her fears.

"Oh, I see. Look this isn't a good time. As I said, Marjorie and I are trying to relax by the pool here. Why don't I call you later on when it's more convenient? Or what about Adele? She's terribly good at this kind of thing, what with having Ruby and all of that. It's so long since I had you, I'm not very au fait with all this kind of thing. In my day, women didn't make phone calls from the hairdresser's and discuss such delicate issues. Be careful of yourself, Serena. People will think you're brash, or even worse, needy."

"Okay, sorry for bothering you. I just needed to talk to somebody. I shouldn't have rung." Serena felt like she'd been slapped in the face. Although she might have known her mother wouldn't be interested. When was she ever? As a child, if it hadn't been for Mrs Murdock her nanny, she'd never have been shown any love or attention. Her nanny had been more of a mother to her than her own mum. And any time that she *had* devoted to her children had always gone to Adele. Serena was always left feeling like she was out on her own.

"Don't be like that, Serena. I'm just walking inside. I can't talk about that kind of thing with Marjorie sitting there. Listen, it took Daddy and me years to have you and your sister. In those days we didn't go trotting off to clinics being poked and prodded. Just relax and it'll happen. Don't get yourself in a state, darling. You're only married a wet week anyway. It's not as if anybody will be asking questions for quite a while. Enjoy being married. Go on nice holidays. Look after Paul and don't concern yourself with all that baby nonsense. It's not all it's cracked up to be. All those sleepless nights, and all the vomit and crying and nappies. Just take your time. You'll see – it'll happen when the time is right. Now I must fly, I can't leave Marjorie sitting by herself. I don't want to appear rude. Bye, darling, kissy kiss!" The line clicked and her mother was gone.

"Serena, what can I do for you today? The same colour as last time, or do you suddenly want to go pillar-box red?" Tom had appeared to do her hair.

"Hello, Tom. No, I'll stick with warm chestnut, thank you, darling." She took a deep breath and fixed her face into an even smile.

By the time she popped into the nail bar for a quick gel refill and fought her way out of the car park and sat in the traffic back to the house, it was nearly five thirty. Bustling in the door, she made herself a large gin and tonic to calm her nerves. Her Moschino dress was laid out in her dressing room. It was black with a shocking-pink piped trim around the square neckline. It came to just below her knee and the boning in the stiff satin fabric accentuated her perfect size-ten figure. As she downed the gin and tonic, she wished for the first time in her life that she was too large to wear the figure-hugging dress.

Stroking the gorgeous dress, she allowed her mind to wander. She imagined what her children might look like. Would they take after Paul? Tall and strong with those pale-blue eyes, or would they have big pale-green eyes and sallow skin like her? Would her daughter look like Ruby? The image of her niece flashed through her mind. She hadn't seen Ruby properly for ages – she must call her and take her for lunch. She loved doing that. They'd go to the shopping centre and Ruby would show her all the coolest and latest trends, and tell her who fancied who.

A sense of deep longing flooded her. She would give her eyeteeth to have a Ruby of her own. She already knew what she'd call the children: Samuel for a boy and Lydia for a girl. Twins would be lovely. A boy and a girl all at one time. That would be just perfect. She could get matching wooden cots, one dressed in pink and one in blue. She'd have a little prince and princess all in one pregnancy. It would get her off the hook with having to go through all the torture of birth twice. People would be envious and impressed all at the same time, if she was to have twins.

She glanced at her diamond-encrusted gold watch and realised Paul would be there in ten minutes. She refilled her glass and hurried to dress herself. She gently pulled on her sheer silk tights. Wolford, of course. She shimmied into her Moschino dress and finally stepped into her exquisite Jimmy Choo satin shoes. She finished the outfit with a pretty diamond choker Paul had given her on their honeymoon. It was like tiny diamond daisies all linked together by gold buttons. It was stunning and classic.

She knew she had it all. A successful husband, a beautiful house, plenty of money, designer clothes to beat the band, more diamonds than Marilyn Monroe. But suddenly none of it seemed to matter. She realised she really wanted and needed a baby to complete her life.

She was feeling slightly better after her couple of little drinks and, as she heard Paul's key in the door, she fixed a smile on her face. He wouldn't need to see a face that would stop a bus when he came home. She'd made up her mind to call Ruby tomorrow and organise a nice day with her. That would ease the hollow ache she felt inside.

"Hi, sweetheart, I'm up here getting dressed!" she called down to him.

He ran up, taking the stairs two at a time. He appeared in the dressing room, undoing his work shirt as he walked.

"Hi, honey! God, you look beautiful. I'll be the envy of every man, woman and child there tonight!" He grabbed her bum as he kissed her and walked on into the en-suite for a quick shower.

"Thank you, darling. Your tux and shirt and shoes are there for you!" she called in to him.

"Thank you! What would I do without you? We need to go in five, there's a car arriving to pick us up!" He jumped into the shower and the smell of his favourite Molton Brown shower gel permeated the room through the steam of the shower.

* * *

Like all the functions they went to, Paul dreaded it and found the mingling part painful. Serena shone and skilfully guided him around the room. They had an unspoken rule between them that she would look after him. Her arm linked his as she tactfully reminded him who people were.

"Hello, Julie, how are you?" she prompted him with the lady's name. "You're looking stunning in blue, isn't she, Paul?" She was the wife of the other main sponsor that night. It would have been very awkward if he'd forgotten her name.

"Thank you, Serena, I wasn't sure about it. Are you sure it's not too much?"

The dress was ghastly and made the woman, who had dyed orange hair, and over-enthusiastic fake tan look like a cross-dressed orangutan but Serena assured her she was the belle of the ball.

"Nicely done, darling. Good one," said Paul after they had left Julie.

Serena winked at him as she swiftly grabbed another glass of champagne from a passing tray. An hour later, as they all filed in for dinner, Serena felt a lot better. It was amazing what a few glasses of bubbly did to make her feel less anxious. The baby-issue anxiety was eased, if only momentarily.

At least at these big functions, she had a purpose. Paul needed her. She was of use to him. That made her feel warm inside. Quashing that niggling empty feeling she always got from her mother's rejection, she held her head high and worked the room. Tonight, she was not the ignored younger sister of a woman who had no time for her, nor the annoyance of a daughter who disturbed her mother and Marjorie as they tried to assume a horizontal position in front of the pool. She was the height of glamour, sophistication and Paul was proud of her. As the room assembled and people took their seats, she quickly checked her make-up in a tiny fold-up mirror from her pretty evening bag. Patting her shiny hair, she spritzed herself with her favourite, Chanel No 5 and took her seat. Luckily they were in a five-star establishment, so the waiters came and poured the wine quickly.

The cool white wine was further balm to her wounded heart.

"Could you please be kind enough to bring me a bottle of Gigondas for my husband?" She shoved a fifty-euro note into the waiter's hand. "Keep the change, thanks so much, darling!"

But, as they sat in the taxi on the way home, Serena's pleasant buzz had evaporated and she realised that no matter how much she drank that night, she couldn't fully shake the feeling inside. Drink was kind of her friend. She used it a little bit like a security blanket. Most times it enveloped her and tucked her under its wing and soothed her. Tonight though, the brandies she'd polished off after the bubbly only served to make her feel edgy and miserable.

"What's up?"

She started. She hadn't realised Paul was watching her as she sat in her own dream world.

"Oh nothing, I'm fine. Just tired. The night went well, didn't it?" She forced a smile and tried to appear nonchalant.

"Yes, it did, but there is something wrong, isn't there? Have I done something to piss you off?" Paul took her hand and kept staring at her.

"Let's leave it until we get home? My m-o-t-h-e-r!" she mouthed, and nodded towards the taxi driver. God forbid that someone should overhear that she wasn't living the perfect life. She didn't know who that man was – he could tell anyone her business.

"Whatever." Paul shrugged and looked out the window.

Serena felt her heart thumping. She had mentioned to Paul that she'd stopped taking the pill. He knew she was planning on starting a family, but they hadn't really sat down and discussed the whole issue. Not at length. He really had no idea how important the whole thing was to her. She'd have to own up and spill her heart out. But she wasn't sure how she should go about being heartfelt with anyone, especially when she knew she was going to come out of it appearing to be less than perfect.

17

tweeting@angiebaby.com
OMG 1+1=1 baby . . . I'm gobsmacked

As she perched against the edge of the bathroom sink, Angie wished she'd known the last two times she'd done a pregnancy test that there was no such thing as waiting ten minutes for the second blue line. More like ten seconds. The nanosecond the stick got wet, the line appeared. Not a faint, is-there-a-line-there-or-not scenario. Oh no, it was clearly etched in place, as if it had been drawn there with a marker pen.

Angie had fleetingly known she was around her fertile time. She had of course lied to Troy that she was on the pill. She sat on the edge of the toilet and stared at the plastic wand in her hand. She was going to be a mother.

Christ, what was Mags her own mother going to say? Denis her father would never be able to meet her gaze ever again. What was she going to tell Troy? She hardly knew him! She'd have to call Rachel and try to track him down. She really didn't like the idea of a forced relationship with this guy she didn't know. They hadn't clicked and besides she knew nothing about him. She hadn't actually *planned* getting pregnant as such, as in she hadn't gone out that night deciding to go for it with the first willing accomplice but deep down she knew she'd thrown caution to the wind – wittingly.

She decided to get some air. Although it was November, the weather was still quite mild. Putting her coat on, she slammed the apartment door, not really knowing what to do with herself. She meandered towards the sea. The salty air helped soothe her thumping head.

She tried to imagine the conversation she'd have with Troy. What would she do? Arrange to meet him in a city-centre pub, sit him in the corner, ask him if he'd like a pint and a packet of peanuts and say, "Oh by the way, you're about to be a father."

No, she couldn't do that. She continued to stroll and think. By the time she'd walked the full length of the beach and back, she was certain. She had no reason to tell Troy. It wasn't as if she'd ever see him again. All she had to do was act slightly cleverly about it all. Then he'd never need to find out. The only link she had with him, which was vague, was Rachel.

She'd wait a few weeks before telling Rachel and she'd tell her it was a guy from work. She'd never know and that would be it, all sorted. The baby would be well and truly hers.

Satisfied she was making the right decision for herself and the baby, she went home and did what all newly pregnant mothers do. She went on the internet and frightened the living daylights out of herself. She signed up to two sites which would email her on a weekly basis to update her on how the baby was progressing. Or the foetus as it was now called.

She also went through the phone book and found the well-known Mountrath Clinic in the salubrious Dublin suburb. She looked at their website and decided she would call them first thing in the morning. She liked the sound of Dr Sullivan, one of the gynaecological specialists. With a bit of luck, he'd take her.

If she had worked it all out correctly, her baby should be due in July some time. She could take her maternity leave then, so she'd have more time afterwards rather than before.

Feeling slightly shocked but totally delighted, she sat on the sofa with her knees tucked up to her chest and thought about her baby.

Would she be tempted to find out if it was a boy or a girl? She honestly didn't mind either way. "As long as it's healthy," she'd heard so many pregnant friends say. How true it was. She really didn't mind either way.

She really hoped the baby was healthy. What would she do if the child had special needs? Would she be able to cope? It was of course a chance she'd have to take.

"I'll love you no matter what," she said out loud to her tummy. She felt all warm and cosy inside. She had the same feeling of excitement she used to have as a small child on Christmas morning. She just knew she was going to love being a mother..

* * *

"Mountrath Clinic, Dr Sullivan's rooms!" the lady barked.

"Yes, hello, I'd like an appointment please. I've just found out I'm expecting." Angie wasn't sure what she should be saying.

There was a lot of clicking and the sound of paper being moved about. "Right, you can come on Tuesday at eleven thirty."

"Fine. I wonder –"

"See you then." The secretary didn't do small talk and had already hung up.

18

tweeting@rubytuesday.com
Goodbye, life as I knew it. Instead of independence I'm even more dependent.

At ten o'clock Ruby signed the "going out" book in school and handed the letter from her mother to the form tutor, explaining she had a dental appointment.

"I hope you didn't tell anyone where you were really going," Adele snapped as she pulled out of the school car park.

"No, Mum, they think I'm going to the dentist. Don't worry, I haven't blown the cover." Ruby leaned on her hand and stared out the window.

Moments later they had pulled up outside the Mountrath Clinic. It was a huge scary building. The secretary was a snotty cow who looked down her nose at Ruby. She spoke over her head to her mother, almost acting as if she wasn't there.

"I really appreciate you taking Ruby on Dr Sullivan's books," Adele had muttered in an undertone to the secretary. "I realise he's very heavily booked up but I really want her to have the best care possible and seeing as I attended him myself . . . It's all unfortunate enough, without having to sit in one of those dreadful public hospitals." She sniffed as if she sensed a bad smell even talking about the public hospitals.

"That's no problem, Adele. You do know that Ruby will have to deliver in the maternity hospital though, don't you?"

"Yes, I'm aware of that situation, but at least we have some comforts in the interim." Adele prodded the back of Ruby's shoulder and ushered her over to sit on the sofa.

* * *

Parking at the private clinic, Angie suddenly felt quite alone. Maybe she would have been better to tell Troy. Even though they didn't know each other now, maybe they could develop a relationship? Taking a deep breath, knowing it was too late for today's appointment at least, she gathered her courage and approached the receptionist at the big white shiny desk.

"Hello, I'm here to see Dr Sullivan." She surprised herself with how scared and unsure she sounded.

Luckily the girl was more interested in the nail file and bottle of pink lacquer she was fiddling with. "Second floor, suite seven," she drawled.

Angie used the stairs and found herself in the middle of the second floor. Following the signposts she found the right room.

"Hello, I'm Angie Breen, I have an appointment with Dr Sullivan at eleven thirty," she whispered to the secretary through the sliding glass partition.

"Hi, Angie, take a seat. Dr Sullivan will be with you shortly. There are a couple of people ahead of you, but you shouldn't be waiting too long." She smiled and gestured for Angie to go into the waiting room.

As Angie entered, she was struck by the diverse selection of women who were sitting there. They ranged from a young girl who looked about fourteen to a woman who looked about sixty. The young girl was probably just there with her mother, and the older woman might be there due to gynaecological problems, Angie decided.

The waiting room was compact and quite dark. Done up in dark wood in deep maroon and navy colours, it was almost like being in an old cinema. In the corner, built into the sofa, was a coffee table which housed some magazines. Angie picked one up, and gratefully buried her nose in it. Occasionally glancing over the top, she had another little survey around the room.

Then sound of voices through the heavy wooden door caused everyone to look up.

"See you in three weeks, if we don't meet in the hospital before that." Dr Sullivan was ushering out a lady with a very large bump.

"Ruby White, please!" Dr Sullivan called the next patient.

To Angie's astonishment the child stood up.

"Are you coming in too, Mum?" she said to her stony-faced mother.

"Of course I am," said her mother as she stood up with a sigh and followed her daughter into the examination room.

Just as the mother and daughter shut the door to the consultation room, another lady arrived in the waiting room and sat down. Angie lowered her magazine to look her over. She was stunning. She had shiny hair, like a polished conker. Dark skin, which was perfectly made up, with shimmering glossy lips. Her nails were the same colour as her lips and immaculate. She wore a wrap dress in navy and white, and perched on the sofa beside her was the latest Chloe must-have handbag.

Angie felt more than a little nervous as she waited her turn. She suddenly felt anxious in case that glamour puss surveyed her and noticed she wasn't wearing a wedding ring. The older woman was pretending to be asleep, so Angie didn't try and chat to her. What if one of them probed her and asked awkward questions?

Get a grip, Angie, she thought. It's none of her bloody business what you do or who you are. If she asks, just cut her off curtly.

She needn't have worried. The stunning woman seemed to be happy to avoid any conversations. She was too busy flicking impatiently through a magazine, tutting about the fashion on the pages.

* * *

Ruby was silent and shaking when they walked into Dr Sullivan's room.

"Sit down, Ruby and Adele," he said, smiling gently. "How are you both?"

129

"We've been better, to be honest." Adele looked worn out.

"Shall we do a quick run-through of the questions I asked you to answer on the form while you were waiting?" He turned to Ruby. She nodded. He felt desperately sorry for both women.

Adele looked like she'd been run over by a truck, Ruby was like a rabbit in the headlights.

Ticking each question as Ruby answered, he read with speed, finishing up with "So you think your last period was eight weeks ago, is that right?" he asked Ruby.

"Yes, Dr Sullivan." She looked at the floor as she spoke.

"Okay, come on in here and we'll put some gel on your tummy and see if we can find a little heartbeat. I"m going to use a little machine called a Doppler. It won't hurt and it will hopefully pick up baby's little heartbeat." He held out his arm to motion the way.

Ruby went into the adjoining room and climbed up onto the examination table which was covered in paper from a big white roll. The surface was hard and the paper slipped about as she scrunched into place.

"I'm just going to lift your jumper – can you move your tracksuit bottoms down a small bit?" Ruby pushed her bright yellow Juicy Couture waistband down, so Dr Sullivan could squirt some gel onto her tummy. It was freezing cold and made a kind of farting noise. It was clear, with no smell. She didn't know where she was supposed to look as Dr Sullivan placed a cold metal wand thing onto her tummy and pressed down.

"Take a deep breath in for me, Ruby." He was twiddling with a machine which looked like a mixing desk the DJs used at the nightclubs.

Then, it happened. From total silence, came the loud, steady thudding of a heartbeat.

"From week six, we can hear the heart but this is good and strong," Dr Sullivan explained. Wipe your tummy and come back into the other room." He smiled at her kindly as he left.

Ruby could hear her mother and the doctor talking in hushed tones. She wiped the goo off herself, slunk into the room and sat down quietly.

"Of course that's up to yourselves. All I can do is provide the best care possible for the mother and baby," she heard Dr Sullivan saying.

"Thank you for seeing us, Dr Sullivan." Adele stood up to leave.

"Goodbye, Ruby. My secretary will tell you when to come back. You'll have a scan and some blood tests done in a few weeks. See you soon and take care of yourself."

"Thank you, Dr Sullivan," she answered with her head hung low as he ushered them out.

Then the worst thing imaginable happened. Aunt Serena was sitting there in the waiting room. Of all the people in the world that Ruby felt she would hate to lie to, Serena was right up at the top of that list. Ruby felt like her legs were going to give way.

"Aunt Serena!"

"Ruby, Adele, what a coincidence!" Serena got up to greet them.

Ruby was surprised to see that her aunt was blushing furiously, obviously embarrassed at being caught in Dr Sullivan's office.

She followed them out of the waiting room and into the secretary's office.

"I had an appointment – just for a check-up – with Dr Sullivan," said Adele, "and Ruby had a half day from school, so she came too." Then she turned the tables on Serena. "Have you got something to tell me?"

"No, nothing like that, just a quick check-up, the same as you. I'd better go in case he calls me. I'll talk to you again. Bye, Ruby darling. Would you like to go for lunch on Saturday? I could pick you up at eleven?" She stroked her niece's arm.

"Eh, no I can't sorry. I'm going to a friend's house for a sleepover and I won't be free." Ruby looked at the floor.

"During term time? I thought you weren't allowed?"

"It's her friend's birthday, a special occasion." Adele nodded towards the waiting room. "You'd better go."

"Okay, chat to you later then." Serena breezed away, feeling more than a little flustered and slightly suspicious. Ruby was usually thrilled to see her and would jump at the chance of going out. Even if she did have a sleepover, why didn't she ask to do it another day instead?

* * *

Angie continued to turn the pages of the magazine, although she wasn't really looking at any of it. She kept thinking of the poor child who'd just left. If she were *her* daughter, she'd be kinder and more understanding. She'd looked terrified and bewildered. Angie decided she would try to be as understanding and open as she could with her own child.

"Angie Breen, please!" Dr Sullivan was standing there with another paper file in his hand. "Go on through there, Angie, I'll see you in just a second." He gestured towards the consultation room.

Angie walked in and sat nervously on the edge of one of the big wooden chairs. The room was much brighter than the waiting room. Out the window she could see the sea and a park, with mums and children and dogs running around. The main feature of the room was a huge mahogany desk, with a leather-covered twirly chair. The far wall was covered by a large bookcase, which housed old-fashioned leather-bound books.

"Now, Angie, sorry to have kept you waiting. I'm Dr Sullivan. What can I do for you?" He slotted in behind his desk and rested his elbows on the table, with his two hands laced together, and regarded her.

"Well, I'm around eight weeks pregnant and I'm here for a check-up. I'm not sure what I'm supposed to do next." She felt a bit silly and very nervous. It suddenly occurred to her that he might want to do a horrible internal examination.

"Okay, that's fine. Basically, all we can do today is listen for a heartbeat and check your blood pressure. I'll arrange for you to have a scan. I generally like them to be done at around fifteen weeks. I'm just looking at your details. You're over forty, so I'm obliged to offer you an amniocentesis test." He looked at Angie kindly.

"What does that involve?" She felt truly terrified.

"It involves me inserting a small needle through your abdomen to obtain some of the amniotic fluid, or the fluid which is in the pregnancy sack. We then use this fluid to answer some questions. It can tell us if there are any major abnormalities with the foetus. I must warn you, though, that the procedure does carry a small risk

of miscarriage. It's totally up to you whether you go ahead or not."
He stared at her for a second before getting up and gesturing
towards a small side room. "Come on in here, Angie. If you'll just
lie up on the couch, I'll put some gel on your tummy and we'll listen
for a heartbeat." He nodded towards the examination couch.

Frightened of the unknown, Angie edged her way onto the
couch. She was dying to ask if she'd have to endure internal
examinations, but she was too shy.

"I'm really scared about the birth," she heard herself blurt out.

"Most women are, but try not to worry about it at the moment.
You've quite a way to go before all that happens. I'm told by most
of my patients that by the time the baby is due they're so fed up of
being pregnant they're no longer worried about the birth. They just
want the whole thing over and done with. With a bit of luck you'll
feel the same way." His voice was calming and soothing. He wasn't
condescending or dismissive. He had the right balance when it came
to talking to his patients. He didn't try to be their friend but at the
same time he wasn't cold.

"I've heard loads of women talk about births and how they had
wanted an epidural," she said, "and by the time they convinced the
nurse to give them one it was too late. I don't want that to happen
to me. I'm not looking for an experience which will haunt me for
the rest of my life." She shuddered at the thought of it all.

"As I said, you've a long time to wait so try to keep all the nerves
at bay for now. I will do my best to make sure all your wishes are
carried out at the time of the birth, how's that?" He squirted some
cold clear gel onto her abdomen.

"Okay, I think. I'm sorry to sound like such a nervous wreck but
I'm on my own having this baby. The father won't be present and
I'm not from Dublin. You're the first person I've spoken to about all
this. I suppose I must sound like a madwoman!" She giggled dryly.

"You don't sound mad at all. There are plenty of organisations
for single mothers, if you feel you'd like some support or someone
to talk to?"

"No. Thank you, but no. I wouldn't be into that sort of thing.
Telling strangers my business. I'll be grand."

She was silenced by the loud thumping noise which was emanating from the wand in the doctor's hand.

"Okay, Angie, this Doppler should pick up a nice sound for us, if I can just locate the foetus. That, my dear, is your baby." He smiled and his eyes crinkled at the corners as he too listened to the steady, fast thudding.

"Is it supposed to be that quick?" She was astounded.

"Yes, the foetal heartbeat is a lot faster than ours. That sounds like a good healthy little fighter in there. From the sixth week this little device can pick up a heartbeat and as you can hear this one is loud and clear." He removed the ultrasound wand and wiped the gel away using a white paper towel.

"Follow me inside when you're ready." He walked back into the main room and sat behind his desk again.

Feeling quite wobbly, a little tearful and very overcome, Angie shuffled into the room.

"With regards to the birth. We don't deliver babies here at the clinic, so I send all my patients to the local maternity hospital. It's a public hospital, with the option to go in a private room, should one become available. It's not the prettiest of places but the equipment and expertise is second to none. I'd like you to go there the day before you come back to me in a few weeks' time. You can have a scan and a number of routine blood tests. I like my patients to have their bloods done just before I see them, so I can have the most up to date result possible. The hospital will process the bloods and email me the results. They will give you a couple of pictures at the time of your scan to keep for your scrapbook. Your scan will be put onto a disc that looks just like a DVD, so make sure you bring that along to me at your next appointment. They'll email me all that information also, but it's good to keep the hard copy on file here too. Have you any questions?" He sat up straight, with his hands clasped and waited for her to speak.

"I'm sure I'll have a million and one questions when I've left here, but for now I feel a bit muted with shock after hearing the baby's heartbeat." She misted over again.

"It's all very emotional the first time. It's kind of reassuring too. Do you feel it's made the pregnancy more real for you?"

"Yes, I suppose so." She really felt like a moron. Not used to being so stuck for words or so out of control, Angie needed to go home and take it all in. She needed to go and buy some literature on pregnancy too. The next time she came to see Dr Sullivan, she'd be better prepared. She'd write any questions she had in a notebook. She hated this feeling of meekness.

"Well, it's good to meet you and start your journey with you. Good luck with the scan and bloods and we'll see each other here soon, all going well."

As he ushered her out, Angie noted the "all going well," phrase he'd tucked into the sentence. Lots of women miscarried, so she could understand why he had to be like that. She said a silent prayer that she would manage to carry her baby full term. It was going to change her whole life. Being a mum was something she'd always wanted. The only fly in the ointment so far had been the lack of a father. But she'd overcome that problem now.

Fleetingly, she felt a niggling stab of guilt for not telling Troy. But he'd probably just be shocked and put out. It was probably better in the long run that she was doing this without him.

She'd have to tell her parents sooner or later, and Rachel too. Aside from them, the rest of the world could just find out as the news trickled out. Trickle it would too, pour more like it. She knew the gossip mongers were going to have a field day at her expense. But she really didn't give a toss. Let them have their day. At the end of it all, she'd have a baby. Smiling as she left the clinic, she felt happier than she had done for years.

* * *

Outside in the car, Adele turned towards Ruby.

"Here's what's going to happen, Ruby. You will go to school for another couple of months, until you begin to show too much. You will have to repeat third year and sit your Junior Cert next year. There's no alternative. I think it will be best all round if we pass the baby off as mine and Daddy's. It's not going to be easy but it's the only way you or that poor child is going to have any kind of a normal life. We will raise the child as our own. You will refer to it as your brother or sister. I'm only forty-one – people will believe I've had a baby." Adele tapped her nails on the steering wheel as she trotted this out.

"No, Mummy! The father may still show up. He might want to raise the baby with me. Besides, people will notice I'm pregnant and you're not. We'll have to tell Aunt Serena and Katie and Granddad so would that mean they'd all have to lie? I told Mariah too." Ruby looked alarmed.

"Why did you tell that girl?" Adele was suddenly putrid with rage. "Her family have done enough damage, without having her blab our business all over town."

"She's my best friend, Mum. I had to tell someone and she won't tell a soul. Anyway, she's not talking to me anymore. She fancied Yaakov and she's furious that I went off with him." Ruby looked at the floor to hide the lies. She was growing increasingly nervous of Mariah finding out the truth. She was beyond pissed-off at the thought that Ruby had slept with Yaakov without telling her. What on earth would she say when she realised this baby was actually going to be her half-brother or sister? She sincerely hoped that, when Damo left Noreen, Mariah would eventually come around to being able to forgive her.

"Daddy fully intends having words with Damo McCabe, so he'll make sure Mariah stays quiet too. We'll go down to the house in Spain towards the end of the pregnancy. You'll have the baby in Spain. You and I will stay there for the summer. The baby is due in July, so by the time we return in September for school you'll have had time to get over the pregnancy and birth. You can change schools then. At least all won't be lost. Dr Sullivan has agreed to see you until you go to Spain. Meanwhile, you must promise me you won't speak to anyone else about this." Adele kept tapping the steering wheel as she delivered instructions to her daughter.

Ruby sat in silence and tried to take in what her mother was saying. They wanted to take her baby? They wanted her to step aside and keep quiet and never tell anyone the baby was hers? How was she going to live in the house with the baby and never tell him or her the truth?

"Mummy, it can't work. I'll have to tell the baby when it's older that I'm its mother. We can't all live a lie. I can't expect Mariah to lie. Why can't we just tell the truth? I'll face up to my responsibilities. I'll do whatever it takes. Please, Mum, don't make me do this!"

"Ruby, your father and I have talked about this until we were blue in the face. Believe me, we have run through every option we could think of. You might think it sounds bizarre now but when you have a bit of time to think about it and get used to it, you'll realise it'll be the best idea for everyone. Especially you and this baby, God help it. I'm afraid the decision is made."

Ruby bit her lip and tried to remain calm. She needed to behave like a grown-up, if she stood any chance of being listened to. Having a tantrum and crying loudly was not going to gain her any Brownie points. She needed to talk to Damo again. This was all getting out of hand. Her parents were going to be even more angry than they were now if she didn't set them right soon.

"But what about Aunt Serena? She saw us there today, she's going to notice. I can't keep saying no if she wants to see me. I can't imagine going to Spain or doing any of this without telling her. Please, Mummy, don't make me do this. She'll be so hurt if we shut her out." Ruby began to cry in spite of her best plans to control herself.

"Leave Serena to me. I'll have to think about her. The last thing we need is her finding out and marching around with her nose in the air, smugly thinking she's the Queen Bee and I'm her drone."

* * *

"Please sit down, Serena," said Dr O'Sullivan. "I have some news for you, stemming from our tests." He sat behind his desk and motioned for her to sit in the chair opposite him.

"Oh, already?" Serena's heart was skipping beats with nerves. Her palms began to sweat and she wished she could take a quick drink from her handbag.

"You have a condition called 'endometriosis,' have you heard of it?" he asked.

"No," Serena looked horrified.

"It's quite common. It's easily surmountable. It's a condition where threadlike projections come from the womb and attach to the surrounding areas. It could explain why you haven't conceived."

Serena felt like she was going to die of shame. She couldn't believe she had something *wrong* with her. This was disgusting. How was she going to cope with this? All she could think of was pouring herself a drink to steady her nerves. This was an outrage. Paul was going to be so shocked that she had this dreadful thing growing inside her. Her mother would have a field day if she heard about this. She could just see her, raising her eyes to heaven and sighing to Adele that it was typical of Serena to have to cause trouble.

"It can be treated very successfully with some lasering. We do this laparoscopically, which effectively means we make a tiny incision in your lower abdomen, insert a thin prod with a laser attached and burn off the endometriosis. It's good news, Serena. Once the problem is rectified, you shouldn't have any further problems conceiving. Everything else looks perfectly normal." He looked pleased with himself.

Serena's humiliation had turned to anger. As usual, her own insecurities were getting on top of her and she was seething. How could this have happened to her? Why was she being punished? Now she was going to have to go and have an operation. It wasn't fair. She managed to smile at Dr Sullivan, as he seemed to expect it.

"I can book you in for surgery in a few weeks, if that suits you. You need to come in the night before and stay one, maybe two nights after the procedure, all depending on how you feel."

"Right. So soon? Is it dangerous, this endo thingy?" She suddenly had a picture of herself in a headscarf, with no teeth, rotting in a wheelchair.

"Well, in your case, the endometriosis is just a bit of a hindrance.

Removing it will mean you don't have such painful periods and they shouldn't be as heavy as now either. Do you suffer with a lot of pain, or put it this way, would you take many painkillers around the time of your period?"

"Well, I never feel well. I would be more likely to go to bed early with a brandy and port. But, who says I'll have to stop that?" She tossed her glossy head back and giggled.

"Well, I'd hope you would stop if you were pregnant. Also you'll have to abstain from alcohol twenty-four hours before and obviously after your surgery. But that won't pose as a problem for you, will it?" He was staring at her.

What did he think she was? An alcoholic? What a cheek! Did he think she looked like a tramp in a smelly old overcoat with a bottle of cheap wine stuffed into a paper bag?

"Of course that won't be a problem!" She sounded a bit snippier than she'd intended. "No, that's perfectly understandable of course." She put on her most enticing smile and saw the man visibly relax as he showed her out of the consultation room.

"My secretary will sort you out with some dates there. See you soon."

A short time later, Serena sat in the car, the date was marked into her diary. That was fine, she could do it. It was only a minor procedure anyway. Nothing to worry about. She'd just have a small mouthful of vodka from her teeny-weeny flask in her bag. Not that she really needed it. But she'd just had a shock after all. After a quick snifter, she dialled Paul's number.

"Hi, darling, I'm going to have to go under the knife. It's all been terribly traumatic for me."

She explained the whole scenario to him. He was sympathetic and sweet and told her how brave she was. She nonchalantly mentioned she wasn't allowed to have any drink before or after. Paul just accepted that information as if it was normal. More than the surgery, the thought of not being able to have a couple of glasses of wine filled her with dread.

"A day without wine, is like a day without sunshine," she loved to say. But it was true. A little drink never hurt anyone and it was fun. What was wrong with having fun? Nothing. This whole drinking ban was ridiculous. For God's sake, she wasn't in school. It wasn't as if she was performing the surgery herself. All she had to do was lie there, unconscious, for crying out loud! Why did she need to be drink free to be a vegetable on a surgical slab?

19

tweeting@themercedesking.com
Regrets? Me? Nah, I'm the Mercedes King . . .

Every time Damo shut his eyes to go to sleep he saw Ruby. He'd see her tear-streaked cheeks and her shaking hands as she dropped the bomb which was haunting him.

"I'm pregnant."

He'd heard Mariah and Noreen talking in hushed tones in the kitchen, so he knew the news had hit.

"Well, don't you go getting any ideas, my girl. She might be your best friend, but you don't need to do everything together, you hear me?"

"Lay off, Mum, what do you take me for?" Mariah huffed noisily.

Damo strode into the kitchen angrily. "Talking like that about Ruby isn't going to help matters, Noreen. Don't you think the kid is going through enough at this rate?"

"Damo, all I want her to realise is that having a baby at her age isn't any fun. We managed, just about, but it was bloody hard. I know!" Noreen jabbed herself in the chest for emphasis.

"She'll be grand, it'll all work itself out. These things do. To add insult to injury, her lot aren't as well equipped as our families to take this kind of thing on. The father of the child is nowhere to be found, and all my sources tell me he's gone back to Balooba-land or wherever the hell he sprang from."

"Do you not have records on him from when he applied for the job?" Noreen looked stricken.

"No, I don't. Sure these fellas all give you the name of a flat and a pay-as-you-go mobile number. He could be from bleedin' Toy Town for all I know or care. With most of these lads, if they're any good it's a bonus, and half of them just don't show up after a couple of months. Then you know they've either robbed a till or been caught not paying rent. This is different though – this time it's too close to home for my liking. And I've a missed call from Harry, Ruby's father. This is a pain in the arse that I don't need at the moment, so I don't need to come home and listen to you two gassin' on about it!"

Damo went and took a quick line of coke, then called Ruby's father. Better to get the conversation over with, and then, as far as he was concerned, it would be all finished with.

Harry answered on the first ring. Jaysus, Damo thought, does he sit on top of the bleedin' phone all day?

"As you can only begin to imagine, Adele and I are just about going out of our minds here. Would you do me the courtesy of meeting for a coffee, so we can try and trace this kid?"

"Eh, yeah. Sure, whatever suits you."

Less than an hour later Damo found himself in an office opposite Harry. Dressed in a navy suit, with stripy tie and shirt, Ruby's father sat with his hands clasped and his face set in a serious grimace.

"I'm not even getting into the fact that you were in charge of our daughter the night this sorry mess began. Ruby is obviously in charge of her own actions." Harry closed his eyes and tried to remain calm. "Now, what I would like is any information on the guy she was with that night."

"I can't help you there. I've no forwarding address for him. I've spoken to his landlord and anyone who knew him. The lads he lived with are all Eastern European and want to be the first to know if we find him, as he owes them all rent." Damo looked at this Harry fella. All tense and stuffed into a suit, henpecked-looking. Wouldn't know fun if it bit him on the arse. Damo pitied him. Locked up in that house with his face-ache of a wife, going to this dog-box of an office, working at a computer day in, day out, for what?

"Right. If you hear anything obviously I want to hear from you. The main reason we need to find this clown is to make sure he knows the score. We don't want him appearing out of the blue in years to come and messing up our lives any further. What I need to ensure is that he has no legal comeback and stays the hell away from our daughter and this baby in the future." Harry rubbed his temples.

"I wish I could say or do something to make things better for you all." Damo held Harry's gaze and put on his most sincere face possible.

"If you'd looked after our daughter the night we entrusted her to you, then this problem would never have arisen. But hindsight is a wonderful thing, isn't it?" Harry laughed bitterly.

Damo stood up, tall and straight. "Listen, I'm going to take responsibility for this child. I would feel better. I'll give the money and all towards its keep. Not that it's my fault that your daughter got herself into this mess but I won't have it be said that I didn't offer to help yous out here."

"I beg your pardon?" Harry looked like he wanted to strangle the other man.

"I'll give a few quid each month, lighten the load. Pay for one of them nannies or a nice crèche, where it can speak French or Spanish, whatever Ruby wants." Damo was bored with all this – besides he'd got a text from one of the gig promoters to say that one of the big American acts was looking to come to The Orb later on. He needed to get his head together for that. This guy was a string of misery and seemed to want to sit and drag this whole thing out for hours.

To say that there was a lot of shouting from Harry's office over the course of the next few minutes was putting it mildly. The snooty secretary shifted uncomfortably in her chair outside the office.

By the time the door was flung open by her boss and the dark-haired man with the medallion strode out, things had reached fever pitch.

"Don't say I never offered to help." Damo flung his hands up in the air and stomped out muttering.

Harry kicked the door shut. It was Christmas week, and instead of looking forward to spending time relaxing with his wife and daughter, he was dreading it. Rubbing his temples he felt more hell, hell, hell than ho, ho, ho.

20

I can't stand waiting. My fingers are tapping, my breath is bated. Come on, come on . . .

Paul was having a glass of wine, inhaling the aroma of roasting chicken mixed with the alpine freshness of the beautiful tree Serena had decorated.

Paul sighed happily. "I love the blue and silver theme you've chosen. It's really striking. The pine smell just carries me back to all the Christmases of my childhood. It's such a magical time, isn't it?" Stretching his legs out he began to relax, enjoy the comfort of his own living room. In fairness to her, Serena never usually hit him with pressing matters the second he came home from work, but tonight was different. She was pacing up and down in front of the lit fire, clenching her fists and sighing deeply.

Serena knew it would be wiser to wait until Paul had finished his wine, kicked off his shoes and taken off his tie, but she had been home alone for hours waiting. It was only a few days to Christmas and she knew it probably wasn't the right time to hit him with all her deepest darkest thoughts. But the familiar smell of Paul's aftershave and the sheer presence of another person was too much. She had to talk.

He was surprisingly kind when she did blurt it all out. "I'm sure there'll be some straightforward explanation, darling. You did the right thing by going to get yourself checked out." He put his arms around her and rocked her back and forth.

He was a bit surprised, to say the least, at being hit with this. Serena was usually so in control and never this needy. A small part of him kind of liked being the protector. But at the same time, he wasn't interested in this becoming a huge issue. He'd heard of people who had to go down the whole fertility-treatment route. As far as he knew it involved time, money, energy and a lot of emotion. He didn't think now was the right time to tell Serena that he wasn't that pushed either way about the whole kids issue. She was very wound up about it all, so it mightn't go down well to suggest they were fine the way they were, just the two of them.

"Paul, I have to say something to you. What if it's not me? The problem may lie with you. What if I go and have all this stuff burnt off and we still can't conceive?" She was staring at him with tears in her eyes.

"Well, we'll cross that bridge if and when we need to." He smiled at her but inside he wasn't a bit happy. In fact he was a bit pissed off at her insinuation that he wasn't functioning properly. What was she suggesting? That he was firing blanks? Not likely. He was fit and healthy and above average intelligence. He was sure he must be in perfect working order. He thought he'd better make the right noises for the time being and hope this whole thing would solve itself. "Just to check, why don't we do a bit of practising?" He raised an eyebrow suggestively and pinched her on the bum.

"Paul, is that all you can think of? Can't you see I'm upset and finding this all very taxing?" She stomped off and slammed the door to their en suite.

Bloody women! He was being patient and hadn't said anything controversial. He might as well stick his dick in a meat-mincer for all the use it was going to get tonight.

* * *

The following day, Serena was out having a Christmas lunch with Noelle. They were at the best table in the house, beside the window, where they could see the passers-by and, more to the point, everyone could see that they were dining at Chez Franc. They'd had a delicious meal of fresh fish, asparagus tips and a gorgeous bottle of wine. Noelle was all on for a bottle of bubbly.

"Why end such a great lunch? When we're finished these Irish coffees I'm ordering a bottle of champers. I'm not paying that Filipino nanny for no reason. It's so exhausting being a mother, Serena. Christ, enjoy your time before it all happens to you. I was in such a hurry, with my blasted body clock going tick-tock and all that. Mark my words, it's no easy job." She motioned to the waiter to come over.

Serena thought about her own predicament. Feeling calmer after her lunch and a couple of glasses of wine, she was able to think more clearly. She did want a baby. She really did. She would go and have this surgery done, if it meant she could be a mother. All she had to do was envisage Ruby and her decision was made. Oh, the concept of having a Ruby of her own was delicious! She needed a little private celebration.

"A bottle of vintage Moët, please, " she said to the waiter. "It's on me. I just love Christmas – when better to spoil ourselves?" she added and winked at Noelle.

"Ooooh, I'll drink to that! I love celebrating." Noelle squealed.

"Here's to a very happy Christmas and an even better New Year!"

The girls raised their glasses and toasted each other. "So tell me how you found this Filipino nanny. I might just be needing one in the not too distant future. We haven't made that decision for certain yet but, in case we do, I want to be prepared." She leaned forward to hear all the details.

21

tweeting@angiebaby.com
Did you know a foetal heartbeat is between 120 & 160 beats per minute?

Christmas and New Year had passed peacefully for Angie. She'd gone home for a couple of days and used the American colleagues as an excuse to keep her visit short. She had decided to keep the pregnancy to herself until after her scan. She wanted to be certain everything was all right before she revealed her news to her family.

"I'm not too impressed with that lot, Angie love. I know they like to work you hard, but it's Christmas. Have they no sense of family or religion?" Mags had been more than a little bit cross.

Angie had almost buckled and told her mother the truth. "This lot are more into Thanksgiving by all accounts. It can't be helped, Mammy. It won't be for that much longer at least. Once we hit the end of June I'll be back to normal." In her head Angie knew that was about as far from the truth as could be. By June she'd be almost due her baby. Things were never going to be the same again.

Today, as she made her way across the road, avoiding the constant flow of heavy traffic she felt butterflies in her tummy. The enormous archaic grey building would have made Angie feel anxious or intimidated if it wasn't a maternity hospital. She was off to have her scan. As the rain was trying to turn to sleet, she was greeted by a huddle of women in bulky dressing gowns, fuzzy animal-head slippers complete with bobbly eyes, and fags. She tried not to stare at them as they pulled on their cigarettes with their baby bumps sticking out.

"That lift is a nightmare – I had to walk down three flights of stairs to come out for a fag," one human chimney commented to the other.

"I know. You'd think they'd sort out a smoking area nearer the antenatal floor," the other chimney huffed.

Angie had to hold her breath so she didn't spit out that they shouldn't be smoking while pregnant in the first place, but it was none of her business what other people did with their bodies. *But it's not just them, it's the unborn babies, who have no choice,* the nagging voice in her head was saying. Angie had never smoked and was thrilled when the smoking ban had come in, making it illegal to smoke in a public place. She hated the smell of smoke on her clothes and in her hair after a night out before the ban. The thought of inflicting cigarette smoke on an unborn child filled her with horror and made her feel more nauseous than ever.

Angie was exhausted. As the American project was reaching its crescendo, she was working even more crazy hours. That was why she hadn't been home to Cork to see her family more. She had vowed to herself that she would go home and face the music as soon as she had this scan over and done with.

She followed the huge overhead signs, showing her where Out Patients was. She walked up the wide staircase and breathed in the antiseptic smell as she went. The floors were covered in pale grey shiny stuff, with darker grey tiny tiles like those of a swimming-pool going up the walls. The large lines of strip lighting overhead added to the bleakness of the place. Going up her sixth flight of stairs, she was beginning to see why there was such a huge queue for the tiny lift on the ground floor.

As she passed the floors, she could hear babies' cries, echoing through the vast spaces. It gave her the necessary boost she needed to walk to the seventh floor by herself. She wasn't going to be on her own for much longer. She'd have a little companion, a little boy or girl to share her life. The idea filled her with joy. Reaching the seventh floor, she pulled open the huge heavy door, which was surrounded by wood with a thick meshed glass strip down the front. Heat hit her with a whoosh. The yellow arrow pointed her in the right direction. The large group of women at different stages of pregnancy let her know she was in the right place.

Finding the ultrasound check-in, she knocked softly on the door.

"Hiya!" The young girl was smiling and fresh-faced. She looked too young to know anything about babies, let alone work in a hospital.

"Hello, I'm Angie Breen, I'm here for my first scan." Angie flushed with excitement.

"Grand, fill this in – you can take the clipboard with you. Now it's vital that you have a full bladder, love. So make sure you keep drinking the water from the dispenser in the waiting room, and don't go for a wee until after your scan. If your bladder isn't full enough, they'll only send you back out and you might end up sitting for ages. Then your wees will want to come and you'll have to do Riverdance all around the room, if you know what I mean!" The girl giggled.

"Okay, thank you." Angie tried to join in with the giggling but she did feel a bit queasy with all the bladder talk. Suddenly it all seemed very medical and a bit scary.

Walking to the adjoining room, Angie took a seat on a brown plastic chair, just like the ones she'd sat on in the canteen in school many years previously. Popping a plastic mug from the side of the dispenser machine, she filled it with water and proceeded to fill her bladder to the brim.

The radio crackled in the background. The room was the same bland colour as the hallway, except the tops of the wall and the ceiling were a putrid shade of yellow. It must have been on sale the day the decorator went to buy it. Nobody in their right mind would actually choose that colour willingly.

Nurses appeared with surprisingly regularity, carrying cardboard files, and called out names. Although there were at least ten other women in various stages of pregnancy in the stuffy room before Angie, the queue seemed to be moving quickly. She took a book out of her bag and decided to try and relax and have a good read. She was glad she didn't have to touch any of the magazines on the chipped round wooden table in the corner. They looked dog-eared and almost soggy from use.

Less than an hour later, a small round nurse with skin as black as coal called her name. "Ms Angie Breen, if ya please!" She smiled and revealed the whitest teeth Angie had ever seen.

"Dis way, darling."

Angie followed her meekly.

"You lie on the bed for Martha and we'll get a look at this little un." She busied herself with a machine which looked like it had fallen off the *Starship Enterprise*. Pressing a million and one buttons, Martha waddled over and laid her soft black hand on Angie's arm. "Lift your top and roll down the skirt and we'll say hello to this little mite." She raised her shoulders and smiled.

"I think my bladder is full enough," said Angie. "I feel like I want to pee so badly." She had to concentrate on the ceiling as the same gel that Dr Sullivan had used with the little Doppler machine was squirted onto her tummy. The cold wetness was making her long for the toilet even more. This time though, as well as the heartbeat, there on the television was a moving thing. It was a bit hard to recognise but it was squirming about and it was pumping up and down.

"Helloooo, Baby Buntin'!" Martha laughed, a big loud excited belly laugh. Showing her tonsils and all her perfect teeth.

"Oh sweet Jesus, I don't believe it!" Angie stretched her hand out to touch the screen. She couldn't see with tears. Taking the tissue Martha offered her, she wiped her eyes and blew her nose.

"That there," Martha pointed to an area, "is Baby's head," she circled her finger, "and here we have an itty-bitty arm, there a leg, here the other arm and here the other leg. I'm going to zoom in on the leg and measure Junior's thighbone. That's gonna tell Martha how long baby's been hiding in Mamma." She grinned as she worked, sounding like a Caribbean person from the Lilt ad on the telly.

Angie could barely breathe as she watched her miniature little being moving and pulsating on the screen. She felt a rush of love like she'd never known possible. It was the most wonderfully overwhelming experience of her life so far. Why did all the women who'd had babies not run and shout from the rooftops about all of this? It was amazing and exhilarating.

"When was your last period, sunshine?" Martha asked her.

On hearing Angie's answer, Martha calculated; "So the due date for your baby is the eighth of July. Well done, Mamma!" She held her hand up for a high five. "Now, do you want to know the sex of the baby? I can't be certain as of yet. Most health carers agree that you need to be sixteen to twenty weeks to be sure, but if you're particularly anxious I can try to see?"

"No, thank you. I think it'd be better to have a surprise at the end of it all." Angie had thought long and hard about this question. A part of her thought that because she was on her own she would like to know. Just so she could bond more with her unborn child. She could also pick a name with more clarity. But then she decided that the surprise was going to be ruined if she found out. She honestly didn't care what she got, just so long as it was healthy.

"Okay, honey-bee, just look away for a minute until I tell you when. I don't want you to see the sex of the baby. Sometimes it's as clear as day and there's no denying it!" Martha instructed.

The scan took a further ten minutes. At the end, Martha printed off some photos and handed them to Angie.

"Well done, darlin', you did good. So far you're a great mamma. Keep going this way and that baby's gonna be a lucky little mite," she chuckled as she wiped Angie's tummy and helped her sit up. "You fix yourself and I'll just transfer the scan on to a disc which you need to take to your next appointment with Dr Sullivan. Then you can head off. Take care and I'll send the full report to your doctor via email. Everything looks great. All fingers and toes present, all organs functioning perfectly. Are you having an amniocentesis test done? It's the policy of this hospital to offer one once the mother is over the age of forty."

"No," Angie answered with gumption. She'd decided she didn't want to check for abnormalities. She was keeping this child, no matter what. So she wasn't going to jeopardise her pregnancy by having the test done. Dr Sullivan had told her that amniocentesis tests carried a small risk of miscarriage.

Within minutes, Martha had copied her scan onto a disc and handed it to her. "Okay, all you need to do now is go to the other end of the corridor to have your bloods done. Good luck and enjoy the rest of your pregnancy." She patted Angie's hand and sat back at the desk and began writing notes.

"Just as long as I can make it to the toilet without creating a river, I'll be happy!" Angie grabbed her things and dashed to the loo.

Although it wasn't the nicest thing in the world to have a tight band strapped to the top of her arm and a needle jabbed into the inside of her elbow, the blood test was quick and necessary. Right at that moment, with the black and white pictures still in her hand, she'd have agreed to lose a limb if it meant her baby was going to be healthy.

She'd have to tell her boss soon, not to mention her family and friends. Oddly, she was in no rush to tell everyone her news. She wasn't scared or ashamed or anything like that – but she'd enjoyed the quiet knowingness of the last while. The shit would probably hit the fan in more ways than one when she made her announcement. Her parents were old-fashioned and just plain old. They were probably going to find the whole thing quite upsetting. She'd have to deal with that. Her boss was going to think of how long she'd be missing from work. But she'd put it all off for long enough. She vowed she would go to Cork next weekend and tell her boss before she went.

At the end of the day, she didn't care what anybody else thought. It was all about her and the baby at this stage. Even if she was shunned by her family and fired from her job, nothing could dampen the feeling of sheer joy and unadulterated happiness she felt inside.

22

tweeting@themercedesking.com
What a great day to be alive . . . beat the January blues this evening only at The Orb . . . doors open at 9.00p.m. sharp.

tweeting@rubytuesday.com
I never knew it was possible to feel so alone in a busy world.

It was Saturday afternoon, the house was mercifully silent, and Damo was having a quiet cup of coffee in the kitchen when the doorbell rang.

"Bloody typical!" he muttered out loud as he padded out to the front door, dressed in his tracksuit bottoms, sport socks and a tight white Ralph Lauren T-shirt. "I give Noreen and Mariah a fistful of notes to go shopping and do I get any peace? Oh no, it's let's piss Damo off day, isn't it?"

He groaned inwardly when he saw who was there. "Ruby, how're ya, love? Happy New Year to you. Nice Christmas? Eh, Mariah's gone shopping with her mammy."

She stormed into the house yelling. "I know, I texted her to see where she was! What the hell were you playing at with my father? Christmas in our house was hardly destined to be the best one ever, but you had to take it all a step further and make sure he was even more furious, didn't you? Happy New Year? Happy? Not likely."

"Yeah, right, come in. I was just havin a cuppa, I'll make you one if you –"

"No, thanks. I want a hell of a lot more than a cup of instant coffee, Damo. I want to know what your intentions are. Do you actually love me? When are you going to stand by me and this baby?" Her eyes were rimmed with tears and she looked about twelve.

"Ruby, Ruby, Ruby. Take a seat. Take a chill pill. Calm yourself down. Listen, I told you what I think you should do. You need to let me sort this out. Go to London, get the job done, splash out on yourself, come home. *Bam*!" He clapped his hands loudly, making Ruby jump. "Problem solved. This doesn't need to be so complicated, sweetheart." He delivered one of his knock-'em-dead smiles.

Ruby dissolved into tears.

"What now?" Damo rubbed his temples. He really was beginning to get very tired of all this bullshit.

"I thought you cared!"

"I do."

"But I thought if I gave you a bit of time, you would realise you want to be with me. That we could be a real family!" She lunged forwards and wrapped her arms around him.

"Whoa there a minute, darling! I *have* a real family. I don't wish you any ill, seriously. But you and me, it was just a bit of gas, a laugh, bloody great while it lasted. But we aren't going to be playing house, sweetheart. I obviously didn't make myself clear. I don't want to ruin my life or yours with this baby. So the offer still stands. I'll sort you out or, if you insist on going ahead with this pregnancy, then what I said to your father will be honoured – I'll drop you a few quid and I'll stand by that." Damo sniffed, wanting the whole conversation over and done with.

"I don't need you stepping in!" said Ruby. "My mother wants to take my baby and bring it up as her own." Ruby tried to calm herself. She stood up straight and her face went blank. "I'm sorry, I shouldn't have come over here. Maybe my mother is right – the baby will be better off as theirs. I'll go to Spain and do what they want. God knows it'll be better to be out of Dublin and away from the prying eyes and the mad looks I'm going to get." She turned and ran down the hall and out the front door.

Ruby ran and ran until her throat burned. Stopping just around the corner from her house, she leaned against a fence and tried to catch her breath. Maybe if she kept running like this, she'd lose the baby. That would solve it all. That way she wouldn't have to have an abortion – it would be God's will. She hadn't envisaged that her life could get any worse than that moment when she'd done the pregnancy test. But this was a whole new nightmare. Damo wasn't going to leave Mariah's mother. He didn't love her. He didn't want to be with her. She couldn't imagine how she was ever going to get over this. She wanted to curl into a ball and die. How could she have misread the signs so badly? She felt numb with shock.

* * *

God didn't choose to take the baby away, however, so Ruby went for her first scan. Herself and Adele were on dreadful terms. Ever since Ruby had realised Damo didn't love her, she'd wanted to expire. Nothing was worth it without him. She tried to convince herself she was better off without him, that he was only a lying cheater, but she really wasn't convinced, not deep down. She admired him, with his cool clothes, the club, rubbing shoulders with the stars, his fast car and the way women all fell at his feet. Beside him, the boys her age seemed clueless and childish. Right at that moment in time, she felt sure she would never get over Damo – ever.

So now, here she was sitting in the waiting room at the maternity hospital. There were two other girls who looked around her age. They didn't speak to each other though. It wasn't that kind of atmosphere. Adele was assuming her new, glazed and pained look. Ruby stared at the tiled floor. They weren't waiting long before her name was called.

A small thin austere-looking nurse who looked about sixty-five ushered herself and her mother into a room full of equipment.

"Lie up onto the bed there, please, dear." The nurse sat in front of the machine and began to write. She didn't look at Ruby.

She explained what she was going to do and turned the small screen towards Ruby so she could see what was going on.

"The gel will feel cold. Okay, here we go." She squirted the gel onto Ruby's tummy and began to dig into her with the ultrasound probe. The sound of the heartbeat came thundering through, followed by a lot of grey grainy flickering movement on the screen.

"There's your baby, Ruby. Can you see the outline of the head and there's the spinal column?" The nurse was pointing at the screen. Ruby nodded but really she couldn't see what the nurse was talking about at all. It just looked like a bowl of tadpoles squirming around in a bag of grey jelly.

"Some new mums find it hard to relate to the baby on the screen – how do you feel?"

The nurse, who had seemed a bit scary at first, was actually making a huge effort to include Ruby. For that she was extremely grateful.

"I don't really feel like that's inside me at all. I just feel like I'm watching the telly." Ruby smiled and stared at the screen, trying to comprehend that this was her baby. She wondered if it would look like Damo. Fresh, false hope sprang anew. Maybe if it was a boy and it looked like Damo, he'd love it and want it after all. Surely he'd change his mind about her and the baby if he saw it.

"Do you want me to try and tell what sex the baby is? I can't actually guarantee I'll be able to tell at this early stage. But some mothers have a total fixation with wanting to know. We understand that too. So I could try to see if you're very keen?" The nurse looked at Ruby.

"No, we want the surprise at the end," her mother answered for her.

"With all due respect, Granny, it's up to Mum here if we find out or not." The nurse raised one eyebrow fleetingly at Adele and looked back at Ruby.

"Yes, I want to know." Ruby looked at the nurse with excitement.

"Ruby!" Adele scolded her sharply.

Ruby's smile faded when she saw the raw anger in her mother's eyes.

"Forget it." Ruby was barely audible.

Her mother smiled with satisfaction at the nurse. For the rest of the examination, the atmosphere was strained and quite hostile between the mother and daughter.

Ruby just kind of switched off. She didn't understand half of what the nurse was rabbiting on about and her mother was huffing and puffing in the corner like a tired horse. She really just wanted to go home and hide in her bedroom, where she could daydream about living with Damo in a house in the South of France. They could drive around in an open-topped sports car and he would put his arm around her, pull her towards him and kiss her, telling her she was the love of his life.

"Baby will be due on July the seventh." The nurse typed some more information into the computer and handed Ruby a couple of photos of the baby. "I just need to transfer your scan information onto a disc, which you need to take to Dr Sullivan's office at your next appointment, and you're good to go. Are you having bloods done today too?"

"Yeah." Ruby looked at the floor with a blank expression.

"So you need to follow the signs to the phlebotomy department at the very end of this corridor. Here's your disc." The nurse went to hand it to Ruby, but Adele intercepted and shoved it in her handbag.

"Knowing Ruby it'll get lost. Better if I take some control of this situation." Exhaling loudly, Adele ushered Ruby out of the room.

By the time they got home an hour and a half later, Ruby was exhausted. She couldn't believe how much she was able to sleep at the moment. School was awful too. She couldn't tell anyone about the baby. So she felt shut away, like she was in a soundproof, Perspex box. Where everyone could see her but not hear her.

Her parents had forbidden her to go to Mariah's house until they decided what was going to happen with regards to Damo. She'd phoned Mariah's mobile a couple of times but, every time, Mariah hit the red button and she was shunted to voice mail.

"Mariah, please call me. I need to talk to you. Please," Ruby begged.

But no return call came and when she returned to school the next day, Mariah avoided her like the plague. In the café at lunchtime, Ruby was too afraid to go to where Mariah and the usual group of girls were sitting. Ruby tried to catch Mariah's eye and ask her to come outside for a chat.

As she sat by herself on a bench outside, she felt hope rise when Mariah came towards her.

"Don't come near me, Ruby White! How could you? You let me go around thinking I had a chance with Yaakov and all along you'd already slept with him and not told me. You're not the girl I thought you were!" Mariah turned to walk off. "So stop calling me and stop talking to me, right? I don't want anything to do with you. And another thing, if any of our friends find out what you did, I will make you suffer. You've made a fool of me once but you won't get the chance to do it again. You lied to me and told me you weren't into him, and I was stupid enough to believe you!" Mariah stormed off.

So that was final and Ruby felt more isolated than ever.

She missed her Aunt Serena too. Her mum had said she'd tell her but not until she was ready.

"I'll have to bide my time, Ruby. Not only will Aunt Serena be utterly disgusted with your behaviour, but Grandma and Grandpa are going to be confused and not to mention mortified. In my day, only girls of a certain ilk ended up in your situation. Do you have any idea how *wrong* this whole situation is on so so many levels?" That look was there again. The face like Adele was sniffing sour milk. The purple shading climbing up her mother's face, followed by the inevitable hand-waving, to try and somehow fan the shame of it all from herself.

"Whatever about Grandma and Grandpa, could we not just tell Serena? I know she is offended that I haven't been out to lunch with her. Every time she calls I have to lie. It's not fair to her, Mum. Besides, I just miss her." Ruby sighed deeply.

"I would try and get used to that if I were you – missing her, that is. I know your Aunt Serena better than anyone. The minute she hears you've blotted your copybook, you won't have to worry about lying to avoid invitations. She won't want to know you, let alone take you around shopping centres or trendy bistros." Adele wagged her finger. "All the lunches and treats will stop, you mark my words!"

Ruby wanted to smack her mother's face. Just because her mother didn't get on with Aunt Serena, she tried to make her out to be a she-devil. But Ruby knew better. Ruby saw a different side to Serena. Doubt crept into the young girl's mind all the same. Would Aunt Serena be ashamed of her? Would she not love her anymore?

Her mum began to pace up and down. "It will probably be another ten weeks before you show too much to hide it – you can get a bigger school jumper and skirt. Realistically, after that, it's going to be too risky. Someone will notice. The other fact we have to consider is that I ought to tell people that I'm pregnant now. If we want to make the story realistic. Jesus, Ruby, I hope you're happy with your actions!"

Adele beat Ruby to it, by hauling herself up the stairs to her room.

Ruby was left standing in the hall on her own. Fresh tears sprang from her eyes and she crumpled to the floor. Crouched on the bottom step of the stairs, she buried her head in her knees and sobbed. Lonely, scared and sorry sobs.

23

tweeting@serenasvelte.com
Thank God for the simple pleasures in life . . . crisp fresh bed
linen with a glass of crisp white wine.

There was a noise coming from very far away. It was seriously annoying. It wouldn't go away. It was moving her arm too. It was shaking her repeatedly.

"Stop it, please." A drowning dull voice came from Serena's mouth.

"Hello, Serena, can you hear me?"

She tried with all her might to open an eye. It complied for a second and promptly shut itself again. The light was so strong. Jesus, what had she been drinking? She tried to remember where she'd been the night before. Paul didn't have a big function, did he? She hoped she hadn't been too drunk.

"Serena, your surgery is all over with. Well done, you've made it through, you're in recovery." The nurse was standing right in front of her face. Serena remembered now. She was having all that thread stuff burnt off her uterus. It'd bloody want to have worked. She'd had to go to a lunch with two friends and not have a drink. Not a drop. It had been the most boring lunch she'd ever been to – in fact she'd left after an hour. Christ, she'd never realised how stupid Lea was! She'd kept repeating herself and talking rubbish.

She was glad she never did that when she was drinking.

At least this annoying operation thing was over with now. She could get pregnant immediately and get her life back on track. She really had planned on being well into her first pregnancy by now. But it couldn't be helped. Paul said that life could throw things at you and she supposed he was right.

She felt she'd had her fair share of hassle by now. Another day or two in hospital and she'd be back in action.

As they wheeled her in her bed back to her private room, she noticed a sharp digging pain in her stomach.

"Oh sweet Jesus, what the hell is wrong with my stomach? I'm in pain here, you know!" she barked.

"On a scale of one to ten, one being low pain and ten being unbearable pain, where would you rate yourself?" The nurse didn't look behind as she helped the porter manoeuvre the bed.

"What? Pain is pain. I can feel it. It's not nice. Do something about it. Rapidly. That's what you're here for," she groaned and brought her knees up to her chest to try and ease the feeling.

"Try to stay still and flat. We'll organise an injection for you as soon as we get you settled. There's a good girl," the nurse answered calmly.

"An injection? I need a bloody anaesthetic at this rate. Have you any idea how much pain I'm in here?" Serena yelled as the bed sped on. "This is supposed to be a private clinic! Why am I feeling like I've had my insides gouged out with an apple-corer? What kind of instruments did they use? Farm machinery? Och, my bloody shoulder is in agony too! The idiot was supposed to work on my womb. Did he look at the wrong chart or something?"

"That pain in the shoulder is common unfortunately, after a laparoscopy. It's the gas they use to raise the tummy up while the surgery is done. It often gets trapped in the shoulder on the way out." The nurse ignored her rudeness and remained calm.

Back in the ward, the nurse busied herself taking Serena's blood pressure.

"Well, if I have to sit here, can I at least have something to relax me, like a chilled glass of white wine?" grumbled Serena. "The heat in here can't be good for any one."

The nurse gave Serena a rather shocked look.

"Well?" Serena demanded. "This is supposed to be a private clinic, isn't it? Unlike the public hospitals that I see on the news, this place boasts a reputation for looking after its patients. What's wrong with asking for a drink?"

The nurse remained calm and polite. "Yes, Serena, it is a private clinic, not a hotel or a bar. It's not a good idea for you to drink alcohol after an anaesthetic. It would make you feel very nauseous, apart from the fact it would be dangerous. I'll give you a quick needle now, and that will help with the pain. Hopefully you'll feel a lot more comfortable in a few minutes."

"Jesus, this is like being on a school tour with the nuns," Serena muttered caustically.

Luckily for everyone concerned, Serena took a sleeping tablet. Along with the strong painkillers the nurse had injected and remains of that day's anaesthesia, she fell into a deep and silent sleep.

* * *

Next morning she woke up full of life again. By eight o'clock, she'd finished her breakfast and had her shower and was ready to go home.

"Paul, hello darling, I'm ready to leave this dreadful place now. Can you swing by and collect me?"

"Well sure, but has the doctor told you it's okay for you to go home?" He sounded concerned.

"Not yet, but I'll just tell them I'm going now. I've had enough of being treated like a naughty child. I want to go home to my own bed, with my own things. I'm not into this whole hospital lark. The bed is unmercifully uncomfortable and it has a plastic mattress." Her voice was rising shrilly as she spoke. "What do they think I am? An incontinent old bag?"

"Just stay calm, Serena. I'll be there in fifteen minutes. I'd imagine you'll have to wait until the doctor releases you though, so don't get your knickers in a knot." He smiled as she went off on a tangent again.

When she decided she didn't want to do something, woe betide the poor beggar who got in her way. That was, of course, one of the reasons why he loved her so much. She was always totally direct.

By the time Paul got to the clinic, Serena was sitting in an armchair beside the bed. She looked pale and drawn and was slightly stooped over.

"Hi, honey, how are you feeling?" He bent to kiss her.

"I'm fine now you're here. The doctor was just in. I can go home which is a relief. I've to take these antibiotics and rest. He wanted to know if I'd be sure to take it easy at home, because otherwise I'd have to stay here, which is a bloody joke. There's no chance of any relaxation in this place. They spend their time bursting in and out the door connecting me to monitors and blood-pressure machines. It's like being an exhibit in the zoo, and as for the questions. They wanted to know about my toilet habits this morning. Who do they think they're talking to? I'm not an animal. I certainly am not about to discuss things like that with a perfect stranger. Let's go." She struggled out of the chair and shuffled towards the door.

Paul packed her things into her Louis Vuitton holdall and hurried down the hall after her.

"We need to stop at the chemist on the way to fill this out," she said, waving a prescription at him.

"No problem, you sit tight and I'll get it. Will I phone your sister to come and sit with you? I have to go the office, and I've two guys over from the UK so I'm not going to be home before eleven tonight. I feel awful leaving you like this." He glanced sideways at her. "Maybe Ruby would pop in when she's finished school. She always cheers you up?"

"Not at all, Adele will be busy with her golf today and Ruby will have homework or study of some sort, anyway. I've had enough of people annoying me. All I need is to be left alone. I'll watch television in bed and I'll heat up a ready meal later on. I've had my coffee and porridge this morning, so I'm not hungry." She sat back and tried to relax. No one had told her the pain would be so bad. She felt like her insides had been scraped all the way around with a wallpaper-scraper. "Keyhole surgery" made it all sound so minor but in reality she was in agony.

By the time Paul got her settled in bed she was exhausted. She waited for him to leave before she painfully made her way down to the kitchen. She poured herself a glass of white wine from the fridge and brought it upstairs to bed. Her antibiotics had "avoid alcoholic drink" written in big black letters on the sticker. Wine didn't count though. They only meant things like brandy or other strong drinks. The wine would help with the pain and it would relax her muscles. She propped herself up in the bed with pillows and turned on the day-time chat shows. Sipping her wine, she felt a lot happier.

"A day without wine is like a day without sunshine . . ." She closed her eyes and took a deep drink of the cool liquid. That was better. Things were looking up. She was back in control.

By seven o'clock that night, she'd polished off a full bottle of white wine. She wasn't feeling great though. She felt sore and muzzy and a bit sick. She'd heated up a portion of lasagne, but hadn't felt able to eat it. It smelled too much like cat food and it looked too sloppy.

Knowing she needed to eat, she managed to force herself to eat some toast. Just then her friend Noelle phoned.

"Hi, sweetie! Oh, you sound dreadful! Are you sick?" she crooned.

"No, just a bit tired, what's up?" Serena actually felt pretty appalling. The toast was like eating polystyrene. It was dry and scratchy on her throat and she was having to make herself swallow it.

"Listen, Marie-Claire my Filipino lady has just told me her sister wants a live-in job. I thought of you immediately. Do you want to meet her? I'd recommend having a live-in, it takes all the pressure off," Noelle babbled. "It also means the house will be spick and span any time Paul needs to bring guests home. If you're even considering going down the baby trail, you'll need the help then. My girl is a wonder and I'm sure her sister, Lucinda will be of the same ilk."

Serena really didn't need to have this conversation right now. The way she felt, she wasn't planning on having any babies – ever. Ruby would have to suffice as a surrogate child. If she felt remotely like this after having a baby, it wouldn't be worth it. But she wasn't about to tell Noelle that she'd had that dreadful stuff burnt off her womb, nor was she going to miss the opportunity to have a live-in helper.

"She sounds great, sweetie. Can you tell her to come and see me next week?" Serena just wanted to put the phone down and get herself a brandy and port. That would make her feel better for sure.

"That's the hitch. She desperately needs a job starting immediately. As in, tomorrow. So if you were interested, she'd really need to see you then. Sorry to put you under pressure but if you don't need her I'll pass her on to Patricia – she was looking for someone too."

The thought of someone else getting the live-in help was enough to make Serena snap. "Tell her to come over tomorrow at twelve and I'll talk to her then. Now I don't mean to be rude, Noelle, but I'm in the middle of dinner here, so I'll fly. Thanks so much for thinking of me – you're a doll!"

Serena slammed the phone down and doubled over with pain.

She only managed a few sips of brandy and port before she vomited. Feeling totally wretched and scared, she fell into bed like a wet rag.

* * *

She felt marginally better the next morning. She'd slept like a log. She hadn't even heard Paul come in the night before nor had she heard him leave that morning. After a shower, she dressed in a soft cosy tracksuit and phoned her husband.

"Hello, Sleeping Beauty! You were dead to the world so I didn't want to wake you." Paul sounded hassled.

"Oh, I'm so much better today," she lied. "I've a little thing I wanted to run by you." She filled him in on the idea of having a helper for a while. "It would be a weight off my mind. The cleaning lady we have is very unreliable and any time we have a dinner party I have to pay an extra person to come and clean up. Also, when we have the baby she'd be vital," she finished.

"Right." Paul sounded like he was only half listening to her. "Listen, darling, I'm up to my gonads here. I'll leave it up to you.

Just make sure she has references and she'll have to agree to sign a contract." He really didn't want to talk about it. "Bottom line is, you're more than able to organise the house and all that stuff, so you go with your own instinct on this. Okay?"

He was gone. Serena was delighted, Paul needed her to organise all these things, so she'd be in charge. It would be quite nice to have "staff" in her house. The more she thought about it, the more she liked the idea.

By the time the Filipino lady arrived at twelve, Serena had made a list of all the duties she needed to be carried out, from ironing to watering the plants.

The small girl at the door was meek and sweet. Serena brought her in and showed her around. She simply nodded when Serena pointed out what she wanted. She refused tea or coffee and sat nervously on the edge of her chair when Serena showed her the list.

"Now my husband insists you must sign a contract. Is that okay with you?"

"Yes, Miss Serena," she nodded.

Oh, this was marvellous altogether, Serena thought to herself.

"Right then, I think you should start as soon as possible. By the way, I love the 'Miss Serena' thing. I wouldn't have insisted upon it, but seeing as you seem to like it, we'll stick with it, okay?" She clapped her hands with delight after she showed the girl out. They had arranged that she would bring her things and move in the following day.

Serena was thrilled to have "staff". It would go down very well with the girls. She was feeling a lot less nauseous and sore too, so she felt she might just be able to think about having a baby soon. The hospital had told her to wait for two months before trying, but depending on how she felt she might just go ahead sooner. She'd give it a few weeks and see how good this Lucinda girl was.

She needed to celebrate, so she opened a bottle of wine. She'd have a little glass while she was making her lunch. She drank half a glass and popped an individual quiche into the oven. Things were looking up. She just needed to get over this operation, get pregnant, have the baby and she'd be well on her way to implementing the plans she'd had in her head when she'd got married. Everything would be perfect. This whole surgery glitch was but a fly in the ointment.

She decided to phone her sister to tell her all about it.

"Adele, how are you?" she beamed down the phone.

"Is everything all right, Serena?" Adele snapped.

"Yes, fine. I just wanted to tell you about the new live-in helper I've just hired." Serena arranged herself on a high stool in the kitchen, all ready to tell her sister about it.

"I can't talk to you at the moment, I'll have to call you back. I have much more pressing issues to deal with and, quite honestly, I'm not in the frame of mind for talking about cleaning ladies!"

Well, some people were just plain rude, Serena thought, hanging up the phone.

24

tweeting@angiebaby.com
Papa please don't preach, because I'm definitely keeping my baby, wish me luck!

Angie's heart was beating like a drum when she pulled up at her parents' farm. The familiarity of home enveloped her like a hug. The old farmhouse, with peeling paint, faded curtains and years of trailing ivy lacing its way up the surround of the blue wooden front door all gave her a warm feeling inside. As usual her parents came rushing out to greet her, the dogs were barking and running around in circles with excitement and her mother was tutting at them affectionately. Denis, her father, lifted her off the ground, proving that even women aged forty weren't too old to get a bear hug from their daddies. Mags, her mother, held her face in her hands and kissed her.

"Come in out of the cold, child. I've a stew on the Aga for you. We're thrilled to see you."

Denis took her bag and they ushered her inside.

"Knowing you, you haven't had a decent meal since Christmas – all you young people think about is work and going to dances," her mother fussed with a smile on her face.

Angie grinned. This was the only place on the planet that she could still feel like she was eighteen years old.

Mags bit her lip. "I'm not criticising you, love, but you're looking a little heavier than usual. I hope you're not living on takeaway food. I can imagine it must be difficult to have to think about cooking a healthy dinner after a long day at work. But, you are looking after yourself, aren't you?"

"Ah, you know me, I'm a divil for the easy option! Let's sit and have a bit of a catch up." Angie swallowed hard.

Now that she'd come home to deliver her news, she was really nervous of her parent's reaction to her pregnancy. They had always supported her, but they were in their seventies and they weren't worldly-wise people. She was terrified of upsetting them. She was so excited and thrilled about the baby that she really hoped the news wasn't going to cause any distress to them. Their love and support meant the world to her.

The smell of the stew and the warmth of the kitchen engulfed Angie when she walked in. One of the cats was curled into a soft stripy ginger ball on top of the closed Aga. Angie patted her fuzzy head as she passed. The farmhouse was the same as it had been for twenty years. The old flagstone floor, the faded flock wallpaper and the big scrubbed wooden table, which comfortably sat ten adults. No designer chrome-legged tables or straight-backed leather chairs here. Philippe Starck would probably have a coronary if he was forced to sit on the mismatched, heavy seats.

One of the lads who helped on the farm was sitting at the table eating a plate of stew. He'd been away when she visited at Christmas.

"Howa'ya there, Angie! How's the big smoke treating you? D'ya like living up in Dublin?"

"It's all good, Brendan. Busy and fast-moving and dirty, but that's Dublin. I like it but I wouldn't settle there to be honest with you. Nobody knows anyone. It's all too big and rushed. Not like round here, where you could go on your own into the pub and know someone would sit and chat to you."

Mags served her up a fine plate of stew and Angie resigned herself to waiting until Brendan finished his dinner and left before she could tell her parents her news.

As soon as he did, she took a deep breath, put down her fork and began. "I've something to tell you both," she said and looked at her parents who were sitting either side of her, hanging on her every word. "I hope you'll be happy for me," she added.

Denis and Mags looked at each other and back at her, both their crinkled, weather-beaten faces open with smiles.

"What is it, child?" Mags asked.

"Mammy, I'm having a baby." She paused but they said nothing, just stared incredulously at her. "The daddy isn't going to be involved, so I'll be rearing it on my own. I hope you can both be there for me and, more importantly, for the baby." She looked from one to the other expectantly, hoping with all her heart that they wouldn't mind.

"Oh, right so." Denis was scratching his head and looking a bit embarrassed and uncomfortable with the conversation. "What do you think, Mammy?" He looked to his wife for a hint of how he should act.

"Is this what you want, love?" Mags asked, her hands shaking from shock but her face fighting to hide her concern.

"Yes, Mammy. I know it's not ideal that the child won't have a father. It's not what I would have planned but that's my lot and I'm more than ready to be a mother to this child."

"Right so," her mother answered. "Now it might take us a little minute to get used to the whole thing but if you're happy, then the child will be welcome and loved, won't it, Daddy?" She looked at her husband.

There was a brief pause as Mags and Denis took stock of the situation.

"How long have you known?" Mags looked down at Angie's obviously swollen tummy.

"I'm sorry, Mammy, I knew at Christmas, but I just wasn't ready to tell yet. I'm sorry I hid it from you." She looked at the floor in shame.

"I'm only sorry that you didn't feel you could talk to us. I hate the idea that you've been coping with this news by yourself." Mags dabbed her eyes and swallowed, forcing herself to smile.

"It's not a reflection on you or Daddy. I have always felt I can tell you anything. I just needed more time. Can you understand?" Angie looked stricken.

Mags was finding it hard to hide her shock. "So when is the baby due then?"

"July." Angie held her mothers' gaze.

Wanting to keep things calm, Denis pipped up. "The main thing is that you've told us now, pet. Sure isn't it all out in the open now?" He tried to sound as cheerful as possible.

Angie felt a rush of love for her parents. She knew this was a bitter pill for them to swallow. They were devout Catholics and firm believers in the institute of marriage, so it would be a far cry from what they'd have hoped for her. But they loved her and she now knew they would love her baby too.

"We'll get used to it, won't we, Denis?" Mags steadied herself.

"Thank you, Mammy, and Daddy too. I know this isn't easy for you to take on board. You're the best. This baby will bring us all so much joy, just wait and see." Angie stood up and went around the table to hug her parents.

They sat for a long time talking about Angie's plans. She explained about her contract and that she was going to have the baby in Dublin. She showed them the scan picture.

"Well, I never saw a photo like this." Denis was astonished at the technology. "We're looking forward to meeting you," he told the picture.

Angie smiled. She was lucky to have such grounded and loving parents. They might not be the most trendy or travelled people (the only time they'd been out of Ireland was to go to Blackpool on a bus tour) but they were good, kind and decent. They'd worked hard all their lives and made sure that herself and her brothers were well cared for and well provided for.

When the time had come for their children to move on, they'd sold a piece of land so they could give each of them a little nest egg to start them off. They were simple people, with a lot of love for their children.

"Sure women raise children on their own all the time nowadays," Mags said. "It's not even unusual, sure it's not?"

"Not really, Mammy. Listen, I know you'd prefer if I was married and had a husband and a daddy for the baby, but God has decided I'm to be a mother without all that. I think I'll be good at it. I'll do my very best anyway and sure the child will have two grandparents, so that makes three at least." It was a lot more than God that had decided she should get pregnant, she fleetingly admitted to herself.

Her father sat back and watched her talking. She was glowing. He'd never seen her happier. He was so proud of his only daughter. She had a good head on her shoulders. She'd done so well with her job. She was always a go-getter. Denis had hoped she might meet a nice fella who would look after her when they were gone. But, if she had this child, then she'd never be alone. So in a way that was just as good.

Angie read his mind. "There's nothing stopping me meeting a nice lad at some stage. Plenty of people have children and go on to meet someone these days."

"That's true – all these second marriages and all that," Mags interjected.

Angie slept like a baby that night, in her own childhood bedroom. The same rosebud wallpaper, although a little yellowed and curled at the edges, was still on the walls. The old familiar smell of her room and the sound of nothing but the trees blowing in the breeze outside was like a lullaby rocking her to sleep. It was ten thirty before she even stirred next morning, which was unheard of for Angie – at least since she'd moved to Dublin. Used to the noise of the city and the gruelling work schedule she was having to follow, it was a rare treat for her to be relaxed enough to lie on.

Pulling on an old squashy pink dressing gown and a pair of sheepskin slippers, she padded down to the kitchen. Her mother was busy baking scones.

"Good morning, sleepyhead!" Her mother hugged and kissed her.

"Mammy, thank you for being so good about the baby. I've been so worried about telling you and Daddy. I didn't want to upset you. I didn't want you to feel ashamed of me. I'm sorry I left it so long to tell you. But I needed the time to get my own head around it all."

"We'd never be ashamed of you, love, Daddy and I have never been anything but proud of you. Fair enough, in an ideal world it would be good for you to have the support of a partner but, if that's not to be, then that's that."

Mags was looking at her searchingly. They hadn't pushed her for information on the baby's father. Although she didn't want to get into too many details, she felt she owed them some sort of an explanation.

"He's not married or anything like that, just so you know," Angie said. "He just didn't want to be involved with the baby, so I've told him that he'll have to stand by his decision. I won't allow him to dip in and out of the child's life. That'd be worse. So I'm going to do this on my own." She looked at her mother to see if she was going to accept the story.

"I see, but he might change his mind when the child is born, love," her mother said gently. "Men aren't very good at knowing how they feel until they see a baby. They don't have maternal instincts like women. Would you not let him meet the child and decide things then? I just don't want you to have any regrets later on."

"I won't, Mammy. I've thought long and hard about it. This is the way I want to do things." Angie was firm.

"But what about the child? What if he or she blames you for keeping the daddy away in years to come?"

"I'll have to cross that bridge when I come to it." Angie bit her lip. She had of course thought of that. But every time she did, she quashed it all. Troy probably did have a right to know he had fathered a child. Deep down she knew he did, but then where would she be? Sending a child on the train up and back from Cork to Dublin? Having to share the child with a man she didn't know? Only spending every second Christmas with her baby? Having to consult him about what school the child went to or what religion it should be? It would all be fine if they were a couple and knew each other. But they didn't. They lived in opposite ends of the country. It just wouldn't work. *But he has a right to know, it's his baby too,* the nagging voice in her head piped up.

Shaking all thoughts of Troy and what was morally right and wrong, she zoned back in on her mother.

"Okay Angie, you know what's best for you, but do keep in mind this might come back to haunt you in the future if you don't try to get that man to make an effort with this child. At least, if you can hold your head up high when your child asks about its daddy, then you're not open to any blame."

"I know what you're saying, Mammy. I'll keep it in mind," Angie conceded. Millions of women in America went to clinics and used donated sperm. What she was doing wasn't any different.

Except she knew it *was* different. Those men all consented to having their sperm used. Troy had no idea she was using him as a donor. Maybe it was because she'd told her parents, or maybe it was due to the fact that she was away from work, but she was thinking about Troy constantly. Maybe she wasn't doing the right thing in keeping quiet. Unable to ponder any longer, she ate a quick breakfast, dressed warmly and took the dogs for a walk. As she stomped over the fields, her head cleared and all she could think of was the baby. Her baby. She had butterflies in her tummy when she thought of it.

As if on cue, the baby kicked. So this is what all the maternity books had described. That fluttering in her tummy. Like tiny butterflies having a party. None of the books had portrayed quite how much those little movements would connect with her heart. Nothing she'd ever experienced in her life had come close to this feeling. And this was only the beginning. Angie couldn't begin to imagine how she'd feel when she actually held her baby for the first time.

"Hi, Baby, I can't wait to meet you!" She rubbed her tummy as she walked. Smiling with satisfaction, she trudged on, knowing that for now she was keeping this baby all for herself, whether it was right or wrong.

25

tweeting@themercedesking.com
Beat the recession, cocktails 2 for the price of 1 Mon –
Thursday at The Orb. The only place to be seen this evening.

tweeting@rubytuesday.com
A problem shared is a problem halved right? If I tell the
world, does that mean my problems will disappear?

Damo was cruising down the motorway in his beloved Merc. He'd learned to take all the Ruby stuff and put it in a box in the back of his mind. The whole thing was beginning to wreck his buzz. The sooner she went off to Spain with her mother the better. He had a couple of new young ones starting at the club this evening. Twins from Brazil. He reckoned they'd be on for a bit of after-hours fun. That'd cheer him up, get all this hassle out of his head. These girls were twenty-four too, a bit older, so he reckoned they'd have more sense than Ruby. He was going to steer clear of really young ones from here on in. More hassle than they were worth.

* * *

At that same moment, Ruby had just arrived at Serena's front door. She knew it wasn't going to do anything to help the situation her mother. They were supposed to just vanish off to Spain like two fugitives, without telling a soul. But if anyone could help her and be

176

on her side, it was Serena. She needed an ally and someone who might be able to talk some sense into her parents.

"Darling, what a lovely surprise! Come in – oh no, what's wrong? Don't cry!" Serena had to almost support Ruby as she'd fallen into her arms outside the front door.

"I'm sorry, Aunt Serena," Ruby sobbed. "Mum will kill me if she knows I'm here but I had to talk to you!"

Ruby noticed a tiny-framed girl whizzing past with a bucket and duster as Serena led her to the drawing room.

Flopping down on the soft cream sofa and wiping her tears away, Ruby took in the scent of polish and fresh roses. She adored Serena's house. It was clean and minimalist. Her own home was far too traditional for her liking, but Aunt Serena was so with-it and cool. She always had the newest Prada handbag or shoes. Ruby wanted to be just like her when she grew up.

"Aunt Serena, has my mum called over the last few days to talk about me?"

Ruby looked wan and exhausted, Serena noticed. "No, honey. Why, what's happened?"

"Please don't hate me!" Ruby started to sob again, her thin arms wrapped around herself in misery.

"I could never hate you, my love! Tell me." Serena had the most awful feeling in the pit of her stomach. If someone had hurt Ruby, she would see to it that they paid.

"I'm pregnant, Aunt Serena."

The words rang through Screna's head, bounced around a couple of times and caused an immediate numbing almost anaesthetic effect. Emotion, speech and all previous function escaped her.

"Serena? Say something. Oh God, you hate me, don't you? You think I'm a little tart. I didn't sleep around! It was one time and I honestly didn't think I could get pregnant. I'm sorry – please say you don't hate me – please!" Ruby flung herself at Serena and wrapped herself around her, burying her head in her shoulder.

It took a couple of seconds for Serena to engage her brain. Instinctively she rocked and hugged the young girl, stroking her hair. The tears couldn't be helped, Serena just let them flow.

"It's all going to be okay, baby girl. It's okay. I'm here. You poor, poor darling! It's okay," was all she could muster.

Of course she was shocked by the knowledge that her beautiful little niece had obviously been behaving in a manner that was far from innocent but, unbeknownst to Ruby, the biggest kick in the teeth was the fact that this mere child was able to get pregnant before she could.

Reeling from the unfairness and the irony of the entire situation, Serena dug deep and pulled every shred of responsibility she felt towards the girl, and used that to talk.

"How long have you known about this?" Serena stroked the girl's cheek.

"I missed my period in October," Ruby sobbed.

"And your mother didn't think to tell me? That makes sense of why you didn't want to spend any time with me. I thought you might have hit a stage where you didn't want to hang out with your silly old aunt. I knew there was something going on when we called over on Christmas Day. I should have asked you or said something. I haven't set eyes on you for almost three months. I feel like I've failed you, sweetheart. I've been so busy with this and that, but it's no excuse. It all makes sense now I presume your mother wanted you to stay away from me and hide all this." Serena felt rage stir up inside her. "Do your grandparents know?"

"No. Mum said we have to keep it all quiet or the plan won't work."

"What plan?"

As the idea of Adele and Harry adopting the baby was put to Serena, there was a deathly silence. The situation just got worse and worse. Serena had to stop herself from grabbing the phone and calling her sister and abusing her from a height.

"What do you think I should do, Aunt Serena?"

There it was. The question of the century. Serena felt herself float again. It was all like a sick joke. Were God and all the angels and saints trying to have a laugh? Somewhere, were there people pulling the strings of life, wetting themselves laughing at the cruel little joke here?

"I'll have to talk to your mother. What do you want to do, darling?" Serena allowed her gaze to drop to Ruby's tummy. She still wasn't showing much, but now that she knew what she was looking for, a tiny little rounding was visible.

"I want things to work out with the baby's father. I know the circumstances aren't ideal. I know I'm young, but that doesn't mean I don't understand what love is. I'm not the first young girl to have a baby, and I know I won't be the last. Who's to say things couldn't work out with the baby's father?" Ruby was getting more upset by the second. "I'm on Easter holidays so we're going to Spain tomorrow, just to meet the doctor who will deliver the baby and to organise ourselves. Then we'll come back and head over there again later when I get bigger." She sighed. "I really thought it was going to work out with the baby's father. Maybe it still can." She bit her lip. "I really thought he loved me, Serena."

"So you told him, did you?" Serena probed gently.

"Yes, and he didn't want to know." Ruby told Serena briefly how it had all happened, leaving out the name of the father and of course the details of the cocaine and the fact that she still harboured a longing for Damo.

Serena listened and made very little comment beyond saying, "Oh Ruby, you poor love!" periodically.

Clicking into adult mode, Serena convinced Ruby to allow her to drive her home. She couldn't possibly pretend to her own sister that she knew nothing about this. Not that Adele had considered *her* feelings for even a nanosecond but this wasn't about them. This was about Ruby.

"Don't cause any more shouting, Aunt Serena, please," Ruby pleaded as they screeched up to the house, feeling the awful tightening sensation in her tummy raising up its ugly head again.

The front door flew open and her mother was standing with her hands on her hips, looking furious.

"Oh, I see, so you've called in the cavalry, have you?"

"Grow up, Adele. Let's not let our own lack of tolerance for each other make Ruby feel any worse than she already does. This isn't a game, let's go inside and try to be civil, if you know how!" Serena spat.

The tension in the room was dreadful. For the millionth time in the last few weeks, Ruby wished she was on a desert island, away from all of this. She pictured herself and Damo, on sun loungers somewhere delicious like Hawaii, soaking up the sun with brightly coloured cocktails with sparkly umbrellas stuck into them.

"You have no right to pitch up at my home, with *my* daughter and tell me what to do, Serena. I know you think you can be the Queen of Sheba with those vixens you call friends, and with that drip of a husband of yours, but I am your older sister and you will not disrespect me in my own home." Adele let the built-up anger of the last few weeks flow like a river of spite.

Serena didn't even sit down. She was so stunned by her sister's viciousness that she couldn't speak. "Whoa, back down a second. I'm not here to wage a war with you or anyone else. I just think we should all calm down a bit and listen to what Ruby wants here. I understand you're upset, the situation is far from ideal, but –"

"How could you possibly understand? The only person you care about is yourself. You've never been any different, Serena. Anything you wanted, Daddy got it for you. Now you've moved on to Paul. You say jump, he says how high. You have no idea what it even means to feel hurt, pain or disappointment. Don't you dare march into my home, with my daughter, acting like the knight in shining armour who is going to save the poor little mistreated girl from her wicked mother. You might get to play Wonderful-Aunt-Serena when it suits you. Fine. Ruby adores you. But you don't get to come in here, all whistles and bells, and tell me how to deal with *my* child," Adele was yelling now. "Harry and I are doing what we believe is best for *our* daughter. Period."

Adele marched across the hallway and opened the front door. Holding her hands up in resignation, Serena began to leave.

"No, wait, Aunt Serena! Don't leave me here! You promised you would try and talk. You said you would help me!" Ruby began to sob uncontrollably.

"I'm so sorry, Ruby darling, but your mum is just too angry at the moment. I can't be here when she's like this. Stay in touch with me and we'll chat when things calm down a little. I love you, baby girl, remember that." And Serena walked out.

By the time her mother managed to slam the front door shut, Ruby had fled to the safety of her bedroom. Burying her face in her pillow, her head felt like it would burst she cried so hard. She'd been so sure Aunt Serena would be able to get through to her mother. Now she felt truly alone. She was never going to get anyone to listen to what she wanted. Her life was as good as over.

* * *

The following day, the flight to Spain and subsequent car journey all passed with minimal communication between mother and daughter. Ruby was grateful to listen to her iPod, Adele read the same two pages of her book over and over again.

Using a hired car, they drove directly to the clinic.

It wasn't a big old-looking building, like Irish hospitals, but small, modern with everything looking pristine. The walls, the floors, the doors, the ceilings were all white. It was like one big shiny white cell. It was quiet, unlike the normal hustle and bustle of a hospital. All the doors were shut as Ruby and Adele sat on two white leather chairs waiting to see the consultant.

"Sit up straight, Ruby. You need to try and create a good impression here, we're hardly sending out a good image to begin with, what with your," Adele wagged her fingers around in a circle, "situation!"

"Sorry! I didn't realise I was being interviewed or that I had to sit in a certain way to be allowed to give birth here," Ruby huffed.

"You know what I mean – you can only make one first impression. Don't embarrass me in front of this consultant, please, that's all I ask," Adele sighed.

"What? Any more than I already have, you mean?" Ruby glowered at her mother.

Two doctors padded past, neither of them greeting Ruby and her mother. They both wore full-length white coats and white soft-soled shoes. It was much scarier than the Mountrath Clinic back in Ireland, thought Ruby. At least there the doctors were all dressed in normal clothes. Here they all seemed much more austere and serious.

"I don't know if I like this place, Mum," Ruby whispered.

"You'll be fine, Ruby. I've researched this and by all accounts this is the best place you can be. You'll have a private room and you'll be well looked after. Now be a brave girl and don't start whining." She patted Ruby's knee. She couldn't face this consultant with Ruby bawling her eyes out. That just wouldn't do. Besides Adele was still smarting after the way that rude midwife had spoken to her at the scan in Dublin ten weeks earlier.

"If the baby gets any bigger, how am I going to give birth to it? It's huge already and I look like I have a football stuffed up my jumper," Ruby whispered.

"It's just because you're so thin and slight, not to mention young, so it shows all the more. You'll be fine. I'll make sure they give you an epidural. I had one when I had you. They're amazing, like having a magic wand waved over your pain. The best policy is to try not to think about it too much for now. You've a while to go yet, Ruby." Adele stroked her daughter's hand for a second, then folded her arms and looked straight ahead.

They met the Spanish consultant, Dr Alejandro, who was olive-skinned with oiled-back dark hair. He spoke broken English and had a tendency to meander off in Spanish. Ruby's grasp of Spanish was minimal. Although they'd had the apartment in Spain since she was born, all the other people in the complex spoke English. The only Spanish she knew involved ordering food and drinks and buying things in the shops.

They signed all the forms and arranged for Ruby to come and have a scan. Although she'd had one in Ireland, Dr Alejandro wanted to do one for his records.

He also asked Ruby to make out a birth plan and bring it in for the next appointment.

"If you do, then it will be easy for us to understand how it is you would like to do this birth, *comprende*?" he asked.

"Okay." Ruby was shy and withdrawn.

Adele then explained what was going to happen when the baby was born.

"We have all the papers drawn up here, to show that Ruby is

signing the baby over to myself and her father. My husband has a good solicitor, so he is looking after the procedure."

Dr Alejandro looked at the papers and sat back in his chair. "You have organised counselling for Ruby with all this?" he asked.

"Well, no. She can talk to me or her father if she needs to. She's also very close to my sister, her Aunt Serena, so she has more than enough support in place at home." Adele was blinking and staring at the doctor as if he'd offended her.

"No, that's wrong. Señora, you must arrange for her to see a person who is not your family. She must understand what she is doing. She is young, yes, but that does not make it okay to tell her what she must do with this baby." He was firm.

Afraid to risk an argument, Adele agreed to allow Ruby see an independent counsellor at the clinic. The appointment was made for the following week. Ruby was on her Easter holidays from school, so nobody would think it unusual for her to be in Spain for ten days.

"You will not attend the session, Señora. Ruby will speak with my colleague alone. She must have some time and space away from you and your husband to decide what she will do." Dr Alejandro was adamant.

There was silence in the car as Adele drove down the motorway towards, Marbella. As they passed under the familiar white archway, with "*Marbella*" etched into it, Ruby spoke.

"Mummy, are you happy with Dr Alejandro's idea of me speaking to a psychologist?" She was biting her lip.

"Not overly, Ruby. Those people can tend to put ideas into your head. I don't want anyone confusing the issue here. Contrary to what that man believes, Daddy and I are the people who know what's best for you. You're less than sixteen years old – you have your whole life ahead of you. We are not going to allow you to ruin your life." Adele's hand flew up to her mouth and she stifled a sob. "I told my friends I was pregnant yesterday." Tears ran silently down her cheeks as she turned the car into their complex.

"What did they say?" Ruby could feel her heart beating rapidly.

"They were a little surprised to say the least, but of course they all congratulated me and wished me well." As she turned the car off,

Adele leaned against the steering wheel and cried. Her whole body shook as she allowed herself to release her sorrow.

"Oh Mummy, I'm so sorry for putting you and Daddy through all of this. I never meant for this to happen." Ruby joined her mother and burst out crying too. She pictured Damo in her head, how confident he was, his wicked smile and how he made her feel.

Albeit awkwardly, due to the confines of the small car, the two women hugged, patting each other on the backs and rocking from side to side. "We'll be okay, just you see, Daddy and I will make this all right. You go and talk to whatever doctor you need. Do whatever you feel helps. We'll be behind you all the way. I love you, Ruby. No matter what, always remember that." Adele hugged her daughter again, feeling like she was going to die of a broken heart.

Herself and Serena had never been close, but Adele knew she needed to talk to her sister. She felt dreadful about throwing her out of the house, and she knew deep down that the one thing they shared if nothing else was their love for Ruby.

26

tweeting@serenasvelte.com
There is a ball of emotion, sitting in my stomach, threatening to rise and choke me, this is not the way I had it planned, where did I go wrong?

Serena was sitting in the coffee shop around the corner from her house. She'd gone for a walk and the sleet had driven her inside for shelter. She had never felt more hopeless. The shock of Ruby's news was still only sinking in. She'd told Paul the night before and he'd been pretty stunned, but had done the truly male thing and put it in a little recess of his mind and continued to eat his dinner.

"How can you eat at a time like this?" Serena had dropped her cutlery loudly onto the table.

"Don't get me wrong, I'm pretty damn shocked, believe me. But Ruby isn't our kid, I haven't eaten since eight o'clock this morning and at the end of the day, Serena, it's not our problem," Paul had sighed.

Serena had to bite her tongue. There was no point in herself and Paul falling out. It was bad enough that she and Adele were on such bad terms.

"Paul, I honestly don't want to start a row here, but apart from the fact that Ruby is one of my favourite people in the entire universe and she is going through hell on wheels, you are obviously

185

failing to make the connection, that this whole *pregnancy*," she balked at the word, "issue might just touch a raw nerve with me." She could feel the tears welling up in her eyes.

"What? Oh right. Sorry. I know it must be hard for you. But Adele and Harry will do what's best for Ruby and you'll be pregnant before you know it. Sure, the two kids can grow up together. It'll all work out, you'll see," Paul took her hand and tried to mollify her.

"If only it was all that simple, Paul!" She pulled her hand away, scraped her chair back and stormed upstairs, slamming the door behind her.

It was months since Serena had been in hospital for her little operation. She'd felt tired and sore for quite a while afterwards. She'd heard the anaesthetic took quite a while to leave your system, so she was prepared for that. But she really thought she'd be pregnant by now. This issue with Ruby was the final straw. She had to make things move along more quickly. Sulking in the bedroom and fighting with Paul wasn't helping. She splashed cold water on her face and marched back to the kitchen, where Paul was finishing his dinner.

"What do you think we should do about the baby issue?" she demanded as he took a mouthful of wine.

"Erm, well . . ." He tried not to snort the wine out his nose as he reluctantly tuned into the conversation. Being a man, he wasn't very good at all this baby talk. Really, he would prefer if Serena wouldn't mention things like that but he couldn't bear to see her upset. At the end of the day, if she wanted a baby then that's what she should have.

"I mean, after the operation, I thought I'd be pregnant by now but it's dragging on a terribly long time, don't you think?" She plopped down on a chair and faced him.

"Yep, absolutely. So what will we do about it?" He hadn't thought about how long it was taking at all. He just enjoyed the trying to get pregnant part. As long as that didn't stop, he was happy enough.

"Well, would you consider going to a fertility clinic to be tested?

I'll arrange it all. It could be on a Monday or whatever day suits you. What do you think?"

She was looking at him with big green eyes, like Bambi searching for his mother. Instinctively, he wanted to yell, *"Fuck no, I'm not going to sit with anybody in a white coat, who wants to poke my man bits or discuss what I do with them!"* Every man knew about the plastic bottle and the cubicle with the dog-eared dirty mags. He just knew that after the awkward questions he'd have to go into a room on his own and produce a sample. What if he turned out to be firing blanks? What then? Would Serena leave him? She was still looking at him, he realised.

"I suppose I'll go, if that makes you happy," he said, trying to smile.

The inevitable happened. Serena was her usual efficient self and managed to get Paul an appointment almost immediately. That was how, exactly a week later, Paul found himself in a room with an armchair and not much else. At least, with the development in technology, there was a flat-screen TV and a selection of movies.

"Just chose a movie and when you're finished, pop the sample jar into the small hatch over here." The nurse pointed to a kind of tabernacle in the wall.

Doing lots of coughing and not much talking, Paul grimaced at the lady and stood in the room, wishing he could be anywhere else on the planet. At his request, Serena was not with him.

"Ah no, don't come," he had said. "I'd prefer to get it all done on my own. I'm not very good at this kind of thing, so it would be easier if I can eat, shoot and leave as the joke goes." He was trying to sound nonchalant about the whole thing. In reality, he'd never found anything so difficult in his life. If it were for anybody except Serena, he'd have told them where to go. But, he knew the lack of a baby in their home was pure torture for his wife, so he had to do his bit.

Selecting *Sexy Sirens*, he put the DVD into the machine. The sound burst out of the tiny surround-sound speakers.

"Fucking hell!" He nearly jumped out of his skin with fright. He tried to find a remote control to turn it down a bit. There was none to be found, so he cringingly went about his business.

It was more difficult than he'd ever anticipated. He was also terrified someone would walk in, although he figured he would hardly be arrested, seeing as he was doing this for medicinal reasons.

What felt like hours later, he managed to produce a sample. He placed it in the tabernacle, shut the little wooden door and strode across the room to leave. Then a fresh fear came over him. What if he met someone he knew from business or one of their friends? Terrified to come out of the room, he broke into a sweat. Glancing at his watch, he realised he was late for a meeting. Closing his eyes and taking a deep breath, he pulled the door open. As he strode towards the reception desk, the nurse greeted him.

"All done?" she boomed, smiling.

What the hell was she smiling about? And why did she have to shout so loudly? Did nobody ever tell her that this was all dreadfully cringe-worthy? Just because she worked here and was used to it didn't mean it was normal.

"Yes, thank you. I'd better be off now. Late for a meeting and all that." Paul didn't meet her gaze. Jesus, she was like Barbie on acid, all made up and loud and bouncy. It was so bright and shiny everywhere. Paul couldn't wait to get out.

"We'll be in touch. Give us about three weeks before you phone in, all right?" She smiled wildly again.

"Great, super. Thanks, bye now." Paul ran out the door like a scalded cat. He hoped to Christ his sample produced healthy little buggers. If they told him he had to ever step foot in that place again, he'd have to contemplate chopping his todger off. Anything would be preferable to being submitted to the overly pleasant nurses and that awful room. He wished he'd worn a false moustache and glasses that morning.

As he sat into the car, his mobile rang.

"Hi darling, how did you get on?" Serena asked.

"It was hideous, Serena. Please don't ask me to go there ever again," he barked.

"Poor darling, were they rude to you?" she soothed.

"No, no, quite the opposite, alarmingly enough. I just found the whole place creepy and invasive. They ask far too many questions and they smile too much." He shuddered as he sped out of the place.

"Well done all the same, honey. I really appreciate you doing all this. Let's hope everything's all right," Serena oozed.

Well, if it wasn't, if all his fishies were as dead as dodos, then so be it. He wasn't going to discuss it right at that moment in time, but as far as he was concerned he was finished with all that stuff. If Serena wanted a baby that badly and she wasn't getting pregnant by conventional methods, they could adopt. Plenty of people did that. It would be much simpler. They could fill in some forms and get a baby. It couldn't be that difficult. There must be millions of babies looking for a good home. He'd bide his time and, if the problem continued, he'd make that suggestion. Or, he fleetingly thought, maybe they could have Ruby's baby? That would kill two birds with one stone.

Serena put down the phone from Paul and cried. She knew he hated the idea of the fertility clinic. She was so grateful that he'd gone at all. She'd been terrified he'd make an excuse and not go. He was a darling to do it all for her. She sincerely hoped everything would be all right. She hoped for Paul's sake that the problem didn't lie with him. She didn't want him to be angry and resent her for making him get tested. She'd heard of relationships breaking down when one person was deemed infertile.

27

tweeting@angiebaby.com
*I feel like a beach ball with eyes. Should I just wear a duvet
cover or is it actually possible to feel "normal" while pregnant?*

Angie was just about to leave the office for the night, when her
mobile phone rang.

"Hello, this is Una from the maternity hospital in Dublin. Can I
speak with Angie Breen, please?"

"Speaking." Angie had a sudden wave of fear. Please God don't
let there be a problem with the baby. Don't let them have found
some awful disease in my blood.

"Great, I'm in charge of co-ordinating the antenatal classes here
at the hospital. I am trying to organise a single mums' class and was
wondering if Thursday nights would suit you? I see you have your
name down for evening rather than weekend classes."

"Yes, that's right, Thursday is fine with me. How many people
usually join each class?" Angie was suddenly a bit nervous.

"Well, I have four others confirmed so far – we probably won't
make it any more than six." She sounded cheerful. "So I'll see you
here next Thursday at seven thirty all going well."

"Okay," said Angie and hung up.

She hated that "all going well" phrase they all used. It implied that she might have a miscarriage at any moment or that she might be hit by a bus before next week.

Still, she couldn't help feeling a quick flutter of excitement. Especially now that her parents and friends knew about the pregnancy.

Knowing she had no groceries, she stopped off in the local supermarket. Taking a convenience trolley or "a sad-bastard trolley" as Rachel dubbed them, she slumped around trying to pick nutritious and healthy items. Of course that all went horribly wrong when she found herself on the biscuit aisle. She'd never particularly like biscuits until she'd become pregnant, but now it was like they called and waved at her when she saw them. Deciding she deserved a few treats, she stuffed a couple of packets of Jaffa Cakes into the trolley. Knowing that there was no way in hell she was going to start cooking a meal from scratch, she made her way to the ready-meal section. Just as she'd put a few dinners into the trolley, she stopped dead. She got such a shock she felt the room spin. The bright strip lighting was dazzling and the corny panpipe music slurred in her head.

Dressed in a sludgy green parka with fur around the hood, brown cords and mangy suede shoes, muttering to himself, there was Troy.

Rooted to the spot for several seconds, Angie made a slightly squeaky whimpering noise. *"Fuck, fuck, fuck,"* she babbled, as she tried to turn the SB trolley around. Of course it was one of those ones with a mind of its own, so the back wheel flipped out and ran over her tocs. Hopping and cursing she booted around the corner to the next aisle. Just as she thought she could exhale, she saw him rounding the other corner.

"Bollox," she whispered. The only thing for it was to abandon the trolley altogether. Pulling up the collar of her coat, as if that would work as a disguise, she tucked her bag under her arm and walked away. Vowing to invest in a moustache and glasses kit, she made her way outside.

Terrified he would appear soon, she flagged a taxi and jumped in. She only lived five minutes away from the supermarket so she was sure the driver was cursing her.

Feeling safer at home, she sat on the sofa and tried to calm down. She was fairly sure Troy hadn't spotted her, but it had been too close for comfort. What the hell would she have said if he'd seen her? She'd have to be ready with a lie if she ran into him again. There she was thinking Dublin was this big impersonal place, where nobody knew anybody else, yet she'd nearly been caught out.

Men are pretty thick when it comes to pregnancy and that kind of thing, she thought. Troy would probably never put two and two together. Even if he did, she could say she was only three months gone, as opposed to well into her second trimester. She could drop in a name of a new boyfriend. He'd buy it surely?

After dialling for a takeaway, she phoned Rachel. They hadn't spoken for weeks, which happened from time to time. It was high time she told her.

After making her announcement, Angie held the phone away from her ear.

"You're fucking joking! I can't believe you're up the pole!" Rachel was shocked and surprised. "Who's the father? Are you still together?"

"No, he was one of the American crew, he's gone back to the States," she ventured. "I'm not going to tell him."

"What! Ange, you can't do that, girl. Jesus, just because he lives thousands of miles away doesn't give you the right to keep him in the dark like that. That's iffy beyond belief. I'd rethink that one if I were you. What are you going to do when the kid's older and wants to know where its daddy is?"

Rachel sounded stunned. If she only knew the truth, she'd have a complete conniption. It confounded the fact for Angie that she'd have to keep the father's identity to herself.

Everyone else seemed to think she was wrong to keep father and child apart. But at the end of the day, she was the mother, and she thought she was doing the right thing.

She slept very fitfully that night. Images of Troy flashed through her mind. The baby must have known she was uneasy, as it kicked the living daylights out of her all night. By the time the alarm clock went off at six, she felt like she'd done five rounds with Mike Tyson.

Peeling herself out of bed, she felt almost hung over. She knew Rachel would have spread the news of her pregnancy. She was the equivalent of the *News of the World* when it came to gossip. In a way it was a relief, it saved her having to tell everyone.

"The secret's out, Baba." She patted her tummy. When the baby responded with a swift kick, she laughed out loud. Sod it, she thought. Nothing in the world matters more than this baby. The rest of the world can bugger off. I'm having this little person in my life. I'm going to cherish and love it and nobody is going to dissuade me from doing what I feel is right.

By now it was the last week of April. Even though it was still cold, the light had changed, and Angie's winter woollies seemed too heavy. She decided she'd better go and invest in some maternity wear.

Managing to escape from the office for a while, she skipped into one of the many maternity boutiques in Dublin. The first one was too scary. The clothes were utterly vile. The tent meets Granny's curtain-fabric look. She wasn't that huge yet, she just looked a bit like the girl who ate all the pies. When she tried on some of the tents in the shop, she looked and felt awful.

Stepping into another shop, she felt her heart quicken. The clothes were gorgeous. Nicer than the stuff she'd been looking at for "normal" people. The girls were so cheerful and helpful.

"You'll need a couple of outfits for work, so let's mix and match. If you're careful, you'll be able to muddle through on maybe five items," the assistant beamed.

Why did the assistant have to look like a stick insect? Mind you, the whole world looked skinny when you were carting a beer belly around with you.

"I knew my tummy would grow, of course I did, but nobody told me that everywhere else expands too." Angie turned to the side to scrutinise herself.

"I'll just give you this pillow to pop under the top, to give you an idea of how that suit will expand with your growing shape." The stick insect passed her a squishy round blob.

With the padding in place, Angie felt like she was going to vomit.

"Sweet Jesus, tell me I'm not going to look like this," she whined. She looked like an elephant. The cushion made her look enormous.

"No, no, of course not. Nobody gets that big. It's just to give you an idea," the stick insect lied badly.

"Right, I'll take the black suit. Do you make lagging jackets in summer fabric? I need something that will make me feel thin. I reckon the bigger the tent I put on the smaller I'll feel." Angie surveyed the flimsy summer print dresses on the hanger in the dressing room.

"Actually, if you wear more fitted things, you'll feel and look a better shape. If you go for the loose fitting draped look –"

"I'll look like a pumped-up hippo?" Angie finished. Even her hands and feet were looking like dough balls. If she looked like this now, what the hell was she going to look like towards the end? She'd have to invest in one of those electronic disability carts to get her from A to B.

"Once you can't see your feet anymore, you know you're well on your way," the other assistant piped up, smiling.

Angie felt miserable. It must have been a sudden rush of hormones, but she felt uncharacteristically touchy and narky with the shop assistant. Why the hell was she smiling like that too? Was she a sadist? Did she work in this shop to make herself feel thinner and more gorgeous? A good idea, fair enough, but not at my expense thanks. Willing herself to think pleasant thoughts Angie tried to look neutral rather than scathing.

"On my first, I thought the pregnancy would never end. You kind of forget what you looked like before, don't you?" the assistant said.

"Have you had more than one?" Angie regarded the svelte blonde with the shiny red nails and unlined skin.

"I've three at home. The reason I set up the shop was because the clothes that were available when I was pregnant on my first were so awful. I felt suicidal by the time I was due. I shuffled into the hospital in my sack dress, feeling about as attractive as a bout of cold sores. I vowed, if I survived the birth, I'd open a trendy maternity store."

The fact that this modellesque creature had done this insane body expansion three times over and still looked like that, made Angie want to shake her. Instead, she let the lady pick out some pretty outfits. The girls oohed and ahhed at Angie and told her she looked stunning.

"I just won't look in the mirror too much. I get a shock every time I see myself. I forget that I've expanded until I go into the bathroom at work or walk by a shop window. I think, Christ who's that fat cow, and realise it's me," she finished, looking a bit ashamed for all the moaning.

"I know how you feel," the stick insect joined in. "I used to scare myself too. But believe me, you can bounce back afterwards and look just the way you did before. My daughter is only six months old and I'm already back in my jeans."

Angie knew she was trying to be reassuring and kind, but she just made her want to kill herself. But then again, Angie had never looked like this girl. Even when she was swaying langers drunk in front of a mirror in a semi-darkened nightclub, she knew she didn't look like her.

At least she didn't have to take her clothes off in front of a man at the moment. That was beyond her. How did women in relationships manage looking and feeling like this? She was briefly grateful that she wasn't going to be scrutinised by any man.

She cast her mind back to a work colleague in Cork who'd come into work crying one morning, because her husband had made a joke about her being like a walking mountain. The thought of it filled her with anger. How dare that git talk to his wife like that! By the time she'd fumbled back into her clothes, her face had taken on a nice purple hue. Okay calm down, relax, deep breathing, she told herself. There was no point in having an epileptic fit over an event which had happened years ago – to someone else.

Christ, her hormones really were working on overtime. Another plus point for not being in a relationship currently. She'd probably end up on her own anyway, if there was someone there to fight with – she reckoned she'd be tearing his eyes out right now.

Glancing at her watch, Angie realised she'd been in the shop for over an hour. Paying quickly, she rushed back to the office. She'd told her bosses the previous day about the baby. She'd been met with the goldfish stare, followed by a smug, "typical-women" type look.

"Well, I suppose it was just a matter of time. All the good women go off to have babies at some stage," one of the Americans piped up.

"Well, I suppose the population might just cease if we didn't, and seeing as men haven't yet mastered giving birth, we women will just have to continue, won't we?" Her eyes widened and her lips pursed.

There was a brief silence in the room, until one of the men remembered his manners.

"Erm, congratulations by the way. When is the happy event?" he ventured.

"I'm due at the beginning of July, so it won't mess up this deal, if that's your concern." She felt like blubbing and running out of the room.

"That wasn't what I was getting at, honestly. That's truly wonderful news, Angie. Your husband must be very proud," he said, trying to soothe the mood.

"Thank you, and I don't have a partner. I'll be raising this child on my own." Her heart was beating like thunder as all eyes turned to her. Although they were all spending a lot of time in the office together, because she was the only female they never had personal chats. She knew nothing about any of the men and they knew even less about her.

"Oh right, sure. Of course, excuse me. I shouldn't have assumed." Her colleague coughed awkwardly.

"Let's just get on with our work," said Angie. "You all know now that I'm not just eating too many pies. My work won't be affected and I'll be able to finish out most of my contract. The only thing I will ask is that I can attend my gynaecologist. That will only be every three weeks at most." She hated mentioning baby doctors in a room of men, but what could she do?

"Oh yes, for sure."

"Absolutely."

"No problem there."

They all muttered and it was obvious to everyone in the room that the "baby" discussion was well and truly over with.

It was astonishing to Angie but ever since she'd told them, the men were treating her differently. Just like today. She said she was popping out for a few minutes, which she never did. She was met with a chorus of "of courses" and the men then averted their eyes.

"I'd swear they think I'm going to give birth on the desk," she laughed to Rachel when she called her.

"You should hold your tummy and make grunting noises, and then wave your hand and yell, 'Sorry! False alarm!'" Rachel laughed.

By the time she was back at her desk, with her shopping bags stuffed under her coat in the cloakroom, she felt happier. When she sat down now, the baby bump kind of sat on her lap. The baby was kicking all the time, especially when she was either sitting or lying down.

On cue, the baby had a lovely little dance. Angie instinctively put her hand on her abdomen. The phones rang, the computers whirred and the office continued to run. Nobody else in the whole world could feel this little person. Only she and the baby were connected. Yet again, Angie thanked God for giving her this chance to be a mother.

28

tweeting@rubytuesday.com
My life is in the toilet, in every sense of the word, I am too old to be young, and too young to be old.

R uby was doing the thing she spent most of her day doing at the moment – peeing. Even if she didn't drink much water or Diet Coke, it made no difference. She'd tried everything but the pee just kept coming. All night she was up and down to the bathroom like a yo-yo. The baby was kicking all the time now too.

Their ten days in Spain were almost up, as she arrived back at the clinic to see Dr Alejandro before returning home to Ireland.

"Hello Ruby, come on in and sit down. This is the last time I will see you for a while. Your mother tells me you will return when you are thirty-two weeks. So I am interested to know, how did you get on with my colleague, Dr Miguel, the psychologist?"

"Okay, I suppose." Ruby looked at the floor.

Dr Alejandro felt desperately sorry for the thin pale and terribly scared little girl who was sitting in front of him.

"Did you talk to him?" he probed.

"A little. He asked me if I was happy about giving my baby to my parents." She picked at a loose thread on the sleeve of her hoody.

198

"And what did you tell him?" Dr Alejandro leaned forward. He was very concerned about this whole issue. He felt the poor girl was being pushed into relinquishing her baby. She was very young, ideally she was not ready to be a mother, but sometimes life wasn't ideal. He felt strongly that her parents needed to give her a chance to make up her own mind.

"I told him that my parents are only doing what's best for me and the baby. If they didn't care it would be worse." She didn't make eye contact with the doctor. Her thin face looked drawn and her shoulders slumped. The defensive pout and slumped teenage posture only made her seem more pitiable. "It's my birthday today. I'm sixteen." She kept her eyes on the floor.

"Happy birthday! I'm sorry – I should have noticed from your notes." He smiled kindly.

"I'm not exactly having the type of birthday I'd envisaged. I haven't heard from any of my friends, my parents are both treating me like a criminal and, to top it all off, the highlight of the entire day is an appointment. Sorry, I don't mean to be rude to you." She flicked her eyes up to his for a moment.

"I'm sorry you're having such a bad day. But, Ruby, remember you have a right to say what you want to do." Dr Alejandro stood up motioned to her to lie on the examination table, so he could check her pulse and feel her tummy.

She had never been big into food. She wasn't a junk-food merchant and wasn't overly interested in sweets. But since she'd been pregnant, she didn't feel like eating at all. She had to force herself to eat. Breakfast was usually a glass of water and a piece of dry toast. If she finished a sandwich or a bowl of paella at lunch she was doing well. She picked at a salad or piece of grilled chicken at teatime. Even the Easter egg her parents had given her was still sitting unopened in its box.

"You need to try and eat more, Ruby. You're very thin." Dr Alejandro held her gaze. As he checked the baby, he could see her ribs above the bump. Her pelvis was visible and the tops of her arms were like sticks. Under the T-shirt she was wearing, he could see her collar-bones protruding and her shoulders poking upwards.

"The baby will be fine. Babies just take from the mother. That is how even women in famine countries can deliver babies. The baby will even take from your bone marrow if it has to. But you must try to build yourself up a bit. You need to have your strength for the birth and afterwards," he ventured gently.

"The birth will be one day, after that my mother will take the baby, so I can relax and take it easy. I won't be like other mothers. I won't have a baby to take care of." She kept her eyes averted as she spoke.

"Have you any more questions?" Dr Alejandro felt dreadfully sad. He wanted to hug the poor child and make her feel better.

"Why am I getting these marks?" she asked shyly.

"They are actually bruises, because the baby is kicking you so much. You are very thin and because you are so young, your own body is still growing, so the baby doesn't have so much room to move."

Ruby liked Dr Alejandro. He spoke to her in a normal way. He treated her like an adult.

"Is there anything else I can help you with today?" Dr Alejandro stood patiently waiting for her to speak.

Ruby longed to ask him a hundred and one questions. He looked to be around Damo's age. He might be able to give her a few tips on how to make sure Damo wanted to stay with her forever. But it was all too dicey and, besides, he might tell her mother.

By the time she came out to the waiting room, Adele was getting impatient. What on earth were they doing in there? Why was all this taking so long?

Adele ushered Ruby out of the hospital. Everywhere they went, now that Ruby was getting bigger, people stared. She wasn't the type of sixteen-year-old who could pass for twenty. She was child-like, with an elfin face and big frightened eyes. Away from the influence of her friends, she'd lost any sign of cockiness and, due to the heat, she wasn't wearing make-up. She was also reduced to vest tops and stretchy skirts or tracksuit bottoms and flip-flops.

"Why don't we buy you some pretty maternity dresses?" Adele suggested. "We're going back to Ireland tomorrow, and you'll need some loose clothing. Let's try a maternity shop and see if there's anything you like."

"I'm not going into one of those shops. The stuff is for older women. I feel gross enough without looking like a total loser. And I don't want maternity clothes for my birthday present," Ruby sulked.

"I'm not suggesting you get the clothes as your present. We could go to the jeweller's too and get you a nice necklace." Adele tried to remain upbeat. She felt like pointing out that the shop catered for older women due to the fact that they were the correct age for having babies. But she bit her tongue. There was no point in having another row, especially on Ruby's birthday. "But you might find something more comfortable."

"Mum, just get off my case. I'm doing what you asked. Keeping our dirty little secret. I'll go along with all that, because it's my own fault. But I won't look like dork in front of my school friends just to please you." Ruby's eyes flashed, the anger and resentment flooding from her every pore.

Adele was shocked and taken back by the venom her daughter obviously wanted to pour all over her. She took a deep breath. "I've spoken to your father about school, Ruby. Your bump has grown too big. We're going to get you a tutor when we go home. Just for the few weeks that are left before we come back here for the birth. School would be too dicey – you're very obviously pregnant now. So at least you won't have to worry about things being awkward with your school pals." Adele waited for another explosion from Ruby.

"Whatever." Ruby shrugged and put on her don't-talk-to-me-anymore face.

Not for the first time, Adele wondered if they'd ever get through this. Would their lives ever be happy again? She missed her husband and their friends. She missed living her normal life. Being able to interact with people in a natural way. They were all living such a web of lies, she was afraid to even talk to her friends too much. She'd alienated Serena and she hadn't even told her parents. The pressure was building. She felt she was a bubble which was about to pop.

29

I am thinking of changing my name from Damo to Demented . . .

Back in Ireland, Damo was having a hard time keeping things going. The takings in the club were seriously down. This recession was a curse. He'd had a hard enough time dealing with the smoking ban a few years back, without having this whole economic downturn to add to it all.

He'd had a blazing row with Noreen. She'd been sitting up at the kitchen counter, having her usual fag and cup of tea, with a big grin on her face.

"What are you looking so pleased about?" He kissed her on the forehead.

"I was at the bingo with the girls last night and some news has hit the street!"

"Right, what's that then?" Damo had no interest in gossip, but he'd pretend the odd time, to keep Noreen happy. She loved an auld bit of news.

"Well, word is that Ruby's *ma* is pregnant. So Jill was saying. God love them, they're going ahead with adopting the child and raising it themselves. Wouldn't you think in this day and age that they'd just let her have the child and be done with it? Fair enough, they'll end up doing the best part of the rearing, but for crying out loud, why the big hoo-hah?"

"I hope you didn't open your mouth about it all." Damo paced towards her, eyes flashing.

"No, I didn't say a word. I was just delighted with the chat. What's up your arse? Normally you've no interest in anything I tell you, especially if it's gossip." She smiled uneasily.

"What else did Jill say?" Damo was standing at the kitchen island with his clenched fists resting on the marble.

"Since when are you so concerned with other people's business? Ah, I get it. You think I'm going to want to go again, is that it? Or you're afraid that our Mariah is going to go off on one now, looking for a little baby, just 'cause Ruby's getting one," she smirked. "Well, you can relax, Damo. I'm done and dusted. I've enough to deal with, without another babby on the scene, and I've warned Mariah that she needn't come home here with a bun in the oven." She shook her head and flicked on the kettle. "Cuppa?"

She was met with a deadly silence. She turned around and Damo was gone. "Damo?" she called. She heard the front door banging. "Fuckin' men! And they say women are odd!" She opened a packet of chocolate biscuits and sat on a high stool and began to flick through her magazine.

Damo flung the car into reverse and sped out of the driveway. He'd no idea where he was going but he had to get away from Noreen. So the word was out. That bitch of a mother of Ruby's was going ahead with the lies and taking that baby for her own. That was okay but his child would be growing up right under his nose. He wasn't sure how he felt about that.

He thumped the steering wheel. He didn't need this bleedin' complication. He'd enough going on, he had a family, he hadn't asked for all this hassle. For the first time in his life he felt the need to get pissed. Not just a bit merry, but rat-arsed. Out of his tree. Blotto. He turned his Merc towards Blackrock. He'd go to the club and have a few pints. None of the staff would be there for a few hours, so he'd have the place to himself. Glancing at his watch, he saw it was only four o'clock. Usually in a time of stress he'd opt for a quick line of coke. It would steady his nerves and give him a little pep in his step. But he didn't feel like the clean hit his coke gave him. What he needed now, was the obliterated sensation he'd witnessed so many punters displaying night after night in the club, from too much alcohol.

He parked the car outside The Orb and went in. The smell of stale booze and sweat hit him when he opened the side door. The windowless building was shabby-looking without the coloured disco lights. The carpets were covered in sticky black stains and stamped-in chewing gum. The seats, which he'd had recovered only last year, were manky too. The dance floor was the only semi-clean place. The wooden floorboards were painted with high shine varnish, to reflect the lights.

Striding behind the bar he grabbed a pint glass. Fuck it, he needed a quicker hit. Putting it back, he pulled down a wine glass from the slotted rack above his head. Shoving it under the wall-mounted alcohol dispenser, he took a double shot of vodka. Taking a deep breath, he raised the glass to his lips and jerkily downed the booze.

"Fuck, that's disgusting!" He thumped the bar. Within fifteen minutes he'd forced himself to drink a further three measures. Knowing he'd be sick if he kept going, he poured himself a pint. As he tilted the glass and guided the amber liquid down the side of the tumbler, he was brought back to the time when he'd started out. Before he owned his own bars and clubs. Before he lived in a posh house. Before he drove a big Merc. Before he'd ever done a line of coke. Before he'd fucked up his life, he realised with bitter disappointment.

With the pint in his hand, he strode towards the office. Leaning against the doorjamb, he closed his eyes and rubbed his face with his free hand. When had he become such a stupid bastard? All the money, the girls, the drugs, the cars. Hanging around with stars, being the main man – it had all gone to his head.

He drank his pint, spilling it on the front of his shirt and all over the floor. With force, he threw the glass at the far wall. The noise of it smashing was great. "Yeah! That's more like it!" he yelled. He picked up the table next and flung it across the room. It hit the wall and one of the legs cracked the plaster. Curling into a ball and lying on his side in the foetal position, he held his head in his hands and cried like he'd never done before.

30

tweeting@maternityunit.com
A healthy mum is a happy mum, remember your 30 mins of exercise every day!

The hospital was warm and smelled of disinfectant. The faint crying of babies and general hustle and bustle added to the expectant atmosphere that oozed from every corridor. Ruby followed the signs for the second floor. Just behind her, another pregnant lady seemed to be shadowing her.

"Sorry, I'm not stalking you – are you going to the antenatal classes too?"

Ruby thought she looked fairly easygoing. She had a country accent. "Yes, it's my first time." Ruby felt all shy and embarrassed.

"I'm Angie, by the way."

"I'm Ruby."

The two women shook hands.

"I'm kind of thankful I didn't hear any anguished cries or pain-filled yells," Angie confided as they entered the room, the three other women who'd already arrived looked up at them.

Feeling suddenly shy, they took a seat.

"When are you due?" A girl who looked no more than about twelve asked Ruby, totally ignoring Angie. She was wearing a tracksuit and was going for the bump-out-for-all-to-see look. Chewing her gum and staring at Ruby, she waited for a reply.

"I'm due the first week in July, what about yourself?"

"Middle of June. What about yourself, love?" She nodded her head towards Angie.

"I'm actually due the first week in July too, funnily enough." Angie smiled at Ruby.

"Ah Jaysus, that means I'm up first. All the rest here," she gestured towards the others, "are due in July like yourselves."

The other women, one who looked around Angie's age and another who looked a little younger, waved awkwardly. Luckily, a midwife burst through the door and took over.

"Hiya, ladies, I'm Una. I think I spoke to most of you on the phone. What we normally do is a quick fly around the class, you all introduce yourselves and then we go for a wee trot around the relevant wards. Who wants to go first?" She dumped a pile of paperwork onto a desk and looked up, while trying to straighten her hair and fix her clothes. "Sorry, it's been one of those days and I'm like I've been dragged through a hedge backwards. Maybe you'd like to introduce yourselves as I get a bit more organised. Just your name and when you're due and anything else you might like to add."

"I'll go first." The young girl stood up, full of confidence. "I'm Leona and this is my first. I'm eighteen and from a family of six. I live in the flats quite close to the hospital. Two of my sisters have babies at home. When this one pops out, we're going to try and get another flat off the council. Me ma's place is burstin' at the seams already. But what can ya do?" She seemed cheerful and accepting about the baby coming. "I've no da for this baby on the scene. He fucked off the second he heard I'd a bun in the oven. Prick!"

"Erm, right. That's lovely, Leona. Good girl, you sit yourself down there. Who would like to go next?" Una looked a little shocked to say the least.

"I'm Angie and I'm on my own too. It didn't work out with the baby's father. My baby is due in July and I can't wait."

"Great, thank you, Angie." Una relaxed a little. "Who's next?"

"I'm Sandra," said one of the others. "I actually have a husband but he won't come with me to these classes, so that's why I'm on my own."

"Well, that's actually more common than you might think, Sandra. I know society expects the men to attend all births these days, but some of them are better off elsewhere. We'll look after you all, so none of you need worry, when the time comes." Una was a bit more organised by this time.

"I'm Ruby. I'm on my own because the dad lives abroad." Ruby barely stood up and spoke just above a whisper.

"Good girl, Ruby, thank you." Una smiled warmly at her.

"I'm Brenda. I'm here on my own because my husband died," a small blonde girl said quietly. She looked exhausted and haunted.

"That's so sad, what happened?" Angie felt a rush of sympathy for the poor girl.

"Cancer. It was all very quick. He was only diagnosed two months ago. He died three weeks later." She shrugged and tried to smile.

"Now, that's fuckin' rough. By the sounds of it, our lot are just spineless, but your fella dyin' is a terrible thing. God love ya, you win. No arguing with that." Leona shook her head and exhaled loudly.

In spite of the sadness, all of the women cracked up laughing.

"Ah sorry, love, I've a mouth like a foghorn – me ma is always tellin' me to keep me trap shut. I didn't mean to upset anyone. Sorry, girls," Leona raised her eyes to heaven, "trust me to drop a clanger."

Luckily, Leona had managed to break the ice. As they all moved out of the classroom towards the pre-labour wards, they all felt connected with each other already. None of the areas contained labouring women, so they weren't subjected to any animalistic noises, but the tour was still quite scary despite the fact the purpose of it was to make them feel more secure and relaxed.

Back in the safety of the classroom, the midwife showed them a skeleton and pushed a doll through the pelvis, demonstrating how the bones move to allow baby through.

By the end of the hour and a half, all the women were quiet, with slightly green complexions.

"Jaysus, all that birth stuff makes me terrible squeamish." Leona piped up. "Hey, anyone fancy going for a drink?"

Shyly the other women regarded each other and nodded. A short stroll from the hospital, the five women waddled into the nearest bar. Used to seeing heavily pregnant women and celebrating fathers, the barman greeted them warmly.

"Two Diet Cokes and three sparkling waters, please," Angie ordered.

There was an awkward silence for a few seconds, until the barman came with the drinks.

"Well, girls, one way or the other, we're on our own, as per fucking usual. Men are fucking useless, but we'll soldier on. To women!" Leona raised her glass.

In spite of the fact that they'd only just met and barely knew each other, their "condition" was pulling them together. They all smiled and clinked glasses.

"As long as we don't all vomit after listening to Nurse Freak-show, with her birthing skeleton," Leona went on. "Jaysus, she's a face like a slapped arse. I'll bet she's never even had a shag, never mind a baby. I don't know if we need to know all this stuff. I'm just planning on taking every drug they have on offer. Her with her 'wait and see how you feel'! Fuck that! How the hell does she think it's going to feel? There's no million-euro reward and no fucking medals. Drugs, drugs and more drugs. That's what I think, anyway!"

Nobody could keep a straight face with Leona around. She said it like it was and anyone who didn't agree could hump off, as far as she was concerned. Downing her Diet Coke, she announced that she had to leave.

"See yous next week, girls, nice meeting yous," she said, then waved and bounded off.

"God she's a scream, isn't she?" Brenda laughed.

"She certainly is! She's got the right attitude. But I wouldn't like to cross her," Sandra giggled.

"I was worried I'd be ten years younger than everyone else," Ruby smiled, "and I was so terrified of drawing attention to myself. I needn't have worried!"

The others regarded her. She was like a little elf, petite and delicate, and obviously very well brought up, with a soft South Dublin accent. She looked out of place in the city-centre pub.

"I'd better go," she said. "My mum is collecting me and she'll be worried if I'm not outside the hospital." She shrugged her shoulders.

"Say no if it doesn't suit you all, but seeing as we're going through all this together, would anybody be interested in going for a pizza after the class next week?" Angie asked quickly.

Ruby's face lit up. "I'd love to."

"Sounds like a great plan," Sandra smiled.

"Yes, count me in too. I can do with all the support I can muster right now," Brenda said.

The ladies said goodbye and went their separate ways. Angie was delighted to have met them. Although she wasn't going to be living in Dublin after the baby was born, it would be nice to have some other women in the same position between now and then. If nothing else, she felt, Leona would keep them entertained.

31

tweeting@serenasvelte.com
Grub, girlies, gargle, gossip, oh yeah, bring it on . . .

Serena put the finishing touches to her make-up and stepped back to look in the full-length mirror in her dressing room. Her Seven jeans sculpted her long legs and, teamed with brown high boots and a faux fox-fur cropped jacket, made her look stylish and elegant.

Slipping her pearl and diamond earrings into her lobes, she grabbed her Gucci handbag and strode out the door. Her taxi was waiting to take her to restaurant Patrick Guilbaud, a wonderful Michelin-starred restaurant in Dublin city. She was meeting three friends for a long lunch – Noelle (her apparent VBF), Julie and Patricia.

She sincerely hoped they wouldn't ask her about babies. Herself and Paul weren't even that long married, but it didn't seem to stop people. She was astonished at the snide little dropped hints, here and there.

"Any pitter-patter of tiny feet yet?" the wife of a colleague had asked her, in the middle of a bloody function.

A sea of faces had turned to stare at her expectantly.

"Not at all, sure we're only married a wet week. We haven't even thought of going down that road yet!" She'd waved her hand in the air to appear nonchalant. Inside she felt like yelling: "For your information, I've been under the knife, we're going to a fertility specialist and I can hardly breathe I want a baby so badly, you nosy bitch!"

She knew people didn't mean to be nasty, but fertility problems were rife these days. Surely anyone with an ounce of cop-on would know not to say such a personal thing to another woman? But no, plenty of mean, dozy cows had put her on the spot. None of them would dare say it to Paul, of course – the men never got put in that position.

Serena arrived at the restaurant fifteen minutes early. The gorgeous French waiter took her coat and showed her to a low table surrounded by soft, squishy armchairs.

"A bottle of pink champagne, please. There will be three other women joining me, so if you could bring four glasses. Please open a second bottle when this one runs out, and put the two bottles on this card separately." She handed him her American Express card.

"Of course, Madam." He bowed politely and took her card.

She rubbed her hands together excitedly as she waited for the champagne. She didn't want anyone to object to the price of the bubbly, so this way she'd be able to have a few glasses and not feel guilty. Nothing kicked off a meal like a glass of champers. She quickly texted Ruby to ask how she was. Although she wasn't exactly on brilliant terms with Adele, they had met briefly as she'd collected Ruby for a coffee when they'd returned from Spain.

The Ruby situation was a total disaster. Adele had taken her out of school, and was having a tutor call to the house each day. She wasn't allowed to see any of her friends. She was changing school in September and the poor girl didn't seem to know which end was up. Serena had promised to take Ruby to an out-of-the-way area for a bit of diversion, where nobody they knew would see them.

Ruby had been so thrilled to see her but the second they'd driven off in the car she'd burst into tears.

"I feel like a prisoner. Mum is demented, she has to hide too, or her friends will see she's not pregnant. This whole situation is dreadful, Serena. I'm going to the maternity hospital in the city centre for antenatal classes. The other girls are really nice, and they invited me for pizza after the class next week, but Mum said I can't go, in case I'm seen. I have to go to the class via the back door and come straight out afterwards. I went to the pub for a coke with them last night and Mum went mental. What will I do, Serena?" Ruby had held her head in her hands and bawled.

In the end, Serena had gone to a petrol station, bought takeaway sandwiches and cans of orange, and they'd driven up the mountains for a picnic.

"Do your grandparents know yet?" Serena bit her lip.

"Yes, Mum rang Katie last night while I was at the antenatal class." Ruby pushed the uneaten sandwich back into the clear plastic box and squeezed it shut.

"What happened?" Serena could just imagine her mother, sighing and tutting and acting like the problem was all created just to annoy *her*.

"Mum just told me, yet again, how many people I've disappointed and destroyed with my careless behaviour," Ruby whispered.

Serena had hugged her and told her she would never stop loving her and that she would always stand by her.

"Thanks, Aunt Serena. You'll be the coolest mum when you decide to have babies." Ruby had wiped her eyes. Little did she know but her aunt's fresh outburst of tears was nothing to do with her.

But, being a practical and controlled person, Serena was forcing herself to rise above all these problems. Her friends would be there any minute and they'd expect her to be polished, cheerful and ready to be pleasant. She quickly sent Ruby a little message.

Hope u r ok 2day. Out 4 lunch but text if u need me. Remember I luv u x x S

Serena had put her phone in her bag and had just had her glass topped up for the second time when the girls arrived.

"Helloooo, girls!" Serena was feeling on top of the world. The bubbles were working their magic. She'd enjoyed sitting by herself and relaxing in the opulent surroundings. She was now more than ready for chats. "Come and have a wee drinkie. I've been tasting the pink champagne, just to make sure it's all right for you all." She air-kissed her friends amidst plenty of squealing and complimenting. "You're all looking gorgeous as usual! Sit down. Oh, Noelle, you brat, new Gucci handbag?" Serena admired the buttery soft leather shoulder-bag.

"An eye like a hawk this one has, doesn't miss a beat," Noelle teased, thrilled her new purchase hadn't gone unnoticed. "I did the dog on it too!" She pointed a perfectly formed false nail towards the floor. Swivelling her foot on a pointy heel, she showed off the matching boots.

"Ooh-la-la," Serena exclaimed, "who's been a naughty girl?"

"I know I just had to but Nigel is going to have a face like a slapped arse when the credit-card bill rolls in. I'll have to make sure I look after him well this month, if you know what I mean!" She winked and giggled.

After the two bottles of champagne, the ladies moved into the dining room. They ordered their food and bottles of red and white wine.

It was all going swimmingly until Noelle mentioned Lucinda.

"How are you getting on with her? Isn't it such a relief to have a live-in helper?" She arched an eyebrow.

"Yes, Lucinda is a dote. She's so helpful, especially when I have to entertain for Paul at home. The house is always spotless and she's a whiz at the whole waitressing thing. You were such a sweetie to put her my way." Serena smiled, uneasily sensing there was more to come.

"So, now that you have some help in place, will you be joining us on the mummy front?" Noelle blinked innocently while smiling widely.

Serena felt like she'd been punched. She actually surprised herself at how taken aback she was at the question. "Who knows, sweetie? I might just decide to spoil myself for a little while longer. I mean I adore the thought of a little Paul running around, don't get me wrong, but I'm having such a blast right now, I feel a baby might burst my bubble. Besides I always have Ruby to spoil and keep me company. Does that sound dreadfully selfish of me?" She smiled but inside she was seething. She felt like slapping that bitch's smug face.

Her front worked. Noelle wiped the smile off her face and fiddled with her hair self-consciously.

"Oh, right. I see, well no, of course you could never be selfish, darling. It's just I thought you might be thinking along the baby lines, but you have all the time in the world. You're not even in your thirties yet. Nowadays that's still very young to start a family." She sniffed. "Just because I wanted to have my first before I was thirty doesn't mean everyone thinks that way."

Sensing the growing tension, Julie interjected. "Has anyone been to Lake Como? We're thinking of going this summer."

As the conversation turned towards holidays and everyone became well and truly engrossed, Serena excused herself.

"I'm just going to the ladies', excuse me."

Walking calmly from the restaurant, she made her way to the bar, which was conveniently en route to the toilets.

"A double brandy, please," she demanded, while rooting in her bag for cash. Shoving a fifty-euro note at the barman, she tapped her nails on the counter impatiently, while looking towards the restaurant in case one of the girls was following her.

The barman, as it was a Michelin-star establishment, was placing a paper doily down, followed by a little glass jug of water, before placing a large balloon-shaped glass in front of Serena.

"Come on, come on," she muttered. As soon as the amber liquid was poured into the glass, she snatched it and took a large gulp. Bracing herself, she took another large mouthful. The liquor burned her nose and throat. Although it was unpleasant to drink quickly, the fiery sensation brought with it a certain soothing sensation. Tipping her change into her bag, Serena smiled fleetingly and distractedly at the barman before clicking off to the ladies'.

Once the cubicle door was firmly shut, she folded the toilet seat down and sat onto it with a thud. Her shoulders slumped forwards as she desperately fought back tears. Why did the baby issue have to haunt her everywhere she went? Was she ever going to be a mother?

She needed to get a grip on herself. She was damned if she was going to let Noelle know what was going on. She'd just love to wallow in her pain.

By the time she retouched her make-up and made her way back to the table, the brandy had hit her. She was feeling muzzy and luckily she didn't care as much. In fact, she wouldn't have cared if a ten-foot truck came crashing through the restaurant and mowed them all down. Brandy had a habit of making her feel that way. It was like a little touch of anaesthetic in a glass.

32

tweeting@serenasvelte.com
Great expectations? I hope so, watch this space . . .

It was almost five o'clock by the time Serena and the girls began to filter out of the restaurant after their lunch. The sun was shining which made the drunken buzz feel more than a little odd. After all the usual air-kissing and waving, Serena headed towards Grafton Street.

"I can guess where you're going now, Serena – off to try and outshine me! Well, good luck with that!" Noelle called after her as she staggered off towards the taxi queue.

Serena's eyes narrowed. At times she could just box that woman.

The high-class pedestrian shopping area housed the most salubrious stores in Dublin. She'd go into Brown Thomas and buy herself a little treat. The huge store carried all the top designer labels, with all the latest trends. Noelle wasn't the only one who could appear with designer bags and matching boots. Paul Davenport's wife was entitled to buy whatever the hell she wanted. Unlike bloody Noelle, her husband wouldn't need servicing just because she'd treated herself. She'd go and buy a much nicer bag and shove it up Noelle's nose the next time she saw her. *"Try and outshine me, good luck with that,"* Serena mimicked bitterly.

217

As she was marching purposefully towards the store, she noticed a tiny children's boutique. Swaying slightly as she tried to steady herself, she realised she was quite tipsy. Assuring herself it was just the rush of fresh air after being inside all afternoon, she lunged towards the door. Of course it had nothing to do with the fact that she'd drunk several glasses of champagne, three brandies in total and the guts of a bottle of wine to herself.

The shop door was locked. "Blast," she muttered, trying to peer in through the glass. Suddenly the door buzzed and she staggered forwards. As she entered, the heels of her boots sank into the thick carpet.

A pretty young shop assistant came towards her, smiling broadly at her. "Good afternoon, feel free to browse. If I can be of any assistance, please don't hesitate to ask." She stepped back behind the counter.

The shop was compact and smelled expensive. The tiny clothes were divided into boys and girls. To the left were the girls things, boys were to the right. The clothes ranged from newborn right up to age ten. Staggering towards the boys' things, Serena picked up a hanger containing a tiny pale-blue outfit. Miniature elasticated wasted, velour trousers, with a matching popper-fastened cardigan. Underneath was a soft cotton cream top with a little Peter-Pan collar. Clipped onto the top was a pair of the smallest socks Serena had ever seen. She could just imagine a teeny-weeny little Paul wearing this outfit. Stroking it gently, she moved towards the girls' side.

In the same range she picked out a petite sugar-pink velour dress. Underneath were matching knickers and a cream top. The doll-like tights were the final straw. She had to have them.

"What a lovely choice! They're really classic outfits, aren't they?" The assistant smiled at her. "No pressure, but just to let you know, both outfits have matching coats if you'd like to see them?"

"Okay." Serena looked over her shoulder in case anyone should spot her.

The assistant brought out two tiny pea coats, one in the baby blue, one in the pale pink.

"I'll take them both." Serena began to root in her bag for her credit card. "I'm having twins, this is the first thing I've let myself buy," she lied.

"Oh how gorgeous, and you obviously know you're having one of each. Isn't that just perfect?" the girl smiled. If she'd noticed Serena's perfect figure and flat stomach, not to mention the noxious smell of drink, she didn't let it show. Instead, she gently wrapped the exquisite little outfits in soft tissue paper. Slipping the parcels into a beautiful bag, she tied the cream satin ribbons at the top to secure the whole thing.

"That's 320.00 please." She took the card and swiped it through the machine.

"Good Lord, I'm going to be broke at this rate!" Serena was enjoying the game.

"Well, these clothes are really special. If you need basic stuff, like cotton Babygros and vests and that kind of thing, I know some brilliant websites if you'd like me to write them down for you?" the assistant offered.

"Yes, how kind, I'd love that, thank you!" Serena flashed her widest smile.

Armed with the bag and the names of the websites, Serena left the shop, feeling like she was walking on air. Flagging a taxi, she bundled herself inside. It took until she got home and up the stairs to her bedroom to realise that she was only fooling herself.

Paul was away for the night on business, so she wasn't expecting him home and her Filipino help was out visiting her sister for the evening, so she knew she had the place to herself.

Opening the ribbon on the pretty bag, she slid the tissue-wrapped parcels out. Carefully opening them, she spread the divine little outfits out on her bed.

With her hand up to her mouth, she tried to stifle the sobs. Stroking the velvet softness of the velour fabric, she let herself go. Rocking backwards and forwards she stared at the tiny pieces of clothing and cried. She cried for the babies she longed for to fill these clothes. She could barely breathe and her throat felt dry and tight. Her chest heaved as she poured every moment of sadness into the miniature pieces. Her face awash with tears and snot, she staggered downstairs to the kitchen. Rubbing her face roughly with kitchen paper, she clumsily opened a bottle of wine.

Pouring herself a large glass, she perched on a stool and flicked open her laptop. The web addresses the shop assistant had given her were already etched into her mind. She typed in the first one. A mirage of stunning little baby things popped up on the screen. She felt her heart steady as she drank her wine and scrolled through the items offered.

As she concentrated on the pages of baby things, she felt less and less upset. Just like in the shop, she found herself in a happier place. A world where she was indeed expecting twins. Before she knew it, she'd grabbed her credit card excitedly and tapped in her details. Once she started, she couldn't stop. She ordered everything from vests to tiny booties. If all came to all and Paul found the stuff, she could easily say it was for Ruby's baby. Paul knew she would buy Ruby the crown jewels without thinking twice. So this would be no different.

Feeling happier than she had in ages, an hour later, she closed the laptop and went back upstairs. Her eyes were heavy from both the crying and the wine. Grabbing the little outfits, she hugged them and curled up on top of the duvet and went to sleep. For the first time in a long time, she felt at ease and relaxed. Allowing herself to fall asleep in the world she wished she belonged to was so much nicer.

* * *

The next morning, she woke to Lucinda clattering plates out of the dishwasher. Why the hell did she have to bash everything around so much? When she had babies here, she'd have to learn to be quieter. Feeling pretty seedy after the indulgence of the day before, Serena decided to put on her Juicy Couture tracksuit and go for a walk.

Carefully stashing the baby clothes in the back of her wardrobe, she quickly waved into the kitchen at Lucinda as she grabbed her mobile phone and some cash.

"I'll back shortly," she called over her shoulder.

As usual, Lucinda didn't answer. She wasn't the chattiest creature but that suited Serena in a lot of ways. She couldn't bear to live with Miss Personality or even worse someone who wanted to be her friend. Jesus, no. She wasn't in the market for a new best buddy.

Sticking a pair of ear-phones into her phone, she activated her iPod. Music filled her head as she took deep breaths and allowed the clear air to cleanse her. Not being a true athlete, she swiftly got bored with the walking and all the health buzz. She'd just go and have a quick cappuccino and walk back. That'd do. She wasn't in the market for looking all sweaty and red. She hadn't spent over 300 on her tracksuit for it to end up all smelly and manky. It was nine thirty in the morning and she figured the café would be nice and quiet. She ordered her coffee and grabbed an *Irish Times* from the counter. Spinning around, she was disgusted to realise the place was awash with women and buggies.

"It's a bit Buggy City in here, can you please find me a table," she snapped at the lady on the till.

"Find a seat wherever you can, love. You'll be lucky to find a free table at this time. It's just after school drop-off. All the mammies come in for their little cuppa and a chat." The lady waddled off with a J-cloth.

Just perfect, Serena thought. That was all she needed. A bloody coffee shop full of screaming toddlers. Having to double up with an older gentleman, she perched on the edge of the wooden chair. Shifting the newspaper in front of her face, she tried to concentrate on reading. As her cappuccino was put down on the table, she was forced to remove her cover.

At the table beside her sat four women. They had hair like haystacks and not a screed of make-up between the lot of them. They wore shapeless T-shirts and cheap jeans or cut-off trousers on. There wasn't a designer handbag in sight. In fact, they all had those dreadful bulging nappy bags slung over the handles of the buggies.

Serena shuddered. It was all so depressing. The buggies were another matter. The one closest to her was caked in mushy biscuity stuff. The netted part underneath was overflowing with soiled bibs and toys and packets of wipes. The little girl in the buggy hung sideways out of the seat and stared at her.

"Hiya," the baby squeaked, smiling and showing little white teeth on the bottom and pink gums on the top.

Serena stared at her. The least her mother could do was wipe the child's face. She was covered in butter and jam. In her little pudgy fist, she held a mushed-up ball of soggy toast. "Hiya," the baby ventured again. "Hiya."

Silence.

The baby held her gaze. "Hiya."

Her mother turned to Serena and gave that oops-a-daisy, isn't-she-a-scream-type look. Serena had to bite her finger to stop herself from yelling. Why did mothers all do that? That bloody smug, knowing look? Where did they all learn how to do it? Because every one of them did it. That self-satisfied, isn't-she-a-scamp-but-we-all-love-her look!

Serena drank a huge gulp of hot coffee and felt the liquid burn the hell out of her oesophagus. Coughing and spluttering as her eyes watered, she tried to stand up and leave.

"Oh, poor you, that coffee can be scalding. I know that feeling though, you need the old caffeine fix, so you gulp it," the mother smiled.

Serena smiled falsely and excused herself. Was that another thing that happened to women who had babies? That they felt they could be everyone's mother? That they could comment on a stranger in a café, in that smug, conviviality way? She felt like shouting, "You're barking up the wrong tree, Mrs! I'm not one of you. I'm not in your baby club. I'm defective. I can't do what you do. I can't produce a baby and, what's more, I can't sit in horrible shapeless clothes and coo at a filthy little sprog, while pushing a disgustingly dirty buggy around! I'm what they call too posh to push!"

Maybe that was it, Serena thought as she marched towards her house. Maybe she was just too particular and fussy. Perhaps if she too went around not giving a toss about how she looked or where she went, she too could be a mother? She jumped as her mobile rang. Paul's name flashed up on the screen. She couldn't answer it. She'd have to call him back later on when she felt less deranged.

She couldn't afford to let this baby or rather lack of baby, make her appear to behave like a freak. Paul didn't need a mental case and a nervous wreck as a wife. If he found out how crazy she was becoming, he might leave. Then she'd be truly in the shithouse. No husband and no children. She'd have to hide away and never show her face again.

After showering and changing into a comfortable pair of jeans and a soft cashmere sweater, Serena phoned the fertility clinic. Her heart skipped a beat when they confirmed that Paul's fertility results were in.

"You'll have to make an appointment with one of the specialist, as we can't give you results over the phone," the secretary explained.

"Right, give me an appointment as soon as possible, please." She felt sick. What was she going to tell Paul?

"Now, we have a cancellation with Dr Rutland tomorrow morning at eight if you and your husband could make it?"

"Yes, we'll be there. Thank you."

Serena hung up feeling a hundred times better. She called Paul and told him about the appointment.

"Do I need to be there or can you just tell me about it later?" he asked, chancing his arm. "If I never have to step foot in that place ever again, it'll be too soon." He shuddered as he thought of the shiny happy people, floating around as if the whole hellhole was a normal place.

"Yes, Paul, you do need to attend. If not for me, for yourself. Don't you want a baby?"

Oh shite, he thought. This was all he needed, Serena going off on one about how he was to support her with the baby thingy. "Yes, darling, of course I want a baby, I'll be there." He hung up and stretched in his office chair. Scratching his chin, he wondered did any man really sit and dream about having a baby? Well, he didn't get it at all if he was brutally honest. He supposed he'd love the child if it came along, sure he would. But all this trouble and hassle? Nah. It wasn't really up his alley. Still, if it made Serena happy, then he'd go along with it all. Anything for a peaceful life.

Feeling more like herself, with a sense of hope in her heart,

Serena logged on to the computer. Browsing, she found a whole lot of new babies clothing websites. She spent a gorgeous hour, clicking and ordering things. She saw a stunning nursery set. An old-fashioned wooden cot, with matching changing unit and tiny wardrobe, all painted in egg-shell white. There was an optional fine net canopy to hang from the ceiling. Knowing Paul would notice it, she resisted. She'd have to wait until she knew she was pregnant before she bought it. Glancing at her watch, she realised it was already twelve thirty. Clapping her hands, she poured herself a glass of white wine from the fridge, to drink as she prepared a salad for herself.

* * *

By the time they arrived at the clinic the next morning, Paul was feeling pretty uneasy. As they approached the reception desk, he jiggled with his loose change in his pocket and gritted his teeth.

"Good morning, may I help you?" It was the squeaky Barbie-on-acid young one again.

"Hi there, we're here to see Dr Rutland, Serena and Paul Davenport." Serena was firm and direct with Barbie.

"No problem, Mrs Davenport, just take a seat and Dr Rutland will call you in shortly." Barbie did one of her big pink smiles.

Serena ushered Paul over to the sofa area. Their backsides were barely on the chairs before a small woman, with grey hair scraped into a severe bun appeared.

"Mr and Mrs Davenport?" she snapped, with her eyebrows raised.

"Yes." Serena met her stare with an equally chilly gaze.

The tiny woman walked off, as Paul and Serena scrambled after her.

"Sit." She perched on a chair behind a huge desk. She was child-like she was so small. Tiny hands and bird-like features. She put on round wire-framed glasses and, clasping her mini-hands, she looked at them.

"Mr Davenport, I've examined the results. When a man's sperm count is at a level lower than ten million per millilitre of semen he is deemed infertile by the World Health Organisation. You are well above this mark. You produced a healthy and active semen sample. In my opinion, from what I see here, the problem does not lie with you." Her face remained stony. She didn't move or flinch.

Paul felt relief flood over him. At least it wasn't his fault they weren't getting pregnant. He'd been terrified that Serena would want to leave him if he'd been defective. Not to mention the embarrassment if any of the lads had ever found out his tackle wasn't in correct working order.

"Mrs Davenport, I've looked at the ultrasound and the laparoscopy investigation result. I see that Dr Sullivan over in Mountrath found some endometriosis. He treated that by lasering off as much as he could. Correct?" She looked over her glasses at Serena.

"Yes." Serena didn't smile.

Paul shifted in his chair. The tension between the two women was palpable.

"You are here to try and find out why you are not conceiving. Correct?"

"Obviously," Serena snarled.

"Right, in order to help me form a better picture of what's going on here, I need to ask some simple questions regarding your general health." She looked up again.

Serena stared back with her arms folded, chewing on her lip.

The questions went well, until Dr Rutland touched on the alcohol issue. "How many units would you consume a day, Mrs Davenport? Assuming a standard glass of wine is equal to two units." She waited, pen poised, staring at the questionnaire.

Silence.

"Do you understand the question, Mrs Davenport?" She looked up.

"Yes, of course I do. I'm just trying to work it out." Serena felt like the walls were closing in on her. "We'll come back to that. Knowing how many glasses of wine I drink is hardly relevant. We're talking about fertility here."

"Well, when we take into consideration that the safe level of alcohol consumption for women is two units per day, it's of extreme importance. If you are consuming large amounts of alcohol, it has been medically proven that this will decrease your chances of conceiving." Dr Rutland held Serena's gaze.

"Oh for goodness sake, a few drinks never hurt anybody! You can't honestly sit there and tell me that by having a couple of glasses of wine I'm preventing myself getting pregnant? Look at the millions of teenage girls who get blotto and end up pregnant all the time. That's the greatest load of poppy-cock I've ever heard! Not that it's any of your business, but I have a sixteen-year-old niece who is pregnant after a drunken rumble currently, so don't sit there and tell me that alcohol has any diverse effect on conception."

"Those teenagers, like the niece you refer to, don't have fertility problems. You do, Mrs Davenport. I would suggest you start right away and cut out all alcohol completely. You need to follow a healthy diet. I can give you some booklets and printouts. Steer away from convenience foods and lean towards fresh food. Now that the endometriosis has been cleared, an alcohol-free period could possibly help you. All the rest of your investigations and tests were clear. I'd advise you to try this for two months and if you still haven't conceived, make another appointment." She sat very still, like a cat about to pounce on prey and waited.

"Is that it?" Serena screeched. "I've to go away and eat rabbit food and drink water for the rest of my life and then I'll have a baby? You call yourself a fertility specialist? Are you insane?" Serena was standing up and shouting by this time.

"Serena, calm down, darling!" Paul was looking from his wife to the doctor. "All Dr Rutland is suggesting is staying away from alcohol for a while to see if that makes a difference. It's not a big deal, is it?"

Serena felt like the world was standing still, as all the eyes in the room were on her. Would she be able to spend the next two months without a glass of wine? She could do it, no problem. But did she want to? Hell no. A day without wine was a day without sunshine. What was she going to do at all the functions? How would she meet friends for lunch? Her whole social life would come to an abrupt end. She realised the bitch of a doctor was talking again.

"You won't be able to drink when you conceive, so it will prepare you for that," she said with a smile.

"Don't smile at me like that, you old witch!" Serena had finally snapped. "You're so delighted with yourself, ruining the only fun I have left. A witchdoctor you should call yourself, you snotty old bag!" Serena sat down on the chair with a thud and burst out crying.

"I think we may have touched on a slight problem here," said Dr Rutland. To give her due, she didn't take offence to Serena's abuse. Nor did she continue to argue with her. Sitting still in her chair, she waited for Serena to calm down.

"Sorry, Paul. Sorry, Dr Rutland. That was abusive and rude of me." Serena looked like a lost child.

Paul put his arm around her and pulled her to him. Exhaling loudly, he realised that another huge problem that had nothing to do with infertility had been going on right under his nose, and he'd missed it.

* * *

Serena felt so ashamed. She was still in shock that she'd totally lost the plot with that horrible doctor woman. Paul was looking at her with sheepish terror.

"We need to have a big long talk, Serena. Let's go for some lunch," he begged.

"You must have a ton of work to do, darling, we can talk later on when you get home," Serena suggested.

"I've nothing to do that is more important than you. We'll have a quick bite to eat and then I can go to the office." He was adamant.

As they sat down in the little pasta restaurant, the first thing Serena thought of was a bottle of wine.

"A bottle of Chablis and a large bottle of sparkling water, please," she ordered with a smile.

"Cancel the wine, please, we've changed our minds," Paul held her gaze. He wasn't smiling.

"But . . . I always . . . oh, right." Serena looked at the floor. "Paul, listen. There's no problem. I mean, just because I enjoy good wine, and I . . ."

227

Paul was staring at her. No expression on his face.

"Serena, I always knew you liked a drink, but I think I've been turning a blind eye to the extent of this. Exactly how much do you drink each day?" He fiddled with the cutlery.

Serena felt a deep panicky feeling bubbling up from within. "Not much. Just a normal amount." She smiled and tried to hold his gaze confidently.

"What's a normal amount? For instance, last Friday, what did you drink?" He stared, barely blinking.

Serena started to feel really nervous of him.

"Well, that's not a good example. I went out for a boozy lunch with the girls. So that's hardly a good day to pick." She tried to sound nonchalant.

"Go on." He held her gaze.

"Well, we all had a couple of glasses of champers, followed by a couple of glasses of wine with lunch," she finished.

"And what about brandy? You love your brandy."

"Oh yes, I did have a brandy coffee, instead of a dessert. The others were having one and I didn't want to be a stick in the mud." She felt like she was back in school, with an angry teacher.

"And then you came home and had some more wine, I suppose?" Paul didn't flinch.

"I can't remember, to be honest. Paul, why are you so angry?"

"I'm not in the least bit angry, Serena. I just want you to admit to both me and yourself that you have a drink problem."

The room began to spin. Serena felt like the walls were closing in on her. She felt scared and strangled and surrounded. Did she really have a drink problem? Surely not? All she did was enjoy a few glasses of wine. What was wrong with any of that? Everyone else did the same! Surely everyone she knew wasn't an alcoholic too?

"Serena, I'm going to arrange for us to go and speak to someone. We need to get you back on track. We need to establish if you are sinking here. If you need help, now is the time to get it." Paul reached out and took her hand.

She let him. Inside she was screaming. She felt like boxing him in the face. What the fuck did he know? If she was an alcoholic, then so was he. He drank all the time too. Why was it okay for him and not for her? Why was there one rule for him and a different set for her? He was turning into a right boring bollox. What did her want her to be, a nun? Would he prefer if she had no friends and sat around all day like a boring git waiting for him to come home?

If she did nothing all day, and couldn't occupy herself, he'd probably leave her. When had she ever gone out and made a show of him? Never. When had she looked unkempt and smelled of booze and sweat? Never. When had she fallen off her chair or shouted like a drunkard at a function. Never. Paul had a lot to answer for.

But, as she looked into his eyes, instead of the usual love, she saw pain. Feeling a terrible sense of loss and bewildering shame inside, she knew she owed it to him to at least speak to someone. Surely if they went to see a professional, they'd help him to see that she was perfectly normal. That's what she'd do. She'd go along and they'd make him see sense.

When Paul decided something there was no stopping him. He'd only dropped her home a few minutes when her mobile rang.

"Darling, I've arranged an appointment with a guy called Dr Blaze he's in the Mountrath Clinic. He specialises in addiction and he's agreed to see you. He has a cancellation for next week. Will you come with me?" Paul sounded exhausted and strained.

If she said no, what would happen? Then he'd be convinced she was an alcoholic. It would be better to go along and clear this up, for once and for all.

"Sure, I'll go with you, if that makes you happier." She tried to sound upbeat and relaxed. She couldn't wait to hang up the phone. She felt like hiding in the back of the wardrobe with a big sheet over her head.

She needed a drink. As she strode to open the fridge, she stopped. Before today she never would have thought twice about pouring herself a glass of wine. Why should she? There was nothing wrong with a little refreshing drink from time to time, was there? She wasn't an alcoholic for Christ' sake. Alcoholics either lived on the streets and drank out of brown-paper bags or else they spent their time in pubs, from early in the morning, drinking pints of cheap beer. Alcoholics were dirty and unkempt. They didn't wear designer clothes, with couture handbags and shoes. They didn't go to the hairdresser's every few weeks. They didn't have gel nails applied. They didn't wear impeccable make-up each morning. They certainly didn't go for bracing walks while listening to bouncy music on a state-of-the-art iPod.

No, all this alarmist talk was simply getting to her. She loved wine. Loved the cool sensation as it ran down her throat. The range of flavours, from oaky to spicy. She knew her wine too. It wasn't as if she drank any old shite. For instance, she'd never drink those vile little screw-capped mini-bottles of cat widdle they served in scruffy pubs.

No, Paul and this Dr Rutland were simply barking up the wrong tree. Dr Rutland obviously couldn't pinpoint why she and Paul weren't conceiving, so she'd suggested all this alcoholic stuff to keep them off the scent. The more she thought about it, the more it made sense to her. She'd just have a small glass of wine to calm herself down. If Paul and anyone else wanted to shoot her for a drop of wine, then she'd hold her hands up and wait for the bullet. The whole thing had been sensationalised by an incompetent woman who didn't know her job.

Sneering at the thought of that jumped-up little Hitler woman, she closed her eyes and drank a big soothing gulp of Chablis.

Just to keep relations until it was all sorted out, Serena washed and put the glass away before Paul came home. She would put a large bottle of sparkling water into the fridge for dinner. She looked at her watch. It was only five thirty. How come the familiar crunching of the gravel outside was announcing Paul's return? She ran upstairs and gave her teeth a quick brush.

This was simply ridiculous. It was like chewing gum and crunching mints when she was fourteen, to hide the smell of forbidden cigarettes. Paul wasn't her father, for Christ's sake, he was her husband. Her partner, her equal. Still, it was just easier not to upset him while he was being spun this pile of bullshit by Dr Bitch-cow.

33

Angie was beginning to really suffer as she neared the final stages
of her pregnancy. May, that year, was hot and sticky. People
were appearing in extraordinary outfits. By rights in Ireland at that
time of the year, all the summer stuff was in the shops, but nobody
dared venture out in it. This was different. The sun shone, the skies
were blue with the odd wispy cloud tootling by. But, above all else,
it was actually warm.

"Is it just because I'm the size of a water buffalo or is it bloody
boiling?" Angie moaned to Rachel on the phone. She was finding
the heat appalling. "My ankles are enormous, my hands are like
paws, I feel like I'm being stewed in my own juices!"

"I can't wait to see you. I can't imagine you with a big bump,"
Rachel giggled.

"Well, I'm delighted I'm such a source of amusement for you!"
Angie felt rotten. "Sugar, I have to go, I have to see my gynae at one
and it's half twelve. By the time I get out there I'll probably be late."
She ended the conversation quickly.

Realising she'd left it too late to use public transport, Angie

231

hopped in a cab. As they travelled towards the clinic, she rubbed her tummy.

"When are you due?" the driver called back, looking in the rear-view mirror.

"I've only nine weeks to go," she answered proudly.

"Ah that'll fly in, love. I've two at home, four and eight. Big now, but I remember when our first came along, we thought it would never happen. It's the best thing in the world. Just you wait, it's amazing. Find me any person who looks at their own child and doesn't fall instantly in love!" he chuckled and shook his head.

Angie felt the butterflies in her tummy again. Every time she thought about the baby coming, she got so excited. Even though she was hot and uncomfortable and not getting much sleep, not to mention the constant peeing, it would all be worth it.

As usual, Dr Sullivan hooked her up to the Doppler ultrasound machine so she could hear the baby heartbeat. The methodical thudding of her baby's little heart filled her with fresh hope.

"That's all good, Angie. Your blood pressure is fine and the urine is all okay, no proteins present. You're in great shape. Well done." Dr Sullivan smiled. "Now, you're into your last couple of months, so I'm going to step up the visits. I'd like to see you every two weeks until the birth."

"Okay," Angie squealed and clapped her hands. The whole thing was surreal.

"Have you any questions or worries about the birth?" Dr Sullivan asked.

"No, I think I'll see how I go. If it all gets too much, I can opt for an epidural, can't I?"

"Yes, for sure. You just need to make sure you don't leave it too late. Having said that, first babies usually take a little longer than subsequent births. That first baby has to do all the work, getting through the birth canal," he smiled.

"You probably think I'm insane but I'm really looking forward to it all." She looked a little shy.

"Well, that's a great attitude to have, it'll stand to you. The more relaxed the mother is, the better the chances of a smoother birth.

Once you can keep your cool and listen to the team of nurses and midwives, that can help hugely."

Angie felt like she was walking on air when she left the gynaecologist's office. Well, she was more waddling on air if the truth be known. As she stepped into the elevator she caught sight of herself in the mirror. She must have looked like she was going to pass out, because the lady beside her piped up.

"You'll be back to normal before you know it. I felt like I'd never look like me again. But you do. It's amazing what the body can do!" She smiled and excused herself at the next level.

Angie was astonished at how many people just spoke to her. Just like that. People she didn't know, offered advice or kind words, or asked when the baby was due. It was a whole new world to her. This baby was opening more doors than she ever thought possible. It was like she'd finally joined a secret club, which required a baby by way of membership.

As she meandered back to the office, she daydreamed about all the mother and baby groups she was going to join. She'd recently decided that she was going to take a year out when the baby came along. Due to both her pregnancy and the savage hours she'd been working, she'd spent very little money since she'd moved to Dublin. Coupled with the ten-thousand-euro lump sum she'd been offered to move, she had plenty of money to allow her to spend precious time with her baby.

After all, she figured, this child might well be her one and only, so she wasn't going to miss a second. As she walked along with the sea on one side, she breathed in the cleansing salty air.

Another great thing about being pregnant was that she had a set wardrobe. Angie had read tons of articles in the past about having a "capsule" wardrobe – where you go and buy bits and make sure they can mix and match. Of course she'd never done that. In fact, she was pretty brutal at dressing herself. Since her day in the maternity shop with the three ladies, she'd stuck to what they'd said, and it worked.

So she was full of marvellous intentions of finding a shop in Cork and doing the same thing, whenever she got her figure back. If it ever came back. Being able to see her own feet would be a good start.

She was starting to get tired too. The bump meant that she was now sleeping with seven extra pillows. Who needed a man, when she could create her own out of cotton and feathers? Her pillow partner didn't break promises or let her down either. He never said he'd call and not do it. He didn't argue with her or make her feel bad about herself. Fair enough he didn't bring her out for a drink or a posh meal either, but she was off booze and the Chinese around the corner delivered.

The sleeping thing took rather a lot of arranging all the same. She was propped up with three pillows, her previous single one being useless at tilting her to avoid heartburn. Next came two pillows lengthways between her thighs. Next came a pillow under the bump, finally two behind her back to stop her rolling backwards.

She had got to know the little Indian man in the haberdashery shop near the office. For three days in a row, she'd gone in and bought a pillow. He was very sweet and friendly but certainly not what Angie had in mind as a nomination for man-friend material. The third time she went in, his little face lit up.

"You come to see me again, lovely lady?" he lilted.

She was a bit confused at first. "Erm, yeah, I need another pillow, please." That was the other thing nobody had told her about. Your brain turns to mush when you're pregnant. You forget things all the time. Walk into rooms and have no clue what you're doing there. Try to speak and the words have gone on holiday. Attempt to argue a point and end up crying. Not to mention the bumping into things. Jesus, if she banged her bump off another cupboard, edge of a desk, door frame or banister she'd cry.

"I know you come in here to see Prakash." He winked at her. "Prakash like to see lovely lady too!"

Angie started to sweat. She was sure Prakash was a total tiger in the bedroom and very attractive, but she really wasn't in the market for a special friend right now.

So she'd paid for the pillow and waddled out as fast as her bump would carry her. When she discovered she needed more pillows, she'd decided to bite the bullet and go to Argos. It was a blessed relief as she barely had to speak to another human being, never mind being leered at. Thinking along the overkill rather than skimping lines, she'd pre-ordered five pillows on line. With a taxi waiting outside, she exited looking like a live lagging jacket.

"Jaysus, love, are you inviting the Irish team for a sleepover?" The driver took the bulky pillows and squished them into the boot.

That was how she was now lying almost comfortably in a bed which felt like it was made of marshmallows. Exhausted and a bit sweaty after the excursion, she closed her eyes. She was almost asleep when the nagging need for a wee began.

"Please no," she slurred to the pillows, feeling almost drunk with exhaustion. She was terrified of moving, in case she never got comfortable ever again. She tried to think of something else. That worked for about ten seconds, until the baby started to kick. That was it. The baby must be sitting on her bladder. She fumbled herself free of the pillows, swung her legs over the edge of the bed and levered herself to a sitting position.

That was pretty much the ongoing nocturnal pattern for her. She'd be having a great snooze and a lovely dream, when the wee monster would knock on the door.

The other alarming fact was the size she was reaching. When the stick-insect in the shop had told her the cushion was only a prop and she wouldn't get that big, she'd lied. She was now surpassing the cushion and reaching a new record in largeness.

In one way it was reassuring and satisfying, as she knew the baby was thriving and growing. In another, it was terrifying and unnatural. How on earth was a thing the size of a small whale going to fit through a very small space? She was well aware that millions of women had managed this feat, but she still couldn't get her head around it.

Rachel was no help either. Not being a mother yet either, she was probably the worst person to talk to. Angie had heard some horror stories from other mothers, involving cutting, stitches, sitting on frozen peas and walking like John Wayne. But Rachel was the worst. She was a definite candidate for a full anaesthetic should she ever need to give birth.

"I've heard that some women end up pooing all over the doctors," she said in one of their conversations over the phone. "Jesus, I'd rather run barefoot up Croagh Patrick than have that happen to me. How would you ever walk down the road with your head held high after crapping on a doctor?"

"Thanks, girl. You're a rock. Not only are you freaking me out, but you're actually telling me things I'd never in a million years have thought of. Things I could live till a hundred and three and not need to know. Now, how would you like to be the godmother?" Angie tried to steer Rachel away from matters of bottoms and goo.

"Are you serious?" Rachel screamed.

"I think so, but you'll have to promise to be sensible," Angie warned.

"My arse, I'll be the cool one. I'm going clubbing with him or her. I'll provide the fags and beer when the child's fourteen and not allowed do anything fun. I'm going to be cool Auntie Rachel!"

Already Angie was worried. She'd never thought of her child going out drinking and smoking and going to clubs. In fact, she'd never even envisaged the child being able to sit up, never mind going on wild rampages with Rachel.

"Give it a chance, the child isn't even fully formed yet and you have it turned into an alcoholic," she laughed.

"So have you told the daddy yet?" Rachel was brilliant at dropping bombs.

"No, and I'm not sure if I will. I've told you before, I'll wait until the baby is here safely and then I'll think it through." Angie wanted to put the phone down now. She hated even allowing thoughts of Troy to enter her head. It was all so much easier when she could just think of the baby as hers.

"That man has a right to know. You're not the Virgin Mary. There's no Immaculate Conception here. You're not God either, so you can't act like Him!"

"Rachel, drop it for now, please. I never said I was Mary or God or Joseph or any of the rest of them, but I am this child's mother and I will make my decision when I'm good and ready, okay?"

"Ooh, touchy, touchy. Bit of a raw nerve?" Rachel goaded.

"Just drop it. You'll raise my blood pressure and I'll end up with oedema and protein in my urine, otherwise known as pre-eclampsia!"

"Ya wha? Have you been reading those freaky pregnancy books again? Right, I'm going. All that stuff is beyond me. I'm going out for an Indian in a while and I won't be able to eat if you keep going on about that kind of thing."

34

tweeting@maternityunit.com
*Always remember, ladies, those pelvic floor excercises can be
done at home, in work or on the bus! We can't encourage you
enough to hold that position, as often as you can!*

Ruby stood in the bathroom staring down at herself. She had
weird marks on her skin – they looked like she'd slept on a
wrinkled-up sheet. They were red and purple and all around her
tummy and on the tops of her legs. Pulling on some underwear, she
waddled into her parents' bedroom.

"Mum, what's all this?" she called.

Adele was sorting some summer clothes into a suitcase. They had
only a week and a half left before they were due to leave for Spain.

"Oh, I had them too, they're stretch-marks. I've heard they're
hereditary. It's just because you're in your last trimester now. Your skin
is like a balloon, and as your tummy inflates, it leaves those funny
marks. You have to expect this sort of thing, Ruby. They should
fade afterwards. There are brilliant creams on the market now too
– we'll get you some down in Spain."

Ruby was really wanting this pregnancy to be over. She missed
her friends and she missed being a normal person. It was really hot
in Ireland already – she couldn't imagine how stifling it was going

to be in Spain. According to the weather forecasters it was the hottest May on record since the sixties.

Too afraid to go to Mariah's house, Ruby resorted to phoning the landline. To her delight Damo answered.

"Yup, hello," he crooned.

"Eh hi, Damo, this is Ruby."

"Ruby, looking for Mariah, are ya?" He was glad she couldn't see his face. He knew he must look like he'd seen a ghost. Luckily he was on his own in the house.

"No, I wanted to talk to you actually. I've been wanting to talk to you for ages. How've you been?" She tried to sound all cool and grown up.

"Yeah, good. Cool, lots going on, you know yourself. Listen, I'm on the way out the door, I'll get Mariah to call you."

Ruby's heart sank. He didn't even want to have a conversation with her. She started to cry. "I told you I want to talk to you, Damo. I'm going to Spain to have our baby. You haven't bothered to even call me. My parents still know nothing. I feel like I'm going insane."

The silence was only broken by her intermittent sobbing.

"Calm down there, darling. Listen, what do you want me to do? I can organise some money for you. Do you need cash? Let me know the deal and I'll sort it, yeah?"

"I don't want money, I want you. Don't you care about me at all? Don't you care about the baby?"

"Of course I care. Hey, you're a great girl. What we shared was real special. You know, sometimes things don't work out the way we want and your parents are on to something with their plan. If we just leave things as they are, it's the best-case scenario for all this." He was trying to sound calm.

"Best for who, Damo? I thought you really loved me. You told me you'd never met anyone like me. You said I was special. You don't care if I live or die, do you?" She was shouting now.

"Ruby, Ruby, calm down, my darling. You're getting it all wrong. We're from a different space in time, you and me. It could never work, don't you see? We both have our own roads to follow. We can't make this happen, much as I would love that. There are too many people in our way. Sometimes love isn't enough. Sometimes we have to take the harder road, make sacrifices, you know?" He was rubbing his head as he spoke. Fuck this for a lark, he needed to get rid of this kid for once and for all. This was just dodgy at this stage. He'd be the bollox in all this if she crumbled and started talking.

"So you do love me then?" Ruby gulped.

"You know I do. What's not to love? You're beautiful, clever and way too good for me, darling. You need to find someone who will be able to give you all the things you need. I have too much baggage. Noreen is getting on now, and Mariah, Elvis and Alexis would be crushed. Your parents would never understand. We can't do that. Much as I love you and, God knows, I do, sometimes we have to sacrifice our love for the sake of others. But I will never forget you and I will never love another woman the way I loved you."

Ruby agreed to think about what he'd said and hung up. Running herself a bath, she locked herself in the bathroom and allowed herself to cry again. Damo did love her. She knew it. He couldn't have behaved the way he had if he didn't care. When they'd been together, the way he'd looked at her, what they'd done together – she just knew he loved her. But maybe he was right. Maybe their love was just too complicated. She knew it was special and different to any other love, but why did it have to hurt so much?

At seven thirty that evening, Ruby was putting on some lip-balm in her room when Adele found her. She noticed her daughter's eyes were dark and she looked drained and miserable. There was a change in her – she looked even more stricken than she had for weeks. Perhaps it was because they were finally going to Spain. The enormity of what was happening was bound to be hitting her by now.

"Are the people in your class going on for pizza tonight as usual?" Adele asked on an impulse.

"Yes, they are. Please, Mum, the restaurant they're going to is the other side of the city. It's small and dingy. Nobody we know would step foot in it. I would be able to feel normal, even for one evening."

"Okay then, I'll let you go. But no wandering around on your own and I'll swing by and collect you at ten. I'm not getting out of the car, mind you. I've no interest in being stared at or made to feel uncomfortable. Make sure you keep our business to yourself. It's amazing how news travels in this city. Just keep it light and breezy and then you won't have to lie."

Ruby's face lit up. "Oh, thank you, Mum! You're the best!" Ruby was longing to be with the other antenatal mums. She didn't feel the need to be anyone different with them. They didn't ask awkward questions and they never made her feel like an outsider.

* * *

Angie found herself looking forward to the antenatal class. She was going for a pizza with the other girls. She had got to the stage where she had no interest in going anywhere. She was just too big and lethargic. But at least these four girls would understand how she felt. If she was beyond exhausted, she could say so and they would appreciate how she felt.

The antenatal class was fine, in so far as the midwife told them how to recognise if they were in labour and what to do. They'd all got a sheet with the hospital phone numbers, including a direct line to the midwives, who could advise them if they were worried.

"Are there any questions?" the midwife asked.

They all looked at each other and shook their heads.

"Great, let's get the hell out of here," Leona piped up. "No offence, Una, but we're going for a pizza and I'm bleedin starving as usual." She patted her belly.

Minutes later, as they sat at the round wooden table with the red-and-white checked tablecloth, the smell of fresh dough making their mouths water.

"Will we get a couple of large ones to share or do you all want your own?" Brenda asked.

They agreed to share a ham and pineapple and a pepperoni, along with garlic bread and coleslaw.

Soon they had a feast to chomp through.

"I've been eating my body weight in Crunchy Nut Cornflakes," Leona began. "I've bleedin' dreams about the little feckers. I never used to like them and I'd say as soon as Junior here comes along I'll never want to look at a single one again." She stretched another cheesy slice of pizza onto her plate.

"This stuff must solidify in your stomach and sit there for a week," Sandra mumbled through a mouthful.

"But it tastes marvellous going in," Angie sighed as she ate another dripping slice of garlic bread.

Ruby sat with wide eyes and ate only a slice of garlic bread and sipped still water.

"Do you feel sick still?" Angie asked her kindly.

"I have no appetite at all, I haven't had from the beginning." She was speaking so quietly they all had to lean in to hear.

"Do you know, I think I recognise you from Dr Sullivan's clinic. Did we pass each other ages ago in the waiting room?" Angie shovelled another slice of pizza in.

"Yes, I knew I recognised your face from somewhere." Ruby brightened slightly.

"So what are yous all planning on calling the babies? I'm thinking of Angel for a girl and Keefer for a boy," Leona said.

"I keep changing my mind," Angie said. "I go through days where I love the name Kevin, then a week later I decide it's terrible and I wouldn't name a goldfish that. I think I'll have to wait and see the baby."

"If I have a boy, he'll be Barry after his daddy," Brenda said sadly. "If it's a girl, I really can't decide, although Barry had always liked the name Sarah." She looked like she was a million miles away as she sat swimming in her own thoughts.

"That must be really shite for you," said Leona. "Did you believe he was going to actually die?"

"Maybe we shouldn't talk about that," Angie said.

"No, I'm glad you're talking about him," said Brenda, looking at them sadly. "My family and friends don't seem to know what to say to me, so they solve it all by not mentioning him at all. It's like he never existed. That's the worst. It makes me feel like he's been forgotten. That he's been totally wiped out. Believe me, that hurts a hell of a lot more. You're okay, Leona, I'm happy to talk about him."

"Ah sorry, love, I'm as thick as pigshit at times," Leona giggled, quite unperturbed by the whole conversation. "I'll get meself into trouble sooner or later. Don't think me gob is connected to me brain most of the time."

"To get back to the subject of baby names," said Sandra, "I have Karen for a girl, after my mother, and George for a boy after my husband."

"What about you, Ruby love?" Leona nodded towards her.

"I, eh, I haven't thought about it." Ruby looked at the floor.

"Wha'? I don't believe you. Jaysus, I do be lookin' in magazines and on the telly and everywhere for names. What about the baby's daddy? Does he have any names he likes?"

The silence made everyone freeze.

Looking up in shock, Leona's hand flew to her mouth. "Ah fuck, there I go again, puttin' me foot in it. What did I tell ya earlier? I always do it. I'm sorry, love, I'm a nosey cow – don't answer if you don't want to. Ah, Jaysus, Ruby, don't cry, you'll set me off an' all!" Leona stood up and went over to give Ruby a hug.

"Oh no, I'm so sorry!" sobbed Ruby. "Sorry, everyone – I'm making a scene – I didn't mean to cry." Her hands shook as she tried to control herself.

They all regarded her kindly and waited for her to calm down a bit.

"My situation is different to all of yours. I'm not keeping my baby, you see." Ruby looked even younger than her sixteen years. Her eyes huge in her face.

"Oh Ruby, we had no idea!" Angie put her arm around her.

"If the truth be known, I hadn't a choice. My parents' lives have been ruined by my stupidity, you see, so they're doing what's best for me." She shrugged as the tears coursed down her cheeks.

"Well, if you don't mind me saying, I think that's the biggest crock of shit I've ever heard!" Leona spat.

"Shush!" Angie warned her.

Leona cringed. "Oh sorry, I'll just put me head in me handbag – don't mind me, Ruby love."

"Well, the baby will be raised by my parents, as their child, so he or she won't be gone-gone. Just not mine." Ruby blew her nose. "I'm so sorry to ruin your dinner. My mother would kill me if she knew I'd told you all." She looked terrified as she thought of the possible consequences. "None of you will say anything, will you?"

"No, not at all," said Angie and they all held their hands up, promising to keep the news to themselves.

"What goes on tour stays on tour, what?" Leona added.

"I really thought he loved me. I still think he does but it's just complicated, you know? We can't be together – sometimes love isn't enough," Ruby quoted Damo.

"Ah yeah, they all say that," said Leona, nodding. "A shower of randy gits, the whole lot of them. They promise you the sun, moon and stars until they get their leg over, then any sign of trouble and they're gone. I know, girl, I know."

"No, it's not like that, Leona. He really does love me, he still does, but we can't be together. It would hurt too many people."

"If you want to believe him, then you go right on ahead, love. Maybe I'm just too negative. I've come to the conclusion that they're all bastards. I know yous mightn't agree. Like your hubby couldn't help dying, and your fella is still around," she pointed at Brenda and Sandra. "But the ones I meet, in any case, are pricks."

Angie steered the conversation away from Ruby, sensing the young girl had had enough to contend with that night.

"None of us sitting here are doing the expected thing, if we're all being frank. I'm on my own, so is Brenda, so is Leona."

"And my husband will only look at the baby when it's clean dressed and looking like a Pampers ad," Sandra added kindly.

"I'm scared about the whole thing to be perfectly honest," Brenda said. "When I found out I was pregnant, Barry was so excited. He was great with kids and he just loved the idea of having his own. I was nervous from the word go. I just hope I'll manage. I'm so glad I've got this child coming, don't get me wrong. God, it's a gift and a piece of Barry, which I will nurture and love. It means he'll never be totally gone. But, because of that, I feel a huge pressure in a way. What if I make a balls of it all and the child ends up being a menace to society? I don't want to let Barry down or spoil his memory in any way. Do you know what I mean?"

"It's a huge pressure now that you point it out, "said Angie. "But look at how strong you've been so far. You've had such a sad and terrible time, and you've coped. You're going to be an amazing mum to this child. Barry will be watching over you too. Always remember that."

"Sure the women do it all anyway, love. At least your fella has an excuse not to help, being dead and all that." Leona chomped on the pizza, totally unaware of the shocked faces at the table. "As much use as an ashtray on a motorbike, me ma always says. She's right too. Either they spend their time in the pub, down the bookies or on the golf course if they're posh. That baby will be perfect, just the same as all our babies. Sure look at me. I'd no da growing up and I turned out fine." She patted Brenda's hand.

The four other women burst out laughing. Leona was a tonic. Just the type of person you needed to have around in a time of crisis. Her outlook on life was fantastic.

"I was thinking, when you have the baby and bugger off back to the sticks," Leona told Angie, "we could come on the train and visit you some time. Let the nippers all meet and then they could have little pen-pals when they're older."

"That's a super idea, I'd love that. You're all welcome any time in Cork. It's not quite the sticks, though, you cheeky cow. It's a big city!" Angie tried to look offended.

"Me arse! Once you've grown up in the flats in the centre of Dublin, everywhere else is the sticks. Sure if I manage to get to Stephen's Green, I feel like I'm in the country. Ah, Jaysus, me signet ring is all clogged with bleedin' cheese!" She shook her hand to try and free her large gold ring from pizza topping. "I for one will defo come and see you and the babs in Cork. It'll be deadly to tell everyone that I'm going to visit a friend in de country. Sounds like a thing that they'd do in the movies, doesn't it?" She looked all thrilled with herself.

In spite of the rocky start to the meal, Ruby enjoyed the other women. It was great to have one evening when she wasn't being the hidden-away freak she'd actually become. Just before ten o'clock, she reluctantly gathered her belongings.

"I'm being collected at ten, so I'll say my goodbyes now. I'm going to Spain in just over a week and my mum says it won't suit for me to come to any more classes." She smiled tightly unable to hide her dissapointment.

"Jaysus, it's well for some! Bring us back a tight-arsed bullfighter, will ya?" Leona giggled.

"I actually won't be back until after the baby is born," Ruby answered meekly.

"Oh, I see. Well, the best of luck with it all. I hope it works out for the best. I'm sure you'll be fine." Angie stood up. She wasn't sure if she should give Ruby her phone number or offer to meet up in a couple of months. Afraid of saying the wrong thing, she simply hugged the young girl.

All the women hugged awkwardly, the baby bumps making it all a bit challenging.

"Thanks for listening and I hope you all get on really well with your births. Good luck with it all." Ruby forced a smile. She really liked all the ladies – they seemed to understand her and none of them judged her. None of them looked at her the way her parents did. None of them seemed to think she was a menace to society. She wished she could stay in Dublin and have the rest of the classes with this group. Instead, she walked into the night air and found her mother revving the car crossly.

"God love her," Angie lamented after Ruby walked out. "She looks so lost, doesn't she?" The others all nodded. "I did actually see her on my first appointment with my gynae. Her mother was with her and to say she was snappy with the poor girl is putting it mildly." Angie exhaled.

"That's the beauty of growing up in the flats," said Leona. "Nobody expects anything else but for you to be up the pole by eighteen, but in her world, where it's all posh accents and snooty schools, you're like a leper with a bump at her age. I'll stick to me flats!" Leona held her hands up.

Although the others giggled, they secretly agreed with Leona.

At last Angie glanced at her watch and grudgingly announced she'd have to go home. She was finding it harder and harder to get up for work in the mornings. The pillow-swapping and constant shifting was beginning to get to her. Why was it that she'd spend the entire night trying to sleep and get comfortable, trotting in and out to the bathroom, being kicked to death by the baby and as soon as it was time to get up, she was comatose? It just wasn't fair. People rabbited on about the lack of sleep when you have a baby. It couldn't possibly be worse than all this. At least when the baby was born, she'd have someone there to keep her company. Right now, she was lonely. She had nobody to talk to. Nobody to tell her how well she was doing. Nobody to be excited with. She needed to go to a baby shop and buy the essentials: a pram, cot, basic clothes and some stuff for herself for the hospital. She'd been putting it off, as it all seemed a little bit sad, by herself.

As she was moving outside, Brenda came after her.

"If it doesn't suit you, please just say so, but I was wondering if you might be free at the weekend to accompany me to Mothercare or one of the baby shops? I could ask one of my family or Barry's mum, but I'd rather go with you if don't mind." She looked incredibly sad and vulnerable.

"Oh, what a coincidence! I was just thinking I should go myself and that I'd like some company! I've nobody at all to ask. My family and friends are all in Cork, so I've been putting off going alone. We could go to one of the shopping centers and have a bite of lunch while we're at it!" Angie instinctively hugged the other woman.

Swapping phone numbers, they agreed to meet early on Saturday morning in Blackrock shopping centre.

"I'm delighted to have your number now," said Brenda. "Sometimes, especially in the evenings, I long for someone to talk to. If I call a relation they always sound so strangled and sad. Would you mind if I rang you the odd time?"

"I'd love you to. I'm on my own too. I've nobody to chat to and it'd be great for both of us to be able to share our little moans." Angie hugged her again and promised to phone her the next night.

"I hope you don't think I'm like a lunatic stalker or anything. It's just that I happen to know you're also by yourself. I do have family who would be only too thrilled to accompany me to the baby shop but they'd all be snivelling into the Moses baskets. This might sound utterly selfish to you, but I'd actually feel guilty if I enjoyed the experience, with one of them watching me. Seeing as we don't know each other that well, and you didn't know Barry, you won't expect me to cry over ever bootie I buy. Does that make any sense to you at all?"

"You bet," said Angie. "Often it can be easier to talk to someone you're not that close to. And let's face it, if you discover I'm a mad lunatic, you can rest assured I'll be buggering off back to Cork soon, so you won't have to wear a moustache and glasses in Tesco's to avoid me!"

* * *

That Saturday, Angie and Brenda met in the shopping centre at nine thirty.

"First things first. Coffee and sticky buns!" Brenda linked Angie's arm. Anyone watching them would assume they'd been friends all their lives. "We're a bit like two Wheebles, waddling around here!"

Feeling spurred on by the caffeine and sugar, they marched into Mothercare. The prams and buggies on the shop floor looked more like complex machines than child-friendly devices.

Flagging down an assistant, they asked for advice. Two hours later, they emerged feeling quite confused.

"Jesus, you'd nearly have to re-mortgage the house to have a baby these days!" Angie looked at the receipt for all her stuff. She was having it all delivered instead of lugging it around herself. "Mammy put us all in the same Silver Cross pram. We'd one wooden high chair and that was about the height of it."

It was fun all the same, and very exciting. They'd picked out little vests and Babygros, all in white. The girl had been very helpful with the "mummy" stuff too. Sanitary towels the size of bath towels, disposable knickers, feeding nightdresses, with button-down windows at the front. Nipple creams, healing creams, breast pads, nursing bras, the list of hideous paraphernalia for the mothers was endless.

"It's not glamorous by any stretch of the imagination, is it?" Brenda giggled.

"Those disposable knickers are the limit for me. I'm now glad I won't have a man near me after I've had this child," Angie laughed. With her hand shooting to her mouth she looked at Brenda aghast. "Oh Christ, I'm sorry!"

"Please don't start tiptoeing around me! I've got that with everyone else I know, just say what you want to say. I'm not going to top myself because you're making a joke."

"Okay, fair enough. I'll just open my trap and continue to put my foot in it. Although I've a long way to go before I beat Leona." They both giggled at the thought of the younger woman.

By the time they'd finished their lunch, they were both exhausted.

"My legs are like tree trunks. Do you find your ankles look like an elephant's after you've been walking for a bit?" Brenda was surveying her feet, with difficulty.

"For sure. I barely have any knees anymore either. In fact any part of my body that used to be boney is now covered in a thick coating of dough-like fat. It's not exactly attractive, is it?"

They decided to go to Brenda's house, which was ten minutes from the shopping centre. Angie followed her in the car and pulled up outside the house. It was a normal semi-detached: front door, one window downstairs, two windows upstairs. The door was painted cream and the front garden was neat and the bordering flowerbeds were awash with colour. Little primulas and pansies dotted the area, making the garden pretty and cheerful.

Brenda punched in the alarm code. "Come on in." She flung her bag and coat on a chair in the hallway. "Chilled drink?" she called over her shoulder.

"Yes, lovely, thank you," Angie felt suddenly shy. She always felt like that in someone else's house, if she hadn't been there before. She glanced around, terrified of appearing too nosey.

"Go and have a little look around if you like," said Brenda. "I hate when you go to someone's house and they don't let you see anything. You have a wander and I'll get us some juice."

She wandered into the sitting room. The first thing she was drawn to was Brenda's wedding photo on the mantelpiece. She and Barry looked so happy and in love. He was a tall, strong-looking man, with a really smiley face. His eyes were almost non-existent, they were so squinty when he smiled.

Angie felt sadness stab her heart and make her physically hurt, at the thought of this lovely man being taken away so cruelly.

"Here you go." Brenda had appeared quietly behind her.

"Oh Brenda, I'm sorry!" Angie was crying, she couldn't help it.

Brenda put the juice down and they hugged – albeit awkwardly with the two bumps in the way.

"I miss him desperately. I still can't really believe he's gone." Brenda picked up the photo and stroked the glass gently. "You just never know what's around the corner, do you?"

By five o'clock, the sun was still shining and they'd moved outside to sit on loungers. Angie agreed to stay for dinner – they would order a Chinese. Both women were relaxed and able to talk with ease. As Angie sighed, allowing the sun to seep into her bones, she hoped herself and Brenda would be friends for a long time. They just clicked and it was obvious that they needed each other. Angie hoped they'd stay in touch after she'd gone back to Cork.

"What about your baby's father? Does he not even wonder how you are? Has he even made contact with you?" Brenda asked.

"No, I told him that if he wasn't willing to commit from the outset I didn't want him dipping in and out of our lives. It wouldn't be fair to anyone. And he agreed." Angie bit her lip. She longed to tell someone the truth. She was close to spilling the beans but she didn't know this woman well enough yet. If they continued to be friends, she would tell her. She felt she could trust her. She didn't seem to be the type of person who would blab her business around. But she'd have to be wary of who she told. Ireland was a small place – people all knew each other. It wouldn't take long for news to travel, if she told the wrong person.

As her due date approached, she felt more and more protective and possessive. She really didn't want anybody else to take her baby, even for one night. If she told Troy, there was a chance that he wouldn't want to know. But, on the other hand, he might be very keen on being part of the child's life. It was a chance she wasn't willing to take. She wasn't up for sharing this baby, especially with someone she didn't know.

35

tweeting@serenasvelte.com
Not feeling so svelte today, anger is not a friend of mine.

Serena was sleeping fitfully these nights. She was still really angry about all the accusations. She was looking forward to meeting this Dr Blaze. She was hoping he was less of a freak and more interested in the truth. The sooner this whole mess was sorted out the better.

Feeling quite bleary-eyed, at last she found herself sitting in front of a small round man. Everything about him was round, from his body and head to his little wire glasses. He had a tiny bristle-infested chin, and all Serena could do was stare in a trance as the little brush bobbed up and down when he spoke.

"What, in your own words, seems to the problem?" He cocked his head to one side and looked from Serena to Paul.

"Well, we were in with Dr Rutland as we've been having a bit of trouble conceiving," Serena began. "From where I'm sitting, she couldn't find anything wrong with either myself or my husband, so in desperation she turned the tables on me and suggested I was drinking too much." Serena pulled her jacket down and sat bolt upright.

"Why do you think you're here, Paul?"

251

Paul shifted in his seat and glanced sideways at his wife. You could have cut the atmosphere with a knife.

"Well, that's the nearest we've got to conceiving – a pregnant pause," Serena shook her head in disbelief as she saw Paul struggle to find the right words.

"This isn't easy for me, Serena," Paul said quietly, "but all I want is what's best for you. Since it's been pointed out to me, it actually makes sense. I think that you may have a problem with alcohol, darling."

"Oh sweet divine Jesus, not this claptrap again!" Serena waved her hand in the air and glowered at Paul in disgust. He could see her green eyes flashing with rage.

"Why do you say claptrap, Serena?" Dr Blaze asked calmly.

"Because that's exactly what it is. I'm not an alcoholic. Do I look like a down-and-out? Do I have a problem conducting my day-to-day life? No. Of course not. I'm one of the most organised people I know. My house is spotless, I am fully in control. When have I ever let you down, Paul?" She turned towards him with hurt, fear and anger emanating from every pore.

"You haven't ever let me down, darling. It's not about that. Okay, maybe you're not an alcoholic, but you must admit you do rely heavily on alcohol."

"May I interject for a second, please?" Dr Blaze produced a piece of paper and laid it on the table before them.

They both leaned forward to examine the page. It was a questionnaire about alcohol use.

"Can you go through the list together and try to answer the questions as honestly as possible. Remember my only aim is to help. There are no judgements and no aspersions cast in this room." Dr Blaze smiled encouragingly.

Serena held his gaze for a second before looking at the page. He was calm and not in the least bit smug or condescending. She began to read the list.

1. Do you feel you must drink as part of a social event, or else it's not fun?

2. Do you lie or make excuses about how much you drink?
3. Do you ever drink and drive?
4. Do you say you can cut back or give up drinking, but never manage to actually do so?
5. Do you ever drink alone?
6. Do you ever wake up feeling like you need a drink?
7. Do you ever feel bad or guilty about your drinking?
8. Do you get the shakes or the sweats if you stop drinking for a few days?
9. Do you have a very high tolerance for alcohol?
10. Does your drinking affect your work or personal life?

As she read, Serena felt like a pair of hands were slowly closing around her neck, squeezing tighter and tighter, putting pressure on her windpipe, stopping her from breathing. She tried to remain calm. She tried not to allow these questions affect her. By the time she got to the one about drinking alone, she froze.

"What's wrong with drinking alone? I wasn't aware there was a law against it!" She had meant it to sound scathing. She had intended on ridiculing the whole idea. But her voice didn't comply. It burst forth, sounding more strangled and terrified than she'd ever imagined possible.

"Most people don't feel the need to drink alone, Serena," Dr Blaze put in gently.

"Why, but, I . . ." Her body took on a whole new uncontrollable, involuntary life of its own. She began to shake so badly her teeth chattered. The tears streamed down her face and not just little lady-like drops. Oh no, big plopping wet ones. Her nose was running and she was rocking back and forth.

"It's okay, darling, no one wants you to suffer. We just want you to be well." Paul was horrified and felt like the world's most shite husband. "How the hell have I missed all this for so long?" he whispered.

Dr Blaze simply sat and let the couple hold each other. It was ten whole minutes later before he spoke.

"Serena, alcoholism can often cause people to make negative

assumptions. Alcoholism is not a moral weakness or a character flaw. It is an illness, which can be treated very successfully with a wide variety of interventions. The first, and biggest step, was coming here today."

There was pin-dropping silence in the room. Serena stared at Dr Blaze. She looked like a startled chicken on the outside. Inside her brain was working like a video machine in fast forward. She was desperately trying to think up a witty and intelligent response. With intense inner fear, she admitted to herself that there wasn't one.

"I don't understand," she said, her voice was weak with shock. "I've always lived my life the way I do now. Have I been wrong forever?" She stared at the doctor like a puppy. One that had been beaten with a large stick and left in the corner of a shed to lick its wounds in confusion.

"Most alcoholics have a long record of alcohol abuse. It's not your fault though, you must remember that. And, Paul, you must understand that."

"But Paul drinks a lot too. Is he an alcoholic as well then?" She looked at Paul and couldn't bring herself to hold his gaze, so she looked at her lap dejectedly. Deep down she knew the answer. He didn't drink all the time. Sometimes when they went to a function, he'd drive and not touch a drop. Some nights he'd refuse a glass of wine with his dinner. Sure he enjoyed a drink, but the difference was that he could take it or leave it. She now realised she couldn't. She always had a drink. At every God-given opportunity. Every day.

"Serena, that's not actually true. If I have a big speech or even a presentation the following day, I won't have a glass of wine with dinner. I find alcohol clouds my judgement, so I often drive when we go out. I know you may have never taken this on board but I don't drink every day." Paul hated saying the words, but he knew he had to be honest with Serena.

Dr Blaze spoke again. "Just because you don't walk around in your dressing gown, muttering to yourself, with rollers in your hair and a burnt-out cigarette in your mouth, doesn't mean you're not an alcoholic, Serena. In fact, people in your position, who have a high-quality life style, with the funds to lead a glamorous day-to-day existence are nearly more at risk in my opinion. If you were a down-and-out, drinking cheap liquor from a paper bag, it would be easier for you and everyone else to see what is happening. But ladies who lunch, who look and smell beautiful, don't portray the same image. So it's much more difficult for us all to face the fact at times." He left another big silence.

Paul broke the ice.

"Serena, look at me." He turned her face towards him. "I love you. More than anything in the world. I know you want a baby and of course I'm going along with that. If and when we have a child, I'll love it too. But right now, you are enough for me. I love you that much. If we never have a baby, so be it. I'll still have you. Please let's try and work this out and get you well. I'll do anything I can to help you. If we have to sidestep on the whole function thing for a while, that's fine. I hate them anyway as you know. We don't have to drink alcohol at home. Please, let me do this with you. Will you?"

His beseeching eyes and his outpouring of pure and honest love for her touched her beyond belief. Once again, she crumbled and felt her body ache inside. It was both the most wonderful and most dreadful moment of her life so far. The mixture of stabbing pain mixed with fear and dread was in some way made bearable by the knowledge that Paul loved her and wanted to help her.

The biggest question was whether she was able to help herself. Would she be able to live her life without drinking? It all seemed so bleak and boring. How the hell would she go to a function or a wedding or a christening or a dinner party and not have a glass of wine?

She suddenly felt a slight glimmer of hope. "Would it work if I promised to only have one glass of wine a day?"

"Do you think that would work for you?" Dr Blaze sat very still.

"Em, well, it might. It just sounds so much less boring, doesn't it?" She tried to smile.

"Would one glass be enough?" said Dr Blaze. "Or after a couple of days, would you maybe think that moving on to two would be better? Then by next month, it might move onto three, with an allowance of more when you go on a night out. Suddenly, you're back to square one. It's a pattern, Serena." He sat still and silent again.

"But I could promise not to go past one glass." She wanted to hold onto the security and keep the demons at bay. "I just can't imagine never being able to have a drink, ever again." There, she'd said it. "It just sounds so final, so bleak, so awful. How will I ever have fun? I'm going to be the boring one at the party. People will shy away from me." Serena's face grew redder and she began to break out in a sweat. Her voice rose. "They'll think I'm like a narky old aunty. The unmarried one, who sits in the corner at weddings, tutting and smelling of mothballs and wee, only moving to give out or fix her headscarf!"

Paul and Dr Blaze didn't speak.

"A day without wine is a day without sunshine. I'm destined to live under a cloud forever. Is that what you both want for me?" She was yelling now, like a petulant child.

"All anybody wants is for you to be well." Dr Blaze didn't try to argue or defend his corner.

"But I . . . You don't . . ." She trailed off. She felt sick inside. This was her worst nightmare. She honestly thought she was coming here to sort all this out. To stop all the nonsense talk. To put a lid on the whole, ridiculous situation. To find the way of fixing the non-baby issue. Not in her wildest dreams did she ever think she was going to be affronted like this. She'd never have come if she'd realised they were all going to gang up on her.

"I run a treatment programme which you are very welcome to join. You can see me on your own at first and, if you feel comfortable with it, you could join some group therapy if you wish?"

She felt boxed into a corner. What was she supposed to do? Her mind was whirring at a hundred miles an hour.

"I think we should leave it at that for today," said Dr Blaze. "Would you both come and see me again the day after tomorrow?"

Thanks be to God, he was going to let her go. If she could just get the hell out of here, she'd feel better. She was never stepping foot in this place again. There was no bloody way she was spending the rest of her life sober. Fuck that. Sure, she'd think about the fact that she might drink a bit much sometimes. Okay, she'd cut down a bit. Fair enough. But there was not a hope in hell that she was turning into a boring, dreary old bag. Even the fucking nuns drank wine at Mass, for Christ sake!

Right now, she needed to get herself and Paul out of this man's way. She'd make Paul see that she didn't have any issues with alcohol. Everything would be all right. Now that they knew Paul wasn't firing blanks, the baby thing would probably just sort itself out. With a bit of luck, she'd be pregnant shortly and then they'd all be distracted by the baby and leave her the hell alone. She usually basked in the limelight but this kind was not what she had in mind. Quite apart from the fact that it was all a farce, she took exception to being questioned and made to feel like she was doing something damaging or even dangerous. For crying out loud, society was full of murderers and rapists, people who were bad with a capital B. She was a middle-class, attractive and intelligent woman. She was not going to be made to feel like a criminal for simply enjoying her life.

Even getting out of that room made her a little more hopeful. She politely said goodbye to Dr Wank-bag and left.

"I'm so proud of you, darling," Paul began, as they sat into his car. "They say that admitting you have a problem is the first step to recovery. I can't believe how well you're doing with this. I'm so sorry I didn't see it all before now. I want you to promise me you'll keep talking to me. Keep telling me what's going on in your head. That way, I just know we'll get through all this." He was nodding enthusiastically.

As Paul reached across to the passenger seat to pat her leg, Serena was as stiff as a board, her green eyes flashing, her lips snarling. She felt like a volcano was about to erupt inside her.

"What the fuck is wrong with you, Paul?" she seethed. "Do you honestly think that I'm a bloody alcoholic?"

Paul pulled up at the traffic lights and faced her. "Yes, Serena, I do think you're an alcoholic," he answered calmly.

She hated his calmness. She hated the way he was looking at her. With all that hurt and concern in his eyes.

"Oh piss off, Paul! Stop acting all holier than thou!" she spat. "You're hardly Mr Perfect yourself. You're not exactly Mr Teetotal. Get off your high horse and give me a break. Who suddenly sainted you and made you so perfect?"

"I'll tell you what, we'll both give up booze for a month and see how we get on. How's that for a plan?" He drove on with his eyes fixed firmly on the road.

"We will in our holes, give up for a month! Why the hell would we want to do that?" She was getting more and more angry. "What's it going to achieve?"

"I think it will achieve a lot. Can I just ask you, what would you do if you found out you were pregnant? Would you give up drinking then?" He stared straight ahead.

"Why are you trying to catch me out all the time?" she screamed.

"I'm not." Paul rubbed his face and exhaled. He felt so inadequate that he hadn't seen all this coming. What kind of a crap husband was he that he hadn't realised what a decaying can of worms was waiting to be opened? They had a difficult road ahead of them and he just hoped they'd survive it.

36

tweeting@rubytuesday.com
Head-melted.com – why oh why did I let my brains fry, all it took was just one look, why oh why . . .

Ruby was sitting in her bedroom at home, trying to pack her last couple of bits for Spain. As she looked around her room, at her rack of CDs and her posters of U2 and Katy Perry, she wished things were different. The next time she sat here, she wouldn't be pregnant any longer. There would be another person in her house. A boy or a girl that she had grown and given birth to.

She thought about Damo. She tried to reason that he knew what he was talking about. She wanted to believe that he did love her. That he would like to be with her, but couldn't.

Putting her hands on her huge tummy, she looked at the enormous bump with disdain. All this was the baby's fault. If it hadn't decided to embed itself in there none of this would be happening to her. She might have had more time to be "Fun Ruby". To make sure that Damo fell totally in love with her. Sometimes she would lie in her bed and pretend it wasn't there. She'd think about going to McDonald's with the girls, or trying on clothes in A-Wear.

She remembered the excitement of the night they'd gone to the Beyoncé concert, followed by the nightclub. The sound of the base beat, the rhythmic thudding on the polished dance floor. The rainbow of the strobe lights, hitting the mirrored walls. How her head had been swimming, then with one deep breath of magic dust up her nostril, it had cleared – or so she'd thought.

She could still be that happening, clubbing diva. But she'd ruined it all. She'd shattered her parents' lives along with her own. At first the idea of her parents taking the child had horrified her. But as her abdomen had grown and her freedom was taken with it, she resented the baby more each day. If she hadn't ended up pregnant, she could still be around Damo.

Her parents were right. This child was a curse. It was already ruining her life. Imagine what it was going to do when it was born? It would stay awake all night and scream all day. She'd never be able to go anywhere or do anything if she was responsible for it. It wasn't like the Tiny Tears doll she'd had as a kid. She couldn't shove it in a toy trunk when she got bored with it.

She never thought she'd think it but she actually wanted to go back to school. She wanted her old life back. The sooner the baby was born and signed over to her parents, the better. She had eight weeks to go and counting.

Her father was to follow them over to Spain, two weeks before she was due. He wanted to be there for the birth, and afterwards to take care of all the legalities.

Ruby left a final message on Damo's phone, telling him she was going and that she'd call him when she had the baby. All night her phone lay on the nightstand, silent. She kept hoping that Damo might call at around three or four in the morning, when the club shut. But there was no contact.

* * *

By the time they disembarked in Spain, waited for their luggage, which of course ended up being the last bags on the conveyor belt, both mother and daughter were hot and cranky.

"Can you turn up the air-conditioning, Mum? The car is like a bloody sauna, I can't bear it," Ruby snapped.

"Pregnancy makes you feel warm at the best of times but even I feel dreadfully hot." Adele turned up the air-conditioning as she drove towards their apartment block. "Did you speak to Serena before you left?" She didn't take her eyes off the road.

"No, I texted her and she texted back that she'll call, but she was having a bit of a nightmare with business stuff of Paul's at the moment. Did you talk to her?" Ruby bit her lip. She'd been hoping to see Aunt Serena even for a half an hour before they left – it wasn't like her to brush Ruby aside. Fleetingly she hoped her aunt was okay.

"I'm sure it's some major catastrophe like whom she should hire to cook Paul's dinner this weekend. That woman wouldn't know the meaning of the word 'nightmare'. I don't think I've ever met a more indulged person in my entire life. If she thinks she has problems, she should walk a mile in my shoes," Adele spat. "Enough about her, she just rubs me up the wrong way. I know you and she have a fantastic relationship, but you didn't grow up with her, Ruby. She and Daddy were like the secret service, Mummy and I were just a by-the-way in our house."

After settling in to the apartment and having a cooling swim, Ruby and Adele were relaxing by the pool when large fat raindrops began to fall.

"Blast it anyway!" said Adele as they hurried inside. "Why don't we pop to *El Corte Inglés?* We need some basic provisions for this baby." She sighed, wrapping her towel around herself. Not even the sun could act normally and shine today.

"I've no interest in going to baby shops – I'll wait here and watch TV."

"Oh no, you won't, young lady! You're coming with me. Why should I have to do it all?" Adele wagged her finger.

"It's your baby, remember." Ruby shrugged.

Adele shut her eyes and counted to ten. If she opened her mouth, she'd start yelling and she was terrified she would say things that could never be taken back. Sensing she'd gone too far, Ruby threw a caftan over her bikini and grabbed a denim jacket.

They bought a pram and travel cot and a bag of baby grows and vests.

"There's no point in buying a big wooden cot for here, we'll do that when we get back to Ireland," Adele said. "What do you think of this pram?"

"Yeah, whatever. I'm not going to be sitting in it or pushing it, so you decide," Ruby shrugged.

"Well, I'd like to hope that you'll help out and take a sisterly interest in this baby, Ruby. If I was really giving birth to this child, I'd hope that you would want to have some input into its life." Adele was beginning to despair with Ruby. First she was opposed to herself and Harry raising the child as theirs, now she seemed to have relinquished all responsibility altogether. It just hammered home to Adele that they'd been right all along to plan the adoption of this baby.

Ruby's total lack of interest now showed how unable she'd be to look after this baby. Yet again, Adele wondered how the hell they'd ended up in this awful predicament. They'd sent her to one of the best schools in Ireland. They'd paid through the nose to keep her there. Dressed her in designer clothes, brought her to Spain for the summer, up to the ski slopes in the winter. They'd paid more to that livery yard for her pony than most people spent on a mortgage. Where had they gone wrong? Adele had always assumed that these things only happened to underprivileged girls. Not girls like Ruby. She would never get over the shock of it all. Whatever about herself, poor Harry would never be the same again. He idolised his only child and the thought that she'd done this was almost more than he could bear.

All she could do was remain calm and hope to God that their time in Spain would be relaxing. At least they were away from the prying eyes of the neighbours. They knew several families in their complex, but thankfully none of them were around. Most people went down for May, then went back home and didn't return until September. July and August were unmercifully hot and even the locals tried to avoid the heat.

37

tweeting@serenasvelte.com
I give up, I can't do this any longer. I need to find a better
place.

Paul dropped home around eleven, ostensibly to pick up some
papers but actually to check up on Serena. He had been doing
that occasionally lately, always nervous that she would guess what
he was at. There was no sign of Serena and he wondered if she was
still asleep – he had left her in bed that morning.

He still hadn't got over the shock of finding out how much pain
she had been concealing. He should have known she was suffering
so badly. He should have seen the devastation going on behind her
polished exterior. Sure, he knew she didn't get on with her sister, and
her parents had very little to do with her, but *he* was her husband
and he'd let her down.

He was still astonished at the degree of her anger. After the initial
meeting with Dr Blaze, she'd stormed upstairs as soon as they got
home, saying she wanted to soak in the bath.

Looking around, wondering what the hell to do next, he had
opened the kitchen cupboard and surveyed the contents. There was
everything from orange liqueur, tequila, gin, vodka, to several types
of brandy. He'd found a large cardboard box in the utility room,

and began to stack the bottles into it. Next he moved onto the wine. Although he enjoyed a glass of wine, he certainly wouldn't miss it. He was going to do everything he could to help Serena. He figured that having a house full of booze wasn't going to be of any benefit. At least, if all temptation was removed, she stood some kind of chance. Within half an hour he was sweating as he piled the last box into the large boot of his car. He'd store it all in the office until he thought about what to do with it.

Of course, she had been furious when she discovered what he had done and had raged at him for hours – for treating her like the inmate of a rehab clinic, for treating her like a child and so on. When he refused to bring back the alcohol, she had rushed off to the off-licence and stocked the cupboard again.

Since then she had been exercising great control in his presence and hardly went near the drinks cupboard at all. But he knew she must be consuming the alcohol in his absence and topping up the bottles constantly.

He sighed deeply. He felt they were making no real progress at all.

He ran up the stairs, taking them nimbly, two at a time.

"Serena?" he called. No answer. "Serena? Where are you, honey?" Silence.

She wasn't in the bedroom. Their bed was unmade so it looked like she had just got up. He knocked on the en suite door. "Serena?" No answer and no sound of running water. He opened the door and saw her slumped in the bath, her face ghastly white. A small brown pill container was rolling around on the floor – empty.

"Jesus, Serena! Can you hear me?" He swooped down, hooked his arms under hers and pulled her out of the bath. She was cold and limp. Her head was lurching forward but he could hear her faint breathing. "Oh God, no, don't do this to me, Serena! Hang in there!"

Dragging her into the bedroom, he managed to heave her onto the bed and wrap her up in the velvet throw. He ran back to the bathroom, grabbed the medicine container and shoved it into his pocket. Then he noticed an empty litre bottle of vodka was perched near the tap end of the bathtub. Cursing loudly he ran back to Serena and scooped her into his arms.

Utterly terrified and not knowing what else to do, he bobbed down the stairs and out the front door, grabbing his car keys off the hall table as he passed it. He opened the back door of the car with difficulty, almost dropping her in the process, and slid her into the back seat. Kicking the door shut, he leapt into the car.

As he sped up the road, he called directory enquiries.

"Hello, directory enquiries, Mark speaking, how may I help you?"

"I need A&E in St Vincent's hospital!" Paul shouted.

"Would you like to be connected?"

"Yes!" Paul shouted.

Luckily the phone was answered immediately.

"Do you know what medication she's taken?" the nurse asked.

"I don't know but I have the bottle with me – it's empty but I'm not sure how many she's taken."

"Okay, the main point will be to know exactly what chemical she's ingested. I'll make sure we have a team waiting for you, see you shortly. Drive to the main entrance door." The phone went dead.

Paul drove as fast as the Dublin traffic would allow. Within minutes, he pulled up outside the main door to the hospital. A team of three lunged forwards with a wheeled trolley and pulled Serena from the back of the car. As they rolled her away, he remembered the empty pill bottle and ran after them.

"Wait, you'll need this, I found it on the bathroom floor." Paul shoved the bottle into one of their hands.

Inside, as she crashed through the doors and away from him, he stood looking like a lost child. He felt lonely and helpless. He was a useless bastard. Why the hell hadn't he realised what Serena was doing long ago? He was so busy running his business, he'd missed what was really important. If she didn't make it, he'd never forgive himself. Even the fact that she'd kept telling him how much she wanted a baby. That alone was obviously affecting her hugely. Of course he'd paid that very little attention.

"Please God, don't take her away from me, I promise I'll be a better husband. I'll look after her and help her to get well. I'm sorry, for being such an asshole," he whispered.

It was over an hour later before a doctor approached him.

"Are you Serena Davenport's husband?"

"Yes, I'm Paul Davenport. How is she?"

"She's still in intensive care, Paul. She'd ingested a fair few of those tablets, and most of a bottle of vodka. We performed a gastric lavage, or stomach pumping, which will obviously remove any unabsorbed substances. With regards to the benzodiazepines, which are the type of drug she ingested, they are not normally linked with death. They are however, considerably more dangerous when mixed with alcohol. We've administered an antidote and that should protect the liver and heart from severe damage. She'll need to stay with us for a few days. I'm going to organise for a psychiatric team to assess her also."

"Thank God!" Relief swept over Paul but then came a wave of guilt. He felt like the worst person in the world. All he'd missed doing was handing her the pills to swallow or pouring the vodka for her.

"I'm in shock. I had no idea she was in such turmoil. I should have known." His voice was barely audible.

"Paul, there's no blame being apportioned here. People in crisis can hide things brilliantly. You won't be of any help to Serena if you crumble. She needs you now. We'll make sure she's well physically and we'll get you both linked into a programme to help with the psychiatric side of things. She's one of the lucky ones – it was a miracle that you found her so quickly. I'll speak with you later on. A nurse will come and get you shortly. As soon as she comes out of intensive care, you can see her. Why don't you get yourself a coffee?" With a flurry of white coat the doctor was gone.

Fighting back tears, Paul made his way down the shiny corridor to the café, his shoes squeaking on the polished surface. He ordered a latte and a sticky bun. Like a clockwork robot, he sat at a scruffy round table, on a grubby plastic seat. The café smelled stale and faintly of disinfectant. None of the other diners looked any happier than he did. The coffee was like dishwater and the bun was spongy and tasteless. Shoving them aside, he paid for a newspaper at a little stand in the doorway and walked back to where he'd been. Finding a grey plastic seat, he sat, jigging his leg and waited to be called.

His phone rang repeatedly. He didn't answer. Eventually, knowing his office would be wondering where he was, he called his PA and said that he had a family emergency and to cancel all that day's appointments.

Then, reluctantly, he phoned his mother-in-law.

"Paul, how are you sweetie?" Paul had never particularly warmed to Serena's mother. He found her selfish, false and totally self-absorbed.

"Hello Kate, I'm all right. Listen, I've got some shocking news for you and Jim. Poor Serena has been struggling lately and, the thing is, she's taken an overdose. I'm in the hospital now."

"What do you mean she's taken an overdose?" Kate screamed. "Don't tell me she's a drug addict?"

"No, nothing like that. I'll explain when I see you, but she's been having some problems and I just didn't realise how much it was affecting her. I feel like I've failed her." Paul was struggling to fight back tears.

"Why do you say that? You didn't feed her the drugs, did you?"

"No, but –"

"I'm stunned. It's so, so, common. Don't whatever you do, tell anyone about this, Paul. I don't need our friends looking at us with pity, or thinking we dabble in drugs in our family."

No wonder Serena ended up like this, Paul thought. She'd grown up with a nanny instead of a mother, and now, when she was crying out for help, all that ignorant cow could think of was her own reputation. None of those buzzards she called friends would understand either. Just so long as it didn't interfere with their golf or trip to the hairdresser's, they'd be fine.

"I just thought I'd let you know. She's in St Vincent's hospital if you want to see her. She'll be here for a few days." Paul resisted the urge to shout obscenities at her.

"Oh, right. Well, I can't get there today. If she's still there tomorrow I'll try to pop by. Can't you get her into a private clinic? Those public places are utterly vile," Kate sniffed.

"I'm well aware of that, I'm standing here. Right now, Serena needs care and attention. Where that happens isn't important at the moment. This was the nearest place I could get to. What matters is that she'll be okay, don't you think?"

"Yes, dear. Call me tomorrow. Tell Serena I send kisses – tootle-pip!" She hung up.

Paul punched the wall. That woman was for the birds. Her father was a decent man, and Paul knew he adored Serena, but he was abroad on business. It was up to him now to try and help his wife. He'd get the best team possible. She was in crisis and he was going to stop at nothing to make sure she got better. He wanted his happy and confident girl back. As a final effort to get a member of her family on board, he called Adele. Her phone clicked straight to the message-minder, so he left a brief message and hung up.

"You can come and see Serena now." The nurse appeared.

He was shocked when he saw her. In the hospital gown, with her hair plastered to her forehead, she looked pale and vulnerable. She was sleeping.

He took her hand and kissed it gently. "I'm sorry, darling, I won't let this happen to you again. We'll get through this together." He sat on the edge of a chair and held her hand as she slept.

It was after six o'clock that evening before Serena woke up. The sun was still shining and the noise of the rush-hour traffic outside was penetrating the hospital.

"Paul?" she looked to her husband. "Why am I in here?"

"You took some pills and drank a bottle of vodka earlier. You scared the shit out of me but we got here in time." He smiled gently at her. "You'll be fine."

"I'm sorry." Tears ran down the sides of her face as she lay unable to move in the bed. She felt paralysed, both physically and with mortification at what she'd done.

"No, I'm sorry. I should have known you were so unhappy. I'm going to help you now. We're going to get you through. Please just promise you'll let me try?" He pulled his chair closer to the bed and took her hands.

"I didn't really want to die. That wasn't my intention," she croaked. "I just wanted the hopelessness to fade. I wanted to feel no pain. I wanted to float above all the heartache. Just for a few minutes."

"I'm sorry, honey." Paul was crying openly too.

"How am I going to live if I can't drink? I feel like the light at the end of the tunnel has been blocked off and sealed up. I feel like I've nothing to look forward to anymore," she sobbed.

"It's going to take time. It's going to be bloody hard, but we'll do this. I'll help. We'll do it together," he soothed her. "As soon as you're well enough, we'll go to the Caribbean or somewhere lovely. You can lie on the beach and let the sunshine wash over you."

"And then we can eat food with no wine and go to bed at nine o'clock, sober!" she scoffed.

"We'll get used to it," Paul held her gaze. "You've got to try and get your head around it. We have to see drink as being an enemy rather than a friend. A friend wouldn't put you in this state after all."

"True." Serena thought about what he was saying. She'd never thought of drink as a bad thing. To her, it had always been a fun and cheerful thing, or a comfort. Never something which could damage or hurt her. Paul was making sense. Although the thought of giving up her wine and spirits was hideous, he did have a point.

Right at that moment, she'd never felt worse. Her head was booming, her stomach felt raw and sore. Her skin was tight and itchy. For Christ's sake, she was in a hospital gown, with her hair matted to her head and a drip in her arm. There was nothing glamorous or pleasurable about her current situation. Paul was right. Drink was not her friend. But as with any old friend, she knew it was going to be heartbreaking to say goodbye. She truly hoped she'd have the strength to do so.

38

tweeting@maternityunit.com
Birth plans can be helpful, so take the time to think yours
through, let's work together to make your birth the best for you.

It was the third week of June and the city was hot and sticky, as Angie finished up in the office in Dublin for the last time. At thirty-eight weeks gestation, her baby felt like it must weigh at least a stone by now.

She longed for the country air. As soon as the baby was born, she would go and stay with her parents for a while. She'd have all the freedom she craved, with space to push the pram and get over the birth. She also knew her parents would dote on the child, so she'd have ready-made baby-sitters. Not that she was planning on disappearing. She couldn't even imagine allowing anyone else hold the baby.

The antenatal classes finished up the week before. Herself and the other three went for a Chinese meal to celebrate. Leona was overdue by a week and not too happy.

"I think this child thinks it's an elephant. Don't they stay pregnant for two years or something?" She rubbed her belly in annoyance. "Me ma keeps telling me to eat curry to get it out. I've had heartburn and a dose of the trots, but no fucking baby. So I've gone back to the burgers. I'm dying to get back on the smokes too."

"Did you give up because you were pregnant?" Angie asked, impressed by Leona's abstinence.

"No, not really, it's just every time I smoke I puke. So I got pissed off puking and thought I'd knock it on the head until the baby comes along." She picked at her food.

"Would you not just stay off them at this stage?" Brenda suggested. "Surely you'd be better off not smoking and it costs a fortune these days."

"I know but once I'm stuck in with a baby at night-time, I'll be bored out of me brains, so I'll need something to do. I've a flat coming up with my sister and her baby – she smokes too, so it's something we can do together, you know. We're not really the type to sit and play scrabble. So it'll be a few cans and fags, you know yourself?"

"I wonder how Ruby is getting on?" Angie mused. "At least we're only here, she's in Spain with her mother. I'd say she feels like an oven-ready turkey at this rate. Can you imagine how hot she must feel?"

"She's a nice kid," said Sandra. "I hope she manages okay with the birth. Maybe we should arrange to have a little reunion once we're all settled. I'd say she could do with the support."

Leona was feeling kind of funny. She'd been uncomfortable all day. Wasn't able to eat her lunch and when she'd been on the bus on the way to the restaurant, she'd felt just odd.

She leaned forwards. "I know yous are eating, girls, and I feel sorry for Ruby too, but have any of yous ever felt like yous been kicked in the fanny?"

"Erm no." Angie stared at her.

"That's how I feel all day. Rotten. This pregnancy lark is shite really, isn't it? Fellas get away with murder. They do the business and bugger off. We're the ones left having to get fat and look like we've had a pump up our arses, while they sit in the pub and scratch their balls . . ."

Aaagh!" Leona grabbed the side of the table.

271

"I think your baby's coming, Leona!" Angie sat up excitedly. "Lucky we're only around the corner from the hospital!" She clapped in delight.

"It's all right for yous sitting watching and clapping. I feel like a fucking articulated lorry is trying to drive out me arse here! Ah bollox, me waters have gone, I'm drowning here!"

"I've got a long black coat, we'll put it on you to cover up the wet," said Sandra, standing up. "I'll phone my husband if you like to come and bring you to the hospital."

"Thanks, love, but I don't want any fucking man near me – will yous come with me?" Leona's face crunched as a contraction took hold.

"This baby looks like it's coming soon," Angie whispered to Brenda.

"Too right. I'll go out and flag down a taxi. Will you sort the bill and we can fix up with you later on?"

"Sure. Leona, I must go and pay the bill – just keep calm, love."

"I hope you'll remember to be calm yourself when you're trying to shit a bowling ball!" Leona was gripping the side of the table and gritting her teeth. "Mr China Man is going to kill me when he sees the mess I'm after making of his seat. At least it's red velvet!" She cackled briefly before wincing again.

The pain and obvious terror on the young girl's face made Angie afraid. She'd always thought of the birth as being a nice and calm and uplifting experience. Leona looked about as far from enjoying herself as it was possible to get.

Brenda stuck her head in the door to indicate that the taxi was waiting.

"I'll phone the hospital and let them know you're coming." Sandra was all business.

They put the coat around Leona and led her out to the taxi. Just as she was about to slide in, another whopper of a contraction hit her.

"*Fuuuuuuuck!*" she yelled, leaning forwards to try and bear the brunt of the pain.

When it subsided they all bundled in awkwardly. Within minutes they arrived at the hospital and Leona was put in a wheelchair and taken to the delivery ward.

Not quite knowing what to do, the others just stood in the corridor.

Moments later, a midwife appeared, with a gown and mask on.

"Leona would like someone to come in with her. We can only allow one person, due to insurance," she apologised.

The three women looked at each other.

"I'll go if you like?" Angie scanned their faces.

Sandra held her hands up. "Fine with me, I really don't think I could stomach it."

"Go ahead." Brenda gave Angie a quick hug.

Angie was instructed to wash her hands and the nurse helped her into a gown, put protective covers on her shoes, and handed her gloves and a mask.

"She's fully dilated and labouring quickly," the nurse explained. "I'd say it won't be long before the baby's born."

As they entered the room, Leona called out to Angie. "Jaysus, this is hideous! Come over here and don't be looking at me bits. I'll never be able to talk to you again if I think you've seen me fur-burger – *aaahhh!*" She was gripped by another contraction.

"Push the pain away, Leona," the midwife instructed. "Push right down into your bottom. Good girl, you're doing a fantastic job. This baby's in a hurry to meet you. It won't be long now, pet."

"What about me bleedin' drugs? I'd planned on having everything. This is shite, can you not give me a quick jab of somethi . . . *Aaaagh, help!*"

Angie stroked Leona's head and joined in with the team of three nurses in encouraging her.

"Go on, Leona, push! You're a star, you're flying it, you're doing it, keep going!"

"Okay, pant!" the nurse shouted, holding her hand up.

Leona panted. "Oh Christ, I want to push again," she squirmed.

"Just hold it, darling, you don't want to tear too much!" the nurse called out.

"I want to top meself, never mind tear meself in half!" Leona

273

tried to pant. "This is torture – I'm not a dog, I can't pant anymore."

"Okay, Leona, one big push for me!" The midwife gave her the green light. "Look down, here comes your baby!"

"No, it's like a bleeding alien coming out! Don't put it near me, it's manky looking!" She opened her eyes wide as her little girl slid out into the nurse's hands.

The clapping and whooping in the room was fantastic. Angie hugged her, crying and laughing all at the same time.

"God, that was just amazing. You're some woman. Well done, you're brilliant!" cried Angie.

"That was bleedin' brutal. Never again. Can you stitch up me fanny so I can't let it happen again?"

The nurse cleaned the baby and weighed her.

"Six pounds twelve ounces, a lovely weight – well done, Mum!" She handed the little bundle to Angie.

"Ah look, isn't she deadly?" She flushed with pride as she looked at her daughter.

"Oh, she's just beautiful!" Angie stared at the tiny face.

"Thanks for being with me, Angie. You're a real star. I was getting really scared on me own. I was planning on calling me sister but it all happened so fast."

"Pleasure. You were brilliant. Do you want me to tell the others?"

"Yeah, bring them in sure," Leona said.

"You'll have to wait a few minutes until we deliver the placenta and you might just need a stitch or two," the nurse smiled.

"I'll go and tell them the news," said Angie. "Have you got a name? Is it still Angel?"

"Giz a minute, she's only after arriving. I'll need to have a good look at her first." Leona stared at her baby.

"Of course," Angie smiled. She knew one thing though – it didn't matter what the baby was called – with a Mum like Leona, she'd be well looked after. If she inherited even an ounce of her mother's spirit and confidence, she'd be fine.

Angie went out to tell the others the news.

"How was it?" The other two gathered around Angie anxiously. "Is she okay?"

"She's great. God, she was brilliant – not a drug in sight, and she just flew it!" Angie oozed.

As the three women chatted excitedly in the hallway, inside the labour room Leona's placenta appeared.

"Jaysus, that looks like a big bag of raw mince! That's disgusting – yous can chuck that straight in the bin for a start!" Leona was looking at the bloody mass in horror.

"Do you know, some people fry it and eat it? It's meant to be very nutritious," the nurse laughed.

"I'd eat me own head and suck the sweat out of a rugby player's jockstrap before I'd eat that thing!" Leona giggled.

After she'd phoned her surprised mother and sisters, Leona asked if the three women could come in.

They poked their heads around the door and looked anxiously around the delivery room.

"Meet Madonna O'Brien," Leona announced proudly, cuddling her daughter.

The three women weren't sure if she was joking or not. Luckily they all oohed and ahhed and said what a beautiful little baby she was. It turned out she was deadly serious. The child was in fact going to be named after Leona's favourite singer.

By the time Leona's mother arrived, it was after eleven o'clock. The three women said their goodbyes and promised to visit Leona and the baby.

Angie arrived home and fell into bed exhausted. But she couldn't sleep. The whole miracle of birth and the gorgeous little baby Leona had produced had left her dumbfounded. It was truly amazing, the whole thing. Very soon, it would be her turn. Instead of feeling nervous now, she was excited and looking forward to it even more. She couldn't wait to see what her baby looked like. Was it a boy or a girl? Unlike loads of other mothers-to-be, she had absolutely no inkling as to what sex her baby might be.

Some days she was convinced it was a girl, then she'd change her mind. She might catch a glimpse of a blue car or a person dressed in blue, and decide that was a sign from above that she was having a boy. The truth was that she didn't care what sex the baby was. Just as long as it was healthy, she would be the happiest girl in the world.

Eventually, at one in the morning, she drifted off to sleep. She was sleeping less and less as she expanded. The baby was now pushing her ribs out and dragging her lower back. She was still surrounded by pillows and frequenting the bathroom all night. After this evening, she felt less annoyed by it all. Knowing what a wonderful prize she was going to get at the end made it all worthwhile.

39

tweeting@rubytuesday.com
I've had enough — let it be over already. This is hell on wheels.
3.30a.m. I want my old life back.

R uby had been awake for most of the night. Even with the air-conditioning up high, and the windows open, there was barely a breath of air in the place. At a quarter to four, she picked up the house phone and dialled Damo's mobile number. It clicked on to voice mail. Damn, she'd forgotten the hour time difference. It was already a quarter to five at home. Too late to catch Damo at the club. So she listened to his voice mail.

You've reached the voice mail of Damo McCabe, please leave a brief message after the tone. Thanking you.

Ruby hung up. What would she say?

She must have drifted off to sleep at some stage, because she woke with a start. Although it was still only nine thirty in the morning, the sun was up and Spain was hot, hot, hot. Ruby was uncomfortable in her own skin. She didn't know if she wanted to walk, swim, run, eat, drink or lie in bed. Shuffling outside with an iced tea, she lowered herself onto the sun lounger and felt a sudden rush of heat down her legs.

"Mummy, help!" Ruby screamed.

"What is it?" Adele snapped out of her daydream and rushed out to the veranda.

Ruby was standing with a look of bewilderment on her face. "I've wet myself. I just went to lie down and then it happened. I'm sorry!" Ruby burst out crying.

Adele rushed to her side. Ruby grimaced and promptly threw up.

"It's okay, Ruby. I think the baby's coming." Adele tried to sound calm but inside she was panicking.

"I'm going to the kitchen to get some cloths to clean you up. Wait here." Adele flew into the apartment and grabbed some kitchen paper and a damp cloth.

After she'd cleaned Ruby as best she could, she phoned Dr Alejandro. "Ruby's waters have broken, shall I take her straight to the clinic?" she panted. She felt like her heart was going to come through her chest with fear.

"Yes, bring her here. I am waiting for you," he answered calmly.

Adele grabbed a fresh dress and Ruby's hospital bag, which she'd ended up packing on her own a couple of days previously. Ruby had no interest and had refused to even look at it.

"Let's get you changed and we'll head off to the clinic," Adele instructed, sounding much more confident than she felt. Grabbing her phone she sent a text to Harry, Serena and her parents:

On the way to the clinic, Ruby's waters have broken.

Within minutes mother and daughter were on the motorway, speeding towards the clinic.

"Ow, Mummy, it hurts! This is brutal. Can they make the pain go away?" Ruby was gripping the handle on the inside of the car door.

The terror in her eyes made Adele cringe. If she could have taken the pain on board herself, she'd have gladly swapped places with her daughter.

"Good girl, Ruby. It'll all be over soon," she soothed.

By the time they reached the clinic, Ruby was hysterical. Her breathing was laboured and she was screaming in panic.

Adele ran into the clinic to notify them of her arrival.

"She's in the car and she's screaming. Can you send an attendant to help me bring her in, please?" she begged.

Within minutes, they were in an examination room. Dr Alejandro appeared, in his white coat, looking cool and calm.

"Okay, Ruby, I need you to tell me when the pain started."

He spoke in Spanish to a nurse, instructing her to put a monitor around Ruby's tummy.

As she slipped the monitor on, he took Ruby's blood pressure.

"I noticed the pain a bit last night. But it wasn't bad. I just thought it was those Branson pickle things," she grimaced.

"Braxton Hicks contractions can happen at this time, so you're right about that," he said. "Did the pain get worse this morning at all?"

"Not until the water came out. Since then, it's been much worse. Mummy, help!" she gripped Adele's hand and began to sob.

The nurse and Dr Alejandro babbled at speed, while Adele and Ruby listened anxiously.

"The baby is not happy, Ruby," the doctor said. "The heartbeat is not even and it looks like the baby is in distress. We are going to have to perform a caesarean section at once. When was the last time you ate?"

"Not since last night and I got sick just before we came here," Ruby whimpered.

"Okay, that's all good. I need you and your mother to sign this consent form and we will have to take you straight to theatre."

Ruby was bathed in sweat and writhing in pain. The constant Spanish babble going on around them was just adding to her distress.

As soon as they had signed the form, Ruby was wheeled off at high speed. With a crash through the double doors, she was gone. Adele was left standing all alone. Dr Alejandro had told her they'd call her as soon as the baby was delivered safely. Due to the fact that it was an emergency section, she wasn't allowed into the delivery room.

She phoned Harry quickly to tell him what was happening. He promised to get the first flight possible.

"Phone me as soon as you know anything," he said. "And Adele?"

"What, Harry?" She sounded like she was going to crack up.

"Tell Ruby I love her and I'll see her soon." He choked on the words.

"Okay, love. Talk to you soon. I texted Serena earlier but she hasn't responded – ring her and let her know, will you? I don't need her being all affronted when we get back." She hung up. Adele had never felt so alone or so terrified.

The next twenty minutes seemed like hours. Adele sat on a plastic chair in the hallway, staring at the floor like a zombie. She remembered the day Ruby had been born. It was all far less dramatic and much slower. She'd taken her time arriving. At the time, Adele had wished it had all been faster, but now she appreciated it had all been more natural.

The silence which enveloped her in this sterile hallway was unnerving and strangely eerie. She strained to try and hear if Ruby was screaming. Nothing. She may as well have been in an empty building. There were no sounds from any of the rooms. It was like her daughter had been taken to another planet.

Moments later, a nurse padded towards Adele.

"Can you come this way, please?" She didn't smile.

"Is Ruby okay? Is the baby okay?" Adele was beginning to panic as she scuttled down the corridor.

"Come, please," the nurse repeated.

As they entered the room, Adele heard the shrill sound of a baby crying. Bringing her shaking hands to her mouth, she could barely breathe as she took in the first sounds of life. It was coming from the side of the room but she couldn't see anything. The baby was surrounded by doctors and nurses.

She looked at Ruby. She was lying motionless on the operating table with a mask over her face. Her eyes were closed. There was a sort of box covered in disposable material propped up to block Ruby's view of the surgery that had taken place.

"Ruby!" Adele rushed to her daughter. Standing over her, she stared at her child.

Dr Alejandro appeared wearing green scrubs and matching mask.

"I had to knock her out. She panicked too much. She lost plenty of blood. She had a condition called placenta previa, where the placenta is very low in the uterus. She will be okay but she's lucky you got her here very quickly."

"Thank you, Dr Alejandro. What about the baby? Is it going to be okay?" Adele felt like she'd been run over by a bus.

"The baby looked healthy. You go over there and you can see what you've got." He smiled for the first time.

Adele shuffled hesitantly towards the crying baby sounds. She stood motionless behind the babbling team of medics, a sea of pale green scrubs uniforms all speaking Spanish. One of them noticed her.

"Come!" The mask moved as the lady spoke. Moses himself couldn't have done a better job of parting the sea of bodies.

As they all moved to either side, there lying on the bunched-up paper towels was Ruby's little boy.

He was smaller than Adele recalled Ruby being, but he was so beautiful. He had a shock of dark fluffy hair. His little cross face was all scrunched up like an angry prune. His mini-fists were balled and his legs were kicking out in protest.

"Say hello to your grandmother." The nurse scooped him up and wrapped him in a towel. "Here he is, Señora."

"Oh my goodness, I'd forgotten just how tiny new babies are," she whispered.

As Adele took her grandchild in her arms, all feelings of anger or resentment at his conception melted into insignificance. Nothing in the world mattered more that this little miracle. Why on earth had she been angry? Sure, it was probably not the best time in the world for Ruby to have a baby but now that he was here Adele vowed to cherish, protect and adore him. As tears of love and adoration coursed down her cheeks, all her maternal instincts kicked into gear. Her heart physically lurched at the strength of emotion that hit her like a force.

The baby calmed down and yawned as Adele held him close to her. His tiny face was all perfectly formed, his spiky dark fluff, grazing the tops of his little round ears.

"He's very brown, isn't he? His father is foreign, you know," Adele said to the nurse.

"Yes, he look little bit brown because he have, how you say? Jaundice. He will go into the incubator for a little sleep in the warm and he will be fine yes? May we take him to weigh him and then he need to go to the warm?"

"Oh sure." Adele reluctantly handed the little bundle to the nurse. Every emotion under the sun ran through her mind. From love and pride to overwhelming sadness. She was desperately sad that his birth and upbringing was going to be tainted by lies. Now that he was here, she wasn't so sure that taking him and passing him off as her own was the right thing to do.

Tiptoeing over to Ruby, Adele gazed down at her daughter.

"How are you doing there, sweetheart?" The tears sprang afresh as she stroked her child's head.

"Is it over?" Ruby tried to look upwards but couldn't manage to meet her mother's eyes. She felt like she was really pissed. Her eyes were so heavy, her body was so tired. It was such a huge effort to speak.

"No, darling. It's only beginning." Adele didn't even try to hide her tears.

"Whatever." Ruby took a deep breath and allowed her eyes to close. She wasn't in pain anymore but she could feel the doctor doing something on her tummy. It was a kind of tugging feeling and the underneath of her back felt a bit wet and sticky. She hoped that was from the swabs they were using rather than her own blood.

The bright lights were like an alien invasion above her head. The surgical lights were housed on a round metal disc, which looked almost like a record turntable. All the doctors and nurses had masks on, so it was even more scary. She couldn't see anyone's face, so she had no idea if they were smiling or annoyed with her. At this stage she felt just like she was nothing but a nuisance to everyone. Now she'd caused even more trouble, having a caesarean section. She couldn't even give birth without causing bother. Her mother would probably wait until they were alone in her room before she gave out. Well, let her have her say. She'd just listen and remember not to roll her eyes and just get it all out of the way.

Ruby just kept the thought of going out with Damo to clubs and posh restaurants in the forefront of her mind. All she had to do was get through the next few weeks and they'd be able to go back home and forget all about this nightmare.

The midwife handed Adele a piece of paper a few minutes later. Ruby was ready to be moved into recovery, so Adele gathered her handbag and coat. As they wheeled her daughter into the recovery room, she looked at the printed page.

Sex:	*Male*
Length:	*19.61 inches*
Weight:	*2.49 kilos / 5lb 8oz*
Mother's name:	*Ruby White*

It was only a small printout of routine measurements but it was like a knife stabbing Adele in the heart. Ruby was this child's mother. What right had she to interfere with that? As soon as Ruby was properly awake and able to talk, she needed to ask her what she wanted to do. She'd been wrong to impose her views on her daughter. She was very young, it wasn't going to be easy, but it wasn't a hopeless or bad situation. Looking at that little baby, nothing else mattered anymore.

Adele didn't give a toss now what the neighbours thought. If her friends had a problem with it, then they weren't her friends. It was time for Adele to grow up. Whatever about Ruby facing her responsibility, Adele knew she needed to do the same.

Mother's name: Ruby White

Adele read that part over and over again. Who was she to tell Ruby she couldn't be the child's mother?

By the time Ruby was properly awake and able to be transferred to a private room, Harry had arrived. He and Adele went to the neonatal unit. All the baby had on was a tiny nappy and a little cotton hat. He had white sticky pads on his chest connected to wires.

"Why are those things on his chest?" Adele asked the nurse.

"We need monitor his heart. Not for too long, he very healthy little boy," the nurse smiled. "He just need to be warm for maybe one week."

Harry stood motionless in front of the clear plastic box which contained his grandson. The baby yawned and stuck his tiny thumb in his mouth and settled back to sleep.

"Oh God, he's just beautiful. He's so pure and innocent. So untouched by the ups and downs of life. It's up to us to protect him and make sure he gets all the best chances possible." Harry put his hand onto the Perspex and stared. Almost an hour passed before they could bear to tear themselves away from him.

"Ruby needs us too, let's go to her and see if she's awake." Adele linked his arm and they walked towards the area where Ruby was resting. "Did you talk to Serena before you got your flight?" Adele still hadn't heard from her, in spite of having sent a text.

"No, I got her voice mail, so I just left a message. I didn't try Paul's mobile though. I'll call him later on." Harry shrugged.

Ruby was exhausted. She felt like she needed to sleep for a week. Opening her eyes was such an effort. She put her hand down to her tummy. It was still pretty huge. She'd kind of thought she'd be flat and normal again as soon as they got the baby out. But although it wasn't as hard, it still seemed enormous.

Her parents arrived in. They were full of smiles and being really nice to her. They even looked and sounded a little bit drunk.

"Hi, darling. How are you feeling?" Harry kissed her.

"Hi, Daddy. I'm okay. I feel really knackered though," she smiled. It was great to see her daddy. He seemed less angry with her. Her mum was all teary-eyed. God, she looked terrible. She looked old and her make-up was all seeping down her cheeks. She thought of telling her to go into the bathroom and fix it, but then that might make her cross again. No, it was better to say nothing.

"We saw the baby just now," her mum said.

"I know, they told me you were over there. It's a boy, isn't it?" Ruby examined her nails, biting the skin around the sides. "They said they'll bring me to see him in a wheelchair later on this evening, if I feel up to it."

Ruby was a bit surprised it was a boy. She must have thought it was going to be a girl. Anyway, it wasn't really her concern. She wasn't bothered either way. But a boy might please her parents all the same. They had a girl and look at all the trouble she'd caused, so a boy was probably a better bet for them.

They could send him to one of the big rugby schools and he could be a lawyer or a doctor. Maybe a son could make them proud. She'd failed so miserably and ruined everything, so this might be a new start for them. They could have the type of child they'd dreamed of.

Suddenly she had a moment of anxiety. What if it looked like a mini Damo? Shit, what if her parents looked at him and put two and two together?

"What does he look like?" Ruby stared at her mother.

"Oh Ruby, he's just a little angel. He's not unlike you when you were born. He has dark fluffy hair and a tiny perfectly formed face. You're going to love him!" Adele was all teary again.

Although he was a part of Damo, Ruby wasn't that pushed about seeing him. He'd caused her so much anxiety so far. But then she pictured Damo's face. Maybe this little boy was her key to his heart? Maybe he would take one look at the baby and realise that he wanted them to be a family. She needed some headspace, she needed them all to go away and stop talking at her all the time. Making suggestions, and being all cheerful and over-smiley. She needed to figure out how she could use this to get Damo to love her.

The nurses kept telling her they'd bring her to the neonatal unit as soon as they could move her. She thought it might sound rude to say that she wasn't that interested. She was glad they'd knocked her out. Before they'd given her the injection had been a total nightmare.

The pain was rank. It was like the worst period pain multiplied by a thousand. Then the snappy man had come in to give her an epidural. That was awful too. He'd barked at her and told her to stay still. Then the pain had got worse. She remembered screaming and trying to kick the nurses away. Then it had all gone woozy, like being really drunk.

When she woke up, they told her it was all over.

"You have a son." The nurse had smiled like a moron.

Ruby realised she was waiting for her to answer.

"Great," she'd said, feeling numb.

Feeling around her tummy, she found she was bandaged up, so it was impossible to know what kind of a scar she was going to have. She wondered if she'd be able to wear a bikini again, or low-rise jeans? She had a yellow and a pink Juicy Couture tracksuit her Aunt Serena had bought her, which she was dying to show off to her friends, but if this baby had left her looking like Frankenstein she'd be well pissed off.

As she looked up at her parents, they were huddled together looking all misty-eyed.

"Ruby, we need to talk about the baby," Adele began.

"I'll sign the papers and I won't tell anyone, don't worry." She picked at a loose thread on the bedspread. "I know I've totally ruined your lives but maybe this new kid can kind of heal all the hurt and fix the problems. Maybe all is not lost." Ruby shrugged, her young face stern and pouting. She tried to change the subject. "When will this flabby stuff go away? I didn't think it was all going to be here still."

"Listen, darling, we all need to think seriously about this. I'm not so sure we have the right plan. That little boy is your baby. Not ours. I'm not sure we should go ahead with our original idea." Adele stared up into her husband's eyes and back at Ruby.

"What?" Ruby looked utterly astounded.

"What are you saying, Adele?" Harry looked at his wife in shock.

"Let's not be too hasty. Ruby, go and see your baby when you're ready. Think long and hard about this. Now that he's here, I just want what's best for all of us, especially you, darling. Daddy and I have no right to tell you what to do." Adele began to sob.

Oh Christ. This was not what Ruby needed right now. Why did her mother always have to get on her wick? Why did she have to be so mental and hysterical about everything? They should just get on with the plan and move on. Just when she thought things might get back to normal, now they were moving the boundaries again.

"I'll go along with whatever you decide too," Harry added firmly.

Great. Now they were both looking at her, expecting her to come up with some marvellous plan which was going to save the day. She wasn't the bloody Scooby-Doo gang for Christ's sake!

"I need some time. I'm too groggy and sore to do this right now," Ruby sounded a little more narky than she'd meant to. If only Damo would phone. If she had an inkling that he might want to be a father to this child, it might change her mind.

"Okay, honey," said Harry, "but all we're saying is that we're not making any firm decisions yet. Let's all have a few days and try to settle down. We owe the baby that."

"Yeah, okay, whatever." Ruby held her hand up to signal she'd had more than enough of this random mind-changing teary-eyed parental breakdown.

"Have you thought of a name for him?" Adele asked, blowing her nose.

"Nah, you can decide," Ruby yawned. She really wished her parents would go away. She was wrecked and all she really wanted to do was sleep. She didn't care if they called him Satan. "Listen, you two go on back to the apartment. It's been a long day. I'll see you both in the morning, we can talk about it all then." Ruby just wanted to turn over and block it all out. The needle thing they'd left in her arm was sore. They were giving her saline and painkillers. Along with the effects of the anaesthetic she really wasn't in the mood for chat.

"Okay, well, if you think you're all right here?" said her father.

Her parents looked unsure.

"I'm fine, just go. I'm knackered and I really can't take any more bullshit today," she snapped.

Harry and Adele looked at each other and back at her. The hurt and disappointed look had returned. It was actually nearly better. It was more normal at least. They kissed her and she was finally left alone. Thank Christ.

Drifting in and out of sleep, she couldn't really have a proper kip because the nurses kept coming in and poking her. First blood pressure, then medicine, then asking her about her pain. Then wanting to look at her wound, then asking her question after question. She wished they'd all just bugger off and leave her alone. The only person she wanted to hear from was Damo.

They all kept apologising that she hadn't seen the baby yet. Her blood pressure was still a little high, so they thought they couldn't move her until the morning now. Big swing. She didn't give a shit anyway.

Thoughts of Damo kept coming in and out of her mind. Should she ring him? Maybe she could do that thing where you call a mobile and dial "5" to go straight to voice mail. At least then she could just leave a message to say it was a boy, but her parents were naming him and raising him.

Serena, she could talk to her. She'd understand how she felt. The phone went straight to voice mail.

"You've reached Serena Davenport, I cannot come to the phone right now, please leave a brief message after the tone and I will return your call at my earliest convenience."

Ruby smiled. Loads of people thought Serena was a bit scary. But then again, nobody else knew her like Ruby did.

"Hi, Aunt Serena, it's me. I had a caesarean section – it was all pretty vile. I had a boy. Call me when you get the message. Where are you? Oh and Aunt Serena?" She paused. "I miss you and I love you." Ruby hung up as the tears began to flow.

40

tweeting@themercedesking.com
If anyone wants to know what a total git and a waste of space sounds like, just follow my tweets . . . maybe I should change my name to git-on-a-stick.com???

Damo was at the end of his tether. His head was thumping all the time and he wished he was dead. He knew he was a disaster to live with. Noreen was barely talking to him. He didn't blame her.

After the day he'd got pissed and smashed up the office at the club, one of the bouncers had found him passed out and brought him home.

The following morning, Noreen had tried to talk to him, to ask him why he was hitting the bottle.

"You've never been a drinker, Damo. I lived with a piss-head of a father and I'm not putting up with being married to one," she'd warned.

"Leave it out, will ya? There's a recession going on, Noreen. Sometimes a man needs to vent, ya know?"

Noreen had gone out thankfully. Damo was bringing a big party of TV celebs into the club that evening. Although he'd have to sort them with a few free bottles of bubbly, he was hoping they'd get a bit jarred and the tills would start to fill. If he promised them a lock-in, with a bit of luck they'd stay until the morning and usually that

289

would fuel a bit of frivolous spur-of-the moment spending. Hopefully, they'd be locked and buying bottles of good stuff. Dear stuff. Bottles of Cristal so they could show off. All the better to line his pockets.

For some reason, he kept thinking about Ruby. She couldn't have long to go now. He found himself daydreaming about the baby. Would it be a girl or a boy? When Noreen had the three kids, he'd been at work. He now realised that he hadn't been much help. He'd kind of kept on doing his work and hadn't got too involved.

Yet again, he found himself wondering why Noreen had stayed with him. Fair enough he'd made a good go of his work and they had a grand life, but he was a selfish prick in a lot of ways. He'd been like a tomcat for most of their marriage, not that she had a clue of half the stuff he got up to. Noreen was too innocent and too much of a home bird. She'd never had any interest in meeting any of the stars or having her picture in the social columns of the magazines. At first, years ago, he'd tried to encourage her to be a socialite. To get a boob job, dye her hair and wear the high heels and all that. But she'd no interest.

"If you want to be with a Barbie doll, go and find one. I'm who I am, take it or leave it, Damo. You might have changed but I haven't. Don't get me wrong. I love our house, I like the comfort of the few quid, but I'm not a dolly-bird. If I'm not enough for you, then go."

She was a tough old bird in fairness to her. True to herself, he thought bitterly. Unlike him.

If all this came out, he'd be finished. And rightly so too. He didn't deserve Noreen's love.

He found it harder and harder to get up in the mornings. He'd pretty much stopped his gym work. He used to be pumping weights and on his treadmill every day. He took pride in his appearance. Now he didn't give a shit anymore. Who cared if he was a bit overweight? What was he thinking going around dressed in designer gear? He was a sad old git. Who was he trying to kid? He still ran his clubs, he went to work, he did the books, he paid the lads. But his enjoyment of it all was gone. He hadn't washed his Merc for nearly two weeks. He'd even put it through the electronic car wash the other day. It'd been so filthy he couldn't see out, so he'd shoved it through the car wash after filling up with petrol. Which was something he would have never done in the past. He was firmly of the belief that those brush-wash yolks wrecked the paint on cars. Scratched it to buggery and took the showroom finish off the paint. Leaving it all dull and listless. He'd always hand-washed his cars, using all the special chamois and wax stuff.

* * *

It was after two o'clock in the morning in Spain. Ruby woke up feeling confused. For a spilt second, she didn't know where she was. Then it all came flooding back, as she inhaled the antiseptic smell and felt the hard bed beneath her broken body. She rooted in her pink Kipling bag. Her prized bag, complete with coloured monkeys attached to the zip. It contained her wallet, some lip gloss, shades and her phone.

Turning the mobile on, it beeped to let her know she had a new voice message. Accessing her mailbox, she listened. It was from Serena.

"*Received at 3 p.m.*", the message minder informed her. "*Hi, baby girl, I'm sorry I missed you earlier. I spoke to your mum briefly and she tells me you were amazing.*" There was a pause and Ruby heard her sob. "*Anyway, I hope you know that you are the most wonderful girl. You have made my life so –*" Her voice wobbled again. "*So fantastic. I love you, baby girl. You take care now …*" The line went dead.

Weird, Ruby mused. Aunt Serena sounded so upset. Not just emotional but as if there was something wrong.

Without thinking, she phoned Damo's mobile. It rang out and she heard his voice mail. Tears sprang up and she suddenly felt anger and rejection welling up inside her. Pulling herself together, she took a deep breath after the beep.

"Damo, it's me, Ruby. I just wanted you to know, I had our baby. It's a boy, in case you were wondering. I kept waiting for you to phone, I thought you might even call once, but you obviously don't care about me at all. I'm going to let my parents take the baby and raise him. I think it will be the fairest thing in the circumstances. I wish things could have been different. I know I'll probably regret saying this but I need you to know one thing. I thought you loved me. I was in love with you," she laughed bitterly. "I won't call you again."

Damo's phone logged the missed call and sat on the kitchen counter in the darkness.

* * *

The following morning, Noreen was lighting a cigarette and taking a quick slurp of her tea when she spotted Damo's iPhone. Curiously she picked it up to have a quick look. He never ever left his phone lying around, so she rarely got a chance to snoop through it. There was a missed call. Scrolling, Noreen was amazed to see Ruby's name. As if on autopilot, she dialled the mailbox. Nothing in the world could have prepared her for the message she was about to hear.

Upstairs in their bedroom, Damo was finally asleep. He'd done too much coke the night before and the TV crowd had been mad altogether. Great craic, but they'd nearly drunk the place dry. Not being a boozer, he'd done a good few lines to keep up. In turn he had ended up wired to the moon. His body and mind were knackered. He could hear Noreen thumping up the stairs. Sometimes that woman was so bloody noisy first thing in the morning. He didn't come in bashing around when she was asleep.

"*That's it, Damo McCabe! How could you?*" She was yelling like a madwoman.

Sitting bolt upright in the bed, he held his head with his hands.

"Hey, take it easy, what the hell is wrong with you?"

"*You fucking animal!* I knew you were playing the field, for years. I've known you've been off with young ones. Anything in a skirt. But I turned a blind eye. No marriage is perfect and at least you didn't hit me like me da used to do to me ma. You didn't drink and you gave me and the kids what we needed. I thought it was worth it. But this is a step too far. You should be castrated for what you've done!"

"What the hell are you on about? What do you mean you knew I was playing away from home?" Jaysus, this was all just too much, especially at this hour of the morning. The woman was possessed.

"Don't play me for a fool for a second longer, Damo. It ends here. I just listened to a message on your phone."

"What were you doing with my phone?" His eyes widened in panic. "Who rang?"

"Ruby."

"Ah shite! Noreen, wait. I can explain, this isn't what it looks like, love."

"Don't speak, Damo. Don't open your mouth. She is like one of our own. Mariah's best friend. A bloody *child* for crying out loud. She rang to tell you that you have a son. You animal! Get out of this house and with God as my witness I will drag you through every court and get what I deserve out of you. I will take you to the cleaners, Damo. I will make you pay for what you've done. You utter bastard!"

"Noreen, please! Ah no, not me Paul Smith suits! Ah come on, don't feck me stuff out the window! The neighbours will be looking. You'll be morto at the bingo. Calm down, love!"

"You have made it more than clear that I am not your love, and the girls at bingo will come and help me set fire to any piece of your shit that happens to survive the next hour. So thanks for your concern, but I'm sorting this out. My way."

Damo hauled himself out of bed and went to get his iPhone, which had a cracked face from the force of being flung at the wall. Listening to Ruby's message, he blanched. Holy shit, no wonder Noreen was so angry. Jaysus, Ruby was gone mental. Must be all those pregnancy hormones that people go on about.

Then, in the midst of all the panic, a fact hit home. He had another son. Shit.

41

Ruby could feel a shuddering sensation. It was backed by an irritating noise. Jumping slightly, she opened her eyes. A nurse was standing there smiling at her.

"What?" Ruby asked rudely. "I was sleeping just in case you hadn't noticed!" She tried to turn over in the bed. Her stomach hurt like hell. It was so bad she felt like she'd been stabbed repeatedly. She caught her breath and tried not to cry.

"*Hola, mi niña*, are you sore?" The nurse was strapping a Velcro band around the top of her arm to take her blood pressure.

"The pain is terrible," Ruby winced.

"*Bueno, en un minuto* we go to see *el bebe*?" she said gently.

"Whatever." Ruby still didn't have any inclination to see the baby. So far, all he'd done was cause hassle. First he'd made her parents hate her. Then he'd caused Damo to ignore her. She looked like a deflated balloon and the pain was beyond her worst nightmares. Why the hell would she want to see him? "I'll tell you when I feel up to it," she muttered. She'd just tell them that she wasn't able to move. That'd solve it. The baby could bond with her

294

parents and they could all be a happy little family together. That'd leave her free to get her life back and stop feeling like she was a failure. Her parents had been full of what a cutie he was, so let them love him.

After a painful injection, and more poking and hassle, Ruby felt like kicking the nurse in the face. She was so bloody pleasant too. What was she so happy about? All she did was piss people off.

Ruby tried to lie on her side, so she could put her back to the door. The nurse had insisted she leave the door open, so they could "keep an eye on her". What did they think? That she was going to run out of here dressed in a lame hospital gown? Besides, they had tubes shoved into her, one to drain her bladder, a drip with antibiotics and saline and bandages on her tummy. She was hardly going to the shopping centre or off to the beach in this state.

Then they told her she had to stay here for another four days at least. She wanted to die.

"*El bebe*, he need stay here, for keep warm, no? He need wait here few days. He will need the time in the, how you say, *incubadora*?"

"Incubator," Ruby supplied.

"*Si*, but if he stay so good, he can go home with you. He is a strong little boy. You will him the mama milk?" The nurse motioned towards Ruby's breast. "*Si*? I can bring you pump now?"

"No, I've no intention of breastfeeding. Give him whatever you like. Ask my mother when you see her. She's adopting him, so she'll be interested in what you're doing."

The nurse looked mildly confused. "*No comprende*," she shrugged.

"No milk from mama. You give him bottle, yes?" Ruby prayed the nurse would get the message.

The nursing staff had all been briefed by Dr Alejandro about the adoption arrangement. They'd also been instructed to make sure that the girl was not pushed into anything.

"You must give her the chance to make an informed and definite decision when the baby is born," he'd said.

The nurse felt sorry for her. The girl was full of anger and seemed to want nothing to do with the poor little baby. She hoped that seeing him would melt the heart of ice she seemed to have formed.

"Do you have name for Bebe?" The nurse was refusing to give up on Ruby.

"Listen, lady," Ruby yelled, "you obviously don't get it! My parents are adopting the baby – you need to ask *them* all these questions. It's not my concern. Quite frankly, I don't give a toss what they call him. It's up to them. They should roll in here at some stage. I'm sure you can all sit around and drink coffee and talk about what to call him. But for now, I'm knackered and sore and I'm really not in the mood for talking crap with you or anyone else for that matter, *entiende*?" Ruby snapped her eyes shut.

Sighing and unable to understand most of what the girl was shouting, the midwife decided it would be better to leave Ruby alone for a little while. She was so angry and aggressive. She might just fare better if they stopped pushing her for a while.

Adele and Harry, meanwhile, had arrived at the clinic.

They'd slept well, relieved that Ruby and the baby were both safe. As they'd driven in, they wondered if Ruby might have picked a name for him.

"I just hope she doesn't pick Zonon or Jamiroquai or some very strange name we'd never chose," Adele giggled.

"Well, if she has, we'll just have to grin and bear it. It really doesn't matter what he's called."

"I think he's going to be spoilt rotten by his granddad," Adele smiled.

"I'm already imagining taking him to rugby matches. It'll be great to have another man around the house. I've been surrounded by women for far too long!"

Now, as they entered the clinic, Adele's thoughts returned to Serena and she sighed. "I thought things just couldn't get any worse, and now this catastrophe with Serena. Jesus, Harry, what did I do to deserve all this?" Adele was reaching a stage where she just couldn't take any more.

"Things can only get better, love." Harry put his arm around his wife as they walked towards the neonatal unit.

The nurse said they could hold the baby for a few minutes. All the wires he'd had connected to him the previous evening were gone.

"He is doing so great. He is a little fighter. I don't think he will be too long in here. Ruby maybe go home in four or five days. If he continues so well, he can go too." The nurse opened the incubator and gently lifted the little scrap out. Wrapping him in warm cotton blankets, she handed him to Adele.

She looked lovingly at the perfect little face. He made tiny almost bleating noises. "He's like a little lamb, isn't he?" Kissing his forehead, she passed him over to Harry.

He felt like a giant holding the tiny little being. All he wanted was to protect this little child.

"Hello, little man, you're a real little trooper, aren't you?"

The baby raised his eyebrows, and they both laughed.

"He's listening to you," Adele was overjoyed.

They'd talked for hours the night before. The shock of Serena taking the overdose had actually rattled their cage in another way. They'd decided definitely that they needed to let Ruby decide what way she wanted this to go.

"We've no right to go against her wishes, Harry. If she feels she wants the responsibility of this child, we can still be there for her, but we can't make the decision on her behalf. We can't run the risk of having her backed into a corner like poor Serena has been. When I spoke to Paul, he sounded so remorseful. He kept saying that we all should have been watching for the signs, listening to Serena more. It just made me think about Ruby. We want what's best for her and that darling baby, but forcing her into something might be the worst thing we can do as parents."

"I know. It's all a different story now, and everything changes when you actually see him, doesn't it?"

This little baby was a blessing. He wasn't something to be shrouded in lies or hidden away. If Ruby was willing to be his mother, they'd stand by her decision.

"Feck the neighbours!" said Harry.

"And if any of our friends have a problem with him, then they're not truly our friends, are they?"

After they'd both held the baby, they made their way to Ruby's room.

"Hello, darling. How are you feeling today?" Adele bent to kiss her. Ruby moved her head to the side and pouted. She didn't answer and she didn't meet their gaze. "Ruby? Are you okay?"

"Fabulous."

"How did you sleep?" Harry asked.

"Grand! It's great having a pile of wires sticking into you. Every time I even try to sleep, they come in and wake me up. All in all, I'm just loving it in here." She stared straight ahead.

Harry and Adele didn't quite know what to say or do. Ruby seemed so angry and upset. A nurse walked into the room.

"Ruby, now that your mama and papa are here, we all go to see bebe now, yes?" she asked.

"No."

Ruby wished they'd all just go away. What was she? A prize cow? Why did they all have to stand there staring at her and why in the name of God did they continue to ask such stupid bloody questions?

"Look, I thought I made myself clear this morning. That baby is theirs," she pointed violently at her parents, "not mine, *theirs*! Talk to them about seeing it. I'm not interested. Not now, not later on, not tomorrow, not next week. Now would you all do me a favour and leave me the hell alone."

"Ruby!" Adele was shocked and embarrassed.

"That's it, Ruby. I can understand you are finding this difficult but you are not allowed to speak to people like that!" Harry was really angry. "Nurse, if you wouldn't mind, can you organise for Ruby to see the baby?" He folded his arms and stared at Ruby, warning her not to object any further.

Muttering under her breath, Ruby realised she was beaten. She'd go and see the baby and make all the right noises, and then get them to bring in the papers. She'd sign the papers and then the baby would be nothing to do with her. Perfect.

Feeling a little happier that they might all get off her case, she roused herself and complied with the nurse as she helped her into a wheelchair.

"Just wait until you see him. He's just the sweetest little rabbit," her mother was babbling.

"Whatever." Ruby rolled her eyes and sighed deeply.

As they rounded the corner, Ruby saw the baby in the clear plastic box. His head was turned towards her. His tiny eyes were peeping out. He was sucking his thumb.

"Wow, he's really small!" Ruby exclaimed. "He felt a lot bigger when he was in my tummy." She was wheeled over to him. He looked like he was trying to focus on the side of the incubator.

"What do you think?" Adele asked.

"Yeah, he's a baby all right. Lovely. Great." Ruby stared at him. She honestly didn't feel anything. She had no urge to pick him up or touch him. He was sweet, very small, and his head was kind of fluffy, but she didn't feel like he was hers.

"Can we go now?" She turned to her father.

"Don't you want to hold him? They'll let you," her dad encouraged.

"Ah no, he'd probably get cold," she brushed him off.

She wanted to get away from the baby. She'd kind of thought that if she'd felt a bolt of lightning when she saw him, she would think about keeping him. But she hadn't felt anything. She could've been looking in a pet shop window at a hamster for all she felt. Her parents had been right. She was just too young to be a mother. He'd be better off with them. It wasn't as if she'd never set eyes on him again. He'd be her brother – that was more than enough. Right now, she wanted to go back to her room. She wanted them all to stop staring at her and waiting for a reaction. She wasn't hiding any emotion, she genuinely just felt nothing. She could see her parents' look of hurt and disappointment that she hadn't leapt out of the wheelchair and sung hallelujah, but those kind of looks were pretty much the norm lately. She was so used to acting the wrong way at this stage, she didn't expect anything different.

"I'd like to go back to bed now, please," she whispered, looking at the floor.

Her parents looked at each other and then nodded to the nurse that they'd all leave. Adele lingered for a second, staring adoringly at the little baby. She'd always longed for another child after Ruby was born, but it had never happened. She was all too aware of the fact that this child was bridging a large gap which had been present in her for many years. She was also astute enough to realise that playing this the wrong way could result in losing both her grandson and her only child.

Blowing the baby a kiss, she followed her husband and daughter. The procession arrived back to Ruby's room. She was settled back into bed. She looked pale and tired and wrung out.

Adele glanced questioningly at Harry and he nodded. She wished she could just leave Ruby in peace now but they had decided they had to tell her about Serena.

"Ruby, Daddy and I have some shocking news." Adele bit her lip.

"What?" Ruby looked from one to the other.

"Your Aunt Serena took a drug overdose. She's going to be fine but Paul has been on the phone and she's in a very low state at the moment. She's going to need a lot of time."

"Oh Jesus, I knew she sounded weird! Oh God no!" Ruby started to cry and shake. "She rang me, you see, she left a message on my phone. I listened to it in the middle of the night and she sounded so upset! Poor Serena, where is she?"

"She's in St Vincent's hospital, they're looking after her and she's going to be fine. Adele patted Ruby's hand.

"Things can't get much worse, can they?" Ruby sighed.

The sobering news about Serena jolted Ruby out of thinking about herself for a moment. She had to snap out of this weird state she was in. There was more going on in the world than Damo ignoring her. She needed to make some good and positive decisions about her own life.

Harry sat on a chair by the bed. "How do you feel now that you've seen the baby?"

"Okay, I suppose. He's so small, isn't he?" Ruby chewed her lip.

"Yes, and he needs to be minded and cared for," said Adele.

Ruby closed her eyes and exhaled loudly. Her head was spinning. She genuinely needed time to think. When she saw him lying there in that box, he looked so vulnerable and tiny. She couldn't think straight yet, she'd have to wait and see what she felt in a few days.

The fact that her parents had changed tactics and put the ball in her court was a bit unnerving. It was easier when they were in charge. She really just wanted to be a kid. She wished she didn't have to make all these decisions.

She also had a dreadful feeling about Aunt Serena. From the moment she'd told her about her pregnancy, Ruby had sensed a sadness in her.

"Mummy, is Serena having trouble conceiving, do you know?" Ruby held her head to the side.

"Oh gosh, I've no idea, why do you ask?" Adele looked shocked.

"I hope that my having the baby wasn't the final straw. I hope I didn't contribute to her taking an overdose."

"Don't be daft, Ruby! What can your situation possibly have to do with Serena? She's a grown woman for God's sake, and if she chose to try and poison herself, I can assure you that it had nothing whatsoever to do with you, darling."

Ruby wasn't so sure. Forcing herself to tune back into the whole newborn baby conundrum, she sighed.

"Mum and Dad, you'll have to give me some time. I can't figure out what I should do. I'm so sore and groggy. I feel like I'm being hit from every angle. Every time I open my eyes, there's another person asking me questions. I don't know the answers to all of them. I can't say how I feel, 'cos I haven't worked it out yet. What I really want is to be given some time and space." How had she got herself into this mess?

"Okay, darling, we're going to have a coffee and we'll let you have a little sleep. We'll pop back in a while." Adele kissed her forehead.

They closed the door behind them and she looked around the room.

Once the tears started, she couldn't stop. She gulped and sobbed and tried to make it all go away. She felt like a weight was sitting on her chest, threatening to strangle her. It was so scary and awful. She longed to have a big chat with Mariah or her Aunt Serena. She wanted to pour her heart out to someone who understood her. Not one of these doctors or nurses or her parents. What did any of them know anyway? They hadn't the first idea of what she wanted or how she felt.

Her mother tried to be Mrs Cool Mum, but she wasn't. She couldn't – she was old and pretty embarrassing most of the time. Ruby knew she tried her best but she just didn't cut it. But for the first time her life Ruby appreciated the fact she tried. The reason she didn't act like her friends and walk and talk like her was because she was the mum, Ruby was the child. For a flashing moment, Ruby realised that her mother wasn't someone to hold in contempt, but someone she should appreciate and admire and love.

What would Mariah do? Would she be happy to walk around the shopping centre pushing a buggy? Ruby doubted it. Just imagine, Saturday mornings would never be the same again. Before they'd come to Spain, she'd met all the girls in the shopping centre after their hockey match. They'd had bagels and smoothies, and then hung around the music shop, chatting to some of the guys from the big rugby school. They'd all been talking about the end-of-year disco they were all going to.

None of them would want her to hang around with them if she was pushing a pram. There wasn't even space for a pram in the bagel place. The baby would cry if he was brought out to the music shop. How embarrassing would that be? She cringed at the thought of any of those guys knowing she'd had a baby. They'd all think she was a little tart. That she'd be easy, someone they could just shag and not ever want as a girlfriend. She'd have no hope of ever being taken seriously as a cool girl or a clever girl or someone they'd invite home to meet their families. None of the cool guys from the nice homes would ever want her if they knew.

Just imagine the photos on her seventeenth birthday, her in a sparkly mini-dress, all made up, hair curled and ready for a night out with her friends. Add a small dribbling baby to the mix. No. It wouldn't work. If she decided to keep the baby as her own, she'd have to say goodbye to her whole life as she now knew it. She'd have to press pause on her social life and whole present existence. She knew she was being selfish and immature thinking of all the bad stuff, but she couldn't help it. She was sixteen. Bottom line was that she didn't want to be a mother. Not for a very long time.

She knew she ought to feel guilty about rejecting the baby, but her parents were so in love with him. She could see the adoration in their eyes. They were in a position both mentally and financially to look after the child. She had nothing to feel guilty about, if they took him. It was the best plan for all of them. Damo didn't care about either of them. He was never going to be reliable. She'd been a fool to ever hope he would want her. She was just another notch on his bedpost. It was a bitter pill to swallow but she had to face the fact that she meant nothing to him.

If she promised to help out and baby-sit whenever they needed, that would be good, wouldn't it? She'd always be there to talk to him as well, because her parents were fine and all of that, but they hadn't a clue about lots of stuff. Her mother listened to Barry Manilow for Christ's sake. She'd need to make sure they didn't dress him like a dork or make him too nerdy. She could be his fashion guru and give him tips on how to not get on people's wick, so he'd be popular and happening. She'd be the coolest big sister around. That, she *knew* she'd be good at. But as for being his mum? She just didn't want to go there.

Feeling happier than she had done for months, Ruby squirmed a bit in the hospital bed, and found an almost comfortable position. The combination of the injection and her easing mind meant she drifted into a peaceful sleep.

When Adele and Harry stuck their heads in the door a while later, she didn't even stir.

"Let's leave her for a while, Adele. She must be so exhausted and traumatised, God love her. We'll go and see the baby for a bit," Harry whispered.

Adele blew her daughter a kiss, not wanting to even touch her in case she disturbed her. They stepped back out into the corridor.

"She looks so young and vulnerable lying there asleep," said Adele. "Our little angel, how on earth have we ended up like this? I know the baby is a blessing but, my God, it's a hard lesson for her to learn when she's so young. I thought we'd covered all eventualities. I thought we done a good job of raising her to be aware. Of protecting her and doing right by her. How could we have let this all happen to her?"

"I have thought all the same things a million times since she told us she was pregnant but I've come to the conclusion that we have to accept this and try to move forward. There are no answers and I know we both did our best. It seems pretty rough right now, sure it does, but we'll survive it, Adele. We're all healthy, nobody's dead, quite the opposite in fact. All we can do now is roll with it. We can't change what's happened, even with the best will in the world." Harry put his arm around his wife and sighed.

The couple ambled towards the baby-care unit. They were in limbo, as they waited to hear what Ruby decided.

"Have you any names in mind, if we have that choice?" Harry asked.

"Well, I still love Simon," she smiled at him.

"You always said if we were blessed with a son you'd like to call him that. So it's still in your heart." Harry sighed. All those years ago when they'd yearned for a baby, Adele had her two names picked out, Ruby for a girl and Simon for a boy. Women seemed to all do that, from an early age. He liked the name too but, more than that, he adored the thought of having a son.

Ruby was his sun, moon and stars, no question of that, but it would mean the icing on the cake for him if he could now add a son to his family. Being a granddad would suffice of course, but deep down he would be the happiest man alive if Ruby decided to allow him to be this child's dad.

His gut instinct when he'd heard she was pregnant was firstly to kill whoever had done this to his little princess. He still had moments of fantasy where he tortured the little fecker, Quentin Tarentino style. Possibly removing genitals with blunt objects and dousing the area in sea salt. Secondly, he'd wanted to take all the pain away from her. She'd looked like a rabbit in the headlights since the day she'd told them her news.

She was too young to have to go through this kind of trauma and it had been sheer torture to watch. She still looked so lost and hurt.

He just hoped in time she'd get back to her own self. He longed to hear the front door bang as she giggled and bounded outside and up the driveway, the smell of sickly sweet perfume and hairspray in her wake.

The phone had even stopped ringing constantly. It used to irritate the shit out of him. He'd complained on numerous occasions about not being able to get through to his own house. That if there'd been an emergency, he'd be dead before he'd manage to contact anybody. Ruby would have one friend on the mobile and another on the landline, having a three-way giggle-fest going on.

Right now, he'd give his last euro to hear her doing that again.

As they approached the baby, he felt his heart contract. He was such a beautiful child. Perfect in every way. All he wanted to do was protect him and provide for him. He brought out the cave man instinct in him. This little scrap, whatever Ruby decided, was going to give Harry a new meaning to his life. A new reason to get up in the morning.

42

tweeting@serenasvelte.com
Dismal.com

Serena had just finished vomiting, yet again. She was still stuck in hospital, and the doctors and nurses were so far refusing to let her out. She'd been having hideous withdrawal symptoms. Night-time was the worst. The sweating and nightmares were so vivid she woke up and had to convince herself she was only dreaming. Demons oozed from every pore. Her head thumped, she shook like a leaf, her hands balled into fists and anger flooded through her like wild fire. A vicious anger, that was roaring and choking, rampaging through her, threatening to tip her over the edge. Getting out of bed worked sometimes. But just like now, that sometimes caused her to puke. Pacing the room was good. She'd diversify the walk around her hospital room by playing a game of avoiding the blue squared tiles on the floor. If she only stood on the white ones, then the terrorising panic might go away.

Each hour of each day edged away, slowly and painfully. It was like she had dredged every nerve in her body and every fibre of her being and spilled it all out, for everyone to witness. The paranoia was palpable. She felt like a caged tiger. Like a criminal on trial, except nobody was on her side. She might as well have been in a foreign country, in the dock, with a wig speaking Arabic and bashing a cane down in front of her.

Ruby had called her that morning. She always felt at ease with her niece, and right now they were closer than ever.

"I wish we were in the same hospital, we could share a room or meet in the coffee shop. I'm dying to get out of here. The nurses are nice and all that but I'm so sick of being poked and watched all the time," Serena confided.

"I know, I'm right there with you. At least your nurses speak English, mine can't even understand most of what I say," Ruby answered. "Keep your chin up, if the worst comes to the worst, you can look sternly at them and say in a deep voice, you are the weakest link, goodbye."

Serena heard Ruby giggle. "Oh, it's good to hear you laugh, baby girl. We'll be okay, kiddo. This is a really bad time but it will all turn out okay, you know. You're parents love you and they'll work it out, you'll see."

Serena's head was so sore all the time. She knew she should be the grown-up and give Ruby more advice, but she didn't have the reserves.

"Why did you do it, Aunt Serena?" Ruby's voice was shaky and quiet. "What if Paul hadn't found you so quickly? What if you'd died?"

"Oh Ruby, I'm so so sorry. Believe me, I am. I never meant to hurt you or Paul or anyone else. I was in a bad place, darling. I just wanted the hurt to stop, you know?" Serena exhaled shakily.

"Oh, I really do know, believe me, but killing yourself wouldn't have helped anyone." Ruby hesitated. "Serena, can I ask you something?"

"What, love?"

"Is it my fault you did that to yourself?" She sounded like a four-year-old child.

"Oh God no, Ruby! How on earth could you even think that?" Serena was stunned.

"I saw your reaction when you let your eyes look at my tummy. You want a baby, Aunt Serena, don't you?"

And there it was. The big elephant in the room. Brought out for all to regard.

"I . . . Ruby . . . how on earth did you know?"

"I wasn't sure but I just suspected. You're the best and kindest and coolest aunt, and I know you'd be an amazing mum. All your snooty friends are having babies and I just figured you might want to as well. I'm so sorry if I made your pain worse. Oh God, I just can't believe how much shit I've caused!"

Both women sniffed down the phone to each other, before agreeing to stay in touch and be there for each other.

"Ruby, just for the record, I never felt anything but love towards you, darling. I just felt like even more of a failure that you are so young and even you managed to conceive, even though you weren't even trying. But the bad feeling and self-loathing was all mine."

The hospital was the most depressing place imaginable, and Serena wanted to get out as soon as possible. Most of the doctors weren't what she needed but one in particular hit a chord. She was similar in age to Serena and oozed confidence. With blonde hair and perfect skin, she looked like something from *Vogue*. The minute Dr Folen walked into the room, Serena clicked with her.

"Hi, Serena, pleased to meet you. I've read through your file and it looks like you've a long road ahead of you. All very doable though. You're like me looking in the mirror ten years ago." She stood at the foot of the bed and smiled. Not a condescending, you're-a-sad-victim type smile. A knowing one.

"Really? I can't imagine you looking like this," Serena sniffed. Hackles up, feeling more mortified by the day, she found a lot of these physicians treated patients like statistics. This lady was different from the outset.

"Most people don't imagine a psychiatrist as an addict. What with all those brains and ability, not to mention the D4 address? People with breeding aren't supposed to be alcoholics, right? It's only people who are thick and lacking in social graces, nothing to look at and no stature, who end up on the top of the shit pile, right?" Dr Folen smiled wryly. "In fact, the whole reason I drank my head off undetected for so long was that the crew I socialised with did too. The only difference was that they didn't continue the party on their own. They didn't socialise with the cornflakes and Rice Krispies first thing in the morning. Nor did they attend gala events in their own kitchen, with the star guest being themselves."

Serena drew breath. How had this doctor guessed she'd been drinking on her own at home? Was she one of those psychic weirdos?

Dr Folen continued. "My friends were always happy to go home from socials and parties. They also found the wine at the table sufficient. They didn't need to have a couple of swift ones before they set out, nor did they make trips to the bathroom via the bar like I did."

Serena stared at the beautiful lady. "Did Paul tell you all this?" She was beginning to panic, the paranoia rising and flailing inside her, like an erupting volcano.

"No. Who's Paul?'

She was calm. That unnerved Serena. That awful crawling feeling which started deep inside her chest and crept like a parasite through every muscle and fibre in her body took off again. The sweat began to bead on her forehead. Her mouth and throat were dry and tight. Her breathing was deep and shaky.

"Paul is my husband. Were you talking to him about me?"

"No, I was really talking about myself. The way I used to be. The way I never want to be again. I'm here to 'pitch', for want of a better word. I'm living, walking, talking proof that there's life beyond the bottle if you're willing to let me show you." Her voice was gentle without being pushy.

Serena felt her whole body shudder. Never in a million years could she picture this stunning doctor as being one of those. One of what she was. She found it hard to even think the word never mind say it. Before now, Serena would have judged people by how they looked or spoke. This pretty and obviously clever lady didn't fit in with Serena's preconceived idea of what an alcoholic should look like. Right at that moment, Serena had a moment of dawning realisation. She was at the end of the road of excuses for her own heavy drinking. She knew things had to change.

"You know one good thing about where I am now?" Serena fought back the tears as she spoke. "The only way is up right now."

"Got it in one, girl. If you want me to and if you'll let me, I'd like to help you climb out of the black hole. I know it's nearly impossible to imagine right here and now, but there's a whole new world waiting for you."

"Now you sound like a bloody Disney movie," Serena grinned.

"I didn't know Cinderella had a problem with booze," Dr Folen deadpanned.

"Oh no, she didn't have time, with her OCD, what with all that floor-scrubbing and washing of the ugly sisters' knickers. I'm talking about Sleeping Beauty. She was a divil for the port. Why else do you think she spent her time passed out?"

"Jesus, all these years I never knew that about her!" Dr Folen grinned. "Will I come back and talk to you tomorrow?" She held her head to the side.

"I'd like that." Serena actually meant it.

The following morning, Serena showered and put on fresh pyjamas. The doctors came around and told her she was free to go home if she felt ready. This was the best news ever. Excitedly she rang Paul at work and asked him to come and get her.

"That's fantastic, darling. Give me half an hour and I'll be with you." While he was delighted she was coming out of that awful place, he was also terrified of what he was supposed to do with her. Not wanting to rain on her parade, he decided he'd try and have a word with one of the doctors before he collected her from her room.

"I've no clothes here with me. Can you go by the shopping centre in Blackrock and pick up a tracksuit for me? Size ten should be fine. I need shoes too – runners maybe but a pair of ballerinas or flip-flops would do. In a size thirty-eight. Thanks, darling!" She felt like she was walking on air.

Dr Folen popped her head around the door. "You look happy, what's happening?" she enquired.

"I'm allowed to go home today," Serena beamed.

"So I hear. Can we have a chat first?" Dr Folen pulled up a chair.

"Sure." The smile melted from Serena's face.

"Hey, it's okay, Serena, I've no intention of giving you a big lecture or anything of the sort. I just want to give you a few pointers for going home if I may?" She waited for Serena to answer.

"Okay." Serena felt the sweats starting again. She hadn't thought about what she'd actually do when she physically got out of here. How was she going to cope at home? She suddenly felt very lost and frightened. "How am I going to live without drink?" she blurted out.

"The same way you have over the last week. Serena, you've been dry for a whole week already."

"I have?" Serena looked at her with astonishment. "Jesus, I have."

"I know it's not the same as being at home, but you've done it. All the withdrawals should begin to ease over the next while. The really bad sweating and shaking is over. Believe me, it's a relief when that stops. It's Monday today, so I'm going to ask you to come and see me in my clinic on Wednesday morning. How would that sound?"

"Yeah, fine."

"I think for the next while we'll see each other regularly enough – that way we can keep tabs on how you're doing. We're going to take this one step at a time but when you're ready there's a vast array of programmes we can tap you into to help you make the changes you need."

Paul arrived as Dr Folen was finishing up. Dr Folen seized the opportunity to address them both.

"Serena is doing brilliantly. She's come a long way and still has a big mountain to climb, but she can definitely do it. She'll be seeing me regularly. If she is agreeable, I'd like to see you also, Paul. It makes it all smoother if we're all beating the same drum."

"Right now, I'm not sure if I'm supposed to be beating a drum or strumming a guitar to be honest. Whatever you think will help Serena, I'll do." Paul looked so full of love and concern.

Dr Folen left her card with the appointment time and excused herself.

"Isn't she great?" Serena smiled.

"Yes, she seems very clued in. Here, I brought you some clothes and shoes." Paul handed Serena the bag, looking all proud of himself.

She tried not to cry out loud, like a small spoilt child, as she tipped the contents of the bag onto the bed. Paul had chosen a maroon fleece tracksuit – it was almost July! There was no underwear and no T-shirt. Instead of simple ballet pumps or runners, as she'd foolishly imagined, he'd bought gold basket-weave, plastic as opposed to leather, high heels. They were possibly the nastiest shoes Serena had ever laid eyes on. They belonged on a transvestite at the Eurovision song contest, as opposed to a woman. Coupled with the dreadful tracksuit, with no bra or knickers, Serena would be a sight.

"I even remembered some socks," Paul looked really pleased with himself as he pulled a pair of white towelling sports socks from the inside pocket of his light jacket.

"Paul, I understand that you are a man and so therefore shopping isn't part of your genetic makeup. But I'm just mildly curious here. Have you ever seen me wear that colour? Secondly, do you think I'd normally wear gold synthetic high heels with thick white socks?" If she didn't have to wear the stuff it might have been funny.

"You said dancing shoes, and I thought they looked like disco kind of ones." He looked genuinely confused. "I would have put trainers with a tracksuit myself, but as you've pointed out, I haven't a clue." He looked like an animal that'd been whipped for being naughty.

"Don't worry. It'll all be fine. I might give the socks a miss. It looks warm out," she fibbed. She wasn't able to argue nor was she in a position to soothe Paul's bruised ego.

Reluctantly slipping into the bathroom, she pulled on the tracksuit bottoms. The cheap fleece material was all bobbly and itchy on the inside. The legs were so thick and woolly, she instantly gained at least half a stone in width. Why the fuck would any woman want to wear this? Who in their right mind would pay to be made look wider? The only things women want to expand are either their eyelashes and in some case their boobs. Serena couldn't imagine any surgeon being approached and asked "Can you pump some extra lard into my arse and thighs?" Not likely. The top was the same nasty stuff, except the designer had added a garish stripe down the sleeves. Zipping it up, Serena looked at herself. She looked like she was wearing one of those baby all-in-one sleep suits. She wished this one had the feet part attached. Instead, she slipped her clammy feet (the tracksuit was like wearing a lagging jacket) into the gold hoofs.

If she met anyone she knew, she'd simply die. Emerging from the bathroom, Paul looked at her in confusion.

"This darling, is the difference between designer and disaster," Serena pointed out, just in case he was in any doubt. Pacing past him, she grabbed her few belongings and asked him to take her home. The air-conditioning in the car helped with the prickly suit. She was able to let the zip down a bit too, so at least the air could get in slightly. The material must have been made predominantly with black bags, as it was pretty much airtight. As long as she could hide it under her bed, never to be seen by other human life, she could consider wearing it while on the treadmill at home, it would be the equivalent of wrapping herself in clingfilm and sweating her cellulite to oblivion.

When she walked into her house, she felt overcome with emotion. Tears streamed down her cheeks and she fell to her knees, right there on the hall carpet.

"Oh God, what happened, are you all right?" Poor Paul had no idea what to do with himself. Like most men, he wasn't very good at crying women. He was especially terrible at it, considering Serena was usually so together.

"I'll be fine." Serena scraped herself up off the floor. Feeling a bit like a limp hand puppet, she was shocked herself at how emotional she'd become. The familiar smell and look and feeling of being home had hit her like a sledgehammer. It was almost as if the drink had impaired her senses until now. Wandering around the house, as if for the first time, she took in all the colours and textures.

"I know the hospital was so bland and drab, but it's like a whole new world walking in here, Paul. Does that sound utterly insane to you?" She spun around and went to him, putting her arms around his waist.

"No, it doesn't. But I have to confess I feel beyond guilty about all this, Serena. I had no idea how bad things had got for you. I've been so hung up on running the perfect business and being a success, I'd become so driven that I missed all the signals. I hope you're not going to hate me. I want you to get better more than anything in the world, but I'm terrified that you're going to look at me and think I'm a prick." He searched her eyes for reassurance.

Thrilled to realise she wasn't the only fucked-up person in the relationship, she hugged him tighter and reassured him. "I'll never think you're anything but a wonderful man, the man I love and adore. This whole pile of shit is going to make us stronger. We'll make sure of that. Let's make a pact to mind each other and be there for each other, although I think you're getting the raw deal right now."

"No, I'm not, you've been amazing since the day we met and if you're going to end up even stronger, which I've no doubt you will, I'm on to a winner." He kissed her and held her close.

Paul eventually went off to work.

"I give you my word I won't try to drown, overdose, drink or otherwise maim myself while you are at work." She held her hands up. "Besides, Lucinda is here and she can call the ambulance if necessary!"

"That's not funny but I take your point. I trust you." He waved to her and drove away feeling desperately inadequate. What exactly was he supposed to do here? What would be a useful thing to say? When they met this therapist on Wednesday, he'd have to remember to ask all these questions. He sincerely wished there was a guidebook to tell him how to deal with this situation.

He didn't want to do the wrong thing and mess up all Serena's chances of getting better.

Back home, Serena pressed the answer-machine button.

"Hi, sweetie, where are you?" It was Noelle. *"I've been calling your mobile. I'm trying to organise a lunch over the next two weeks before I go on holidays – let me know when you're around, byeeee!"*

Breathing deeply, Serena listened to the other messages. There was one other invitation to a dinner party the following weekend. Feeling she couldn't face anything like that at the moment, she jotted the messages on a piece of paper and decided to deal with it all tomorrow.

Meandering up towards the bedroom, she found a small pile of packages neatly stacked on the table in her dressing room. Opening them, she found tiny baby clothes and matching blankets, for boys and girls. Fingering the soft and pretty things, she felt slight hope for the first time in a long time. Instead of making her sob inconsolably, it made her feel more determined than ever that she would use the idea of becoming a mother as her goal.

She was going to get better. That was it. Decision made. If she couldn't conceive naturally, she would try fertility treatment. If that didn't work, she would look into adopting. Come hell or high water, Serena was going to be a mum. She was going to get well and be the best damn mother ever.

43

tweeting@themercedesking.com
If my life was a job, I would happily resign. I wish I were someone else.

Damo had gone over Ruby's message a thousand times. He had another son. Sometimes it all felt like a weird and terrible dream. But then he'd realise with bitter regret it was his life now.

Noreen had fucked all his stuff out the top window of the house. Then she'd told Mariah, Alexis and Elvis. He'd tried to talk to them but they'd all shied away from him.

"I'll never speak to you again," Mariah had seethed. "How could you? Ruby was my best friend. You make me sick."

He marched to his bedroom and filled a games bag with a few essentials (the few that Noreen hadn't wrecked), grabbed his shaving gear and some shower gel, and ran down the stairs. There was a small bedsit above one of his own pubs on the north side of the city. He'd move in there.

"Noreen love, I'm going away for a while." He stood looking at the floor tiles, with the bag over his shoulder.

"I'm not your love, and I couldn't give a shite if you're going to burn in hell. You'll be hearing from my solicitor."

Damo felt sick. He walked out, just like that. Got into his car and drove away.

Noreen sprawled across the island unit in the kitchen and sobbed. She was so confused. She wasn't thick – of course she knew he was a fecking dog on heat. She knew he was into the odd drug, but to get Ruby pregnant was something even she could never have imagined. He'd obviously been strutting around like a peacock, knowing that baby was his for the last nine months and hadn't ever thought to do anything about it. My God, he was some prick! In every sense of the word. He was not the man she'd married and not one she wanted to spend even a single day living with again.

Damo arrived in the bedsit. It was musty and damp. One of the barmen had been renting it for a while, but he'd found his own place and Damo hadn't got around to finding a new tenant. The entire space was dank and was furnished with a stained light shade, a dark brown saggy sad sofa, a narrow single bed, a Formica table and two mismatched chairs. The whole place emanated depression.

Sitting on the bed, he held his head in his hands. How was he going to continue with his life? Ruby was still in Spain as far as he knew. He'd tried her mobile so many times but it was permanently turned off so he'd given up. He needed to know if she'd told her parents he was the father. All he needed now was a bleedin' lawsuit slapped on his head as well.

He felt like he was in a black hole, with no way out. No amount of coke or girls with short skirts could help with this feeling.

44

tweeting@angiebaby.com
Oh holy God, I feel like an alien is trying to escape from an orifice which wasn't designed to expel it.

As she slept, Angie began to have a terrible dream. She was in labour and she was in the middle of the Stillorgan dual carriageway. The cars were beeping and swerving around her. Nobody stopped to help her. The pain was terrible and there was blood everywhere.

When the baby eventually come out, it had two heads and was covered in thick black hair. It's four eyes were winking at her and it was smiling horribly, revealing tons of tiny sharp teeth.

Its smile turned to cackles and it jumped up and ran away. Angie was left in a pool of her own blood on the road.

With a start, she woke up and tried to sit up. The room was dark and silent. Her breathing was quick and she was covered in sweat.

"Okay, Angie, it was only a dream," she whispered out loud.

Rolling out of bed, she went to the kitchen to find her wallet. Rummaging around, she fished out the picture of the scan. Her baby looked perfectly normal, with one head, two arms and two legs. Feeling comforted by the "normal" image, she made herself a cup of chamomile tea and walked around rubbing her tummy.

The nightmare had shaken her. For almost the first time since she'd found out she was pregnant, she wished she had a partner. Someone to hold her and tell her it was okay. Someone to soothe her and tell her the anxiety was natural.

She thought of the birth. Her mum had offered to come on the train as soon as she went into labour. But what if she delivered really quickly like Leona had? She desperately wanted to call Brenda and ask her if she'd consider being her standby birthing partner. Just in case. Suddenly, she didn't want to be on her own.

It was the middle of the night so she couldn't call her friend. But she vowed to ask her in the morning. She knew Brenda's mum was going to be with her but she'd offer to be there too, if she wanted her. She thought of the wedding picture on Brenda's mantelpiece. Her situation was tragic. At least Angie had known from the outset that she'd be on her own while poor Brenda had thought she'd her whole life ahead with Barry.

Overwhelming sadness and hopelessness gripped Angie. She cried for herself, for Brenda, for Ruby, for their babies and for every other sad situation which crept into her mind. An hour and two cups of herbal tea later, she was totally wiped out. At least she didn't have to get up for work the next day.

The knowledge that she wouldn't be in the office, surrounded by other people, set her off again. Flicking through a pregnancy and birth book, she read that it was usual for women to "*have bursts of emotion in later stages of pregnancy*". Satisfied that she didn't need to be put in a marshmallow squashy room, in a jacket which fastened at the back, she rolled back into bed.

Flicking on the TV, she settled on an eighties movie, which in comparison to modern-day productions was a joke. She must have got some sleep, as she woke just after seven to the sound of the early-morning breakfast show starting.

Feeling very hot and stiff as a board, she roused herself and put the kettle on. She felt uncomfortable in her own skin, and didn't really know what to do with herself. Wandering into the bathroom, she decided she'd have a bath. Due to the fact she was in an apartment, the bath was one of those tiny ones, designed for dwarves. But it'd have to do. Because she'd nothing else, she squirted some shower gel into the running water and grabbed a towel from the hot press.

An hour later she shuffled out to the lift and wandered towards the shop to buy the papers and a fresh croissant. The weather was already warm and balmy. The rest of the world was rushing to work. She felt a bit like one of those National Lottery ads on TV. Where the winners turn over in bed as everyone else runs frantically to school or work.

She bought the papers, some bread and an ice cream. She was fully aware that it wasn't even nine in the morning, but the chocolate-topped cone seemed like a perfect breakfast. As she tried to walk back up the stairs to her apartment, she felt a dull aching in her lower back, and right under her gusset.

She remembered Leona asking them if they'd ever felt like they'd been kicked in the fanny the day her baby was born. With fierce excitement, Angie realised that this might be it. Not sure if she should alert her mother, she decided to wait a while to see what happened. Was this it? Was her little baby finally coming?

She paced up and down in her apartment, trying to decide if she was going into labour. Realising that she wouldn't know labour if it bit her on the arse, so the whole exercise was futile, she went to sit down and make herself read the newspaper.

As she sat on the edge of the sofa, there was a slight popping noise down below. A warm gush drizzled down the front of the soft biscuit-coloured sofa. The pinkie liquid stain spread like a live animal, inking its way across the fabric.

"Oohhh no!" she mumbled, feeling very shaky and shocked. The poor sofa would never be the same again. The gush was followed by a hard pressing-down sensation. The baby must be pressing on my cervix, she thought, relaying the information she'd read over and over again.

Not quite sure what to do next, she phoned her mother.

"Mammy, it's time. My waters have just gone, all over the sofa, will you come?" And she burst into tears.

"Hush now, child. I'll be there as soon as I can." Her mother's voice was soothing and reassuring. "Brendan is here tending to the livestock, so I'll ask him to run me up in the van. If things go quickly and you're heading off to the hospital, just let me know and I'll meet you there. Try to remain calm, love. Everything will be all right."

"Okay," Angie sobbed. Even though she'd been waiting with bated breath, in fact living for this moment for the last nine months, now that it was here she was overcome.

Raising herself up slowly off the soggy cushion, she sloped into the bedroom awkwardly. She was so confused and worried, she was almost thinking of using a mirror to look in case an arm or leg was sticking out.

Shaking off her sodden trousers, she waddled back to the bathroom to have a shower. It was bizarre but she had a sudden compulsion to sit in water. Remembering she should phone the hospital, she grabbed the phone. Standing semi-naked, she called the number on the list given by the midwife.

"My waters have broken, and I'm feeling very crampy, and . . . aaahh!" The first big pain hit her. It took her breath away and she couldn't speak.

"Just breathe through it and stay calm. I can wait for a minute," the well-versed voice on the end of the phone reassured her.

When the contraction was over, Angie was able to speak again. The lady told her she could have a shower, but not a bath, in case of infection.

"Once the waters have gone, we don't advise baths. You're not in a rush, but get yourself together and make your way in. Seeing as your waters have broken we like to keep an eye on you. Come straight to admissions on the first floor and I'll see you soon."

Padding around like she'd a jumbo jet up her arse, Angie tried to "remain calm". Jesus, it was all right for yer woman in the hospital to tap, tap on a computer keyboard, drink her coffee and chat on the phone and tell her to remain calm. She didn't have the *Titanic* along with the entire ocean trying to escape out her vagina, did she?

As she bent down to pull her hospital bag out from under the bed, another volcano erupted in her tummy. The force and simultaneous pain rooted her to the spot. All her breathing techniques and everything she'd heard at the classes went out the window. The sheer force and utter encompassing grip of the contractions was astonishing.

"Fuck, oh fuck, fuck, fuck," she panted, feeling very out of control.

This one lasted a bit longer and was a bit stronger than the previous one. She felt like she had a hideous and nauseous period pain, far down below. When the contraction hit, it was like someone was pulling a huge rubber band around her tummy and yanking it taut from behind the small of her back.

Not wanting to give birth alone, in her apartment, with no pain relief, she set to work as soon as the contraction abated. Grabbing a pair of white elasticated palazzo trousers, she managed to step into them. Pulling off her shirt, she replaced it with a wrap dress. Then, scrunching her paw-like feet into flip-flops, she dragged the prepared packed hospital bag along the floor behind her and out the door.

Not able to even contemplate phoning and waiting for a taxi, she left the apartment, waddled down the stairs and out onto the road. As she approached the main road, she just missed a cab. Knowing another would be along soon, she walked on, still dragging the bag on the ground behind her. As she readied herself for hailing, another contraction gripped her. Dropping the bag handle, she stood with the palms of her hands against the outside wall of a house, her two arms outstretched. As the pain deepened, she instinctively lowered herself down onto her hunkers, breathing out like a hippo as she went. As she raised herself up to a standing position once more, the pain still gripped her.

"Bastard!" She clenched her teeth and lowered herself down onto her hunkers again. She had no idea what the hell she was doing. None of it was preconceived, never in a million years would she have thought of this as a plan. When that pain abated, she spun around like a madwoman, ready to hijack a passing car if necessary.

An approaching taxi was a godsend. Raising her hand high in the air she decided not to leave it to chance.

"Hey, emergency! Stop! Stop! Stop!" She was well aware that the driver looked more than alarmed and she was probably behaving in such a loony way he might decide to put the foot down and leave her there.

Thankfully he took pity on her and stopped.

"My baby's coming, I need to get to the maternity hospital, please!" She climbed into the back of the car before he even answered her.

The man pressed the triangle to activate the hazard lights and ran around to retrieve her bag from the pavement.

"Is your hubby meeting you there?" The driver jumped in and pulled away.

"Highly unlikely, aahh, fuckity-fuck-fuck, here comes another bastarrrrrd!" The pain ripped through her again.

"Good girl, fantastic, breathe with me now. *In* and *Out* – you're deadly, fucking great stuff – and again, *In* and *Out* . . ." The man glanced over his shoulder and seemed perfectly at ease with a labouring, cursing stranger in the back seat of his taxi.

When the pain stopped again, Angie felt tired and sweaty. "I'm sorry about my appalling language, I don't normally curse like that. My mother would kill me if she heard me."

"Don't worry love, I'm a dab hand at this labour lark. I'm going to open the window a touch, just to keep the cool air on you. Now, take little sips of this." He passed a bottle of mineral water back to her.

Angie didn't want to offend him but the thought of drinking out of someone else's bottle didn't appeal to her.

"Yer all right, it's a fresh bottle – it's pretty hot and you don't want to dehydrate, love."

"How are you so good at all this stuff?" She accepted the bottle and had a sip. It tasted good.

"Ah, ya know, I've six of me own at home. The missus left it all too late on the last one and we ended up doing a DIY on it. Our Seán popped out on the landing carpet upstairs. Bit messy, not to be recommended as a plan, but he wasn't waiting for anything!" He chuckled at the memory.

"I'd bet your wife doesn't think it's a funny anecdote!" Angie felt the inner insanity rising in her again. Another contraction began to rip through her. If she was leader of the universe at that moment, she'd have every man on earth castrated with a rusty ice-cream scoop. She was never, ever having sex again. In fact she was never even being in the same airspace as a man again if she could help it.

The driver was still chatting away. ". . . and of course it was all worth it in the end!"

"What?" Angie barked. "Listen, I don't want to offend you,

truly, but I'm really not in the mood for chatting right now. I'm trying to concentrate on not dying, if that's okay with you?"

"I know what you're feeling, love – you hate the whole male race, am I right?" he chuckled.

Oh sweet Jesus, don't you dare laugh like that, Angie thought. You've no idea how close you are to death right now.

As the contraction subsided once again, normality prevailed.

"I can't understand what's happening to me. When those pains come, it's like I've become possessed. I'm honestly not mean in general." She tried to lean forward to explain things to this stranger who was kindly helping her out in her hour of need. "I'm really very grateful to you for being so patient." She tried to sound like less of a bunny-boiler.

"Don't mention it. I'm well used to labouring women. I'm from a house of four girls. I could nearly deliver a baby single-handedly at this stage if the need arose." He chuckled kindly.

Less than ten minutes later, they were at the hospital. Without being asked, the driver jumped out and ran inside.

Moments later, as another violent contraction hit, he reappeared.

"That's the way, breathe through it, good girl yourself!" he shouted, looking delighted.

This one was the worst yet. Angie cried out in pain. Holding her tummy in agony, she tried to cry. She couldn't breathe and she wasn't able to muster the tears. The sentiment was all there inside her head though.

She was utterly mortified to realise that she was leaking again. She felt like she wanted to die of embarrassment when she remembered she'd put on white trousers. What on earth had possessed her to wear white while giving birth?

A nurse appeared with a wheelchair. The driver was chatting normally to her as he hooked her bag over the back of the chair.

"They're about eight minutes apart, lasting for a good bit as you just saw," the driver reported.

If Angie had been in any position to speak, she would have made some attempt to thank him. But the horrible nasty gremlin version of Angie was attempting to burst out again. So she thought it might be wiser to stay quiet for the time being.

The nurse stuck her head in the car door. "Can you stand up, pet?"

"Yes, but I've got a really embarrassing problem," Angie whispered miserably. "I've kind of leaked all over this man's car and I'm wearing white." She burst out crying. The whole thing was now becoming too much to bear. Just then her mobile phone rang. Fumbling to grab it, she sniffed loudly.

"Hi, love, it's Mammy, we're about half an hour away – where are you?"

"Oh Mammy, it's terrible! I'm outside the maternity hospital, I'm going in shortly. Can you come here? Hurry, I'm scared." She sounded like a strangled kitten.

"We'll be there in a flash. Brendan is driving like a man possessed. Hold tight, I'm on my way. I'm putting the phone down so Brendan can concentrate. See you soon – I love you, you're the best girl in the world."

Angie threw her head back, opened her mouth and howled as another contraction hit her.

"You've got to get yourself out of the car, pet," said the nurse. She turned to the driver. "Would you give us a wee second?"

"Oh sure, I'll wait over at the door in case you need me." He saluted her, as if he was waiting for a signal to go to battle.

"Right, love, he's out of the way. Try and slide out of there. I'll cover you with a blanket." The nurse was kind and calm. "The seats are leather, so I'll give it a wipe when you get out. He'll never know."

Angie wanted to hug her. Bar the taxi driver, she was the nicest person she'd ever met in her entire life. Clunking her legs out of the taxi, she managed to propel her large awkward mass out and into the wheelchair. As promised the nurse covered her and cleaned the seat.

Paying the driver, Angie thanked him and gasped goodbye as another whopper hit her. The nurse bent down in front of her and held her gaze. Steadily she talked Angie through. As soon as it ended, she pushed her to Admissions where Angie signed all the necessary forms and gave her details.

"Let's take you straight into the labour ward and have a little look at you."

Angie was knackered. She wasn't sure if she'd be able to continue much longer. This was much harder than it had looked when Leona did it. God, she'd even more admiration for the young woman now.

"The good thing about the white trousers is that it gives us a good look at what the fluid around the baby is like. It's good and clear, which means the meconium hasn't been passed."

"The whaaaaa . . ." More pain.

"The meconium is the contents of the baby's bowels. If it's passed in the womb, it can be serious for baby." The nurse was still talking while she hooked up some machines and put on gloves.

By the time the contraction ended, she was all ready to examine Angie.

"I'm gently going to have a little feel inside," she smiled.

Angie looked like an animal to the slaughter as the nurse went to carry out her duty. It felt like a big metal digger was trying to gouge out her insides and drag them through her arse.

"What the fuck are you doing?" she shrieked.

"Don't say things like that to the lovely nurse, Angie!" her mother's voice penetrated her head.

"Mammy!" Angie started to whimper. She put her legs down and stared at the nurse. "I'm so sorry! I don't know what came over me. I feel like an alien has taken over my body. It's like it's trying to rip the top half from the bottom half of it," she gulped.

"It's okay, I've heard worse." The nurse didn't smile, nor did she look particularly put out. "You're doing well – you're about four centimetres dilated. You're well on the way now."

"What? Only four centimetres? I deserve to be four hundred centimetres dilated at this rate. Oh God, I don't think I can do this. I don't think it's going to work. I reckon I'm one of those women who can't give birth!" She sounded different. It wasn't like herself. She was all screechy and high-pitched.

The nurse ignored her outburst. "Would you like to have any pain relief?"

"Oh God yes. Give me whatever you've got. All of it!" Angie gripped the nurse's arm.

"Would you like to try some pethidine or are you thinking of the epidural?"

"Epidural, epidural, epidural, immediately if not sooner!"

The nurse alarmingly left the room, promising to page the anaesthetist.

"What if she never comes back and they tell me it's too late?" Angie asked her mother.

"She'll be back, love, you'll see." Her mother folded her trench coat neatly over the back of the chair and set about organising a little compress. Pulling a flannel from her shopping-bag style handbag, she ran it under the tap at the little sink in the corner, wrung it out and began to stroke Angie's forehead gently.

Miraculously, the nurse hadn't been spoofing. She did return, with a man and his silver trolley.

"Look who I found and he's got a time slot! This is the anaesthetist who will put in your epidural, Angie."

As he rattled his trolley full of dreadful Frankenstein-type implements around to the side of the bed another contraction whammed through her. This time her mother continued to stroke her head and the nurse did the breathing with her, coaching her every second.

The pain was all-encompassing. It involved the worst cramping imaginable mixed with a dull thudding ache. The pressure down below was gruesome.

"We'd want to get this in – those contractions look like they're doing their job," said the anaesthetist. "Turn onto your side with your back to me, please."

Angie fumbled and rolled and eventually made it onto her side.

"I'm going to clean the site first and when I say this is cold, I mean arctic," he muttered through the mask.

Angie wouldn't have cared if he'd said he'd have to poke a hole in her skull and pull her brain out on a crochet needle, if it helped with the pain down below.

The freezing wipe of iodine was swabbed up and down her back, making her gulp air with shock.

"Try to bring your knees towards your chest as best you can. I know it's the most awkward-sounding request right now, but I need to have as clear a vision of your spine as humanly possible. I need to work quickly before the next contraction. You must remain totally still, are we clear?"

"Yes." Angie did as she was told.

The initial sting of the needle to numb the area made her gasp. After that it was plain sailing. Within minutes the skilled doctor had administered the epidural. Hooking the line up to a drip, he told her to stay on her side for a further ten minutes.

"After that, turn over onto the other side, to allow the medication to take there too. Good luck. I'll return to top you up in a few hours if necessary." He patted her arm with his clear disposable glove and dragged his trolley away.

A few hours? Was he insane? If she was still in labour in a few hours' time, she'd request that he put her down as opposed to give any more epidural. The thought of putting up with this torture for even half an hour longer was a nightmare.

"Sometimes the epidural can slow things up a little bit, so we'll see how you go," said the nurse. "I'm going to wrap a little monitor around your tummy so we can keep an eye on baby."

The nurse produced a length of dark green Velcro belting and passed it under the small of Angie's back. At the front of the bump, she fastened a little black box. The screen to her left jumped into life. The baby was broadcasting live on the TV.

"Okay, turn onto your other side now and we'll make sure the epidural is evenly distributed." Between the nurse and Mags they managed to roll her over.

The monitor went a bit crazy.

"What's happening?" Angie's eyes opened wide in fear, as she heard the monitor making loud noises.

"That's another nice contraction – your epidural's doing the trick," the nurse smiled.

"But I can't feel it!" Angie looked stunned.

"Magic!" The nurse ticked off some boxes on a chart.

"Jesus, who ever invented this is a bloody genius." Angie was gobsmacked. She couldn't believe how anything could simply remove the insufferable pain she'd been experiencing.

As the contraction ebbed away on the monitor the midwife arrived with a little plastic beaker of ice.

"These are for you to suck if you feel like it. Sometimes with the drugs, if you take gulps of water it can make you sick, so this is the way we suggest. I'm also going to use one to check how that epidural is performing." She picked out a chip and gently dragged it down the front of Angie's belly. "Can you feel that at all?" she asked.

"No, you could be slicing me with a scalpel and I wouldn't know the difference," Angie reported happily.

Astonishingly, it took a further four hours for her to become fully dilated. But she'd calmed down and was actually enjoying chatting to the midwives and her mother.

"Okay, Angie, action stations now, love. You're fully dilated and ready to go into the pushing phase. This can go on for up to two hours and it can get exhausting. I need you to listen to me and do as I say, so we can use each contraction to its full potential, okay?"

Angie looked at her mother. She'd never felt so terrified and excited at the same time before.

"Let's go," she answered.

"Right, girl, here comes a big one. Put your chin to your chest, take a deep breath in and push down into your bottom like you're going to the toilet," the midwife instructed.

Angie had no idea if she was doing the right thing or not.

"Good girl, and again."

The pushing and breathing and panting and yelling went on for just over half an hour.

"I can see baby's head now, you're nearly there!" the midwife shouted.

Angie felt like she was going to burst, both physically and mentally.

"Oh Angie, I can see the baby, it's on the way, love," her mother was crying.

"Push the pressure away, go for it!" the midwife shouted.

Angie shoved her chin down and pushed so hard she felt like her eyes were going to burst like grapes. Although the pain was pretty much gone, she could still feel enormous pressure, like a huge lump of lead gouging through her body. It wasn't sore nor was it the nicest sensation she'd ever experienced.

"And pant, pant, pant. If you push too hard now, you'll tear!"

Like a dog on a searingly hot day, she panted for dear life.

"Give me a nice push now, that's the girl. Look down, Angie, the head is out."

Angie looked down and there, between her legs, was a tiny head and face.

"Oh God, this is like a scene from a horror movie!" Angie stared at the little face which was scrunched up and not moving. It was kind of blue too. "Is it supposed to be that odd shade of purple?" she panicked. "Is it alive?"

"Yes, love, it's all perfectly normal," the nurse answered.

Angie refrained from pointing out that she found nothing in the world normal about any of this.

Moments later, with just one more push, the baby slid out.

The midwife popped the baby onto Angie's tummy as a piercing cry filled the air. "Look at what you've got, Angie, look down."

"It's a boy!" she yelled. "Mammy, look!" She turned to her mother. She'd never in her life imagined such exhilaration was possible.

Angie could barely speak as she cried and laughed and panted and stuttered. She'd done it! She'd given birth! The nurses cut the cord and wiped the little baby's face. Placing a towel over him, they slid him up towards his mother's chest.

"Hello, sweetheart, I can't believe you're finally here!" She laughed and cried all at the same time. Wiping her eyes and nose, she desperately tried to take him in.

"You did it, you clever girl!" Her mother hugged her daughter and grandson. "I'm so proud of you, darling. Holy God, he's the most beautiful and perfect little being. Thank God he's here safe and sound." Her mother stroked the baby's sticky head.

"Do you have a name for him?" asked the midwife.

"I think I'd like to call him Adam. What do you think, Mammy?"

"I think that's lovely, pet. He looks like an Adam too."

Reluctantly, Angie handed Adam to the midwife so they could check him over. The afterbirth arrived intact and Angie finally lay back and stared at the ceiling.

She couldn't believe she'd done it. She'd actually given birth to her own child. No deal in work or exam result or any other important event in her life before now could have come close to the sense of achievement she felt at that moment.

"If I won the lottery tomorrow morning, it couldn't excite me like this," she whispered.

Being a mummy gave her a warm fuzzy sensation which filled her every fibre. This was without a shadow of doubt the most incredible and wonderful day of her life. She felt complete. She had a real purpose in life now. She was responsible for this tiny creature. She couldn't have been more proud.

The midwife interrupted her reverie.

"A fine healthy man he is too – nine pounds four ounces – well done, Mummy!" She handed Adam to her. This time he was swaddled tightly in a blue cotton blanket, with only his little face peeping through. As she cuddled him close, his little blue eyes opened and he stared straight at her. As their eyes locked, Angie felt like her insides had turned to liquid. The rush of sheer love and joy was astounding. She couldn't believe how instantaneous the love was either. She'd read that some women took time to get to know their babies, while others bonded instantly. She knew she was the latter.

She'd heard people talk about the love parents had for their children but right until that moment, until she'd experienced it for herself, she couldn't have fathomed just how deep and special it really was.

"May I take a photo?" her mother asked.

Normally, Angie would rather have her head boiled in oil than have her picture taken, but this was different. Her son would be in it. Smiling from ear to ear, she presented her precious baby to the camera for the first time.

"Happy Birthday, Adam!" She kissed his forehead as the camera flashed.

45

Thank God for who ever invented the power shower. Being clean has never felt so good.

It was eight o'clock in the evening and Angie had just arrived on the postnatal ward. All visitors had been ushered away and the hospital was a lot calmer. The three other women who were sharing her room had introduced themselves. While she knew they'd probably get chatting at some stage, Angie was very content to have her curtain pulled around her bed for a bit of privacy.

Her tiny little bundle was sleeping, his miniature fists tucked under his chubby chin. Angie simply couldn't believe he was hers. The nurses had changed him into a soft white cotton Babygro. Against his suede peachy skin, the pale blue blanket and white outfit made him look like a painting, he was so perfect.

She'd had a go at breastfeeding with the assistance of two nurses earlier. It was all very fumbly and uncomfortable and involved plenty of wrenching and shoving with her enormous swollen boobs. She wondered if every woman's boobs behaved like disobedient water balloons while trying to feed. The sensation when the baby sucked was very weird. It was like a small alien was trying to ingest her flesh. When the liquid eventually came out, she found it fascinating.

"This colostrum is the most important stuff a baby can have. It takes a few days for the milk to come through, so meanwhile the liquid you're producing now is full of protective enzymes and vitamins and minerals. This stuff is super-juice for new babies. We encourage women, even if they can't keep up the feeding at home, to try and do at least the first few days, so the baby can get this magic colostrum."

The nurses buzzed around, evidently finding it all very normal to be grabbing a woman's inflated breast and shoving as much of it as possible into a tiny baby's mouth.

"I know you both think this is very natural but is it okay at all to feel like I'm doing all this wrong and to wish I could just give him a bottle?" Angie looked very anxious.

"Don't worry, pet, most new mums find this strange in the beginning. I promise you'll be a dab hand by next week. You'll be one of those easy-come-easy-go mummies, who can feed a baby while on the phone on the bus."

Angie laughed along with the nurses, but inside she was utterly terrified. She wondered if they'd let her stay in the hospital until Adam was ready to go to school. That way, they'd be able to ensure she didn't kill him or do something wrong.

The next scary part was changing a nappy. It might sound like a very easy and straightforward thing to do and Angie hadn't even considered it being a difficult hurdle to overcome, but the reality was quite another thing.

It was just after nine o'clock and Adam was still only a few hours old. The team of two nurses came around and got all the babies "latched on," which was the technical term for attaching small mouths to large breasts.

"Make sure baby has a small choirboy's mouth, bottom lip curled out, not tucked in and top lip resting on the top of the nipple. Good girl."

Angie got a smile and she sat rigid in the bed, afraid to breathe in case she jerked Adam and made the whole thing go wrong.

Once he'd fed for what seemed like a week and a half, she had to try and wind him. This getting-his-wind-up business was a whole art form in itself. She had to try and balance his little body by placing her huge, giant hand (in comparison to his teeny weenie little fuzzy head) under his squidgy chin. As a result, his little body was like a mini-sandbag, resting on her lap.

"When he has wind trapped, it's easy to tell – just look at the area around his mouth, it'll be slightly blue," the nurse instructed.

Thinking this was all a marvellous plan on Mother Nature's behalf, colour-coding the problems for mums, Angie was confident she'd suss this wind thing easily. It was astonishing, however, how difficult it was for her to decipher whether he was actually blue or just a tad blue-tinged or if she'd just been looking at the light for too long and he was in fact fine. She thought she'd rub his back gently and do the little sandbag balancing act, just in case. The sense of achievement she felt when he burped was beyond explanation.

"Good boy, you belched!" Feeling like she deserved her first gold medal for being a fantastic mother, she unwittingly moseyed towards the nappy-changing area. This was a small warm well-equipped room just off the main ward.

There was another dressing-gown-clad person there, with similar puffy ankles and bloodshot eyes, smiling like a fool, delighted with her small pink bundle. They exchanged a smile and a we're-in-the-new-mummy gang look.

Angie placed Adam on the changing table, all the time trying not to let his very wobbly head fall off his shoulders. His head had a mind of its own. It looked fine and as if it was going to stay put, then, without warning, it would jerk horribly sideways.

With him safe on the changing mat, she began to unbutton the Babygro. That's when the sweating started. How the hell was she supposed to remember how to do those buttons? There seemed to be at least fifty of them and they were in such a complicated sequence, there was no way she'd be able to manage. Putting that aside, she managed to pull his little legs free of the cotton suit. Just as she was about to undo the nappy, he opened his eyes, his face went red and he began to bawl.

"Okay, Adam. It's all right. Mummy is just trying to change your nappy. It'll be so much better in a minute. I won't be a second, hold your horses!" She tried to sound confident. Adam didn't care. He wailed loudly, his face went dark red and then purple. His little tongue was quivering inside his mouth, and the noise he was making was deafening.

"It's amazing how such a small creature can make so much noise, isn't it?" the other mum said. "There's nothing wrong with his lungs at least! First baby?"

"Yes. You?" Angie tried not to look like she wanted to die.

"No, I have two boys at home, but this is my first girl. She's already a much quieter little thing." Slinging the freshly changed baby onto her shoulder, the lady padded over. "Would you like me to help?"

"Oh God, yes, please. I hadn't even envisaged this as being a major calamity." Angie was mortified to realise she was joining her son and bawling too.

"You'll be a professional in a couple of days, it's all so new in the beginning, Jesus, I must've spent the first week crying after I had my son. I promise you it all gets easier."

With practised ease, she laid her daughter on the next changing table and came to demonstrate. She grabbed Adam by the ankles and hoisted his tiny bottom into the air. With the other hand, she grabbed some moistened cotton wool and wiped him clean.

"Holy shit, what's that black sticky tar stuff on him?" Angie was horrified.

"That's the meconium, their first poo."

"Oh, yes, the nurse told me about that."

"It's a bit scary at first but that stops and then they do really runny stuff, which looks a bit like cheap curry." The other woman laughed at Angie's expression.

It was only then that Angie caught sight of the umbilical cord stump. Putting her hands over her mouth, she gasped.

"Oh yeah, it's a bit vile, isn't it?" said the other mum. "On my first, I spent the first few days terrified it was going to pop off when I was changing him. I made my husband do as many changes as possible in the beginning. I had images of his guts spilling out with it, but it actually just dries up and you'll probably find it in the nappy."

She was actually humming as she finished cleaning Adam's bum. Grabbing a nappy from the pile, she showed Angie which end to put under him. She then demonstrated how to open the sticky tabs which would hold the nappy in place.

"Now, little man, all clean and happy."

Adam was still doing that bloodcurdling, tongue quivering yelling. Either the other woman was deaf or she'd become so beaten by motherhood she didn't realise Adam was distressed beyond belief.

"I don't think he's all that happy, is he?" Angie was biting her lip and feeling traumatised.

"Ah he's fine, they all give out a bit when you change them, but remember crying is his only way of communicating right now, so it doesn't mean he's desperately upset or anything. Now the Babygro buttons are a bit of a nightmare in the beginning but like all the rest it'll become second nature to you. You'll soon be able to do them in the dark at four in the morning." She demonstrated how to line up the poppers properly.

Scooping him up, she cuddled him and crooned to him for a second and, miraculously, Adam stopped screaming. It was as relieving as turning off the house alarm, when it's blasting through your head in the middle of the night.

Handing Adam to Angie, the other lady grabbed her daughter and waddled out, waving over her shoulder. A large part of Angie wanted to run after her and ask if she could go and live with her for a while. But she had to be a grown-up now. She was in charge of Adam and she had to learn how to take care of him.

The enormity of that hit her like a sledgehammer.

"Please God, don't let me drop him or smother him or break off one of his legs while changing his nappy," she whispered into her baby's downy head as she made her way back to the ward.

The whole ordeal left her shaken, and she felt at a total loss and utterly inadequate. Crying – again – seemed to be a good thing to do. So she did. Adam joined in again. A few minutes later, the nurse came along and acted like it was completely normal to find a tiny and larger person dueting on the bed.

"Let's get you two settled down for a little rest," she hummed. She swaddled Adam tightly in a blanket and popped him into the little cradle. Pulling back the bedclothes, she eased Angie underneath and tucked her in too. Miraculously, Adam was quiet and slumbering. "Now, Mum, try and get a little bit of sleep. If you've any problems or if you'd like baby to be taken to the nursery for a wee while just press the buzzer." She handed Angie the call bell. Pulling the curtain around her and dimming the lights, she moved on to the next mother. Before long, the ward had been settled down for the night.

Angie was wrecked but sleep wasn't coming. She was buzzing, thoughts flying in and out of her head at a million miles an hour. She couldn't take her eyes off Adam either. Staring at him, she tried to establish if he looked anything like Troy.

She turned it over in her mind, back and forth. Should she tell him he had a son? She knew it would be the right thing to do, but did she want to? Her honest answer was no. She never wanted him to know. She didn't want him coming near her baby. She didn't want to take a chance, even for a milli-second that he would want to share this baby. He was her little miracle. Fair enough, he'd participated in the conception bit but after that Adam was hers. As she tried to banish Troy from her mind, she closed her eyes and attempted to get some rest.

The hospital ward was about as peaceful as a train station at rush hour. There wasn't a moment of silence during the night. One of the babies at least was crying at any given time. The lights were flicked on and off, as the nurses came in to assist.

By the time the breakfast trolley rattled in just before seven the next morning, Angie was relieved. Adam had slept for most of the night. The nurse opened the curtains and the four women were left facing each other.

"Sorry my baby was so unsettled last night," a small blonde girl in the corner, who looked like she'd been run over by a bus, piped up. "She just wanted to feed nonstop. Every time I put her down she cried. I'm knackered."

Angie made lots of "don't worry," and "it could happen to a

bishop," type noises, while inwardly allowing herself to feel a tiny bit smug. She obviously had a fabulously trained baby, who was going to sleep all night and coo all day. She felt very sorry for the other poor cow, with the horse of a child with the insatiable appetite.

The day passed quickly. Her parents came in and her dad was like a peacock, with his chest out filled with pride as he held his grandson.

In the afternoon, the antenatal girls arrived, minus Leona, who had no baby-sitter. Brenda and Sandra were like women preparing for the guillotine.

Brenda perched on the end of the bed. "Tell us everything. Don't leave out one second."

"Oh Christ, it's only now I see the two of you that I realise just how happy I am not to be pregnant anymore," Angie sighed.

"Shut up, you cow, don't rub it in. Tell us. Start to finish."

Angie was thrilled to be able to discuss the whole process in detail. The two women winced at times and fired questions non-stop.

"Would you recommend the epidural then?" Brenda asked, opening the box of chocolates she'd brought and delving in.

"Does the pope wear a funny-shaped hat? I would pay big money for that effect from a drug if I thought it could work in everyday life. In fact, I now understand the appeal of being an alcoholic or a drug addict. I went from being in nasty uncontrollable sickening pain to floaty lovely gorgeousness. I know they said in the classes to be open-minded but I would happily campaign on behalf of the epidural from this day forward." Angie refused a chocolate.

"You're refusing chocolate – are you ill?" Sandra looked shocked.

"I'm just not that hungry, amazingly enough." Angie was too enthralled with her birth story. She was so enjoying being able to tell the girls all about it. Her mother had been there, so there was no need to tell her. Her father would die of shock and embarrassment if she even tried to mention nether regions, never mind birth stories.

Rachel would be useless. She'd been on the phone from Cork to say congratulations and had categorically stated that she didn't want to hear anything to do with goo or gore.

"You're amazing, I can't believe you only gave birth last night, and you're sitting here, all serene and normal-looking. You're an inspiration to us!" Brenda hugged her.

It was almost as if Adam was waiting for the right time, because the two girls were only gone a while when he made his mark on the world.

He started the dark red-faced waaing-type crying. Thinking she had the whole thing sussed, Angie cooed to him and picked him up. Fumbling with her pyjama top, she tried to make him latch on. He was in such a state he wouldn't have latched onto a cow with ten teats, never mind her measly one breast. Her confidence slipped away rapidly and she began to shake. She tried everything she could think of. Pacing around her bed, jigging him. Patting his back. Crooning to him. The noise grew sharper – the baby's mouth seemed to open wider. She pressed the buzzer for dear life.

By the time the nurse arrived, smiling as usual, Angie was suicidal.

"Please help me. He's hysterical. Do you think he might have hurt himself without me knowing it?" She looked like a rabbit in the headlights.

"What kind of a state have you got yourself into, young man?" the nurse said, stroking his cheek. "Let's try and see if he'll have a little feed for you. Shall I hold him while you sit up on the bed and get yourself ready?"

Angie lowered herself onto the bed, feeling shaky and uncomfortable. With trained ease, the nurse positioned him on her breast and the noise stopped.

"When he's had a nice feed, call me and maybe I could take him to the nursery while you go and have a shower and change your clothes. You'll feel much fresher and the little break away from him for a few minutes will help too."

"Thank you." Angie winced as Adam sucked for dear life. For such a small creature, he was like a top of the range vacuum cleaner when it came to food.

The feed seemed to last forever. The nurses had also warned Angie about keeping track of which side she'd fed from last.

"Make sure you alternate the sides, so both breasts are stimulated, that way you'll maintain an even milk supply."

Easier said than done. Angie was finding it hard to remember her own name, let alone which side she was supposed to feed with.

"A little tip is to put a little ribbon or a safety pin on your bra, marking the side you've just used."

This all seemed simple yesterday but today Angie couldn't remember if the pin meant to start that side or if she'd just finished with that side. Oh God, it was all so new and scary.

When he'd eventually finished feeding and had nodded off to sleep, Angie pressed the call button. The nurse came and carried him off to the nursery for a little while. Angie raided her overnight bag and loaded her arms with nice-smelling products and fresh pyjamas, not to mention a large pile of disposable knickers and sanitary towels. Nobody had mentioned the world-falling-out-of-your-bottom syndrome which seemed to be part and parcel of birth.

A young trainee nurse was on "shower duty," as she approached the bathroom. One other girl went in ahead of her, with nothing but a flimsy curtain for privacy.

"I have to stay here with you, just in case you slip or pass out. Sometimes girls can faint when the hot water hits the back of their neck." She busied herself, mopping around the shower area and changing the paper disposable mat on the floor.

A couple of days ago, Angie would have protested at the thought of a strange woman witnessing her showering. Especially in light of the Niagara Falls between her legs issue. But the whole birth thing had stamped any shyness out of her. Leaning against the wall for support, she waited for the other lady to finish.

When she finally got to stand under the hot water, she felt like she was in heaven. Losing the run of herself, she shampooed her hair.

"Don't go overboard with shower gel in there, pet, it can be a bit stingy on the perineum, especially if you've got stitches," the nurse shouted in.

Looking at her full hand of blue shower gel, Angie winced at the thought of soap hitting her undercarriage. She used the gel solely for her underarms. By the time she'd wrapped her hair in a towel, organised a full-on nappy experience complete with disposable knickers made of J-cloth type material, put on fresh pyjamas and found her slippers she was exhausted.

"God, that feels great all the same." She emerged through the steam smiling.

She was back at her bed, trying to pull a brush through her hair when she heard the howling approaching. Spinning around, she saw the still smiling nurse padding over with a very cross Adam.

"I think little man here is looking for a little feed." She handed over the angry red bundle to a shrinking Angie.

"Oh God, I just fed him a few minutes ago!"

"I know, love, but sometimes they don't feed much in the first twelve hours or so after the birth, and then they realise how hungry they are. The first night, they can often trick us into a false sense of security, and then they wake up and want to build up their little reserve tank."

Angie felt her heart almost stop with fear. So last night was not a gauge at all? Adam was only quiet and calm because he was knackered after the birth? Was this yelling crosspatch more a taste of reality? Would she have to change his name to Damien?

By midnight, Angie was like a wet rag in the bed. Adam had fed non-stop all day. Every time she thought he'd had enough and drifted off to sleep, she inched as slowly as she could towards the cot. Just as she placed him into it, he sprang to life. Eyes open, tiny arms shooting outwards, face reddening with rage, fists balled and that quivering tongue and the curled-out bottom lip.

"Sorry, baba, I'll bring you back to me." She desperately tried to make him happy. By one in the morning, she couldn't take any more. The nurse came to help her settle him, first changing his nappy. Angie had already cleaned two nappies filled with the black sticky glue-like stuff.

"How many litres of that tar do they have inside them?" Angie was so tired her eyes felt like they'd had pepper ground into them.

"It should calm down. Will I take him to the nursery for an hour or two to let you have a wee sleep?"

The nurse was kind and all that but Angie felt she wasn't getting the urgency of the whole situation. She handed the cross bundle to the nurse and allowed her to pull the curtain around her bed for privacy.

Knowing she was more tired than she'd ever been in her entire life, she lay back expecting to conk out. But no. That'd be too easy, she couldn't do that. Instead her new-mummy mind went into over-exhausted overdrive. Thoughts of never having sleep ever again mixed with every fear she could conjure up plagued her.

What if Adam was seriously ill and that's why he was crying so much? What if she just wasn't any good at the mummy thing and he died of malnutrition? What if she was so tired and upset when she got out of hospital that she collapsed and Adam was left to fend for himself? What if she was so bad at being a parent that the authorities took him away? The nurses might be phoning social services right now and telling them that they'd managed to get the poor child into the safety of the nursery, but they'd have to come and save him from that dreadful woman.

The two women on either side of her in the ward were sleeping, with their babies in cots beside them. She was a terrible mother already and he was only a few days old. She'd failed him and herself. All these months, she'd been floating around, delirious and excited, when all along she was a bad mother hiding in a naïve and useless body.

"It's all right, dear. Lots of women go through the blues after having a baby. It's dubbed the 'baby blues' for a reason. Most women hit this on day three, so you're right on target, there, there."

An older, matronly, round squashy kind-faced nurse was stroking her hair. Scarlet with embarrassment and shame, Angie realised she'd been howling away to herself.

"Sorry, I'm just so tired and Adam is going to be taken away or else he'll die, 'cos I can't even stop him from crying, and he's going to have to be brought up in a home now, and I don't think I can bear the thought of being without him," she hiccupped.

"No one is taking your son, pet. He's just a bit shellshocked and you're understandably nervous and tired. This is a huge and life-altering thing to go through, for both of you. I know nothing seems normal right now but all this is actually totally normal."

"But why is everyone else coping? How come I'm the only basket case on the ward? All the other babies are asleep or feeding. Nobody else is looking traumatised and sniffling like a moron," she gulped.

"Not right at this moment in time but all women have ups and downs at the beginning. This is a hard job – being a mum is the hardest job in the world. The other thing, love, is that you are on your own. When you don't have a partner, it makes it all much more scary. I know, because I had my first baby on my own. I did subsequently marry and have another child, and let me tell you, the second time was a hell of a lot easier. I knew what to do, but I also had support. Try not to be hard on yourself and I promise you you'll get there, love."

Angie had never felt so grateful towards another human being. This wise and kind lady was like an angel sent to mind her in her hour of need.

"I'm going to be on duty all night, so why don't I promise to keep a special eye on Adam for you? I will bring him to you as soon as he wakes and meanwhile you try to sleep for a little while." She patted Angie's hand and busied herself fixing her sheets. Being treated like a baby herself, even if it was only for a few minutes was like balm to chaffed skin.

Feeling much calmer and a lot less useless, Angie closed her heavy, burning eyelids.

She felt like she'd been hit over the head with a mallet when she was gently woken by the angel nurse.

"Have I been asleep for long?" Angie was confused and stiff.

"You got a good five hours. How are you feeling now, pet?"

"Better, thank you. How's Adam?" She stretched her arms above her head and yawned.

"He's awake and hungry. One of the girls is just changing his nappy and I was going to bring him in to see if you could manage to give him a feed?"

"Thank you, nurse, I'll do that," Angie smiled.

As the nurse returned with Adam a few moments later, Angie felt an uncontrollable rush of love when she saw him.

"Hello, darling," she said as she cuddled him.

She realised it was going to be a long, slow and difficult process, raising this child on her own, but she also knew she wouldn't change her situation for all the world.

After his feed, she and Adam nodded off for another couple of hours. By the time the breakfast trolley rattled into the ward, Angie felt much more in control. She sat at the table in the middle of the room with the other mums.

"Sorry if Adam kept you all awake yowling last night," she said sheepishly.

"Not at all, sure I was saying the same thing yesterday," the small blonde girl reassured her. "I think, when it's not your own baby, you don't even notice the crying."

Although she was still unbelievably tired, the world was still falling out her bottom and her boobs were now leaking, mentally Angie felt stronger.

"Jesus, the things women go through to have a baby is unreal, isn't it?" she commented.

"There should be solid gold medals handed out for every child all right," another mum piped up.

The banter was happy though, and Angie was conscious of the fact that she had now firmly joined the Mammy Club. She was one of them.

46

tweeting@rubytuesday.com
Once I was a daughter, then I was a mother, would I prefer to be a sister?

Ruby woke up and stretched, wondering for a split second where she was. Looking around her hospital room, she felt better than she had for months. With the help of a nurse, she managed to navigate the shower and washed her hair. She called her parents and asked them to come in for a chat. She'd made up her mind about the baby and she was keen to tell them.

"Can I go and see the baby?" she asked shyly.

"Yes, of course," the nurse smiled. "I go with you?"

"No, thank you. I'd like to go on my own if that's all right."

"*Bueno*. You want help, you call Maria, yes? Walk very slowly *y ten cuidado*. You be careful, no?"

"I will."

She knew her parents would be there shortly and she wanted to have a few quiet moments with her baby. One of the midwives in the special care unit lifted him out of the incubator and handed him to her. For the first time, she held him close. She buried her nose in his soft downy hair and stroked his little cheek. He was beautiful. Like a real live doll. He curled his little fingers around hers. His skin was

345

like velvet, so soft to touch. Sitting on a chair in the nursery, she instinctively rocked him. He made little crooning noises and opened his eyes.

When he yawned and stared at her, it was like every sound in the world had been muted. Unable to even breathe, Ruby drank him in. He was a little miracle. Unscathed, free of bad language, bad tempers, mean thoughts or negativity. He represented angelic beauty at its best. He looked very like his father, there was no doubt about that, but he had something his daddy didn't – purity and innocence. His little body was warm against hers as they sat together. Ruby felt her stomach flip. Why oh why did she still love Damo? What was it about him that made her feel this way? She longed to not care about him, to feel numb towards him. But deep down she still harboured hope that he would wake up and realise he was in love with her too.

The nurses discreetly removed themselves from the room. This was the moment they'd all been hoping for. The baby was doing really well and they planned to take him out of the incubator the following day.

When Adele and Harry arrived in Ruby's room and found it empty, they panicked.

The nurse looked delighted. "It's fine, she go to see *el niño, el bebe*. She there now and the girls tell me she is sitting holding him!"

Adele and Harry looked at each other.

"Maybe she's finally come round," Adele searched Harry's eyes for a reaction.

He sat down on the side of the bed. "I know this sounds terribly selfish," he said. "I'm so glad that Ruby's finally accepted the baby but a huge part of me is gutted. I now realise I was beginning to think of him as my son. But being a granddad will be just as good, won't it?" He took Adele's hands and looked at her.

"It might be just as good," they both jumped as Ruby's voice came from behind them, "but it wouldn't be right. I've made my decision. Here's your son." She walked over and held the bundle out to her father. "The nurses have said his jaundice is almost gone. He won't need to be in the incubator for much longer."

"Ruby, I didn't mean . . ."

"It's okay, Dad. This is what's right for us all. You and Mum will give him all the things I want for him. Everything I had. Love, security, support and something I don't have yet, maturity. I'm not ready to be a mother. I hope someday I'll have my own children, when the time is right, with someone who loves me. But right now, this baby needs parents who are able to raise him. He's all yours." Her eyes shone like polished glass but her head was held high and she looked determined.

"Oh, Ruby!" Adele flung her arms around her daughter and held her for the longest time.

Harry held the baby and rocked him, watching his wife and daughter.

"Darling, are you sure this is what you want?" asked Adele. "We can go home and see how you feel. Maybe if you try to be his primary carer for a while and see how you get on?"

"No, Mum, I think it would be better to go ahead with the plan. We'll tell people he's yours. It's in his interest more than anyone else's. I want him to be accepted and loved. I don't want anything to shadow his introduction to our lives. I don't care what you say, there's bound to be at least one or two spanners who'll say terrible things. I don't want that for him. He hasn't done anything wrong."

Adele and Harry were astonished at how grown up Ruby was being.

"Well, let's think about it, sweetheart," said Harry. "You and the baby will be released from hospital tomorrow. After that, we still have three weeks left in Spain before we return to Ireland. It will afford us all the opportunity to work it all out properly."

"Meanwhile, he really needs a name. What did you have in mind?" Ruby asked, stroking his tiny leg.

Adele and Harry looked at each other.

"Shouldn't you name him?" Adele asked, biting her lip.

"Mum, with all due respect, I'm probably not going to pick a name you'd both be comfortable with. Let's face it, if you arrive home with a baby called Scooter or Blaze, no one's going to believe you came up with it. Hit me and I'll tell you what I think." She waited for them to speak.

"Well, we both love 'Simon', but what do you think?" Adele ventured.

"Simon is fine." Ruby looked at him. "What do you think, baby? Are you a Simon?" He slept on like a little bunny in Harry's arms. "Well, he didn't vomit or scream, so I think that's settled. Listen, you guys are going to have to start taking control and making him yours. It's not going to work out for any of us if you feel you have to tiptoe around me all the time. He's your baby, he's my brother. Fact."

"We'll all need to adjust. It's going to take time, love," Harry answered. The look of love and joy on his face was obvious and Ruby knew in her heart and soul she was making the right decision for this little mite.

"There's one more part of this jigsaw that I have to put in place." Ruby closed her eyes. There was an odd silence between herself and her parents. She faltered and almost bottled it.

"What, darling?" said Harry.

"Simon's father."

"What do you mean, Ruby?" Adele's smile was slowly fading. "Have you heard from the Russian boy?"

Her parents looked at each other. Instinctively they moved together as Harry cradled the baby and put his free arm around his wife.

"No. The Russian boy isn't the father. I . . . I lied to you both."

"Pardon?" Her mother was blinking oddly. The silence was viciously uncomfortable.

"Take your time, Ruby," Harry encouraged his daughter. "This is it. We need to get all this out, here and now, for once and for all, if Simon is to have any kind of a proper life. Go on, love, let's have it. We'll work together, I promise."

Ruby mustered up all the courage she could find and tried to speak. All the good ways of saying it failed her.

"Damo," was all that came out.

"Sorry?" Her dad looked confused. "What did you say?"

"Damo McCabe. He's Simon's father."

47

*If I could shut myself away in a box, and make the world
disappear, then, maybe, for just one moment, my head might
feel clear . . .*

Ruby, Adele and Harry had all walked back to the small
dependency unit, where Baby Simon was safely replaced in the
incubator. Unlike the day Ruby had dropped her bomb about being
pregnant, today was calm.

"I didn't think it was possible to feel shocked any more," Adele
whispered.

"I don't understand," Harry sat on a chair and looked up at
Ruby in genuine confusion.

"I thought he loved me. The really sad part is that I still love
him." Ruby remained totally motionless. The only thing that
betrayed her feelings was the stream of tears running down her
cheeks.

"But he's *my* age," Harry croaked.

"I know, Daddy, but he's not like you. He's not like a 'dad' as
such. He hangs out with pop stars, he's a club owner, he *knows*
people. I can understand that you find this impossible to take on
board, but I can't help who I fall in love with."

"Ruby, you're a child. If anything, you should be flirting with lads your own age. That would be hard enough for us to come to terms with. But this man, whether you see him that way or not, is a father. He's your best friend's father at that. He had no right having any relations with you. In fact, what he did is illegal. I can tell you right here and now, we will drag him through every court in the land for this." Harry was still not shouting. Quite the opposite, he was coldly quiet.

"No, Daddy! *No way!*" Ruby went puce and started yelling, holding her hands over her ears. Simon woke suddenly and began to scream.

"Okay, Ruby, calm down, love. Take it easy," Adele said soothingly.

"I love Damo! I wanted to be with him. In fact, every day since I got pregnant, I've waited for him to call. I would go to the ends of the earth to be with him. I would happily live the rest of my life with him, if I thought he wanted me too."

"What does he say to all this?" Adele was alarmingly controlled in her approach.

"He doesn't want to know," Ruby admitted tearfully.

"How convenient," Harry seethed.

"Harry, you stay here and mind Simon. Ruby and I are going for a girls' talk."

Before he could protest, his wife and daughter had shuffled from the room. Simon was still distressed.

"You can take him again. He is almost ready to leave incubator now. It's okay, you take." The midwife smiled and encouraged the man to soothe the baby.

Harry scooped him up and cuddled him close. As he popped the baby on his shoulder and Simon's cries turned to a meek bleating, followed by sucking as he found his tiny thumb, Harry calmed too. As he stroked the baby's back, and the little being almost amalgamated with him, so much of Harry's inner anger melted away. This baby was more important than any argument.

Outside in the corridor, Ruby confronted her mother. "Mum, before you tell me how disappointed and hurt you are, and what an idiot I am, for the record I already know. I'm the one living this nightmare too. I can see that Damo doesn't give a toss about me. But it sadly doesn't stop me from being in love with him. I didn't do any of this to hurt you or Daddy." Ruby shoved her hands into her dressing gown pockets and looked at the floor.

Adele stopped her by putting her hand on her arm. "Ruby, the reason I've been so, so angry with you, is because you were history repeating itself. I had no idea that Damo McCabe was the father but, believe me, it's sent a chill down my spine."

"What do you mean?"

"When I was a little older than you, seventeen to be exact, I fell in love with an older man called Lou Granger. He worked at the tennis club, where your grandparents used to bring Serena and me. From the second I met Lou, I was drawn to him. Your grandpa forbade me to see him. Any time he spoke to me, I was dragged away. After a short time, we were told the tennis club was out of bounds. Your Aunt Serena hated me for that. She was brilliant at tennis, a real star of the club, and she didn't speak to me for months after we were taken out of there." Adele stared into the middle distance as she remembered. "I will never forget the day I found out I was pregnant." Adele couldn't go on. Grief and pent-up emotion choked her.

"What are you saying? Do I have a brother or sister I haven't met?" Ruby could barely get the words out.

"No. I miscarried at eleven weeks. My parents told me that God had taken the baby because it wasn't welcome. That was that. It was never spoken about again. I was told to keep it to myself and never tell a soul, or I would be seen as soiled goods."

"Does Daddy know?"

"No."

"Did Aunt Serena know you were pregnant?"

"No. We were never that close, she was much younger than me and after I caused her to be banned from the tennis club she and my father were like a little gang against Mummy and me."

"But I know if you told Serena she would understand you more. I just know she would be nothing but sorry if she heard what you'd been through."

"It's too late, Ruby. It's all forgotten and a long time ago." Adele wiped her eyes. "I only told you because I want you to know that I do actually understand when you say you love Damo McCabe. I loved Lou. I met your father when I was nineteen and I knew he was a wonderful man and that he'd look after me, but I'm ashamed to say that it took me a long time to really love him. My heart was still yearning for Lou."

"Do you love Daddy now?" Ruby was almost afraid to ask.

"Very much, darling."

"Then you owe it to him to tell him about Lou Granger. You need to free your skeletons, Mum. You can't go on another day running from your ghosts."

"You're right, Ruby. Do you know something?" Adele held her daughter's face in her hands. "For a sixteen-year-old girl, you've a very wise streak in you."

"Not that wise. I've made a total mess of my life." Ruby sighed deeply. "And now Daddy will want to take Damo to court and it's all going to get even more terrible."

"Can you blame him? You are only young – that man should have known better!"

"But I loved him!" Ruby was heartbreakingly sad.

"Let's go and talk to your father and see what comes out of this. As you say, Ruby, it's time to stop hiding. Maybe if we both face up to our demons, some good may come of it all. Are you with me?" Adele held her hand out to her daughter.

48

tweeting@serenasvelte.com
If acceptance is the first step, I'm still learning to crawl.

Wednesday rolled around and Paul and Serena found themselves sitting in Dr Folen's office at the private clinic. The small purpose-built clinic housed plastic surgeons and several "head doctors," as Paul called them.

"It's kind of like a posh supermarket, taking the holistic approach to mind and body. As in, you can get your body permanently fixed and your mind altered at the same time," Paul said, grinning.

Serena wasn't in a joking mood but she loved Paul for trying. Squeezing his hand, she held on tightly to him as they were motioned towards Dr Folen's consultation room.

Serena was looking much better. She had a beautiful silk-mix wrap dress on, with high sparkly sandals, her fake tan was done, her hair immaculate, her make-up on. To an outsider, she was the epitome of effortless glam.

"Come in and sit down, you two. Wow, Serena, you look stunning. How are things?" Dr Folen smiled warmly as she motioned to them to sit.

"I feel okay. I've good hours and bad hours and then one or two bloody awful hours, but I still don't feel as desperate inside as I did."

"That's super. You're doing an amazing job."

Dr Folen chatted to them amicably. If she were attending anyone else, Serena would have been nervous and on the defensive, but this lady wasn't even like a doctor. She was easy to talk to and instantly made her feel at ease with herself.

They went through some of the preliminary stuff. Then for the first time ever Serena admitted how much she'd been consuming. When Paul and Dr Folen didn't fall of their chairs with shock, she felt like a weight had been lifted off her shoulders.

"I can't believe I'm actually telling you both this stuff. It's a relief beyond anything I'd ever imagined to be able to open up. It's been so hard to carry with me all the time. Even I didn't realise how much I was drinking until this week. Most of the time, I automatically reach for a glass to pour myself some wine and have to stop. It's not that I have a terrible nagging ache to drink, I actually don't. When I stop myself and ask if I really want it, some of the time I don't. Other times, I feel like a little nagging parasite has crawled in my ear and is egging me on – *'Just have one little glass – nobody will know.'* But I've resisted so far. 'Cos apart from you guys, and I honestly don't want to let you down, I don't want to let myself down either. I have a goal, you see." She hesitated and looked from Paul to the floor.

"Go on, Serena," Dr Folen encouraged.

"I want to be a mother. More than anything in the world. We've been to a fertility clinic to be tested, 'cos it's just not happening for us. But I now know, I would sell my soul to the devil and pass up a full bottle of Chateau Latour in exchange for my own baby." There, she'd said it. Out loud and in front of Paul.

They talked for a while longer and Paul agreed to do whatever it took to make her wish come true. Dr Folen once again suggested she might like to join AA. But the idea, right at that moment, didn't appeal to Serena in the least.

"I just don't think I'm ready or able to sit in a room full of strangers and talk about drinking. It's just too close to the bone right now. I'm a very private person too – I can't imagine ever being in a place where I'll be able to pour my private thoughts out to people I don't know. I can't see myself being that trusting."

"Well, trust is a huge part of the group sessions. You soon learn that other people are in a similar situation, and it can be good to know you're not alone," Dr Folen suggested gently.

Paul asked some questions about what she suggested they should do with regards to functions and going out. He could avoid them for a while but the time would come when he had to attend some of them.

"That's all a personal timing thing. Serena will know when she feels she can face these things. Meanwhile, you could always go to the odd one on your own if you have to." Dr Folen wasn't sure who looked more stricken at this suggestion, Paul or Serena.

"Oh no, I couldn't possibly go to a thing like that without my right arm here!" He genuinely looked green at the thought.

"Looks like you're needed here, Serena." Dr Folen put the limelight on her.

"I know you hate those things, darling," said Serena, "but I just can't do it all sober, not just yet." At that moment she felt she'd never go out to a social occasion ever again. It was one thing being able to resist opening a bottle of wine at home, but being offered it on a tray and having to be the only one in the room sober was quite another story.

"Remember, Serena, these days with the drink-driving laws it's quite acceptable to announce that you're the designated driver and you'll be surprised how people will just accept that," Dr Folen said. "You might also be surprised to notice how many people in the room aren't drinking either. Not everybody at every function drinks alcohol."

This whole theory of not drinking was so alien to Serena. It was something she'd just never considered. A bit like some people wouldn't dream of having tea without milk and sugar, she never dreamed of lunch, dinner or any function without alcohol. It was all pretty confusing.

"Take my mother, for instance," she began. "She goes down to the house in France either with my father or friends. They'd think nothing of having a cold glass of white wine before lunch. If the mood took them, they'd have a couple of gin and tonics in the afternoon. And wine at dinner and after. Are they all alcoholics too?" She bit her lip. She wasn't trying to be difficult, she was seriously trying to understand how one person became labelled an alcoholic and another wasn't.

"Without meeting your mother and her friends I cannot comment on them," said Dr Folen. "But, be clear, alcoholism is a disease, not a calculated state. It's very hard to think of alcoholism as a disease. It doesn't look like one, there's no rash or twitch. But the most simple definition I use for it is this: it's a mental obsession which causes a physical compulsion to drink. To put it in perspective, do you ever use a clock radio to wake yourself in the morning?"

Paul and Serena looked at each other, wondering what the hell a clock radio had to do with this.

"Yes, I have," Paul answered.

"Okay, good. Do you know the way a song can play into your dream and wake you up?"

"Yes."

"What can that do in turn? Sometimes, that song can stick in your head. You find yourself singing it in the shower. Then in the car on the way to work. By the time you've reached lunch-time and the same damn tune is still buzzing around your head, you're really sick of it. You tell yourself to stop humming it. Just get it out of your head. So you try to think of something else, but it's no use. As soon as you concentrate on the computer or some paperwork – *bam*! The same blessed tune again. Now, when you consider that this tune is there annoying you and you've consciously tried to stop yourself from humming it, to no avail, it's an example of something that's entered your head and you can't control it. It's in your subconscious and won't go away. Equally, an alcoholic has a receptor in their head and all it wants is for you to hum that tune, by taking a drink. Even though you haven't made a decision to want another drink, your body has done it for you. It's a force which you have no control over. The only way to stop that force in its tracks is to quit drinking. If you can cut it off and starve it, the monster will be kept at bay."

There was silence in the room as Serena and Paul digested this information. Neither of them had ever thought of alcoholism as being a disease, or an annoying song, or an uncontrollable animal. It shed a whole different light on the subject.

"So are you saying it's not entirely my fault that I'm such a mess?"

"Serena, you have a disease. A nasty one at that. It's not your fault. You can't help it. But, with work, you can learn to control it."

"Sure, I've been doing such a good job so far," Serena scoffed.

"It's normal for you to feel angry and resentful but you can beat this. You might need some guidance and some help but it's possible to beat this monster." Dr Folen stared at her intently.

"I don't know if you think this is the wrong way to go," Paul glanced at Dr Folen, "but why don't we try and keep our minds and energy on this baby issue. Use that as an objective instead, or would that be very wrong?" He looked rather embarrassed.

"I think that's a wonderful idea, Paul," Serena piped up, looking more animated than she had in days.

"You must be careful of pitfalls, however." Dr Folen looked a little uneasy. "You said you'd already begun some fertility treatment, had you not?"

"Well, not as such," said Paul. "We just had some preliminary tests. I've been told my sperm count is fine." He coughed uneasily.

"I've had some endometriosis removed and according to the gynae there's nothing else wrong with me." Serena looked desperate. "Obviously that was before I realised I'm 'an alcoholic'." She wiggled her fingers in the form of quote marks.

"Well, most fertility clinics will automatically tell couples to cut out alcohol and smoking, first off," said Dr Folen. "So it may be a factor for you. I'm mostly concerned in case you meet with problems conceiving. I don't want you to set yourself up for a fall, which may in turn trigger a bout of drinking."

Serena and Paul talked to the doctor for a further twenty minutes.

"We'll leave it at that for today," she said then. "You're doing extraordinarily well, Serena. If you can continue in such a determined and strong-willed manner, you'll be doing a fantastic job beating this disease."

Dr Folen smiled and shook hands with the couple. With an appointment for the following week, Serena and Paul found themselves back in the car.

"God, I'm knackered!" Serena felt like a deflated balloon after the session. It was so tiring having to delve deep into her mind and come clean about all her drinking. It wasn't that she'd even been aware of her deception for the last few years. Sure, she had times when she'd sneaked drinks, but most of the time she'd been totally open about it. She had never for one second even contemplated the fact that she was walking around disease-ridden.

The sound of the word "disease" filled her with disgust. It sounded dirty and filled with germs. Rancid and crawling. Not polished and pretty, with designer handbags, delicious-smelling leather shoes and tailored couture clothing. Someone with a disease didn't belong in her interior decorated home. An alcoholic didn't suit her style and elegance. An alcoholic wasn't going to make a suitable mother.

She had to beat this bastard. If it was the last thing she did, she was going to win this time. She wasn't used to losing, ever. She'd never been the one who missed the Spanish exchange in school. She always had a beautiful dress at the Hunt Ball. She was the first of her friends to drive a convertible car. She was the one with the most extravagant wedding, with the most eligible bachelor on her arm. She was a girl of high standards and she was not going to be anybody's slave.

Things were going to turn around for her. She was going to knock this booze thing on the head and she was going to be a mother. Come hell or high water. Not today, but very soon, she would tell Noelle and all the others that she was an alcoholic and she had moved on. That drink was no longer a part of her life. When Paul dropped her home, she put on her running gear and hooked up her iPod. She walked purposefully, pulling air into her lungs.

As she got into her stride, with bouncing music flooding her ears, she sucked in the fresh air. *I am an alcoholic, I will banish drink from my life,* she chanted to herself as she pounded the pavement. Each stride she took, she compounded the feeling, as if trying to reach her own inner psyche. When she got used to saying it to herself without wincing and feeling like dying of shame, she'd be ready to tell the world.

She wasn't going to hide away and never go out again. She was not going to allow drink to dictate to her anymore. She was not going to fade away, like Miss Havisham, gathering cobwebs and festering in a world focused on what she couldn't have. Her path had simply changed. Her new direction was going to be difficult, but she hoped she'd have the guts and determination to keep going.

49

tweeting@angiebaby.com
I feel like I haven't slept in days, I'm not sure if I even know when it's daytime or night-time. I never knew the meaning of the word tired before. Nor did I ever realise it was possible to love another human being this much. Thank you, God.

Angie was stuffing her many accumulated belongings into a bag, getting ready to go home. She'd managed to change a nappy and feed him all by herself, and was now ready to be in her own bed and with her own things again.

Her bed was almost clear and her locker cleaned out when a photographer approached.

"You look nice and fresh and happy. Is there any possibility you and your baby might pose for a photograph for the papers?" the man asked.

"Em, I don't think I'm exactly model material, especially right now," Angie answered, smoothing her hands over her jelly-belly and touching her unkempt hair.

"One of my colleagues is doing an article for the *Irish Times* on public versus private hospitals for childbirth. I'm trying to get a photo of a new mum and baby to go with the write-up."

Angie's immediate reaction was to say no way. Firstly, she looked and felt like a sack of shit and, secondly, she was terrified that Troy might see the article and recognise the baby and come looking for Adam.

"A lot of women seem to be of the impression that the public hospitals are akin to having your baby in a war zone and that the care is sub-standard. You just look so happy and your baby is so content, I just thought you might be a good candidate for a positive picture. No worries though. I was warned by my colleague, who is a woman, not to hassle any new mums."

He went to walk away and look for another more willing model.

"Wait! I'll do it. The nurses and staff have been so amazing to me and my son, I'd feel guilty if I didn't put my money where my mouth is." Even if Troy did see the photo, which was unlikely, surely he wouldn't be able to recognise Adam? And it would be lovely for Adam when he was older to have a newspaper cutting of him as a tiny baby.

She sat on the bedside chair and smiled with Adam in her arms. The photographer clicked away and promised to post her a few copies of pictures by way of payment.

Her parents arrived in the middle of it, looking excited.

"Is the child famous already?" Denis grinned at his sleeping grandson.

"You bet, he's taking the world by storm!" Angie was thrilled.

Her parents had carried out the thankless task of removing all her stuff from the Dublin apartment. Angie had realised she didn't want to be on her own with the baby when she left the hospital. So one of the farm vans had been loaded up by Brendan and driven back down to Cork.

Waving to the other women in the ward, Angie scooped up her son and they set off on the three and a half hour journey to Cork.

Adam slept for most of the way. The one time he woke, Angie managed to feed him. It was all a bit of a struggle in the back of the car. Her father also looked like he wanted to jump out the window with shame, at the thought of his daughter producing her breast in the back seat.

He muttered things like, "It's the most natural thing in the world," and "Sure even the sheep do it." But it was obvious to Angie and her mother that he was finding it all a bit hard to cope with.

He wasn't the only one. Angie was finding the breastfeeding a bit strange to say the least. Every time she fed, her stomach and insides contracted. At first she'd thought that perhaps during the pregnancy or labour she'd managed to break something, or that all the stuff that was falling out of her was in fact her entire insides. But the nurse was able to put her mind at ease and assure her that the pain was being caused by her womb going back into place. Nobody had ever told her any of this stuff. That the whole world falls out your bottom, that your boobs become haunted by a mad squirting poltergeist, that your insides move around on their own, that your tummy ends up looking like a large blancmange-type thing and that you spend most of your time crying.

"I suppose if women spoke about all this too much, then the population would cease, wouldn't it?" she mused to her mother.

"You bet, and if it were left to the men we'd all be having gin and tonics with the dodo birds by now – in other words, the human race would be extinct," her mother agreed.

"I don't need to hear any more of this dreadful talk," her father interjected gruffly.

"Sorry, Daddy," Angie giggled.

By the time they arrived in Cork, Angie was wrecked. She got out of the car, with Adam wrapped in a blanket, and waddled into the house. Her mother, organised and thoughtful as ever, had left a homemade chocolate cake on an old glass cake-stand, along with a beautifully set table. Her grandmother's old tea set had gone full circle, fashion-wise. The deep pink peony roses and gilded edges looked pretty and chic against the old scrubbed wooden table. The yellowed hand-crocheted doyleys completed the gorgeous scene.

"Oh, Mammy, this is lovely! Look, Adam, your first cake!"

They sat and enjoyed the fudgy cake, with endless cups of sweet milky tea. Angie sighed happily as she stared at her tiny son. All the getting fat, pain, goo, gore and tears were worth it.

They had a pretty terrible first night at home. Adam didn't settle very well and the only time he'd stop crying was either when she fed him or let him lie on her chest. When he was lying on her chest, she was terrified he'd roll off and fall or that she'd squash him if she fell asleep, so she stayed awake. Every time exhaustion took over, she'd jump awake and frighten the living day lights out of herself. By morning time, she was like a detoxing heroin addict. Twitchy, irritable and a nervous wreck.

Her mother rapped gently on the door and peeped in.

"I've a little cup of tea and a bowl of warm porridge with honey for you. Would you like me to take the little man while you eat it?" She smiled adoringly at Adam, who was of course fast asleep, because it was now morning.

"Thanks, Mammy. I'm so tired! I had a terrible sleepless night." Angie burst into loud heaving sobs.

"Ah, there, there, pet. You'll be all right. It'll take you both a while to adjust. Sure you were only in the hospital for a flying visit. When you were born, the nuns took over and the mammy stayed in bed for two whole weeks. This new idea of shoving people out the door with a tiny baby is terrible. I'll mind you, don't you worry. You have your breakfast and try to rest for a while, there's a good girl."

"I'll organise you a tea towel for your Mother Teresa impression." Angie smiled as she handed the slumbering little bundle to her mum. The sight of his slumped little back and the fluff on the back of his head made her heart wrench with love.

It was astonishing how bloody dreadful she felt. Until now, she'd never known the true meaning of the word "tired". But every ounce of it was worth it when she looked at her little baby.

She barely managed to down her tea and eat a few spoons of porridge before her eyes shut. When her mother brought a cross little man in for a feed some time later, it was like waking the dead.

"I have the papers too – yourself and the little fella are inside – look!"

Angie had thought it would be a small discreet little picture to the side of a demure article, but to her horror, the photo covered a quarter of the page.

"New mother, Angie Breen, with her charming son Adam."

The article went on to outline the pros and cons of public versus private antenatal health care.

Having a mild panic attack, she wondered if many people had seen it. Okay, take it easy, Angie, she told herself. Even if Troy sees this, he would never put two and two together. He's a man for God's sake! Unless he's a total dork and puts the dates he shags people in his diary, he won't cop on.

Besides, Angie was over all that indecision. She'd made up her mind to be both mother and father to Adam. She had to come to terms with her decision. She was home and dry now, he would never know the difference. When Adam was older, she could simply tell him that she had no idea of his father's whereabouts. Which was partially true. Either way, none of this would become relevant for a long time. At that stage, she'd think of something good to say. For now, on the up side, she'd be able to put Adam's first appearance in the newspaper in his baby book.

As she fed her baby, she gazed at their photograph.

"We'll keep this, and they can show it on the telly when you're a number-one-selling recording star. Or maybe you'd prefer to be a politician? Or a doctor?" she crooned.

In her heart of hearts, Angie didn't care what Adam decided to do when he was older, just as long as he was happy.

50

I want to face my demons, but should I do it on my own?

Serena felt a great sense of pride. She was still on the wagon. There was no doubt she felt better physically. She found getting out of bed in the morning much easier. The lack of hangover was a bonus, every day. Her skin and hair had looked good before, but now she simply glowed. The running was doing her bottom and thighs an unimaginable service. She'd never been fat, but now she was toning up beautifully.

Besides all that, her life had just taken a wonderfully positive step forward.

Adele had called that morning and right from the outset, she sounded different.

"Hello, Serena, how are you?"

"I'm getting there, thank you." Serena wasn't in the mood for dealing with Adele and her clipped tones. No doubt she was ringing to give out and Serena just wanted to remain in a positive mood.

"Do you have a few moments? I need to tell you something." Adele sounded oddly vulnerable.

"Yes. What is it, Adele?"

365

Serena had been balancing the phone between her shoulder and ear, as she riffled through her closet for something to wear. But as her sister began to talk she strode into her room and perched on the bed.

As the details of Adele's affair with Lou unfolded, Serena's eyes widened in astonishment.

"Why didn't you tell me?" she asked.

"I was told not to and I was too terrified of annoying Daddy any further. Besides, you were only small at the time – you wouldn't have understood."

"But why didn't you ever tell me since? You've carried this around all this time and never felt you could trust me enough? I always felt you and Mummy had no time for me, that you were a little clique with no space for me, and for all this time I thought it was my fault." Serena wasn't angry. In fact, she felt she had unlocked a secret that had been shrouding her for years.

"I'm sorry, Serena. If it helps at all Harry only found out a couple of days ago. Ruby's situation brought it all to the forefront of my mind, and I knew the time had come to let it all out."

"Adele, that's not what I'm getting at here. I can't believe you've carried this around for so long, without ever sharing with a single person."

"Well, without wanting to start a row, that's a bit pot and kettle, considering your own current circumstances." Adele was gentle in her retort.

The two sisters chatted for a few more minutes, vowing to try and start afresh. The years of pent-up emotion and resentment were not going to fade away overnight, but being open with each other for the first time was great start.

Serena put the phone down and shook her head as she made her way to her dressing room. Today was going to be a test beyond all others. She was meeting Noelle and the girls for lunch. She'd brushed them off a few times too many and it was getting too risky.

"Have we done something awful to you?" Noelle had snapped.

"No, sweetie, of course not. I just haven't been able to make any of the days you've suggested." She tried to sound breezy and even slightly condescending in order to put Noelle in her box.

"You name a day then."

So that was how she'd ended up having to go. It was to a small restaurant in Sandycove, a little seaside suburb of Dublin. At least it wasn't a big swanky place where she'd be expected to quaff champagne.

"What way should I handle this?" Serena had asked Dr Folen at her last session.

"Well, you need to figure out whether you want to tell them you're an alcoholic or not," said the doctor.

Dr Folen was very nice and Serena truly liked her, but she was a total no-bullshit merchant.

Sitting with her hands clasped and maintaining eye contact, she placed the ball firmly in Serena's court.

"Nobody has the right to tell you what to do with your life. It's up to you."

"I know. To be honest, I want to tell them. It's getting to be a burden trying to hide it. I don't want to tell them lies – that wouldn't make me feel any better. They *are* going to notice too – I was always the first to poo-poo anyone who dared to turn up at one of our lunches and not have a glass of vino. I almost took it as an insult if others didn't join me. When I think back I feel ashamed. I even remember arguing when the girls were pregnant, and insisting on pouring them a small drop, telling them not to be so stuffy." Serena bit her lip as she tried to make sense of it all in her head.

"You don't need to make any decisions." Dr Folen had been firm yet kind. "See how it all goes. You never know, it might not even come up in conversation. No need to pre-empt it."

But the conversation with Adele that morning had changed her entire line of thinking. Bottling everything up inside was never going to be healthy. She was not going to be a slave to this disease. She would do her best to assert herself and her new way of life with her friends.

As she walked into the restaurant, she saw Noelle waving to her from the corner. Julie and Patricia were sitting waiting for her also.

Scanning the table, she noticed Patricia was drinking water, while the other two were having white wine. Swallowing hard, she sat in the fourth seat.

After the initial meet and greet stuff, Julie reached towards the wine bucket for the bottle of chilled wine.

"White okay for you, Serena?" she asked absent-mindedly.

"Actually, I won't for the moment, thanks," said Serena. "I'm parched to be honest. I had a massive running session this morning and I need some H2O to get me back on track. The San Pellegrino will do me nicely." She smiled and helped herself to the sparkling water, hoping to God nobody jumped up and exclaimed loudly, "*Serena's on the dry!*"

To her astonishment, Julie simply topped up her own glass and leaned across to fill Noelle's before plunging the bottle back into the ice bucket.

"So tell us all about this new fitness buzz. You look wonderful by the way." Patricia was polishing off a piece of tomato and fennel bread.

"I'm just loving it. I've got a swanky new trainer, easy on the eye to boot. I've never felt better. I'm toning up and have boundless energy. It's just super." Serena cocked her head to the side and tried to assume a self-satisfied look. Outwardly, she appeared to be the same, a confident and beautiful woman. Inwardly, she was quivering in her Gucci shoes and praying she was pulling this off. So much for her vow to be honest and assertive with her friends!

"That's fantastic news," Noelle smiled. "Patricia's right. You look so fresh, I must take that trainer's name."

Oh shit, Serena panicked. There was no trainer. If Noelle pushed her, she'd have to lie. But the conversation took a whole different direction, thankfully.

"I have a wee announcement of my own," Patricia looked like a Cheshire cat. "I've got number two in the oven!" She pointed at her belly.

"Oh, how wonderful!" Serena was so relieved to have the limelight taken off her.

"That's lovely, darling!" Noelle and Julie cooed.

All the attention turned to pregnancy and how dreadful Patricia had been feeling. She went into detail on vomiting frequency, lack of appetite, wanting to kill her husband, then coming the full circle to say how marvellous it all was.

The other two started to talk about all the shopping she'd have to do and then they started to figure out whether or not she should find out the sex at her 3D scan the following week.

"I think, the technology is there so why shouldn't you avail of it? Then you can start shopping right away," Noelle cooed.

A full two hours passed before anybody mentioned the fact that Serena hadn't drunk any wine. She was just about to make an excuse that she had to go, when Noelle poked her.

"So, dark horse. Do you have any news similar to Patricia or are we not supposed to know yet?" She winked, smiling. "Don't tell me you've sat through a full bottle of divine Chablis without touching a drop for no reason. Come on, you can tell us."

Although there were only three pairs of eyes on her, Serena felt like she was on stage in Wembley stadium. Her stomach lurched. The hairs on the back of her neck stood up. This was it. Her moment. Would she tell them the truth or would she brush it off? She could easily cut that Noelle one down to size, by snapping at her to mind her own business. But equally she could seize the opportunity to come clean.

"Well, I do have some news actually," she began hesitantly.

"I knew it!" Noelle clapped while smiling smugly.

"Oh God, and there I was rabbiting on about myself, while you were sitting quiet as a mouse and not saying a word. I feel terrible. When are you due?" Patricia went to give her a hug but Serena gently warded her off.

"I'm not pregnant. At least, not as far as I know."

"What? Well, why on earth did you say you were?" Noelle scoffed bitchily.

"I didn't." Serena looked at her and held her gaze. "I said I had news, which I do."

"Well, out with it for Christ's sake and stop talking in riddles, girl!" Noelle was in full flight, curtesy of the wine and her friend's obvious discomfort.

"I've been unwell for some time now. I've made a decision to cut alcohol out of my life. I'm an alcoholic."

There. She'd said it. Out loud and for all to hear. The silence was deafening. Her three friends looked like they'd been frozen in time. It was as if a pause button had been pressed.

"What are you talking about? I've never heard anything so ridiculous in my life!" Noelle scoffed, clearly ready to have a rant.

"Shut up, Noelle!" Patricia held her hand up to silence her. "Have a bit of compassion, even for five minutes." Probably because she was sober, or maybe because she was simply a good person, Patricia had picked up on Serena's pain. "I'm so proud of you!" she said and flung her arms around an astonished Serena. "That must be such a hard thing to admit. My mother is an alcoholic and for most of our childhood she staggered around pissed. When I was fourteen, she finally gave the bottle the boot. Good for you!"

It was Serena's turn to look shocked. "God, I never knew that about your mum. She always looked so gorgeous and perfect – she still does, in fact!"

"She does a lot of work with AA still. But she's been dry for twenty years now and has never looked back."

"Let me know if I can help at all." Julie was a bit twitchy and looked like she'd prefer to discuss slaughtering animals rather then the demons of drink.

"Thanks." Serena smiled fleetingly at her.

Noelle was outraged. "Jesus, Serena, I can't believe you didn't tell me. How long has this been going on?"

"What do you mean 'going on'? I haven't been having an affair with the vicar, Noelle. I've been having a really tough time and, apart from my mother, who is about as much use as an ashtray on a motorbike, Adele and Paul are the only people I've discussed this with."

"Why? Is it a secret or something?" Noelle tossed her head back and laughed.

"Do you have any brains at all in that highlighted skull of yours?" Serena felt hurt and angry.

"Oh for Christ sake, Serena, drop the dramatics. So what? You can't drink for a while? Big swing, you'll get over it. We all go through times when we know we need to reel it in a bit. It doesn't mean you have to drag yourself around with an end-the-world attitude, honey!" She grinned and waved her limp hand as if to blow the problem into the breeze.

"I always knew you were a spoilt and self-centred little cow, Noelle, but I stupidly thought you were my friend," said Serena. "I can't believe how far up your own arse you really are. I feel sorry for you, do you know that? I pity you. You're a sad bitch, who gets her jollies from putting others down. You've the emotional depth of a puddle!" She felt her eyes burning. She was not going to cry for that wench's benefit.

"Whoa, calm down! Don't yell at me just because you can't handle your booze. All I meant to say is that being an alcoholic isn't the worst thing on the planet. It's not like you've some life-threatening illness or anything. Anyway, that's a bit pot and kettle, calling me selfish. At least I'm woman enough to have a child and give part of myself to another person. You don't catch me swanning around, being Queen Bee and announcing that I don't want a child until I've finished having fun. I suppose you'll go off and have a baby, now you can't get loaded?"

"Noelle, that's enough." Patricia looked stricken. "Don't listen to her, Serena, she's being a brainless twat. Don't let her vile words set you back. You're doing so well, isn't she, Julie?"

"Of course you are. Anything we can do, just shout." Julie nodded, still looking rather uncomfortable.

"Well, I'm out of here. Some lunch this turned out to be," Noelle started to stuff her phone into her bag and raised her hand to get the bill. Yanking the front of her blouse down and looking for her purse, she muttered to herself.

"For your information, just before you go," Serena sounded deadly calm and very much in control again. "I have wished and longed for a baby for some time now. I've been attending a fertility clinic. The only reason I told you I was biding my time was because, once again, you were being a thoughtless bint. I can only hope and pray that I haven't fucked my own body up with drink, and that I will be able to conceive soon. But that won't be any concern of yours. I don't want to see you again. I think I always knew it, but your reaction today has certainly hammered it home. You are not my friend. You don't give a flying fuck about me, and guess what? Right back at ya, babe!"

Serena sat back in her chair and, instead of feeling wretched and awful, she felt freer than she had for a long time. Her determination and refusal to run away sent Noelle packing. Throwing fifty euro on the table, Noelle tossed her head back, snatched her coat, and nearly impaled herself on the back of a chair as she fled the scene.

"Girl power! Jesus, you let her have it!" Patricia put her hands up to her mouth. "I'm sorry. I know I shouldn't laugh but I don't think the Queen of Sheba has ever been spoken to like that in her life!"

"I know, God love that poor sod of a husband of hers. She'll probably beat him senseless with her Berkin bag when he gets home!" Serena threw her head back and giggled.

The other two girls stayed and they chatted for a further two hours. They were so supportive and genuinely concerned. She was warmed inside to realise that they really did want to see her well.

"I feel terrible – here am I gloating about having number two, when you've been having such an awful time," said Patricia.

"Not at all, I'm thrilled for you. Envious as hell but so delighted for you. I hope it all goes well. Who knows, now that I'm focusing on my health, maybe all this hard work will pay off. The poor foetus was probably too drunk to form in my body before. Now that I'm sober, maybe things will work. Maybe my body will comply. The clinic did say that there are no reasons why I'm not conceiving, so fingers and toes crossed and all that!"

The girls were brilliant. They made Serena promise to keep talking to them. Patricia also suggested that Serena have a casual cup of tea with her mother when she felt like it. She was heavily involved in arranging AA meetings in the area and at least she was a familiar face for her to start off with.

"I'd like that. Do you think she'd mind?" Serena asked.

"I'm sure she'd be honoured. She's been there and I know she'd be discreet. Will I call her tonight?"

"Yes. Thank you. Both of you. I wish I'd told you weeks ago. I'm doing well, as in I'm not drinking, but sometimes I'd love a pal to confide in. You've no idea what a relief it is for me that you're supporting me like this." She sighed. She felt utterly exhausted from all the confessing and from the horrible confrontational scene with Noelle. She had no idea what would happen with her. She wouldn't be ready to speak to Noelle for a very long time and she wasn't even sure if she wanted to forgive her. If she was going to be such a bitch, why did she even want her in her life?

The hurt and disappointment was there all the same. They'd been friends since they were knee-high to a grasshopper, and even though she knew Noelle was a selfish wench she still knew a part of her was going to miss her. A bit like having an annoying mole removed. You're glad it's gone, but in a funny way you miss it.

Maybe it was just another part of her life that needed to go. Maybe along with drink, Noelle was a negative influence, which needed to be excised. Right that moment was not the time to make those decisions, however.

She'd had enough today. She wanted to go home and cook Paul's dinner. She hugged the two girls and walked the short distance to her car. It was surprisingly handy having her car sitting right outside. No looking for taxis or having to wait around. She was home in minutes. Flicking open a cookery book, she set about making a chicken dish.

Now that she was sober and had all this energy, she'd begun to really taste and enjoy her food. The running was toning her and yet she was able to eat more than before. A whole new world was opening up to her. It wasn't easy being sober but she was beginning to understand that it wasn't that terrible either.

She smiled as she heard the front door slamming.

"Hi, Serena, I'm home. Where are you?"

Even if she never managed to have a child, she had Paul. He'd been amazing. He was the one constant in her life. Through thick and thin, he'd been there for her. Now that she had new hope of finding some sort of common ground with Adele too, she felt she had so much more to look forward to. Knowing she wasn't the only one with bumps and starts in her life made her feel so much more hopeful that she would be able to overcome her problems. If nothing else, she was ready to try and turn her life around.

51

tweeting@themercedesking.com
If this tunnel in life exists, I think I can see some light at the end of it.

Damo was sitting in the estate agent's office, having just signed a lease on a nice penthouse apartment. He'd been staying in that kip of a bedsit since Noreen had thrown him out. He'd really thought she'd calm down and forgive him before now. He'd even bought her a pair of big thick gold hoop earrings and had the girl in the shop wrap them in gold paper and ribbon, not to mention the flowers and chocolates. He'd gone to the wholesalers to buy crisps for the pubs and had seen the box of chocolates. They were nearly the size of a pool table. Noreen loved sweets and he'd been full sure she'd forgive him if he turned up with them. He nearly needed a wheelbarrow to cart them up to the front door of the house.

She'd fecked the flowers over the hedge into next door and told him to shove the chocolates up his hole. Hardly decent talk for a lady, he'd told her.

"I never claimed to be a lady but one thing I've never been is a fraud. Even if you hitch the entire Cadbury factory to the back of that bleedin' Merc you adore and drag it in through the sliding door into the kitchen, I'll never take you back. You are the lowest of low,

374

Damo McCabe. There's not a scumbag in Dublin as bad as you. You thought that money would make you a better man, well, let me tell you something! When you hadn't a bean, you were a better person than the egotistical, deluded old fool that stands here before me today. You belong in the gutter, Damo. Your parents mightn't have had much, but by God they had something that you never inherited – dignity and respect. Now, get back in your Merc, rev up, and feck off!" Noreen was about to slam the door when she spotted the box from the jeweller's in his hands. "I'll take that! Knowing you, it's probably worth a fortune. I bleedin' deserve it."

As the door banged, Damo noticed the locks had been changed. The cheek of her! He'd thought all these years that she was a nice girl. Well, she was certainly showing her true colours now.

"That's not nice, Noreen. You can't slam me own door in me face. I'll tell the judge you were abusive!" he shouted in the letterbox.

"Tell me arse!" was the last thing he heard from Noreen.

As if his day couldn't get any worse, Ruby's father phoned him to tip him over the edge. He was all posh and using big words, telling him that if he had his way he'd be castrated with a rusty blade and chopped into small bits and buried in the River Liffey in a suitcase. To say the man was less than friendly was an understatement.

"All we want from you is to sign papers saying you relinquish all ties to your son." Harry had paused.

"Eh, right then. What does Ruby think of all this?" Damo was suddenly interested to know if the young one still held a torch for him. He'd no interest in her either way but right now he could do with all the fans he could get.

"Ruby doesn't want anything to do with you again. That, by the way, is her own decision. She asked me to sort all the details. She'll be moving to a different school in September and we hope that, with our support, she and the baby will have a very bright future, in spite of your interference."

"Just send me the paper. I'm at Number 1, Countess Villas. I've secured a nice penthouse apartment for meself. Very swish it is," Damo sniffed.

"Why? Did you long-suffering wife finally kick you out?" Harry jibed.

"Eh, yeah. Just a blip, we all have them. Marriage is a difficult thing, you know yourself?" Damo felt Ruby's father was pleased to hear he was on his own, the prick.

"Well, I hope you and your penthouse are very happy together. You deserve to be on your own. If I had my way, you would be up in court and banged up for unlawful sex with a minor. But my wife and daughter have explained that they want to move forward with our lives, without Ruby being dragged through court. My sole concern, unlike you, is my family. So we are doing what we feel will make the most of our situation. Ruby is adamant that you should not be allowed to ruin our lives."

Damo was more than a little put out by the conversation. Sure, he'd sign all the papers and all that, but he found it quite astonishing that Ruby had changed her mind about him. That kid was obviously being brainwashed by her parents.

Well, he'd get himself settled into the apartment and get down to the club early tonight. There was one of those two-day event concerts going on in a field just outside Dublin. No doubt he'd get a call for a few of the big acts to come to The Orb during the weekend. A couple of lines of coke and he'd be back on top form. He was Damo the Mercedes King. Fuck the lot of them, he didn't need any of them. He'd come a long way. He had money. What more did he need?

52

tweeting@angiebaby.com
Tired? Oh yes. Struggling to wear much more than a tracksuit?
Oh yes. Happier than I've ever been? You bet!

The days and nights ran into each other after that. Adam had very little routine so, in turn, neither did Angie. She just slept when he did and any night that he managed to stay in his Moses basket for more than a four-hour stretch, she was grateful.

Their six-week check-up rolled in. Her parents said they'd accompany her to Dublin, saying that they'd have a day out, shopping and looking around, followed by a bit of lunch, while she attended the hospital. But she felt she needed the break and besides she wanted to catch up with Brenda and the others. She and Adam were planning on spending the night in Brenda's. She was dying to meet little Barry. As she'd planned, Brenda had named her son after her dead husband.

So herself and Adam were going up on the train and meeting Brenda when they were over the appointment. Leona and Sandra were both joining them the following morning for coffee along with their babies. Sandra had a little girl by caesarean section as she had ended up going twelve days over. She was still finding the recovery slow and sounded quite dejected. None of the girls had heard from

Ruby but Brenda had bumped into Una, the midwife from their antenatal classes, and she had told them that the baby had been born. They were all looking forward to introducing their offspring to each other and having a good natter.

Angie waited for an hour and a half to see the paediatrician. By the time it was their turn, she'd decided he was going to be diagnosed with everything from a hernia to a brain tumour.

"He's a fine little fellow and is gaining weight and growing at a normal level. Well done, Mum," the doctor concluded. "You may dress him up and join me at my desk."

"Is that it?" Angie looked astonished.

"Yes, why?" The doctor looked puzzled.

"Well, I was reading your leaflets in the waiting area and I suppose I'd begun to convince myself he might have something wrong. He doesn't sleep very much either." She sounded lame and whiny.

"Most babies don't, I'm afraid," the doctor grinned. "He's as healthy as can be, a great result."

Angie dressed him and put on the layers of blankets and his little sunhat. The amount of stuff she needed just for a day out was a joke. It would have been much easier to be done with it and go for broke, with a large suitcase on wheels. Luckily, she had a rather large undercarriage on the pram, which was a similar thing really. Every part of the pram was stuffed with clothes, nappies and baby paraphernalia. All she'd brought for herself was a clean pair of knickers and fresh T-shirt. Brenda had firmly instructed her not to bring toiletries or anything like that.

"I have everything you could possibly need here, so just bring what you need for Adam." That all sounded very sensible and easy but of course it still required enough stuff to set up a small nursery store. She had the added hassle of the pram wanting to tip over all the time with the weight of the bags, so she needed to balance it. Both in the hospital waiting room and in the paediatrician's office, she'd taken Adam out and the front wheels had ricocheted upwards, nearly catapulting the pram through the roof. Some day she'd get better at paring down to what was really necessary. For now, her new-mother's paranoia meant she needed to be sure, to be sure, to be sure. She marvelled at other mothers, who might have two or three kids and all they seemed to need was a clean nappy stuck in the back pocket of their jeans and they took off.

Humming and allowing herself to feel a little bit proud of her perfect specimen, she bumped him down the hospital steps. Once she was safely across the road, she dialled Brenda's mobile number in order to meet up with her and Baby Barry. Probably because the sun was in her eyes and she wasn't concentrating, she clumsily ran into a passerby with the pram.

"Oh Jesus, I'm so sorry, I wasn't looking where I was going!" she apologised as the poor man rubbed his shin.

"No worries, could happen to a bishop." He was still bent double.

She shifted the pram out of his way and continued to say sorry, grasping his forearm to try and help him balance himself. He stood up and pulled off his baseball cap, with the other hand in the air to show it was all fine.

"Troy."

Angie felt the road and path meeting, as her eyes began to lose focus. She felt like a shoplifter as the shop alarm sounded at the door. Except, this time instead of a dress or a pair of shoes, she'd stolen his child, which in the greater scheme of things was a hell of a lot worse.

"Yes? Do I know you?" He looked at her in confusion, still hopping in pain. "Oh, yeah, of course, Rachel's mate from the Rebel County no less. How's it going? Jeez, I didn't know you had a kid!" He looked kind of mortified as he nodded and distractedly glanced towards the opening of the pram. Shoving his hands into the pockets of his hoody, he coughed uncomfortably and looked at the ground. Angie quickly deduced that he was more embarrassed than she was at meeting again. He was all red and stuttery and looked like he'd prefer to be sharing a pizza with Satan right now, rather than standing in front of her.

"He's only six weeks old – his name is Adam." She felt like a potential murderer who was chatting amicably to her unsuspecting victim while she held a poised dagger behind her back.

"Yeah, cool. Okay, great. So . . . good stuff, then. Yep. Good to see you . . ."

"Angie. My name is Angie."

"Yeah, was just about to say that. Angie, yeah."

Her heart sank. The ball was totally in her court. This guy couldn't even remember her name, let alone put two and two together and come up with three.

"So that'll put a stop to all the mad partying and all that, I suppose?" He still didn't look her in the eye. "Did you get married as well since we last met, or are you just, what do they call it, living in sin?" He snorted and nodded, chuckling forcibly.

"Yeah, the whole nine yards," Angie lied.

"Good stuff. Great, in fact. Yeah. Super. Okay, so, I better get going. Work and all that, you know yourself." He still didn't make eye contact. "Unlike yourself, my life is still trucking along the same old road. No big changes there. Bit boring really. Nothing huge to report. Okay, right. Yeah. Good."

"Nice to see you again," Angie ended the cringing conversation abruptly.

Troy just seemed relieved. "Yeah, you too. Enjoy the whole mother and baby shenanigans then. Right, good. See you then, good luck, take care." He waved in a very overenthusiastic way while moving off.

Angie was rooted to the spot, her blood rushing through her ears. She could so easily let him walk away. It would all be finished. The poor git would never suspect a thing. She looked at Adam. Tiny and perfect. With nothing wrong with him. Hospital approved. The tiny voice she'd quashed for the last nine months suddenly burst forth, like a dragon out of the ashes and roared through her.

"Troy, wait!" she yelled, rather too loudly.

He swung around, with his two hands still shoved into the washed-out hoody. "Jesus, you made me jump! Yeah?" He had the stance of a buzzard, all shoulders and a lank forward protruding neck with his hooded head lurching towards the ground.

"Sorry, I didn't mean to scream like a banshee at you." She felt sick. "Can you give me a minute – we need to talk?" She swallowed nervously.

"Erm, yeah. Sure, whatever you like." He looked at her sideways.

"Do you have a flat in town or a quiet office where we can talk?"

"Not quiet as such. I'm sharing with three others in a flat in Ranelagh and the office is kind of open plan. How quiet were you thinking?" He shrugged and went all red and looked like he was waiting for her to slap him.

"No, that won't do. Listen, just come over here." She beckoned for him to follow her as she went and sat at the bottom of steps leading up to a Georgian house.

He padded over and sat looking at the ground, like an overgrown teenager. He didn't say a word.

"Troy, I need to tell you something which might just shock the hell out of you," she coughed.

"Ooh, God, sounds a bit iffy, Ange. Right, sure, okay then – shoot!" He nodded enthusiastically, hair flopping around messily as he elbowed her in jest.

"Adam is yours," she blurted out.

"Who's Adam?" He looked at her, the sun making him squint.

"The bloody baby!" she shouted. Oh hell, she felt like fixing her hands around his neck and squeezing until he went purple.

"What? No. But why? How? I don't understand, how come you never . . .?"

"I know. I'm sorry. I know it was very wrong of me and I should have contacted you months ago. But I was scared and we hardly know each other, and it's very complicated with me living in Cork and you up here and all that."

There was a massive silence hanging in the air. He stared at her. This time she hung her head and looked at the ground in shame. Standing up slowly, he looked into the pram. Angie felt like the air had turned to syrup. She could barely breathe as she watched him look at his son. Knowing for the first time that Adam was his baby too. The feeling of panic was prickling every inch of Angie's skin. She didn't want to share her baby with anyone and, now she'd told Troy, she was going to have to. A problem shared was a problem halved, she thought bitterly. But her darling precious child was far from a problem and she wanted nothing less that to have him halved, even metaphorically speaking.

"God, he's really small, isn't he?" He nodded again. He shoved his hands back into the kangaroo-pouch pockets of his hoody. His shoulders were slumped forwards and his floppy fringe covered his eyes.

"Is that all you can say?" Angie stood up and rounded on him angrily.

"Well, it's all a bit of a whammer to be honest with you. It's going to take me a while to let it all sink in. Does your husband know the baby's not his?" He looked at her in concern.

"I don't have a husband, you great big pillock!" she snapped.

"But I thought you said ..."

"I was trying to throw you off the scent. I wasn't going to tell you about Adam." She felt desperately ashamed.

"What, never?" His eyes widened.

"No. I'm sorry. Listen, I know I'm a terrible person and I don't blame you for a second if you hate me. But can we try and come to some kind of adult arrangement, please?"

She looked so desperate and haunted, Troy sat down again and put his arm around her.

"Yeah, listen. If I was in your position, not that I would be, seeing as I'm a bloke and all that, but you know what I mean? I can get your drift. I suppose you kind of hit the old panic button inside. Brain malfunction and all that stuff, yeah, it can happen." He was nodding again.

This time, the nodding and laidback hippy attitude was like a balm soothing the rawness of her entire being.

"So you don't hate me?" she sniffed.

"God no. Sure, we hardly know each other, let's call as spade a spade here. This is a tough call, Ange, to be honest with you. I'm feeling a tad like I've had the wind knocked out of me if I'm going to fess up here. Geez, yeah. Wow!"

He looked up at her and she realised the poor bloke had tears in his eyes and his hands were shaking. Even the putty colour that he'd previously had in his cheeks had drained by now.

"Oh Christ, Troy, forgive me. I'm such a cow. I'm a dreadful person. I should have been honest with you from the start, and I should never in a million years have dumped this news on you, here on the side of the street." She put her arms around him and pulled him into an embrace.

A dam burst inside Angie too, and the two comparative strangers held each other and rocked from side to side sobbing. All the while Adam lay in his pram, serenely unaware of the commotion his parents were creating.

"What kind of involvement were you thinking you'd like me to have, just so I can try to get my head straight on it all? I'm kind of a free spirit. My parents are always saying I should live on a desert island." His eyes were red and filled with tears, as he looked at her with doubt and confusion apparent in his expression. He was desperately trying to be his usual self, forcing himself to skit and snort and nod again. In a heartbreakingly childlike way, he ground his fists into his eyes and tried to abate his tears.

"Well, we'd have to work that out with time." Angie felt frozen. She was reeling as she tried to take the moment in her stride.

"Sure, sure. Sorry, I'm probably saying all the wrong stuff here. I don't have a huge amount of experience with women, never mind the whole fatherhood thing. So if I'm doing it wrong, try not to panic. I do a lot of things wrong. Kind of the story of my life, to be honest." He swung his hands awkwardly and held his palms up to the sky. Shrugging, he sniffed and sat there, barely breathing. He looked over at Angie.

She had never felt so confused in her entire life. She realised, with a sinking feeling, that he was waiting for her to give him some direction. He was like a great big lost puppy, and he wanted her to be his mummy, as well as Adam's.

"I don't think either of us is too experienced in the whole parenthood stakes." She gave him a quizzical look. "One thing I'm feeling, though, is that this might not be the most appropriate place to discuss Adam's future."

"Oh, right. Yeah. Oh God, this is a bit of a blow, I have to be honest with you." He nudged her and tried his best to make light of the situation but the tears began to course down his cheeks again.

Oh, sweet Jesus, she prayed. Give me the strength and patience to manage this situation. Please remove all my vicious tendencies and violent thoughts. Please give me the guidance to deal with this person, for the sake of our son.

"Firstly, can I have your mobile number and address?" she asked, sounding a bit like a schoolteacher.

"Good one, sure, I suppose that's as good a place as any to start, hey?"

Finding the back of a receipt to write on, she fished a pen out of the nappy bag. Scribbling his address, she wrote her parents', her apartment address and her phone number and tore that portion off. Handing it to him, she wondered if he'd simply lose it.

"Must remember to take that out before I give my jeans in at the launderette. I'm a divil for washing stuff into the pockets." He shrugged again.

As she was about to expire from sheer panic, a thought hit Angie. This guy was such a feather head, he'd probably play ball whatever way she told him. He was likely to agree to whatever she wanted. If she was pleasant about it and got him to sign whatever documents she had drawn up, he might actually be okay to deal with.

"Jeez, it just occurred to me that my folks might get a bit of a shock when I tell them about this little one. It might be better if I tell them myself, if that's okay with yourself, Angie?" He nodded, looking pensive.

"Well, in fairness, I can't really tell them, seeing as I don't actually know them." She meant to sound sarcastic, which went over his head entirely.

"Yes, of course. Good point. So does this mean you need some kind of money each week to help out? 'Cos that's no problemo. I wouldn't like to shirk any responsibility or anything like that. Wouldn't like to think of you and wee Adam here in any kind of a bind or what have you." He stroked his chin. "Will I take your bank details and you can let me know how much you're thinking of and we can take it from there?"

Angie stared at him like a dead goldfish. Was this guy for real? Did he honestly think they could sort the whole thing out, on a step outside a Georgian house, in time for him to finish his lunch break?

"To be fair, Troy, it might just take a while to crack the system on this one. We might just have to meet up a few times to thrash it all out properly. We'll have to get some lawyers involved too. It's not going to be done and dusted here and now, in all honesty, now is it?" She stared at him, willing him to keep up with her.

"No, no. True enough. Of course not. Goooood. I'm just not great at all this kind of thing, you know? I try, really I do. I make myself think before I speak and all that sort of thing, but it never seems to come out the way it should. I don't get up in the morning and consciously decide to annoy people and do the wrong thing – it just seems to end up that way. As you've probably worked out, I'm a bit of a mess." He looked at her with raw and open honesty. "I'm not a bad person, Ange. I just don't seem to be able to run my life the way the world expects me to. I've never been any different." He shrugged and blew upwards, moving his floppy fringe for a second before it rested in his eyes again.

"I'm sorry, Troy, we don't know each other that well, but even I know you aren't a bad person. This is such a huge thing to be landed with on the side of the street and you're doing fantastically. Really you are."

He stared at her again, waiting for her to tell him exactly what to do. Scratching the side of his head, he was overcome with emotion again. The tears flowed down his cheeks and she could see him visibly shaking.

"I'm sorry about this, Ange. I think I'm a bit shocked. I'm finding this all a bit difficult to take on board. As you said yourself, we don't exactly know each other either. Well, we know each other obviously, as Adam is proof of that, but we don't *know* each other, sort of ..." He trailed off miserably.

"Would you be interested in having access to Adam?" She held her breath as he nodded. Angie had never felt so cruel and yet so terrified of another human being. This was a living hell.

"Well, yeah," he said. "I suppose at some stage, eventually. Listen, I'm going to have to fess up here. I've never actually minded a small baby on my own. So, right at the moment, it might be a bit messy. In fact, it's probably not an option if I'm truthful. As I said,

I share the flat with three others and I can't see them agreeing to a little fella, lovely as he is, staying for weekends and the likes. So it might be better to leave that end of it to you for the time being, if that's okay. You know, if you needed a night out or something, you could tell me and I could come down to Cork on the train. That'd be no hassle at all. I'm sure when he's older we could work on a plan of action at that point. You know, holidays and stuff, if you like." He looked really confused and upset.

"That sounds perfect." Angie felt like she'd won the lottery. If she'd had even the slightest inkling he was going to be so pliable and willing to let her call the shots, she'd have told him months ago. Her instinct was, of course, not to trust him until she had all this in writing. The raging guilt she felt, which was sticking in her gullet like a ball of dough, threatened to choke her. She'd had no right to keep her pregnancy and Adam's existence from him. Especially now that he seemed to be so mild-mannered and accommodating. *But you didn't know that before,* the voice of reason in her head kept suggesting.

"God," he bashed himself on the forehead, "I probably sound like the worst father now, don't I? Should I just move to Cork? I mean, I don't know anyone there and I'd have to find a new job, but I suppose I should really."

The torture in his eyes as he made the suggestion alarmed Angie.

"No!" she said too quickly. "God, no. I wouldn't expect you to change your whole life for us. We'll work it out between us. The baby will need me to be there the whole time for now. As you say, when he's older, it might work out better for him to come to you. I have a spare room in my place, so you can come and visit any time you like," she finished weakly. Please let him agree, she prayed silently.

"Jeez, Angie, you're being really cool about all this. Fair play. Fair play. It's kind of a pity we live so far apart, I think I could really dig a laidback chick like you." He smiled sadly, fumbled in his pocket for a tissue and blew his nose loudly.

Angie smiled back and put her arm around him as they sat on the steps up to a stranger's home. Inside, she was already drawing up the letter she wanted her solicitor to send him. She wanted to make sure he legally agreed to let her raise this child. Unless he had a full lobotomy, it was looking astonishingly like he might actually agree.

Her mobile burst into action, causing her to jump.

"Brenda, hi. I won't be long. I've just bumped into a friend here."

Angie knew she sounded like she was about to die of fright. She'd obviously tell Brenda everything when she saw her but she wanted to keep Troy on the right track here.

"Is everything all right?" asked Brenda. "Did the doctor check Adam?"

"Yes, all that went swimmingly. I'm just with someone at the moment. I'm trying to discuss a very important issue. I'll be with you shortly, okay?"

Brenda copped on that something serious was going on. "Do you need me to arrive? Where are you?"

"No, thank you, honey. I'm just up from the hospital, so I'll be with you soon."

"If you're sure. Call me as soon as you're on your way so I know you're really okay. You sound weird. If I don't hear from you in five minutes, I'll ring back, okay?"

"Right, thanks."

Troy had stood up and was fidgeting like cat on a griddle. He peered into the pram and stared at Adam for the longest time. Angie could barely watch as Troy took in every detail of the baby. All the sound and movement disappeared as Angie went into her own space in time. She hoped and prayed that he wouldn't want to ruin everything. He seemed like a truly decent sort of guy. His heart was in the right place and he had a gentle and easy way about him, but she had no guarantee that he would still be this pliable when the news had sunk in properly.

"Troy, I know what I did was wrong. Maybe it was my hormones or maybe I'm just a terrible person, but I need you to know that I won't cut you off again, unless that's what you want." Angie felt like she was finally free of her fear.

Her mother's words from several months previously came to the forefront of her mind. That Adam might blame her for not letting him know his father. Now that Troy was standing here she realised his gentle nature and endearing emotion would benefit Adam, she was sure of it. He could offer a whole other dimension to the child's life. Adam would get the farming and outdoor element from his granddad and uncles. His daddy could be the city part, the urban edge to him.

Troy broke her daydreaming by touching her arm and speaking gently. "Listen. I'd better get back to work. I have a meeting with overseas clients which was due to start fifteen minutes ago. I don't need to lose my job, especially now that I have wee Adam here to consider. Will you call me and let me know what's what?" He was now brushing off the back of his trousers. He peered into the pram again. "He's a cool little dude, isn't he?" He was nodding again. The colour was coming back into his wan face.

"You bet he is. I know you must feel like you've been hit with a sledgehammer but this little guy here is the best thing that ever happened to me. He's addictive, you'll see." Angie smiled. "The best thing about him is that he always looks at me with delight, even when I haven't washed my hair for two days. He is the best 'job' I've ever had to be honest."

"My job is one place that I can actually do things right. Believe it or not, I have a team of eight working for me. I know I seem like a total waste of space but I'm not a total washout." He looked at Adam again. "I think I might be able to teach him something. I play piano too, just for the record," he shrugged.

"You don't need to give me a CV, Troy. I'm sure you'll be a great dad for Adam. By the time he's a teenager, he'll probably hate the sight of me and only want to be with you." Angie couldn't speak any more.

"Listen," said Troy. "I can see that you're terrified that I'm going to take the child from you. I'm not in the market for ruining anyone's life. I just want to be happy, just the same as you. Things can only get better. Angie, look at me," Troy lifted her chin so she was looking into his dark brown eyes. "It's going to be all right," he smiled. He looked traumatised, but, God bless him, he smiled.

"We'll muddle through," she agreed. "It will just take a bit of communication. But I have to point out here and now that he won't be going up and down on the train in his rock-a-tot. So any toing or froing will have to be kept to a minimum until he's a bit older."

"Ah yeah, maybe until he's at least two."

Angie looked at Troy and was relieved to see he was joking. "I'm going back down to Cork this afternoon. We only came up for the six-week check-up," she lied. "How about I call you tomorrow and we can talk some more?" Angie knew she was being a control freak again, not telling Troy she was staying with Brenda that night, but she needed some space and time before she spoke to him again.

"Yup, cool. Rome wasn't built in a day, as they say. Could I come down your way over the next couple of weeks and have a get-together with the little guy? I don't want to step on any toes or like get in the way, but you did offer . . ." He looked confused and uncomfortable again. He rubbed his forehead and stood looking at the ground.

"Sure. Of course you can. Any time. And you're bang on there. I did say." She found herself starting to speak like him.

"Cool." When he smiled his eyes crinkled up and he looked kind of sweet.

Thank God he's a bit better looking than I remember, Angie thought as she strode away. Some of her mad pregnancy nightmares had flashed up images of a guy with cracked teeth and a slightly unhinged smile. Troy was kind of like a harmless Labrador.

* * *

Troy walked back to his office shaking his head in disbelief. In fact, he knew he was in total shock. It wasn't so bad. To be told he had a son was kind of nice really. He would go down to Cork and see them. He meant it when he said he'd pay his way too. That was the right thing to do in the circumstances.

Just wait until he told his parents and his mates he had a son. He would bet a year's wages that none of them would guess this one. He shook his head and smiled shakily, trying to get his head together. He'd about three minutes to pull himself together before he had to face a room full of anxiously waiting businessmen. He knew he could hardly go into the conference room and say, "Sorry I'm late, guess who I just met? My son! Guess what, he's six weeks old and I had no idea he even existed! Fancy that! So, where did we leave off last time? Coffee, anyone?"

He thought of putting his iPod on and belting out some Guns 'n Roses for a few minutes but he couldn't manage to make the earphones stay put in his ears. His hands were shaking and his mouth was bone dry. He couldn't face going back to the office just yet. He couldn't sit and pretend to be fine. Dialling the work number, he got through to one of his team.

"Troy, hey, man, where are you? They're getting really pissed off waiting for you," Steward hissed.

"Something urgent has cropped up, a family matter. I won't be in the office until tomorrow. It's unavoidable, so make my apologies and I'll deal with the backlash tomorrow. Cheers." Troy hung up. He never missed work and never let them down. They would just have to wait until he was in a better frame of mind.

He would hop on the DART and go and see his mother. He probably shouldn't tell her she was a granny over the phone. She wasn't really like him – she had a tendency to freak over the smallest thing. No, he'd better call in and talk to her at the kitchen table over a cup of tea. That would be the best idea. She might have a few ideas of what he should do too. After all, she'd already done the whole parent trip and all that.

As he paid for his ticket and sat on the green bench in the station waiting for the train to arrive, he found himself overcome with emotion again. God, this was strange really. He'd never have guessed this one when he'd woken up this morning. He was too mild-natured to feel angry at Angie, but he did feel unbearably sad that she hadn't felt the need to tell him before today. If they hadn't met by chance, would she really have kept the baby a secret? He wasn't a demanding or possessive person by nature, but at the same time nobody likes to feel cheated. Was it a poor reflection on him that she didn't want to tell him? Was he that dreadful a person that she didn't think he deserved to even know? Hurt and an awful feeling of failure enveloped him. The roaring sound of the approaching train snapped him out of his thoughts.

* * *

Angie was in a sweat and having a delayed panic attack by the time she found Brenda in the coffee shop in Grafton Street. She relayed the whole story.

"Jesus, what an awful shock for both of you! Was he not angry or even pissed off with you?"

"No, God help him, he just shook and cried. I didn't want to share Adam, that's why I didn't tell him. I'm such a cruel bitch. But if I'm honest, I'd do it all the same way again. It was my choice to go ahead with my pregnancy. My body, my labour and birth. So all I can say is this - if I'm supposed to burn in hell for this, Brenda, so be it. In fact, I'll bring the cocktail sausages and marshmallows."

"Honey, I understand totally. It's the mummy lioness thing. You're protecting your cub. I feel the same way. My little angel is the centre of my universe too. Barry would have been so proud to be a daddy, but that wasn't meant to be. I can tell you, anyone who ever tries to come between me and my little cub will have his face scratched off."

"Oh Brenda, sorry. I didn't mean to go off on one."

"It's really brought it home to me that he's never coming back. I'm really on my own, Angie," Brenda sniffed. "You're right to tell this Troy guy. Even if he's as much use as a chocolate teapot, he is Adam's father, so you should let him contribute in some way."

"Listen, our boys are going to be the most amazing people. We will love them, encourage them and raise them to be sensitive and fabulous." Angie thumped the table.

"Jesus, you make it sound like they'll be taking over the country," Brenda giggled.

"Maybe they will. With lioness mammies like us, watch out World!"

"That's the spirit," Brenda grinned.

By the time they managed to reach Brenda's house, unloaded the fifteen million articles and bottles and bags, they were exhausted.

Brenda's previously pristine and orderly home was now strewn with a baby gym, changing unit, swinging chair, bouncy seat and countless other large contraptions.

"Jesus, the state of your house! I can't believe the change in décor," Angie laughed.

"I know, isn't it amazing how such a small creature can cause such mayhem?"

"I thought my apartment was only like a skip because it was small and has very little storage. But I've changed my mind. The more space you have the more gear you can stuff in. How on earth is a child the size of himself supposed to use all this?"

Angie gazed around the room. It was worse than the baby shop they'd visited while they were pregnant.

"People were a bit overgenerous with the gifts, weren't they? I think on account of Barry's passing, all our family and friends went a bit overboard with the presents."

"Well, I'm glad I kept my trap shut about Adam. Forget the notion of telling Troy or not, we'd never be able to fit in the apartment if I'd got even half the stuff you did."

They had a lovely evening together. They decided to change into their pyjamas, have a Chinese delivered and relax. In between feeding, burping, changing nappies and soothing babies, it was fantastic to be able to talk. Being in a single-mother situation together, they understood each other perfectly.

"I don't think this is a gift I would ever consider giving to anyone else." Brenda had to raise her voice so Angie could hear her over Baby Barry's screams. The electronic rocking seat that playing creepy fairground music was terrifying the poor child, rather than soothing him.

"Doesn't exactly have the effect the manufacturers were aiming for, does it?" Angie giggled.

* * *

The following morning, Leona arrived at Brenda's house. She looked exactly the same, in her uniform tracksuit, with her little girl in an exact miniature outfit. Right down to the pink Nike runners, the mother and daughter were like Mommy and Mini-me.

"Hiya, how are yous all doing? Look, Madonna, it's your boyfriends!" Leona giggled as she bent to kiss both Adam and Barry.

Shortly afterwards, Sandra arrived with her little girl.

"Meet Isabelle!" She looked so proud of her sleeping infant. Dressed in a pink baby grow, she looked like a little rabbit in her rock-a-tot.

"The only one we're missing is Ruby," Angie mused.

Angie really enjoyed the morning and loved catching up with the girls but her mind was kind of elsewhere. All she really wanted was to get back to Cork and get all Adam's legal paperwork sorted out. Troy seemed to be a total pacifist and easy to manipulate but she still couldn't trust him. Until it was all in black and white, she wouldn't relax. Brenda's stricken face yesterday was imprinted on her mind. She knew she couldn't deny Adam a father but her mothering instinct was still surging and urging her to protect her offspring.

* * *

By the time she reached Cork Station that night, she'd made her mind up to return to her apartment in Cork city. She spent a further two days in her parents' house, gathering up her stuff and getting ready to make her final move.

Reluctantly, she'd told her parents the truth about Troy. Her father had taken on that confused and uncomfortable air about him. Her mother had been practical as usual.

"About time, my girl. That child is entitled to know his father and this Troy fella should know and support his son. It's only right, Angie. You have always been a strong-willed little fecker since the day God put you on this earth, but I have to be honest with you, love. I didn't agree with you taking matters into your own hands on this one. I've stood by and watched you over the years. You've a strong head on your shoulders and you've admirable strength of character and a good brain inside that head of yours, but taking a child's daddy and tossing him aside," her mother sighed deeply, "no good could come of that, pet."

Angie bit her tongue. Now that it was all out in the open, all the opinions were flooding in. It was just like when she finished with a boyfriend and everyone finally admitted that they'd all thought he was a tosser anyway. That dawning realisation that people had been tiptoeing around her did shake her up somewhat.

"Why didn't you tackle me properly about the matter if you thought I was doing so wrong by Adam, Mammy?" Angie was getting annoyed now. "You did say so but then you dropped the issue and never brought it up again."

"Angie, I knew it was no use talking to you. From when you were little, if I told you to leave a sick lamb to nature, you would go against me. You'd have it tucked up in a blanket beside the AGA. You'd nurse it for days, barely eating or sleeping yourself . . ."

"And it would die anyway and I'd cry for a week," Angie finished.

"Sometimes, you have to let things take their course, love. Even if it's not what you want inside here." She pounded her chest.

Her parents made Angie promise to return if she was lonely or found it hard to manage. And so she left for the city.

The apartment was nicer than she'd remembered. She walked in and out of the bright rooms, taking in all the familiar things. She set up all Adam's paraphernalia and felt quite at ease and surprisingly delighted to be back in her own place at last.

Adam was a little unsettled that night, waking at least three times. It was all a bit of a blur. In the end, she'd just pulled him into her bed, so the two of them could get some rest. She knew some of the books advised against having the baby in the bed with you and she'd been very careful not to allow it so far. But at times the need for sleep had taken over and she'd relented.

* * *

It was eleven o'clock the next morning before she was organised enough to get herself outside. By the time she'd fed, changed and dressed Adam and done the same for herself, the morning had slipped away. She wondered how the hell other people managed to do all this by seven in the morning and drop the baby to a crèche. The thought of having to do anything like focus on work or a computer as well was simply beyond her.

She was busy having a fight with the pram, which had managed to mangle itself into a non-moving wheel position in the lift, when she bashed into someone, while muttering to herself.

"Sorry, sorry. This thing has a mind of its own," she babbled.

"Take your time," a laughing voice came from behind her. "Long time no see – you've been busy evidently."

Angie swung around. Much to her surprise, there was the guy she'd woken in the middle of the night all those months ago. Christ, this really wasn't her lucky day. She'd always felt that if a day started out badly, it was almost worth hiding until bedtime, as the pattern would just continue. This was proof of her theory.

"Eh, yes. I've been living in Dublin and then I had Adam here. I just came back last night," she flushed with embarrassment.

"I thought I heard a baby crying last night. Now at least I know I'm not going insane," He stood and smiled at her.

Realising she was blocking the lift, she pulled the pram out of the way and whacked him in the process.

"Oh God, I'm sorry. Firstly, I wake you and shout at you while drunk, and now I'm trying to maim you with my son's pram. You'll be cursing me!"

"Don't worry. I'm a bit starved of female attention – even being violated is better than nothing," he chuckled. "Congratulations. I hope your daddy realises how lucky he is!" The last bit was directed into the pram at a now sleeping Adam.

Angie felt her face growing red. She was sweating too and, putting her hand up to her hair, realised in the flurry she'd forgotten to brush it. She also hadn't a screed of make-up on and was wearing a baby-puke-stained tracksuit and a very unattractive mac-in-a-sack type raincoat.

"His daddy is in Dublin and we aren't together, as such. So, no, he doesn't realise how lucky he is. Or maybe he does, depending on which way you look at it." Shut up, Angie, you babbling asshole, she thought.

"I'm sorry, I didn't mean to pry, it's none of my business at all." It was his turn to cringe.

"No, no, you didn't. All I meant is that, I understand what you mean about being on your own, not that I'm alone, due to Adam, but in another way . . ." Angie really wanted to click her fingers and not be there anymore. "Oh God, forgive me, it's only mid-morning but I seem to be having just about the worst day of my life so far!" She shrugged her shoulders and smiled wanly.

"In that case, maybe I could pop over later on, to wet the baby's head and all that? Mark, by the way." He held out his hand and smiled.

Angie shook his hand and looked at him in slight confusion, with her head to the side. "I'm Angie. But, why on earth would an attractive single man-about-town like you want to come to my apartment and sit with a rattle up your arse on my milk-vomit-stained sofa, instead of tripping the light fandango?"

"Well, with a sales pitch like that, how could I even consider anything else?" He burst out laughing and Angie joined him.

"Maybe I could lend you a plastic jumpsuit and a packet of baby wipes and promise you can have an adult drink?" she smiled.

"Say nine o'clock tonight?" he smiled back.

"See you then."

Angie managed to get the pram out the automatic sliding door of the apartment building. As she walked up the road, she had to shake herself to believe that whole episode had really happened. Maybe it was because she was truly happy, now that she was a mother, or maybe Mark was really a baby-snatching masked murderer, but she had actually just secured herself a date of a sort.

All those magazines she'd read had kept telling her she'd meet a man when she least expected it. The first time she'd gone out looking a fright, without spending time and anguish deliberating over what to wear, with a newborn in tow, it was like the tide had turned. There was a skip in her step as she walked towards the city centre. She might even splash out on a new tracksuit for tonight. She sincerely hoped she'd still be awake by nine o'clock. She'd cross that bridge when she came to it.

All negative thoughts melted away as Angie walked the familiar road towards Cork city centre.

Maybe, just maybe, she was going to be okay. Sighing deeply, she cooed at Adam as she drank in the familiarity of her home city. Angie was thrilled to be home.

One Year Later . . .

tweeting@maternityunit.com
*All mothers and babies are invited to our "Teddy Bears' Picnic"
which we hope will become an annual event.*

Ruby ran to grab the letters off the floor as the postman shoved them in the letterbox. Scanning them, she was surprised to see one addressed to her.

*The Maternity Hospital
Dublin*

*Dear Ruby,
I would like to invite you to our "Teddy Bears' Picnic," event, which we hope will be an annual happening. It will be in conjunction with the Maternity hospital. It will be a low-key and relaxed afternoon held in Herbert Park, just outside the city centre, for mums and babies. It will give all the mothers a chance to catch up with the other people from their antenatal class, and of course it will afford you all the opportunity to meet each other's babies.*

Family and friends are all welcome and we hope to see you there.

Yours truly,

Una Cook, Midwife

Ruby wandered down the hallway to the kitchen where her mother and Simon were having breakfast.

397

"Look at this, Mum. What do you think?"

So much had changed since this time last year. Her parents had become Simon's legal guardians and Damo had signed the papers. They'd never heard from him again, which was understandable when Ruby found out he was away for a small holiday in Mountjoy prison. She'd bumped into one of the girls from her old school.

"Yeah, Mariah left the school too – we all presumed you went to the same place together."

"No, we had a bit of a falling-out, so I haven't seen her unfortunately." Ruby didn't elaborate.

"That's a shame, you were great pals. Oh well, that's the way it goes sometimes. See you around, Ruby."

As the other girl waved, Ruby wondered how Mariah was getting on. Maybe one day their paths would cross again and they'd be able to rekindle their friendship. But for now Ruby was concentrating on her studies. She'd joined one of the big city education centres and was working really hard. It was a different format to regular school, less personal, with a greater number of students, so she wasn't the centre of attention nor was she the focal point for gossip. She travelled there and back by bus, and adored the newfound freedom.

Simon was a real handful and wasn't overly fond of sleeping. But Adele and Harry wouldn't have changed him for the world. The atmosphere in their house was totally different. Adele was like a new person. Her relationship with Ruby was better than either of them had ever hoped. Ruby felt much more at ease with her mother and even chatted to her about the boys in her class at school.

"Just take your time, there's plenty of time for all that," Adele warned.

"I know, Mum, but this guy Jim is actually really cute." Ruby had a twinkle in her eye.

Instead of being cross or grumpy, Adele smiled and hugged her daughter. "Well, go on then, tell me about him. What does he look like?"

Harry had already bought Simon a Leinster rugby jersey.

"Daddy, it's about ten times the size of him," Ruby had giggled.

"At the rate he's growing, it'll fit him soon enough, won't it, son?" Harry had scooped up the chubby baby and tickled him.

"So what about this picnic, Mum?" Ruby asked now. "I guess I can't go?"

Adele looked at her daughter and saw the longing in her eyes. "No, I think you *should* go and see the other girls again. Take Simon along to meet all the other babies. It would be nice for you to catch up."

"Oh, Mum!" Ruby threw her arms about her mother. "Thank you!" She laughed happily. She was dying to see the other girls and find out how they were getting on. She would be able to tell them that she was happy and making a go of it all. They'd been so kind to her at the classes and she'd never felt as if they'd looked down on her. It would be great to see them again.

tweeting@angiebaby.com
Teddy Bears' picnic, here I come!

Angie had just opened the same letter. Like Ruby, she thought it was a lovely idea and set about arranging her trip. Dialling Brenda's number, she told her she and Adam would come.

"I'll look forward to that now! It's been far too long since you've been to Dublin," Brenda enthused.

"I know – what with Troy choosing to come down to Cork the last couple of times we've met, I haven't needed to travel up to Dublin to be honest. I'll call him now too and maybe he'll take Adam for a while on Sunday to give me a chance to look around the shops."

Angie had become very fond of Troy and she was confident now that when Adam was older he would benefit from having him in his life.

On the morning of the picnic God must have been smiling down on them all. For once the rain had held off and, although it wasn't quite sunny, it was warm enough to contemplate sitting in a park, out of doors, hopefully without all of them contracting flu.

There was a bouncing castle for older children, a man on stilts making balloon animals and a little refreshments tent serving tea, coffee and biscuits.

Angie and Brenda arrived together, scanning the crowd for a familiar face.

"Hiya, girls!" Leona's familiar lilt came from behind them. "I see I'm the only one who's in the club again!" She pointed at her growing tummy. "In for a penny and all that. Say hello to your fellas, Madonna," she urged her little girl. "This one should be a bit different – the daddy is the chocolate variety, and plays basketball – well, that's what he told me, anyway." She shrugged as she drank her tea.

As they were all congratulating Leona on her news, Angie spotted Ruby walking towards them.

"Look! It's Ruby!" Angie hurried to meet her. "Ruby, it's great to see you! None of us had heard from you and I was really hoping you'd come today!" Angie hugged her warmly. "Who have we got here then?" She bent to look at the little boy, who was sucking a soother and staring at her intently.

"This is Simon. He's a great little man, aren't you?" Ruby rubbed his head affectionately.

"How are you coping? It's hell on wheels most of the time, isn't it?" Leona gave her a kiss on the cheek.

"Well, my parents are actually raising him. So I'm very lucky in that respect. We decided it was the best solution for us anyway." Ruby looked uncomfortable. "I just help out really, like a big sister, I suppose." She pulled on her shades.

"It's well for some! If I left Madonna with my ma, she'd get lost in the mix, there's so many at her house," Leona sighed.

Ruby was beginning to wish she hadn't come now. Leona was nice and all that, but she wasn't on form for being judged by anyone.

"Ruby – hi, love!"

Turning around, Ruby was greeted with a big hug.

"Everyone, this is one of my favourite people in the world, my Aunt Serena." Ruby flushed with pride. All the women drank in the stunningly beautiful woman who so obviously adored Ruby.

"Pleased to meet you all!" She waved warmly. "Hello, Simon. How's my gorgeous little nephew?" She bent to snuggle the baby. The smell of expensive perfume and the air of perfection just rolled off this glamorous lady.

"Your aunt is like a bleedin' supermodel," Leona whispered to

Ruby. "We only talk to one auntie on me ma's side and she's a chain-smoker with missing teeth and a dangerous obsession with the pub and the bingo hall in that order. I had no idea aunties could look like your one!"

"Serena is amazing. I don't know what I'd do without her." Ruby flushed with pride.

Angie's mobile phone rang as they all helped themselves to a cup of tea.

"Hi, love, all fine so far ... Yes, most of the girls are here and none of the babies are having a meltdown yet ... Okay, I will. I'll call you later on when I get to Brenda's house. I love you too."

"Wooo, who was that then? Did you get it together with Adam's daddy after all?" Leona sidled up to Angie, not afraid to ask for the juicy details.

"Eh, no," Angie said, blushing. "Actually, that was Mark – he used to live upstairs from me. We got together just after I had Adam. Hey, everyone, I have a little announcement to make." Angie suddenly felt all overcome with emotion as tears smarted.

"Are you on the baby bus again too?" Leona brightened.

"Not quite, look!" Angie held up her left hand, with the glinting ruby and diamond ring decorating her finger.

"You dark horse, when did this all happen? Congratulations, I'm thrilled for you!" Brenda threw her arms around her friend.

"Well, Mark was going to wait and ask me on Adam's birthday, but he couldn't wait and he popped the question just as we were getting on the train up here this morning." Angie had tears running down her cheeks.

The girls all congratulated her and wished her well.

"Well, you'll all have to come to the wedding." Angie wiped her eyes, bursting with happiness.

"I know I've only just met you all," Serena spoke up, very calmly and slowly, with a look like a Cheshire cat on her beautiful face, "but seeing as this seems to be a session of good news, I would like you all to be the first to hear that I am going to be a mummy too."

"*No way!*" Ruby made poor Simon jump and burst into frightened tears as she squealed and hugged her aunt.

"Yes way! Can you believe it?" Serena danced around in a circle, clapping her hands in delight.

"How far gone are ya?" Leona poked her tummy.

Serena looked a little taken back by Leona's forward poking of her belly. "I'm just thirteen weeks. I had my scan yesterday. I didn't want to tell anyone until the scan confirmed it all."

"Ah, bleedin' deadly, we can be best friends then. Who knows, our babies could end up married in the future!" She elbowed Serena in her Chanel-clad ribs.

All the ladies laughed, although only Ruby knew that Serena's giggle wasn't entirely genuine. Her aunt was looking more than a little alarmed at being befriended by Leona.

tweeting@themercedesking.com
Framed.com

The warm summer day, which was making the "Teddy Bears' picnic," such a success was doing nothing positive for Damo's mood. He'd been sitting in the same spot for the last hour and a half.

He wasn't sure if it was God punishing him for being wealthy or what the hell was going on. He'd been having a great night at The Orb, six weeks ago, when the place was raided by the cops. They'd bashed in the door, smashing one of his really dear coffee tables, and gone straight for him.

He'd been manhandled out of the place in front of a load of girls from the modelling agency. Without so much as a how's-it-going, he'd been shoved into the back of a van with a load of pissed skangers and driven to the police station. He'd shouted repeatedly that he wasn't speaking until he had a solicitor by his side but the big thick culchie of a driver had laughed at him and told him to shut his trap.

That night in the cell had been sheer torture. All weirdos, puking and pissing on the floor. He kept checking his limited edition gold Rolex to see when his legal guy was coming. But night had turned to day before the stiff-upper-lipped git in a cheap suit had come to rescue him.

"I've spoken to the arresting officers, Mr McCabe. In light of your assaulting the two female officers and your possession of so much cocaine, with a street value of over one hundred thousand euro, you're looking at a hefty fine, and a long stretch inside."

"What do you mean, assault? I never touched anyone. I only saw one female officer and she looked like she'd snap me in half as soon as look at me. I only had a couple of crumbs of coke in my pocket and they never even found that." Damo was stunned and affronted.

The kerfuffle that took place behind the solicitor silenced them both.

"Yes, that's him! That's the man. He used to be my husband, so I know him all right, but that doesn't make it okay for him to be selling drugs to my daughters' friends! I want to press charges."

"Noreen, what are you doing, love?"

"Are you sure about this, Mrs McCabe?" A big hulk of a country-sounding garda was standing, assisting Noreen.

"Yes, I am, Garda. This man is a danger to himself and others."

"We are arresting you for possession with intent to supply . . ."

As the huge bag of drugs was produced from Damo's top pocket, he tried to tell them that it had been planted there. That he'd never seen it before in his life. But nobody seemed to care.

"But I'm the Mercedes King," he whimpered.

Noreen had turned up in court to see him. Maybe she was having second thoughts, maybe she'd stand up and tell the judge he was a great man. One who'd made his fortune and bettered himself. She'd tell the judge how good he was to his kids, giving them the best parties around, buying her all that gold.

But instead she'd sat in silence. When his sentence was handed down, he could see her smile. Then the big fella who was leading him away, the same hulk who had been with Noreen at the station, had cocked his head to the side at her as they'd walked past her in the dock.

"See ya later on, Paddy-Joe – I'll be keeping the bed warm for you," Noreen whispered and winked. "Damo, for future reference, you should never underestimate the power of a scorned woman."

The End

‹o›

If you enjoyed *Miss Conceived* by Emma Hannigan
why not try
Designer Genes also published by Poolbeg?
Here's a sneak preview of Chapter One.

‹o›

Designer Genes

EMMA HANNIGAN

POOLBEG

PROLOGUE

Emily

Nobody likes to say goodbye. Especially when you're a mum saying goodbye to your two small children.

This occasion was no different. I knew I had to hold it together just long enough to make it outside. The lump in my throat felt like a basketball. But in the next five minutes I needed to appear positive, nonchalant and above all else, normal.

It was almost impossible.

My son Louis, daughter Tia, and my mum and dad were all in the sitting room of my parents' house. The fire was lit, the heating was on and the freezing sleet outside was obliterated. Cocooned by both the temperature and love, the children were relaxed. I had to make sure that everything was as run of the mill as possible for a Sunday afternoon. Disney movies, Sunday treats – all the things I normally did with them.

It had been my thirtieth birthday the day before. Under the circumstances, I'd chosen to have a small family party, with cake and plenty of sweets. My head was elsewhere, and if it hadn't been for the children, I would have gladly ignored the day entirely.

"Mum, will you come and sit here with us? A movie is starting and it's going to be great fun," Louis pleaded.

Louis was six, with big blue eyes, blond hair that falls endearingly over his eyes and a smile that cuts through to your heart.

"Please, Mum!" He patted a bit of couch between himself and Tia who was five and straight from Central Casting as a cherub, even if I say so myself.

They knew I was going, but young children forget things.

"Please, Mum?"

The pleading in my son's eyes hurt so much I had to grab hold of the back of a chair and steady myself. I closed my eyes and concentrated on blocking out the overwhelming fear, then swooped down on the couch.

"Big kiss for Mummy!" I launched myself at Louis. *Don't let me cry.*

"One from you too!" I grabbed Tia, fragile in one of her favourite outfits – a pink gaudy fairy dress with hard, itchy netting, purple patterned tights and an old gold-lamé evening top of my mother's, which Tia had sniffed out in a long-forgotten wardrobe upstairs. She had hideous dress sense, which I hoped would improve by the time she reached her teens. I felt winded at the thought of her teenage years: would I be around for them?

On the TV, some poor git was trying to present a report on penguins. His obvious struggle with the live creatures delighted the children and in an instant they were transfixed.

Thank God for the invention of children's programmes. In times of need, they can be a mother's best friend.

"Mum and Dad . . . bye."

Woodenly and hurriedly, I hugged and kissed my parents. We didn't speak. Us adults were trying to hold it all in.

"Bye," muttered Dad. For the first time in his life he looked beaten by a situation. He was always very controlled and upbeat. I could tell this was killing him.

Mum, who was my rock and knew what to say in any situation, was like a robot on automatic pilot. There was nothing she could say at that moment and she just stared at me.

Mum and I look very alike. She has European parentage, is very striking with sallow skin against white-blonde hair, and she seems to get more beautiful as the years go by. By contrast, Dad has dark hair and pale, almost translucent skin. I'm a mixture of the two of them with Mum's blonde hair and my father's milk-bottle complexion. My darling daughter Tia is sallow-skinned while my little Louis is almost blue he's so pale. The baby factory clicked on the skin-tone button and made him a shade lighter than me. His skin is flawless, like a porcelain doll's.

Both kids were engrossed in the television as I took a last look at them. They love their grandparents' house, which meant I was spared the trauma of them not wanting to stay while I walked out. I couldn't have coped with "Mummy, don't go!"

Holding back from running, I left the room.

Robbie was supposed to be waiting for me in the hall but he was busy trying to find the batteries for a radio he thought I might use.

Robbie is my ever-supportive husband. He has naturally spray-on-tan-coloured skin, caramel hair and a contagious smile. He runs his own public relations company, is chatty and sociable and yet always in control, which can be bloody irritating. The whole world can be on the verge of ending and Robbie will sit and remain annoyingly calm. Except for today.

I could hear him banging around in the kitchen, talking to the drawers as if they were going to suddenly change from inanimate objects into biddable working beings.

"I know you're hiding the batteries, I saw them the other day," I heard him growl. "So why don't you just make it easier for us all and spit them out?"

Normally when he's angry I sort it out. Right now, I could barely sort myself out.

I reckoned I had a space of about five minutes where I could let rip, so I stepped out the front door whereupon the wind whipped into my face and made my eyes water. Now nobody was watching me try to keep it all together, the way I had been since I'd heard the news.

"Me? I'm fine, totally fine. Honestly. Not a bit worried. I'll be fine."

I wasn't fine, though.

The sobs came from deep inside me. Frightened, grief-stricken, from-the-depths-of-my-soul sobs.

I wasn't feeling sorry for myself, really – I was just terrified that this was going to be the last time I would see my parents and my precious children. Louis and Tia, my babies. *Oh my God.*

Tears dripped down onto my pink fake-fur coat and I stroked the front of it for comfort. But the comfort dissolved instantly because Tia loved it. My baby, Tia. *"You look like a pink furry fairy, Mummy!"* I could hear her tinkling voice running through my head.

More tears streamed down my face.

As a parent, I wasn't ready to die. I wanted to be there to see my children grow up. I wanted to know how they turned out. What they looked like and who their friends were.

I wanted to bake their birthday cakes. Superman for Louis. Sparkles-to-the-Tonsils Barbie for Tia. I wanted to see them stretch and gain confidence and knowledge. I wanted to be there if they needed someone to talk to. I even wanted to be in the firing line when they became teenagers and hated me. I had a *right* to be the one they hated. I had given birth to them, wanting to and intending on being their mother for as much of their lives as possible, and more importantly for all of mine.

But the journey I was on might change all that. I might not be there.

Emily, get a grip, right? Hold it together. You're wasting your make-up. You can't look like you've been dragged through a bush backwards. What would the neighbours say? Think of . . . uh, think of the angels!

I had never been religious. At all. I'm three-quarters Catholic (well, in so far as I wore the dress with the veil when I made my First Communion and the day I got married) and one-quarter Jewish (I have a Star of David on my charm bracelet). I believed in Shopping and the Right to Earn as Much as a Man, but as for the God stuff . . . well, I wasn't so sure.

Yet in the past while – since what my friends were anxiously calling *"my news"* – a wide variety of people had raised my awareness of angels. And I was converted. I'd always been an admirer of all things pink, fluffy and sparkly, so this whole angel theory fitted into my world beautifully.

Laura, a friend I'd been to fashion-design college with, gave me a box set of CDs all about angels.

"We are surrounded by angels," she said earnestly that day as we sat in the coffee shop and she held my hand, snuffling back the tears.

She'd never had to hold my hand before. I was the more balanced and together one in our friendship. During our college days, Laura was always stoned in the corner talking about the colours of our auras.

"You call and they come," said Laura. "In times of need, we can call on specific angels to help us. If in doubt, Archangel Michael is the main man. He's Mr Fix It, Bob the Builder, Superman, James Bond, Mother Theresa, Luke Skywalker and every superhero rolled into one." She beamed at me. "You should try it, Emily."

She was so convincing that I totally believed her.

Standing outside my parents' house, waiting for my husband, having just said goodbye to my family, I realised that desperate times call for desperate measures. I yelled: "Archangel Michael, please help me to get through these next few hours without falling apart!"

Nobody answered.

The tears kept coming. Big, fat, hot blobs plopping down my cheeks, burning my skin against the freezing air. I kept telling myself to stop crying. But I couldn't.

I hadn't cried at all during this whole process so far. Now, it felt like I couldn't stop.

Think of Robbie – you don't want to let him see you crying. Come on, Emily, stop being a wuss. Get a grip for Christ's sake – now is not the time to fall apart.

"Mummy, are you going to get dead?" Tia had asked the day I'd told her I had to go into hospital. She had climbed onto my knee and started "fixing" my hair, while poking the mole on my neck.

I'd touched her soft cheek, wishing fiercely that this wasn't happening to us, because it was wrong for my little girl to have to even think about her mum being dead.

"No, darling, I'm not going to get dead," I said, in the voice I used for discussions on Barbie, Dora the Explorer and why we couldn't buy any more sparkly dust because the bedroom carpet was already full of it.

"Do you have an infection that makes you have a bad cough?" Her eyes were wide with wonder. "Will the doctor have to hide the cold thing and listen with his earphones while you do big breathing?"

I thought of our trips to the doctor where she'd learned how to be a big girl when the doctor used his stethoscope.

"Not quite, Tia. I'm not sick. I'm going to make sure that the doctors take away all the bad stuff before it has a chance to make me sick. Do you think you can understand that?"

She nodded her head, but her eyes were darting back and forth. It was about as clear as mud for her tiny mind. She was too young to absorb the facts and yet there was no doubt she had enough insight to know that there was something wrong.

It was the first time I realised that my heart could simultaneously break and continue to beat at the same time.

She trusted me to be all right and I didn't know if I would be. I didn't know what they were going to find. Nobody did. I had an 'altered gene' that had spelled a death sentence for two members of my family. A cancer gene. Would I ever be coming home to my babies again?

Susie

I could think of nothing but Emily that day. It took a gigantic effort to concentrate on work and actually listen to my clients. That was quite a problem: I'm a psychotherapist so listening is my job.

I was wishing with all my heart that I could be with her. Emily had been my best friend forever. She was much more than that, she was like my sister. I couldn't really remember my life before I knew her. But, despite all that, it was Robbie's place to be by her side today, not mine. That's marriage, isn't it?

I imagined them driving to the hospital. My bet was that he would be silent and she would be playing our special game in her head.

I should explain. As children, Emily and I invented this game and called it "Recipes Rule". We'd sort out our problems by putting them in a recipe and cooking them up, or boiling them down, depending on the mood. I suppose, when we started the game, we were using the cooking metaphor as a tool for venting our feelings. It was our own little way of telling each other how we felt and quelling our worries in the process. Years later, at university, I realised that we had unwittingly invented a very effective therapeutic tool.

The game was created when Emily wasn't allowed to wear a really gaudy Communion dress. After she'd told me all about it, she sat there brooding and then said she'd thought of a great way to punish her mean mummy. With her bottom lip protruding, she proclaimed: "Mean Mummy Mousse: Take one Mean Mummy. Steal her favourite shoes. Soak them in muddy water with worms and rotten leaves. Serve them to Mean Mummy covered in slugs!"

Clapping and thrilled, I'd finished with: "Watch as Mean Mummy says she's very sorry and won't be nasty ever again!"

We'd jumped up and down cheering, feeling that Mean Mummy had been sorted out. Even though Emily still had to wear the boring minimalist Communion dress, the slug-covered shoes had been a balm to soothe us when we felt we'd been wronged and in our heads we were the winners.

After that, "Recipes Rule" became our lifeline. We sautéed strict teachers, boiled bad boyfriends, massacred our poor mothers on many occasions. Suffice it to say, we sorted the world by cooking it and serving it up in a way that we felt was justified.

When Emily discovered her boyfriend was cheating on her at the age of fifteen, she'd cried with embarrassment and hurt pride until I came up with the Cheating Git Casserole.

"Take one boy called David. Add a stunning and clever girl called Emily. Remove David's brain. Make him think he needs to hang around with Sylvia the slut. Chop off David's bits. Put them in a big heavy pot with carrots, onions and gravy. Stew and make him eat said bits. Serve with a toss of the head and a look that tells him you didn't really like him anyway!"

"Thanks, Suze. I still feel like my heart is breaking, but I have to say I'll never be able to look at David again without imagining his bits floating around with chunks of carrot and onion!" Blowing her nose, Emily hugged me gratefully.

I wondered what recipe my poor brave friend was cooking up today.

1

SEVEN MONTHS EARLIER

Emily

Ice-lolly Sundae:
Take two small children, add sunshine, smiles and ice-lollies.
Douse with water from garden sprinkler. Add mud. Allow
kids to wallow. Hose down to remove muck. Dry and dress.

"Oh my God, that sun is hot. Not that I'm complaining, Emily. There's nothing like heat to unknot your shoulders, is there? I could do with a bit of relaxation after the week I've had with your father." My mother lay back on her sun-lounger with a big sigh.

We were in my parents' back garden letting the balmy sun heat our bones. Robbie and I had awful cheap old loungers in our house, so it was much nicer to visit Mum and Dad. I often came over on summer afternoons – if I went back to work, as I was thinking of doing, I wouldn't be able to suit myself as much.

The tweeting birds and smell of flowers would have created a beautiful and idyllic scene if it weren't for Tia and Louis chasing each other across the lawn naked, while yelling abuse and trying to maim each other.

"I've never heard anything like your father," Mum went on. "All I want to do is have the living room painted, and he's been backwards and forwards to the hardware store so many times buying bloody colour-match pots. He still hasn't decided what colour he wants. At this stage I don't care if it's luminous pink with orange spots, just as long as he stops telling me about it." Mum smiled in spite of her irritation, closing her eyes and drinking in the sun. "How is Robbie behaving? I hope he's not as annoying as his father-in-law."

"Robbie's fine. You know him. Once everything is ticking along and he's able to put each thing in its correct box, he's happy. He started going on about the kids' toy room again yesterday. He seems to think that they don't need any toys or DVDs or anything that makes a mess and takes up space. Let him try staying at home for the entire summer with no distractions! I'd say the toy-store vans would be delivering twice a day!"

Robbie and I argued constantly about toys. He thought a hoop and a stick between them was sufficient. I knew the children adored a variety of playthings. It was one of those subjects we should have avoided discussing. We'd never agree.

The roars from the other side of the garden got louder.

"Stop trying to kill each other, kids!" I screamed. "Can't you pretend you like each other for once?"

Of course they completely ignored me and continued to charge about like deranged, shrunken warriors.

"I'll turn on the sprinkler for them – it'll water the parched grass and keep them entertained at the same time," Mum suggested, peeling herself off her comfortable lounger. Within seconds, the fighting turned to delighted squeals and giggles. Tia and Louis leapt in and out of the chilly drops like little garden nymphs, twisting and cavorting, completely taken with their game.

"Was that the doorbell, Mum?"

"Didn't hear!" she yelled, over the noise of the children.

I got up lazily and meandered towards the house, avoiding being soaked by my two little demons. I had a nice slick of sweat across my face, which I tried to mop up with my T-shirt as I opened the door.

"Only me," said my Aunt Ellie. "You're looking ravishing, Emily." My aunt gave me a quick peck on the cheek as she floated past, looking elegant in a swirl of linen and silk, making me feel like a slob in my sweat-soaked outfit.

I cleaned up okay but just then my blonde hair was stuck to my head and I had no make-up on, a mistake when you've got fair lashes. Right at that second I was sporting the boiled ham look. My fair skin didn't exactly take the sun well. I never went brown – I just looked like I'd been fried.

"You can't come to this house smelling of cologne and wearing pretty floaty clothes," I said to Ellie. "You have to sit in greying underwear and smell like a rugby player's jock-strap to sit with us."

"Give me five minutes sitting in your mum's sun trap and I'll suit the description perfectly."

Outside, Ellie sat on one of the plastic garden chairs near the sun-loungers.

"Hi, Lucy! Hi, Monster Munches!"

"Hi, Ellie! Are you going to take off your clothes and jump in the water with us?" Louis begged hopefully.

Ellie was their all-time favourite auntie. She was always in a good mood and although she'd long since hit what she called "the dreaded forties" she could bounce on a trampoline as high as any six-year-old and play hide and seek for up to an hour, no problem.

"Not today, little man, but I'll watch you, if that's okay." She narrowly avoided being hugged by two dripping wet children, producing a bag with ice-lollies as a distraction just in time.

"Would anyone like a cold drink?" Mum asked, wriggling her toes into her flip-flops.

"I'd actually love a coffee, mad as it sounds," said Ellie. "I need a caffeine boost."

"I'll have a water, please, Mum."

By the time the ice-lollies had been opened and the children had fought over them, Mum was back with the coffee.

Then, as we were sipping our drinks, Ellie took a deep breath and said: "Girls, we need to talk. I have some news." She was looking from one of us to the other, and she wasn't smiling.

The children were darting around the garden, playing *Star Wars* by pretending their ice-lollies were light sabres.

Mum and I looked at each other, and I felt my heart sink. Ellie was one of life's happy, light-hearted people. Nothing got her down. Except one thing. I realised there could only be one type of news which could make Ellie look like this. Cancer.

She'd had breast cancer ten years before. Five of the girls from Mum's family had already had breast cancer, Ellie being one of them. Three survived. But Meg died at thirty-eight and Joanne died at forty-one. They left three devastated children in their wake.

"Just tell me you don't have . . . *it* again," Mum implored.

She could barely say the word "cancer". Being first-born in a family of seven girls, Mum was like everybody's big sister. Ellie was the youngest and, due to the fifteen-year age gap, looked up to my mother as her mini-mum.

"It's okay, Lucy," Ellie soothed her older sister, "but you're on the right track."

Mum looked instantly devastated. "Oh, God." The colour drained from her face.

Fear gripped me. I saw my children flash past, spitting sound effects from their tiny, pursed lips, as they swatted at an imaginary being with their ice-lollies. I remembered my aunts finding out they had cancer and I remembered how much pain and suffering they went through before they died.

To see someone you love being taken over by pain and suffering was awful. I was very close to Ellie and the thought of her going through that again was shocking.

"I had a test done recently, "Ellie said. "And it was positive. I am a carrier of a mutation of a gene called BRCA1."

We looked at her blankly.

"What does that mean?" Mum asked.

The two of us stared at Ellie – the kids, the heat and the sunny day forgotten.

"It basically means that I have an altered gene which makes me very likely to develop breast and ovarian cancer," she explained slowly.

"But you've already had breast cancer," I mumbled. My brain and mouth weren't connecting properly.

Ellie's shoulders slumped. "Well, that's why the hospital approached me. They know that we have a history of breast and ovarian cancer in the family, so they asked me if I would take this test." She paused, took a deep breath and went on. "The gene is called BRCA1 – which stands for Breast Cancer 1. They're trying to identify certain mutations of it in as many people as possible. Mutations of the gene are particularly prevalent in people of Ashkenazi Jewish descent, which as we know our grandmother was. I have inherited one of those mutations. If a woman carries the altered gene she has an eighty per cent chance of developing breast cancer."

We sat in a stunned silence.

"She also has a fifty per cent chance of developing ovarian cancer."

Mum's hands shot to her face.

The sounds of my children's happy voices faded in and out of my head. It was like having a bullet of ice shot through my chest. This had serious consequences for Mum and me. And Tia. Innocent and tiny, bounding around in the sunshine, could she be in serious danger in years to come?

As Ellie began to talk again, I managed to zone back in and listen to her.

"Nobody can say our family isn't aware of what cancer can do. Obviously, the more they can discover about this mutation, the closer they come to finding a cure. So I agreed to be tested."

"What did you have to do?" Mum's voice was faint.

"It was a simple blood test. They sent the sample to a lab in England and they searched for this specific mutation, which was present in all of us so far. The reason I'm telling you is that you may want to be tested yourselves."

Ellie dropped her gaze to the ground. I thought she might be about to cry.

"I'm so sorry to be the bearer of such bad tidings, but I had to tell you both."

At that moment I felt for her. It wasn't an easy bomb to drop.

"What about Heidi and Zara?" Mum wanted to know about her two other sisters, who'd both previously had breast cancer. "You said the mutation was present in 'all of us so far'. You mean they had the test too?"

Ellie nodded. "They've been tested and unfortunately they're both positive. I volunteered to come and deliver the bad news. But we didn't want to tell you we were doing it, not until we were sure . . ."

"Poor you, Ellie! Talk about being given a ticking parcel and told to run with it!" Mum's mothering instinct kicked in as she leaned forward and clasped Ellie's hand.

I loved my mum so much at that moment: even in the face of devastating news, she was thinking about someone else.

But Ellie was still concentrating on getting her message across as clearly as she could.

"So, Lucy, if you are a carrier, and only *if* you are, Emily also has a strong chance of testing positive. But you may not be, Lucy. And if you don't carry it, Emily cannot carry it either."

"Then Tia wouldn't have it," I whispered. It was a glimmer of hope for my baby.

Ellie squeezed my hand. "I'm sorry to have to tell you all this and ruin a lovely sunny day for you." She drank her coffee and waited for the news to sink in.

We remained quiet, deep in thought.

Ellie spoke again. "Two months ago, when I decided to go along and take the test, I assumed I wouldn't be a carrier – it's a bit like taking a pregnancy test and assuming you won't be pregnant. That kind of thing happens to other people, doesn't it? So I went back to the genetics lab last Friday, fully expecting to be told I was safe. But they told me I tested positive. I know I've had breast cancer already, but I really thought my test wouldn't come back positive."

Mum touched my hand, the concern for me written all over her face. I followed her gaze as she watched Tia stamping in the soggy, muddy patch they'd created with the garden hose.

"How are you coping with it, Ellie?" I asked.

"Well, I was really shocked when they told me, but when I gathered my thoughts and sat down and rationalised it all, it made perfect sense," she said matter of factly.

"Oh Jesus!" Mum said. She never cursed normally. Nothing was normal about today.

I just stared at Ellie. I wasn't sure what to think or say.

Ellie pressed on. "You need to decide whether or not you want to be tested. If you decide not, you should at least put yourself on a screening programme. The genetics lab sent me a letter following my diagnosis. It's kind of technical but it explains the whole gene thing very well. I've photocopied it and I'll leave it with you – one for each of you. I think it gives a –"

"Look at me, Mummy, I'm a chocolate girl!" Tia appeared beside me spattered from head to toe in thick, oozy mud.

"Oh Tia, what have you done to yourself?" I stood up and tried to grab her but she was too quick for me.

Squealing with delight, she dashed across the lawn towards the dancing sprinkler.

"Okay then, wash all that mud off with the clean water and stop turning the grass into a mud bath," I called, on automatic-mummy-pilot.

Tia had gone behind a tree, curling her arms and tucking her hands into her armpits, shouting, "Ooh, ooh, ooh, I'm a mucky monkey!"

Louis, similarly muddy, joined her and they began to leap about communicating to each other in monkey language.

"Leave them to it, Emily, at least they're happy!" Mum shouted over to me. "We'll hose them down before you have to put them in the car."

Why am I so anally retentive, I wondered silently? Here I am in utter shock, being told life-altering news, and all I'm worried about is my children being covered in mud. Who cares? I could imagine what my friend Susie the psychotherapist would say about my reaction – something to do with focussing on unimportant issues in order to avoid the horrible ones.

Ellie sat with us for about half an hour after that but we couldn't talk as the children kept running over and back to us. They didn't need to hear any of this.

My head was spinning by the time we waved Ellie off. The bright sun and the heat were suddenly too much for me. I woodenly grabbed the children, removed as much muck as I could with the sprinkler, dried them and dressed them.

"I don't want to go home – it's too hot to sit in the car!" Tia whined.

"We need to go now. Say goodbye to Oma now, like a good girl." The children had always called my mum "Oma", the German for grandmother. I'd had an Oma growing up, as my maternal grandmother is Austrian, and when they were born Mum hadn't felt like a Nana or a Grandma. So she'd opted to uphold tradition and become an Oma too.

"Don't forget your letter from Ellie." Mum stuffed one of the white envelopes into my handbag. "I'll ring you later on when we've both had a chance to digest all this."

She waved us off, looking drawn and pale. There was a darkness in her eyes I had never seen before. The sunny day and jovial atmosphere were well and truly ruined.

During the short car journey home, Ellie's words whizzed around in my head. She was so calm and steady about everything. I felt as far removed from calm as I could have been.

Glad to pull into our own driveway, I bundled the kids into the house. I needed to read the letter from the genetic lab and try to get my head around the news.

I closed the sitting-room curtains and turned the TV on to *Nick Junior*. Grabbing a packet of biscuits, I handed them to Louis, who looked delighted with the normally forbidden offering.

"Are these all for me to eat on my own?" he asked, astonished.

"No, share them with your sister. Mummy has to do some work for a few minutes, so you two can pretend we have a cinema and have a bikkie picnic, okay?"

I backed out of the room and shut the door. I desperately needed some space, even for a few minutes, to read the letter and let my brain compute what all of this meant to me.

Perched on one of the lower steps of the stairs, just inside the front door, I stared at the envelope in my hands.

An image of Robbie shot into my head. God, I wasn't ready to say goodbye to my family! Until that moment I'd never had to contemplate such a dreadful thing. It was like a smack in the face. A freezing cold shower, to douse the warmth out of my very existence.

─◄o►─

If you enjoyed this chapter from
Designer Genes by Emma Hannigan
why not order the full book online
@ www.poolbeg.com
and enjoy a 10% discount on all
Poolbeg books

See page overleaf for details.

─◄o►─

POOLBEG WISHES TO
THANK YOU

for buying a Poolbeg book.
As a loyal customer we will give you
10% OFF (and free postage*)
on any book bought on our website
www.poolbeg.com

Select the book(s) you wish to buy
and click to checkout.

Then click on the 'Add a Coupon' button
(located under 'Checkout') and enter
this coupon code

USMWR15173

(Not valid with any other offer!)

WHY NOT JOIN OUR MAILING LIST
@ www.poolbeg.com and get some
fantastic offers on Poolbeg books

*See website for details